CW00983256

PRIMAL]

Book 3 of the Druid Academy Series

C. S. Churton

This is a work of fiction. The characters and events described herein are imaginary and are not intended to refer to specific places or to living persons alive or dead. All rights reserved. No part of this publication may be reproduced, distributed, or transmitted in any form or by any means, including photocopying, recording, or other electronic or mechanical methods without the prior written permission of the publisher except for brief quotations embodied in critical reviews.

Cover by May Dawney Designs.

Copyright © 2020 by C. S. Churton

All rights reserved.

Other Titles By C.S Churton

Druid Academy Series

DRUID MAGIC

FERAL MAGIC

PRIMAL MAGIC

TalentBorn Series

AWAKENING

EXILED

DEADLOCK

UNLEASHED

HUNTED

Available Soon

CHIMERA

Chapter One

I knew he was a werewolf the moment I laid eyes on him. Close cropped hair, long muscles covering the length of his body, deceptive lupine grace to his movements that betrayed the beast barely contained beneath his human flesh.

Of course, it helped that I recognised this particular wolf.

"Hey, Leo," I called, waving a hand above my head. "We're over here."

Fantail market was crowded today – it always was, in the last few days before the semester started. Druids, shifters, and other magic users hurried this way and that, grabbing text books and supplies they'd need once the academic year got started, while sellers hawked their latest wares loudly, trying to convince people that their ground cottam weed was better than their neighbour's crushed variety, or that some dragon's blood would guarantee that your potion wouldn't explode, or that a cloak inlaid with siren dust was guaranteed to catch the eye of their love interest. Still, the werewolf easily heard my voice over the noise, and zeroed in on the table we'd grabbed outside of Talia's tearoom, making the most of the last few days of nice weather we'd get this year.

Beside me, Kelsey blushed and stared down into her coffee, and Sam grinned.

"Ah, young love," he said, to no-one in particular. Kelsey elbowed him in the ribs, hard enough that he winced.

"Hey, no fair using your hybrid strength on me," he complained, and looked to me for support. I just shrugged.

"Hey, you wanna antagonise the half-werewolf, you gotta take the consequences."

Kelsey gave me a grateful smile, and pushed a mug towards Leo as he pulled out a chair.

"Hey, Leo," I greeted the werewolf, and got to my feet. "Me and Sam are just going to grab more drinks."

"But I've still got—" Sam cut off abruptly as I kicked him none-too-gently under the table. "I mean, yeah, I could use a refill."

I practically dragged him away to give Kelsey and Leo some privacy. They hadn't seen each other for a couple of weeks, and while I wasn't sure there was anything officially going on, I knew they both wanted there to be.

There was no-one waiting to be served inside the coffee shop, so we took our time placing our orders. We would have taken our time strolling back outside, too, if I hadn't heard a gratingly familiar voice drift in through the open door.

"Well, if it isn't the half-breed," I heard Felicity say. "Glad to see you're keeping with your own kind, cur."

We made it back outside before Leo did anything to get himself in trouble with the law, but he was already on his feet and glaring down at the all-too-pretty blonde girl and her entourage. I decided to step in before he got himself arrested protecting Kelsey's honour.

"Oh, hi Felicity," I said brightly, and let my eyes flick to Cecelia and the other girl trailing in her wake, who I didn't recognise. "I see you've found a friend. I guess its's true – you really can buy anything here at Fantail."

Her face crumpled into a sneer and for a moment I thought she was going to retaliate – her hexes were a bitch – but instead she turned up her nose and pivoted in a swish of blonde hair, and stalked away. I watched her leave with a frown.

"Felicity backing down from a fight? That's no fun."

"She can't risk it, can she?" Kelsey said, looking far less concerned about the airhead's insults than Leo had been. "Not if the rumours are true, I mean."

"What rumours?" I asked, pulling out a chair and sinking into it. The others followed my lead, and Sam shook his head in mock disappointment. At least, I thought it was probably mock.

"How do you manage to exist in our society, and yet know nothing about it?"

I shrugged, setting my mug down.

"It's a talent. Now spill the gossip before I'm forced to set you on fire."

"So quick to resort to violence," he said wistfully. "And you used to be such a meek girl…"

"I seem to recall you were the one proposing we burned down the academy so you could cheat on your law exam resit," I pointed out. "And quit changing the subject."

"One little fire." He spread his hands innocently. "I just wanted one little fire so I could check my notes. And you call yourselves my friends."

I raised an eyebrow — because the best threats were usually the most subtle ones — and Sam sighed theatrically.

"Fine. But for the record, I really do think you should pay more attention to what's happening in our community. The fun stuff, at least."

"Noted," I said, with a roll of my eyes. Never mind the fact that outside him, Kelsey, and Leo, my only connection to the druid world was my father — and since he'd tried to murder me at the end of the last semester, I didn't think he'd be keeping me up to date on the latest gossip. What could I say? My family life was complicated.

"It's the Four Nations Cup," Kelsey said quickly, probably suspecting that I was going to set Sam's eyebrows on fire. Perceptive, that one. "Every three years there's a competition held between the druid academies in England, Scotland, Ireland and Wales."

"Like the Triwizard Tournament?"

It was Sam's turn to roll his eyes.

"No, not like the Triwizard… Well, yeah, okay. Kinda. Except no-one's going to die. And you have to earn your place."

"Each academy gets two representatives," Kelsey said. "Anyone from the academy can try out, and if you're chosen, you get to visit all of the academies – each one hosts a challenge."

Wow. A chance to see other academies. I knew there had to be others besides Dragondale – Ava aside, pretty much everyone there had been born in England – but I'd never really given them much thought. I'd certainly never imagined I might get to actually see them. Cool.

Wait. Not cool. Itealta aside, I was hardly the most competitive person on the planet, and I only joined the Fire team so I could hang out with the hippogryffs more. Besides, this contest just sounded like a way to show the rest of the communities how little I knew about our world. Humiliation on an international scale? No thanks.

"Well, I'm going to try out for sure," Sam said, flexing his arms. "I've been working out all summer."

"Which is probably why you just barely scraped a pass on your law resit," Kelsey said.

"A pass is a pass," Sam waved her off.

"Well, I won't be trying out," Kelsey said, flicking her red hair over one shoulder. "Everyone says the third year at Dragondale is the hardest, and we need to graduate with good grades if we want to have a chance in our chosen careers. I won't have time to do anything other than study."

A tiny flutter started up in my stomach. What was waiting for me when I graduated as a fully-fledged druid? I'd only known about the existence of the druidic world for two years, and there was so much I still didn't have a clue about.

"As if you need to study." Sam's voice sounded distant, barely breaking through my thoughts.

What sort of careers did druids have? I'd seen some working in shops here in the market, of course, but surely there had to be more out there for me than that. I might not have been the most ambitious person in the world, but that didn't mean I wanted to settle for something that never challenged me. Obviously there were professors, but I wasn't about to move into teaching. It'd be a little embarrassing when half the students knew more than I did.

"Hello, earth to Lyssa?"

I blinked rapidly, taking in Sam's hand waving in front of my face. I swatted it away and glanced round the table. They were all staring at me expectantly.

"I said," Sam reiterated, "do you have all of your books, or do you need to get any while we're here?"

"Oh." I reached into my bag and fished out the book list. "Um, I think I've got them all. But how are we supposed to know what we need if we haven't chosen our subjects yet?"

They were all staring at me again. This time Kelsey's mouth had actually dropped open. Leo chuckled. I looked between them, trying not to let my confusion show.

"What?"

"On the ball as ever, druid girl."

"You should have decided ages ago," Kelsey said, her voice exasperated rather than scolding – presumably because she was used to my last-minute attitude by now. "You've had all summer to choose."

I shrugged.

"Well, I'll just take whatever you two are taking."

Kelsey shook her head.

"We're not taking the same subjects."

I glanced between them.

"You're not?"

"Nope." Sam looked uncharitably smug.

"Well, how do I choose?" I said, a note of panic creeping into my voice.

"What do you want to do when you leave the academy?"

"How am I supposed to know? It's not like we've had careers talks or anything."

"Yeah, that's later this year," Sam said, and frowned. "Kinda backwards, now that I think about it."

"No shit," I snapped.

"Don't shoot the messenger."

I sighed, and tried to stifle the rising panic. Sam was right. It wasn't his fault I hadn't been paying attention. Why the hell hadn't I been paying more attention?

"Look, it's not the end of the world," Kelsey tried to console me. "If you choose and change your mind, you can always switch subjects before the end of the first semester."

"If I don't mind being months behind."

Kelsey nodded, as though being several months behind wasn't a massive deal. It probably wasn't, for her. One of the perks of being academically gifted, I guessed. She could catch up three months' work in a couple of weeks. I, on the other hand, sucked at studying. But that wasn't their fault, either.

"I like gryffs," I ventured after a moment. "Is there something I can do working with gryffs?"

Kelsey nodded again, with maybe a little too much enthusiasm.

"Sure. There are gryff trainers and breeders, and Itealta coaches, and you could even try out for one of the professional teams if you wanted – you're good enough."

Sam frowned.

"Huh, you're sure?"

"What's wrong with working with gryffs?"

"No, nothing. It's just..." He looked at Kelsey for help.

"We always thought you'd want to work for the council, as an enforcer," she said. "You know, after everything with the zombie, and R– I mean..."

"Raphael," I said. "You can say his name, guys. Look, he might be related to me by blood, but that's all. He's not the one who raised me. He's a sperm donor, at best. And he's an ass."

Leo spat out a mouthful of his drink. Family was a massive deal to shifters; I'd probably just broken one of their ancient codes.

"He's not my father," I reiterated. Leo held up his hands in surrender. "Anyway, assuming I survive this year, that'll be more than enough danger for me for one lifetime. I think I'll stick to gryffs."

And now that I thought about it, I really did want to work with the big, surly, intelligent creatures. I never felt more at home than when I was on Stormclaw's back, racing through the skies.

"Okay," Kelsey said. "In that case you'll want Supernatural Zoology. And Advanced Elemental Manipulation is a compulsory subject. That leaves you with three more to choose."

"Or three to drop," Sam said, leaving me in no doubt as to how he'd arrived at his five subjects. We'd taken eight subjects for the first two years, and I could see the appeal of his method when I thought about some of my dullest lessons.

"I think I'll drop History of Magic," I said. Sam nodded his approval and Kelsey scowled.

"That's not how you're supposed to choose," she said.

"So you're taking History?" Sam asked.

"Well, no... But that's not the point. You should think about Botany, Lyssa, it would complement Zoology. And maybe Potions?"

I nodded. That made sense. Certain plants could be hugely beneficial to gryffs if they were grown and harvested properly. And I didn't completely suck at it. It didn't help that Botany came more naturally to Earth elements, and Earth was the one element I didn't control. But half the academy didn't have an Earth elemental power, and they managed just fine. And once you harvested those plants, a decent knowledge of potions would help get the most out of them. My potion work was mediocre at best, but there were worse things to study.

"Okay, Botany, and Potions. I'm dropping Spellcraft."

"You're sure?"

I nodded.

"Atherton hates me." I caught the look of disapproval on Kelsey's face and pressed on before she could launch into a lecture. "I never manage to learn much in his lessons, and with all the extra study time I'll save, I'll be able to work on my other subjects."

She couldn't argue with that. Atherton's hobby was kicking me out of class for no reason, and I'd had to spend hours studying on my own last year just to try to keep up with everyone else.

"Okay. That leaves you with one last subject."

I nodded.

"Druidic Law, or Gaelic," I said. Neither of which were my favourites, but I didn't hate them, either. I mean, any more than I hated any subject that was almost entirely theory. "What are you guys doing?"

Kelsey pressed her lips together in a tight line.

"I'm doing Gaelic," Sam said. "I think my results from last year's Law exam speak for themselves. Kelsey's doing Law because Dougan practically begged her."

PRIMAL MAGIC

"He did not," Kelsey snapped. "Some of us actually have some ambition, and I'm going to need Druidic Law to achieve it."

"What do you want to do when you leave Dragondale?" I asked, genuinely curious. I'd never really considered what my mousey friend would do beyond studying. Librarian, maybe?

"We don't have time for all that," she said, flushing slightly. "I don't think it'll make too much difference which subject you choose, neither of them are necessary for working with gryffs."

"Anyone got a coin?"

No-one did, because currency in the druid community was entirely remote-based, connected to your energy pulse signature. I rooted around in the bottom of my bag, and eventually fished out what I was looking for – a pound coin that had been left there over the summer.

"Heads I take Law, tails I take Gaelic."

I flipped the coin in the air, caught it in one hand, and turned it out onto my waiting wrist. The queen's stoic face stared up at me.

"Law it is. Good. I can't pronounce half that Gaelic stuff."

Sam groaned, and slumped his head forward onto his forearms.

"Gaelic is going to be so dull without you around to cause trouble."

Chapter Two

Welcome to the Dragondale Academy of Druidic Magic."

The tall man standing on the stage in front of us was in his fifties, with short, dark hair and wrinkles starting to set into his face, and the cloak he wore was swirled with a mix of red, green, blue and yellow. As he had every year, he stared out at the rows of students in front of him, and we stared back in obedient silence. Mostly. There were a few excited whispers, probably from the first years. They'd be a little less excited when they realised what a stickler for rules and grades he was.

"As most of you know, I am Professor Talendale, and I am headmaster of this academy. It is my honour to guide you through the following year and ensure that each of you gives your *full* commitment to your studies."

I snuck a glance at Kelsey who was sitting beside me. Was it just me, or did Talendale's tone get more severe every year? Kelsey returned my look with the smallest frown and what might have been a nod.

"You have been given a tremendous opportunity in attending this sacred academy. All enter these halls as equals. How you leave them will be determined by your actions, and your actions alone. Diligence, dedication and determination are the mark of a good druid, and I expect nothing less from each and every one of you."

He paused and his eyes swept the hall, singling out some of the students.

"Those of you entering the third year, this will be your final year at Dragondale. I urge you not to squander it."

Kelsey visibly paled beside me. Great. Just what she needed – another reminder that her whole future hung in the balance. I gave her hand a quick squeeze and she flashed me an anxious smile.

"A reminder that the Unhallowed Grove is off limits to all students, and first years are not permitted onto the grounds after dark. Portalling is only to be attempted under strict supervision. Lessons will be available to third years during this semester."

"So cool," Sam muttered under his breath. "I'm heading straight to Vegas as soon as I can portal."

"You're too young to gamble there, jackass," I said, rolling my eyes. Sam frowned.

"Oh. Well, as soon as I'm old enough, then."

Kelsey glared at the pair of us, and I'm sure if there had been room she'd have moved her chair further away from us rule breakers, lest Talendale had super hearing that could pick up on our whispers. I was pretty sure he didn't, since he continued without giving us so much as a glance.

"There is another matter to which I must draw your attention. This year we will have some guests staying here at Dragondale. Due to some… renovation work… taking place at The Braeseth Academy of Unclassified Magic, its students will be unable to attend this semester. As such, the decision has been taken that one quarter of their number will attend each of the four druidic academies."

"But Professor," a voice burst out, and a hundred heads turned to the hand waving in the air, trying to get a look at the person foolish enough to interrupt Talendale's speech. The student's voice faltered slightly as he continued. "They're not druids."

"Very astute, Mr Howes," Talendale said dryly. "No doubt your powers of observation will serve you well in the future – though I hope, not in the middle of my assembly again."

The guy reddened and sunk further into his seat, to amused chuckles around the room.

"Indeed, our guests are not druids and as such we may need to make some adjustments to ensure they are able to get the most from our humble halls. They will be arriving in a few days, and I have no doubt that each and every one of you will do everything in your power to ensure they feel at home during their stay."

Absolute silence met Talendale's stern declaration, then abruptly his face lightened and the mood in the room shifted with it.

"And finally, to a subject that I am sure has been the centre of much speculation."

Sam elbowed me.

"This is it!" he hissed. "The Four Nations Cup."

"Every three years, the Druidic Academies of England, Ireland, Scotland and Wales come together to compete against each other in an international challenge of magical prowess. This most ancient tradition hails from our tribal days, long before druid-kind was united as one, when each academy would send their best and brightest students to defend their home from those who would conquer us."

He paused, and I couldn't help but wonder what that must have looked like: infighting amongst the druids, and magical wars.

"Now we stand united by the Grand Council, and we remember the sacrifice of all who have gone before by sending champions to compete for the honour of their academy. There will be four trials; one hosted by each of the academies, and each academy will put forward two champions. The nature of the challenges will not be made known until the day of the trial, so potential champions must be confident in all fields of magic. All who wish to partake must submit their name to me, along with a letter of recommendation from a professor of this academy, by the end of the week. A trial will be held to determine who is most worthy."

A dozen hushed whispers broke out across the hall as students speculated wildly about which professors they might ask to sponsor them, and who had the best chance of being selected. The news of the new arrivals seemed to be completely wiped from everyone's minds. Except mine.

"I'm putting my name in," Sam said. "I reckon Thorne will sponsor me."

Talendale cleared his throat, and silence fell across the room once more.

"I urge you to give serious consideration before putting your name forward. This is not a decision to take lightly. You are dismissed."

The scraping and clattering of several hundred chairs reverberated off the walls, along with the deafening din of excited students calling to each other across the room. I made towards the exit through the mass of bodies, with Sam and Kelsey in my wake, and then up towards the Fire common room.

I held my hand up to the door and gave two long pulses of fire energy, two short ones, and then another long pulse, and the door swung open. Inside was a vast room, filled with sofas, armchairs and tables. The floors were stone, interwoven with wooden streaks – roots from the Tilimeuse Tree that sat in the centre of the grounds and communicated with the Headmaster. I wasn't sure, but I suspected its roots ran through every room of the academy, and up all of its walls. It was beyond sacred. No tree, no Dragondale.

The Four Nations Cup was all anyone could talk about, and not just the guys. It seemed like the competition had everyone's patriotic spirit pumping.

"Are you putting your name forward?" Sharna, one of my classmates, asked after the conversation had been going for the better part of an hour.

"Of course she is," Alex said, idly playing a flame across her fingers. "She's like the druid messiah."

I rolled my eyes.

"Having an extra elemental power doesn't make me special. And no, I'm not entering. Kelsey's right, we've got bigger things to worry about this year."

"Than being famous?" Alex gaped at me and the fire on her hands went out. "Are you insane?"

"Maybe." I shrugged. "But I don't want to be famous for being the most incompetent druid Dragondale has ever trained."

"That's not stopping Sam putting his name forward."

Sam pulled out the cushion he was leaning on and flung it casually at Alex, who ducked aside with a grin. The cushion sailed over her shoulder and straight into the hands of a first year – where it promptly caught fire.

"Oh my God, what do I do?" the first year squealed, staring at the cushion, and the flames that were licking at it where it lay on the floor. Luckily, the academy's founders had had the foresight to make our common room ninety percent inflammable stone, so the fire didn't spread. Just as well. This happened at least once a day in here when there were new students getting the hang of their powers. I turned in my seat and held out a hand, directing a blast of cold air at the cushion. The flames went out and I turned my attention back to Alex.

"Look, the last thing anyone needs is me ruining the academy's best chance of winning some glory or whatever. Anyway, it's not like I'd have any chance of getting through whatever test Talendale sets. I mean, I barely scraped a pass on half my subjects last year."

"What are you so worried about then?"

I looked at Sam for support, but he just shrugged.

"She makes a good point. What've you got to lose?"

"Yeah, maybe." I glanced out of the window. The sun was edging slowly across the sky, and the shadows on the ground were getting longer. If I wanted to get down to the gryff barn to see Stormclaw before dinner, I'd have to go soon.

"Is that a yes, then?"

I looked from the window back to the five people watching me closely. My eyes flicked between each of theirs; Alex was leaning forward on her elbows, and Sharna was perched on the edge of her seat. Sam raised an eyebrow.

"Yeah." I smiled. Their enthusiasm was contagious. "Yeah, why not? I'll ask Professor Alden for a recommendation when I go see Stormclaw."

"I'm going to see Professor Swann in a minute," Kelsey said. "She'd write you one. You did so well on her exam last year. And her recommendation might carry more weight, what with her being head of elemental development."

"That makes sense. Wait, why are you going to see Swann?"

She smiled, tucking a strand of hair behind one ear, and held her hand into the middle of our circle, palm up. In the centre of her palm, a small green circle started to glow.

"Ohmigod!" Sharna squealed. "Kelsey, you got your second power!"

"Why didn't you tell me?" I grabbed her and gave her a hug – a gentle one, because Kelsey wasn't always keen on physical contact. Something to do with her shifter side, I think – or maybe she just didn't like being touched. Whichever. She let me get away with it.

"Well, it just happened a couple of days ago," Kelsey said. "And I wanted to be sure. I mean, Professor Swann's time is very valuable, and I didn't want to mess her around, you know, if I'd just imagined it. But I didn't. It's real."

She grinned, her cheeks flaming almost a red as her hair, and I grabbed her hand and hauled her to her feet.

"Come on," I said. "Let's go find her."

This was a massive deal for Kelsey. Her whole life she'd been told that being a shifter-druid hybrid meant she'd never be as good as other druids. As purebreds. Same for her shifter half – she'd never have as much control as full shifters, or shifter-mundane hybrids. The professors had warned her not to be disappointed if she never manifested a second power. She'd never said anything about me having three powers while she only had one, but deep down it had to have rankled.

We found Swann in her lecture room, sorting through her notes for the following day's lessons. I tapped once on the open door and paused in the doorway. Swann was tall and slender, with long blonde hair that flowed half-way down her back, and was never tied back. She was wearing her customary pale blue dress, and a light blue cloak was wrapped around her shoulders – it got draughty in some of these old classrooms.

"Ah, Lyssa, Kelsey," she said with a tired smile. "Please come in. I assume you're wanting me to write you both letters of recommendation for the trials?"

"No," I said, then amended, "Well, yes, for me, anyway. But Kelsey needs to see you about something else."

"Oh?"

Kelsey held out her hand, and the green glow returned.

"I've manifested a second element."

"That's wonderful news, dear," she said, taking hold of Kelsey's hand and examining it. "What an unexpected development! And it seems almost as strong as your primary element. We'll schedule you some extra lessons to help you get the most out of it, and… yes, yes I think we have time for a little lesson right now. Lyssa, you can head off. I'll hand your letter of recommendation directly to Professor Talendale."

"Uh, thanks Professor," I said, taking the hint and making for the door. Kelsey gave me a nervous smile, and I slipped out, leaving her to her lesson. Now was as good a time as any to head to the barn. I hurried through the academy's wide hallways, and out into the grounds. With each step, the excitement and impatience mounted inside me, until I was barely able to keep from breaking into a run. I couldn't wait to see Stormclaw. It had been nearly two months since I'd last seen him, and the foal he'd sired with Redwing. Leo had given me regular updates while he was working here over the summer, but it wasn't the same as actually being around the gryffs myself.

I was half-way to the barn when I heard the beating of wings. Tilting my head back, I could make out a horse-like figure gliding through the sky, with talons for front legs, and a sharp beak on its face. The front half of the animal was covered in feathers – black feathers, each outlined in gold.

"Stormclaw!"

He tucked his wings to his sides and dived towards the earth, thudding into the ground so hard that it shook beneath me, then he opened his beak and gave a loud screech – a reprimand, I was sure, for abandoning him all summer. He held his head aloft, tilting it to one side as he blinked a bird-like eye at me.

The massive creature dwarfed me, so I had to stretch an arm up to scratch his shoulder.

"I'm sorry, boy," I murmured. "I'd have come back if they'd have let me, you know that."

He turned his beak up at me a moment longer, then dropped his head to butt lightly against me, thrumming in his throat. I staggered back a step under the weight of his affectionate nudge, then scratched between his eyes.

"Hope you've been a good boy," I said, plucking a stray feather and letting it fall to the floor between us. At least he hadn't been hospitalising people in fits of temper this summer, unlike last year. At least, not many people, anyway. And it wasn't like Madam Leechington couldn't grow fingers back in a minute or two, it was no big deal.

He butted me again, then hunched down and tucked one scaled talon back against his side, forming a platform. I grinned and scrambled up onto it, and from there onto his back.

"But no dragons this time," I told him, as I shuffled in front of his wings and onto his withers, letting my legs hang down in front of his shoulders. "I haven't forgotten that first ride last year."

He screeched in what might have been amusement, which I didn't take to be a good sign, but before I could give it any thought he took off at a lope, stretching his wings out on either side of him, then leapt upwards and flapped them effortlessly. The ground fell away beneath us and I took a moment to remind my body to stay relaxed and to flow with his movement as he carried us through the sky.

Dragondale's grounds stretched out below us; rolling green fields and multi-tonal forests. Behind us, the greystone academy sat stoically as if it had risen from earth itself, and ahead of us the light glinted off the academy's lake, scattering orbs of light across the ground. And in the centre was the Tilimeuse Tree, the academy's huge, silver-brown primal plant, with branches that reached high above the ground and bore leaves of green, brown and orange, and roots deep underground reaching out to every corner of our magnificent home. It was beautiful. Beyond beautiful, really. The word hadn't yet been invented that could describe the majesty of Dragondale's ancient demesne, where generations of druids had learned to connect with themselves through nature, and where generations would continue to study long after my bones had turned to dust.

In the far pasture I could make out the herd of gryffs grazing in the evening sun, and a distant airborne shape told me that Ava was exercising Dardyr, one of the academy's three dragons. I touched my hand to Stormclaw's neck, because joking aside, I really didn't want another run in with the deadly creatures. Anyone who thought gryffs were cantankerous had never gotten close to a dragon.

Stormclaw complied with my request, apparently no more interested in becoming a dragon snack than I was, and wheeled back towards the barn. The grounds were even vaster than they seemed from up here – I knew of at least six outbuildings that led you to some sort of self-contained dimension not visible from the outside. One of them covered dozens of acres and housed the dragons, so the students didn't have to worry about being eaten – by them, at least. Another housed Ares, the academy's gryphon. The half eagle, half lion was Stormclaw's sire, and the only creature at Dragondale who was more dangerous than the dragons themselves. Fortunately, just about everyone was forbidden from going anywhere near him. He was one of only a dozen left in Europe, and though the rules were allegedly in place to protect the students, I secretly suspected Alden was just worried that eating one of us might give him a stomach upset.

When we touched down outside the barn, Alden was already there, wearing her customary grubby robes and thick leather-like gloves. A short, stout woman, with hair streaked brown and grey that she kept tied back, Professor Alden was by far my favourite teacher at the academy – and not just because I found her subject so interesting, although I'd be lying if I said that didn't play a part. She taught Supernatural Zoology, which meant I spent half of her lessons surrounded by incredible creatures, whose existence I'd never even have guessed at two years ago. Judging by the rows of stainless steel buckets lined up outside the barn, and the questionable smell coming from them, she was preparing the hippogryffs' feeds.

"Ah, Lyssa," she said as I slid from Stormclaw's back, and gave him a heavy pat on his shoulder. "I thought I might see you today."

"Good evening, Professor Alden," I said, because it never hurt to remember your manners around here. And if the last two years were anything to go by, Alden would be saving my hide by the end of the semester. Best to keep her sweet.

"I suppose it's too much to hope that you'll be working with my herd between your lessons again this year?"

I gave her an apologetic smile, and reached for one of the abandoned feed buckets.

"Sorry, Professor, I just don't think I'll have the time."

"Ah, well," she said, wiping one of her gloves down her cloak and leaving a trail of something slimy in its wake. "No matter. Ava seems keen to help out again, and that young werewolf has proved most helpful, though I suppose we'll not see him now that he's returned to his own academy. Now, there's something else I need to speak to you about."

"Oh?" I paused, and Stormclaw butted me impatiently. I set the bucket on the floor in front of him, and he shoved his beak into it, plucking out a gutted fish and tipping his head back to gulp it down whole.

"Well, as I'm sure you realise, Logan graduating last year means that the Fire Itealta team will be needing a new captain this season."

"Oh. I guess so," I said, frowning. I hadn't really given it any thought, truth be told.

"So, will you accept the position?"

"Me?"

"Of course, you. Who else has your experience, and your skill with the gryffs? This will be your third year on the team, and you know the herd better than anyone."

Me, in charge of the Itealta team? The captain? A grin crept onto my face.

"I'd love to, Professor."

Chapter Three

Good morning, everyone," Professor Ellerby said, as we stood clustered in the early morning mist outside of the greenhouse the following day. Unsurprisingly, this class was dominated by Earth elements, with just a few Water elements and two Air elements joining us – luckily neither of them being Felicity. Me, Sam and Kelsey were the only Fires.

"Today we're going to be repotting the Jing-Ru Dock plants. You will be marked according to their successful transition. As I'm sure you're all aware, they are incredibly sensitive to movement, and likely to release toxins if you disturb them too much, so please handle them with care. I do not want any of the plants damaged."

"Just the students, then," Sam muttered, and I stifled a chuckle. Ellerby homed in on us, and I thought we were about to get a lecture, but instead she said,

"Ah, there you are. My three Fire elements. I imagine you're going to be in demand today, making sure the soil is the correct temperature for the Jing-Rus to recover from the trauma." She glanced round the group as a whole. "I know some of you have manifested Fire as a second element, but I do not want any of you attempting to use it in this class until Professor Swann has deemed you proficient – there is far too much potential for you to damage the plants. Is that clear?"

Several of the Earth elements nodded seriously, and I noted the look of disappointment on one of the Air element's faces. The Water elements looked disinterested – no surprise, since it was impossible for a druid to manifest opposing elements. Earth and Air couldn't be manifested in the same person, nor could Fire and Water. Unless, apparently, you were me. Or Raphael.

Kelsey elbowed me in the ribs, and I realised Ellerby had finished talking, and was leading us inside the greenhouse. I tagged along as we moved through the rows of plants, taking care not to get too close to any of them. It paid to be careful; most things in here could defend themselves, and Ellerby always marked people down for needing to go and see old Leech.

We made it to the work area without anyone needing hospital treatment, and Professor Ellerby moved to the bench at the front. Beside it was a whiteboard, but it was empty – apparently we'd be doing this repotting without any guidance from her. No problem, I'd brought my textbook. I dumped it on one of the wooden benches near the back, and Sam and Kelsey took two of the remaining three spots around it.

The bench was ingrained with old soil, which I made a doomed attempt to brush aside before opening my book and looking for the Jing-Ru page.

"Paddy soil?" Kelsey said, sounding uncertain and flipping through her own book. I shrugged.

"As good a guess as any."

"I'll grab it," Sam said, unhooking a bucket from one side of the bench.

"Is this space taken?" Ben Ackerman was an Earth element, and a good one at that. Tall, awkward and generally quiet, he nonetheless had an incredible affinity for plants and their needs. With him at our bench, our combined grade was about to go up a few notches.

"It is now," I said, shoving my textbooks aside to make room for him. I wouldn't need them with him around, anyway. Just as well – it looked like the Jing-Ru plants weren't in there. Ellerby's idea of an interesting lesson.

"Plants are on the bench to your right," the professor called from behind her bench. "Please be sure to note the plant number before transferring it."

Me and Kelsey both turned to look at Ben.

"I'll choose one," he said. "Unless you want to?"

We both shook our heads. Number one rule of botany: always let the Earth elements handle anything that involved the primal energy of the plants. Kelsey went for some water, and I grabbed a ceramic pot from the pile at the back, staggering under its weight as I hauled it back to our bench. Ben was already there, with a large, bushy plant whose stem he was stroking affectionately. The plant seemed to shudder with happiness under his touch. Or at least, it didn't release any toxins, and I figured that was the same thing.

Kelsey put her bucket of water on the floor and Sam got back a moment later with a bucketful of soil. Ben glanced at it.

"Paddy soil?"

Sam nodded, but Ben frowned and shook his head.

"You want saline soil. Paddy soil is too acidic."

Sam rolled his eyes and heaved the bucket away again, and returned a few minutes later with a new one.

"Tip it out on the bench," Ben said. "Spread it out. The Jing-Ru will do better if it's all lightly heated to the same temperature."

With the three of us warming the soil it took only seconds to reach a temperature Ben was satisfied with. Unfortunately, that was long enough for some of the other benches to notice what we were doing, and ask us to do the same for theirs.

"I'll do it," Sam said, and headed off with one of the Air elements.

Ben eased the plant from its current pot, handling it as though it was an explosive that might detonate at any moment, and the whole time I could see his palms giving off the faint green glow of his Earth magic. By unspoken agreement we left him to take care of handling the plant itself – Kelsey probably because she knew it was our best chance to get a good mark for this lesson, me because I didn't fancy getting hit with any of those toxins. Leech would be seeing enough of me once the Itealta season got started.

Kelsey piled the soil into our pot, and just as I was about to tip some water in, Ben shook his head.

"Warm it first, a couple of degrees."

No sooner than I had done that than a student from one of the other tables came over. I rolled my eyes and went with her, wondering whether it would be completely uncharitable to bring their water to the boil.

It was a long class. Every time we heated anything, someone from one of the other benches, or two of them, or all of them, would come and ask us to do the same thing for theirs. The sooner they were allowed to use their second elements, the better. At this rate, we were going to spend the entire semester running around after other people. By the time Ellerby declared our time was up, me, Kelsey and Sam were all red-faced and exhausted. Still, I couldn't help but notice our plant was looking the best of the bunch. Lucky us that Ben had come to join our bench. I said as much, and he grinned.

"Lucky you? Nope, lucky me. I had all three Fire elements prioritising my plant."

I laughed. I'd never pegged Ben as being quite so devious.

*

The rest of our classes that week were no easier – it seemed like every professor was determined to prove to us just how much harder we were going to have to work this year. And as if our increased workload wasn't enough, I had Alden on my case every time I ventured near the gryff barn, telling me that I needed to hold tryouts for our house's Itealta team, and that if I wanted first choice of the unbonded gryffs, then I'd have to make a decision by the weekend. I grudgingly agreed to hold the tryouts on Saturday morning, so I could help anyone on the team who didn't already have a bond with gryff try to form one in the afternoon. Alden shook her head.

"It'll have to be Sunday. Saturday is the trial for the Four Nations Cup."

"It is? Do you know what it involves?"

"No, I don't." Alden pursed her lips in disapproval. "You can't afford to let yourself get distracted, not if you want a career in Itealta. You know that Logan got signed by the Essex Hornets at the end of last season?"

I nodded. The trouble was, I didn't know if I did want a career in Itealta. I mean, with gryffs, sure, I loved hanging out with the misunderstood animals, and I was serious about working with them. But a career in competing? I just wasn't sure it was me.

Alden, apparently in a perceptive mood, took in my face with a glance and sighed.

"I suppose one day of distraction will do you no harm. Just make sure you're ready for the tryouts on Sunday."

I promised I would be, and scurried off to spread the news about the trial for the Four Nations Cup this coming Saturday, but it seemed that someone had beaten me to it — everyone was already talking about the upcoming assessment, and speculating what it would involve. It seemed like Talendale was being tight-lipped about it. Then again, he was tight-lipped about everything, so that was no surprise. Sam spent the rest of the week getting me and Kelsey to grill him about ancient runes and rare plants at every opportunity, convinced the assessment would be a written test, and then groaning in frustration when he got the answers wrong. I, true to my word, tried not to let it distract me, and focussed on getting word out about the tryouts. Half of our team had graduated last year, and if I was going to secure us the cup for the third year running, I was going to have to find some good replacements. It wasn't easy getting anyone to focus on anything other than the trials, but by Friday evening I had twenty-three people signed up to try out for the eight positions. Well, seven – my position wasn't up for grabs, because whoever heard of a non-playing captain?

I left the sign-up form down in the barn for Alden, so she could see I was taking my role as captain seriously, made a quick fuss of Stormclaw, then hurried to the dining hall. It looked like I might even be on time for once – more or less.

There were clusters of students milling about at the entrance to the main hall, talking in hushed whispers as they gradually made their way through the doors towards the end of the food queue. I spotted Sam and Kelsey and caught up to them and nodded a greeting to them.

"What's going on?" I asked. People didn't usually mill and talk in hushed whispers when they were waiting for dinner. Sam bent his head close to me, and nodded towards a group in dark cloaks, standing well back from the rest of the students.

"Look," he whispered. "The Braeseth lot."

A head snapped round to us, fixing us with his dark eyes. He was short and wiry and wore mundane clothes under his black cloak. I frowned. There was no way he could have heard Sam, at least, he shouldn't have been able to.

"It's rude to stare," Kelsey mumbled, tucking her chin down and pointedly avoiding looking at the unclassified.

"I wasn't staring," Sam said, not taking his eyes from the group. The wiry guy stared back, and I rolled my eyes. I didn't need to make new enemies; I had plenty of those already. I offered the guy a smile and walked over to the group, ignoring the dozen pairs of eyes following me. After a moment, I heard Sam and Kelsey behind me.

"Hi," I said to the wiry guy. "I'm Lyssa."

"Kayden," he grunted. Two of his friends – a willowy girl with blonde hair that fell around her face in dull, lank waves, and a gaunt faced guy with a shock of blue hair so pale it was almost grey – hovered protectively behind him, not quite squaring up to us. Friendly.

"So, um, welcome to Dragondale," I tried again. "Our home is your home."

"Sure."

"Are you always this talkative?"

"Are you always this impetuous?"

I hesitated, as if considering his question, then shrugged.

"Yup, pretty much."

His lips curved into a reluctant smile before he managed to quash it.

"That's Kelsey, and Sam. He's got all the tact of a hippogryff, so don't pay him any attention."

"Hey," Sam protested, catching up to me. "I resent that remark. No, wait. Resemble. I resemble that remark."

He grinned and held his hand out to Kayden. The guy eyed it for a moment, and then they shook.

"Good to meet you," Kayden said. "But if you came looking for a front seat at the freak show, you're going to be disappointed."

"Pfft," I said, ignoring his bitter tone. I guess these guys were outcasts every bit as much as Kelsey – and me. "You're talking to the queen freak."

He gave me a funny look, his forehead creasing in confusion like he was trying to work out whether I was taking the piss or not, then the blonde girl muttered something too quiet for me to catch. Apparently not too quiet for Kayden to hear, though. I wondered how else they were different from us.

"You're Lyssa Eldridge," he said.

"That's what I said, isn't it?" I shrugged.

"You're the druid with three elements."

"Ah, there's the look I know and love," I said, rolling my eyes.

Kelsey shuffled her feet, and I caught her eyeing the dwindling line towards Aiden's counter. There was only so far you could push it when it came to keeping a werewolf from her food.

"Come on," I said to her and Sam. "Let's eat."

I gave a parting smile to Kayden, who was still looking at me like I was a riddle he couldn't solve, and then made for the back of the queue. The one plus side to everyone being busy standing around gossiping was that we only had a couple of people in front of us. Once they'd taken their food, I ordered far too much of something decidedly unhealthy – hey, I was going to need my strength for tomorrow – and made my way over to one of the Fire tables with Sam and Kelsey, all whilst mulling over how stupid it would be to go through with the Four Nations Cup trials. As if I didn't have enough to worry about with the Itealta try outs. I was such an idiot. This was going to be a disaster.

"Uh-oh," Kelsey said under her breath, nudging me with her elbow.

"That's not going to end well," Sam said.

I followed the direction of both of their gazes and had to agree. Kayden and his friends were heading for the table closest to the door, one of the Air tables – and not just any Air table. They'd set their sights on the one Felicity was sitting at with Cecelia and Imogen, next to a few empty seats. As I watched, Kayden said something to Felicity, and the airhead's face contorted with derision.

"I don't think so," she said, loudly enough for half the hall to hear, looking him up and down. "We don't allow just anyone to sit with us. Some of us still have standards."

I rolled my eyes. Classic Felicity. Kayden and his two friends shared a look between themselves, apparently at a loss with how to respond. So much for making them feel welcome. I sighed, and waved an arm in the air.

"Hey!" The three of them turned as one, and I gestured to our table. "We've got plenty of seats. Come join us."

Felicity looked our way and sneered.

"What a surprise," she said, her catty voice ringing loud and clear enough for everyone to hear as she spoke to her cronies sitting right beside her. "Lyssa Eldridge to the rescue. Attracting outcasts is her strongest power, after all."

Her insults were wasted on me. I didn't set any stock in her opinions, and I had absolutely no intention of rising to the bait.

"As opposed to your power, which is what, spending Daddy's money?" Okay, so good intentions only counted for so much. It was worth it, watching her face change colour as she pushed herself up from the table. She raised one hand, and I saw the ball of air swirling inside it.

"Look out!" I shouted to the trio of unclassifieds as Felicity drew her arm back to throw. They were right in her path.

"Felicity Hutton!" Professor Swann's voice cracked across the room, leaving utter silence in its wake. Felicity dropped her hand and crushed the airball, but it was too late. Swann had seen her preparing to attack another student. It was hard to keep the smug look from my face as Swann stepped from behind a cluster of students, glaring at Felicity. Swann pivoted on her heel.

"And Lyssa Eldridge."

"What? But I didn't—"

"My office. Both of you. Now."

She fixed me with a glare that left no room for argument, and with one last sorrowful look at my plate of junk food, I traipsed from the hall behind her, past the trio of students. Kayden gave me a curt nod on my way past, and Felicity a dark look that left no doubt what he wanted to do to her. The blue-haired guy clamped a hand on his shoulder and muttered something in his ear that I didn't catch, and I didn't stick around to find out. It wouldn't be smart to let Swann think I was ignoring her instructions. I was in enough trouble as it was. For some reason.

I'd never been in Swann's office before, and I couldn't help but notice it reflected her perfectly: neither hot nor cold, it was delicately decorated, with light blue drapes – she was a water element, after all – and rustic, exposed Tilimeuse roots streaked through the stone walls and cobbled floor. A fireplace sat in one wall near the door, a large window in a second, some sort of climbing plant covered the third, and the fourth... I took a step forward, my mouth open in wonder. A dainty waterfall was running down the final wall, and when the water reached the bottom, it split in two directions, and flowed back *up* the wall in each corner. I looked more closely, but there was no sign of any pipes.

The door slammed shut, and Professor Swann rounded on us.

"What on earth do you two think you are playing at? In the middle of the main hall, and in front of our guests, no less. Are you trying to destroy the reputation of Dragondale? Because let me tell you, you're going about it the right way."

She glowered at us, and I dropped my head under the weight of her disapproval – and I hadn't even done anything.

"Do I need to call your elemental heads in here?"

I jerked my eyes up to look at her. Alden was my head of element, and if she got wind of this, she might pull my position as captain.

"No, Professor," I said quickly. Swann looked from me to Felicity and back again, her expression inscrutable.

"I'm not so sure. I expect better. From both of you."

Oh, to hell with this. I wasn't about to risk my captaincy over something I hadn't even done.

"But Professor," I protested, "I didn't do anything. It was Felic—"

Swann rounded on me, her face furious.

"And I'm supposed to believe that Ms Hutton conjured that airball just for the sake of it?"

"No, Professor," Felicity said before I could argue that I wasn't responsible for her temper. "I didn't. Lyssa—"

"I don't care!"

I'd never heard Swann raise her voice before. Felicity seemed oblivious as she tried to worm her way out of the trouble she'd earned.

"I was provo—"

"You were provoked?" Swann cut across her scathingly. "You are almost a fully-fledged druid. You should know better."

"But she said—"

"I don't care if she said your mother was a werewolf and your father was a hamster. You were about to use magic on another student. It is only because I stopped you that you're not being expelled right now. You should be thanking me." Swann took a breath and continued, her voice calmer but still stern. "I shall have to inform your father, of course."

Abruptly, Felicity looked contrite.

"I'm sorry, Professor. You're right, I shouldn't have let her get to me. It was immature, and I should have better control. I promise, it won't happen again."

"See that it doesn't," Swann said. She turned to me. I sucked in a deep breath and prepared for the bitter taste of humble pie.

"I'm sorry, Professor Swann. I shouldn't have wound Felicity up." Even if she did make it ridiculously easy, I added silently. And even if she had started it.

Swann glared at us both for a long moment, then she drew in another breath, and her face softened with weariness.

"Go. If I see either of you causing trouble again, it will go on your records."

"Yes, Professor," I said, and made a dart for the door before she could change her mind. I did the sensible thing and made straight for my dorm. Might as well get an early night, anyway. I needed to be at my best for the Four Nations Cup trial – in the interest of at least not totally humiliating myself in front of the entire academy. For once.

Chapter Four

When the following morning rolled round, I felt about as far from prepared as it was possible to be. In fact, I was considering dropping out altogether. I mean, it wasn't even like I wanted to compete in the stupid cup in the first place – I just got nagged into it by Alex. A moment of madness, that was all it had been.

"Hi. Are these seats taken?"

I glanced up from the eggs I'd been downing with vigour, having missed dinner last night, and saw the three Braeseth students from yesterday. I swallowed my mouthful in a painful gulp, and shook my head.

"Help yourselves. Not everyone here is like Felicity."

"Yeah, thanks for yesterday, by the way," he said. "We weren't expecting anyone to stand up for us here."

"Why not?"

He gave me a confused look as he set his plate on the table and pulled out a chair. The other two followed his lead.

"You're druids. We're not."

Wow, I guess druids really did have a bad reputation in the other communities. No surprise, if how they'd treated Kelsey and Paisley for being hybrids was anything to go by, I guessed.

"This is Micah and Harper, by the way."

He gestured to the gaunt guy with the pale blue hair, and the lank-haired blonde girl, both who nodded in greeting, though the girl didn't bother to make eye contact or arrange her expression into anything that might be considered friendly.

"Don't mind them," Kayden said. "This is all a little… overwhelming."

He glanced around the hall, which made me wonder what sort of place Braeseth Academy was. A small one, if the two dozen students who'd come here represented a quarter of them.

"Uh, you already know Sam and Kels, right? This is Sharna, and Dean," I introduced them, and then nodded to the girl who'd dropped me in my current dilemma. "And Alex."

"We met last night," Kayden said, scooping some cereal into his mouth.

Oh. Right. While I was busy getting yelled at and missing dinner. I got back to my cooked breakfast and coffee while the newcomers tucked into their food.

"So," Sam said. "What really happened to your academy?"

Kayden froze, his spoon halfway to his mouth, and beside him, Micah went utterly rigid. I stamped on Sam's foot. Truly, the tact of a hippogryff.

"Ow! Come on, it's not really closed to renovations, right?"

"Ignore him," I said. "It's none of our business."

"No, it's fine," Kayden said, setting his spoon back in his bowl. "There's no reason we can't tell you."

He shared a tense look with the other two, until Micah shrugged and looked away. I pretended not to notice the awkward exchange.

"Braeseth isn't being renovated. It was cursed."

"What do you mean?"

"Cursed," Harper said. "Hexed. What is it you don't understand?"

My mouth popped open – I thought Felicity had the monopoly on being bitchy round here – and Kayden shot her a dark look.

"The academy isn't safe anymore," he said. "Dark magic is in every corner, destroying the building and anyone who gets too close."

"That's awful!" Kelsey said, her cheeks flushed. "Who would do something like that? And why?"

Kayden shrugged and went back to his food, and the other two steadfastly ignored us. I groped for a change of subject, and remembered what I'd been thinking right before they joined us. I glanced over at Kayden, since he was the only one who seemed inclined to make an effort at civil conversation.

"So, are you guys taking part in the cup?"

Harper barked a bitter laugh, and Kayden shot her a glare, then shook his head at me.

"That's a druid competition. We're not invited."

"Yeah," Harper said. "Because your 'Grand Council' keeps rejecting our requests."

"Oh. That sucks."

Kayden shrugged, making light of it. Maybe it just bothered Harper more than him.

"Doesn't matter. We've got enough to worry about right now with our studies. We'll be watching from the sidelines."

Was there a slight trace of bitterness to his voice when he said that, or was I just projecting how I would feel in his position onto him? Not that he was wrong about the studying part, though. The cup was a distraction none of us needed. Anyway, it was settled. I'd withdraw, and cheer Sam on from the sidelines with the unclassifieds. He would make an excellent academy champion. He was strong and fast, and just about the most competitive person I knew, and when he put his mind to it, he knew a hell of a lot about the druidic world. I hadn't even known it existed for most of my life. Sam was definitely the better champion. And, well, I'd find some other way to see the other academies.

"Uh-oh, she's got that look again," Sam said, spraying cereal everywhere.

"Ew, gross," I said, slapping his arm. "Born in a barn, much? And what look?"

"The one that says you're about to chicken out." He wiped milk from his chin.

"It's not chickening out. It's just… being sensible."

"It's chickening out," Alex agreed. "And we're not going to let you. Besides, it's too late. Look – Talendale's about to announce the challenges."

She was right, I saw with a sinking heart. The headmaster was approaching a podium that had been set at the head of the hall. He cleared his throat, and I set down my knife and fork, losing all interest in my food again.

"Good morning, students. I see we have–" he glanced down at a sheet on the podium, "–over two hundred potential champions competing today. I am most thrilled that so many of you are displaying such pride in your academy."

"Someone might have told his face that," Alex mumbled from the side of her mouth. I leaned back in my seat. Two hundred. Easy peasy to drop out part way through without anyone paying too much attention.

"You have ten minutes to finish your breakfast, and then we will make a start. All those not competing, including our guests, or those who are eliminated, are invited to watch the proceedings from the Itealta stadium, where the final challenge will conclude."

"Final challenge?" Sam said, looking distraught. "As in, more than one?"

"Excellent deduction skills, Mr Devlin," Talendale said dryly, to laughter from the rest of the students. Sam flushed red and flashed his boyish grin. "If you have no more insights to offer us, perhaps I might continue?"

There were a couple more snickers – mostly from the Air table, I couldn't help but notice – and Talendale pressed on.

"Myself and the four heads of houses will set each of the potential champions a challenge. Fail any of the challenges, and you will be unable to proceed. The winners will be the first two students to complete all of the challenges. Are there any questions?"

"Yeah," I muttered under my breath. "What the hell did I sign up for?"

"Very well then," Talendale said. "Finish your meals and clear the tables, and the first challenge shall begin."

I'd never seen four hundred students eat and clear away so quickly. Before I knew it, Kelsey was patting me awkwardly on the shoulder and wishing me luck, then following the other non-competing students out of the hall.

We settled down into an almost-silence, and Talendale resumed his position at the podium, this time with a stack of envelopes in front of him.

"Each of you please take a seat," he said.

"I knew it," Sam groaned, more quietly this time. "It's a written test. I'm doomed."

Nonetheless, he settled back into one of the seats at the Fire table, and I took the seat next to him.

"A good druid is quick of wit and slow of temper," Talendale intoned. "Through understanding of our world comes understanding of ourselves, and only by understanding both can we achieve true harmony. As such, the first challenge shall be a riddle. When you believe you have the correct answer, come and see me. Be warned, you will have only one attempt. Answer correctly, and you may enter this portal to the next challenge."

He waved his hands to his left and a portal sprung into existence, giving us the barest glimpse of what looked like a dark corridor.

"However, should you answer incorrectly, you will enter this portal to the stadium, where you will finish the challenge as a spectator." He waved his hands again, and another portal opened to his right, and through this one I could make out the stands, already packed with the remaining students and professors.

Talendale glanced around the room, waiting for questions, and when there were none, he raised both hands. The envelopes on his podium shot across the room, one landing in front of each student in the hall.

"Very well. You may… begin!"

I ripped open my envelope, and pulled out the single piece of card inside it.

A blessing to many, to others: a curse
But rare is he whose life it makes worse.
Finish with this over your fiercest foe
Possess it not, and defeat you'll know.
In these halls, its yearning rife
Name the greatest gift of life.

I frowned, glanced round at all the other frowning students, and read it again. *The greatest gift of life.* What did that mean? *Hope? Love?* It didn't really fit though, and I wouldn't get a second guess. I didn't want to go out on the first challenge – I'd already caught Felicity smirking at me from across the hall. There was no way I was going to give her even more excuses to spread crap about me not belonging here. I set my jaw, and read through the riddle again. I'd never been good at riddles.

I stared at it, waiting for the answer to spring into existence in my mind, which proved to be a waste of time. *Think, Lyssa!*

Sam nudged me and I looked up from my scrap of card to a student rising from the Air table. He walked over to Talendale and said something I couldn't make out – presumably Talendale had cast a sound-dampening spell to stop anyone getting an unfair advantage. Shame. I could do with one of those right about now.

We watched with bated breath, but Talendale shook his head, and gestured to the portal on his right. The one that led to the stadium. The Air hung his head, and stepped through.

"One down," Sam muttered. "A hundred and ninety-nine to go…"

I turned my card over in my hands, and the words on it over in my head. Every few moments someone else would get up and give Talendale an answer. None of them guessed correctly.

A blessing to many, to others: a curse. That could mean children, and, *In these halls, its yearning rife,* that could mean freedom. But children's freedom? That didn't exactly make sense. I groaned, and slumped my head onto the table. Who was I kidding? The whole damned riddle didn't make sense. Wait. It didn't make sense. It was like… It was like some of it was missing.

"Hey, Sam," I hissed, glancing around to make sure no-one else was paying attention. I didn't want to get thrown out for cheating if I was wrong about this. "Show me your card."

He gave me a puzzled look, but let me see anyway. I knew it! I snatched his card from him and put on the table, then laid mine next to it. Sam gasped.

"They're different."

"Sshh! Keep your voice down!"

He ducked his head and glanced around.

"Why have we got different riddles?"

"Not different," I said, shaking my head. I slid the cards around so mine was above his. "Two parts of the whole."

I scanned the newly reassembled riddle.

The sound of refusal starts your quest
To plant a tree, this is second best.
It can't be touched but may be held
Its want has entire empires felled.
The more you have, the more you seek
Cherished by both the bold and meek.
A blessing to many, to others: a curse
But rare is he whose life it makes worse.
Finish with this over your fiercest foe
Possess it not, and defeat you'll know.
In these halls, its yearning rife
Name the greatest gift of life.

"Great," said Sam. "But what does it mean?"

"No idea."

"You can hold it, but not touch it, right?" I said, keeping my voice low. Sam grunted in reply.

"What about breath?" I said, scanning back over the notes.

"Dunno. What's the whole thing about the sound of refusal?"

"Refusal," I mused. "Like, 'no'? I guess that doesn't really fit. Second best to plant a tree?"

"Loamy soil," he said, without hesitation. "Second best is heavy."

"Check you out, how long have you been paying attention in Botany? Kinda depends on the tree, though, right? Wait, what's the old proverb? Best time to plant a tree is twenty years ago.

"Second best time is now," he finished.

"No, now... They start the quest. The first letters of the word, right?"

"Okay, then," he said, scanning the sheets. "In that case, 'finish with' has got to be the last letters, right?"

I looked again, and turned the words over in my mind. *Finish with this over your fiercest foe. Possess it not, and defeat you'll know.*

"An edge," Sam blurted. "You have to have an edge."

"In these halls, it's yearning rife. Name the greatest gift of life. No edge? Now edge?"

We both stared at the sheet again, as if waiting for the letters to rearrange themselves into the answer. What did Talendale think we should value above all else? What could the lack of fell empires? What couldn't be touched? No edge... Now edge...

"Wait," I said. "Knowledge. That's it! It's knowledge!"

"Flipping heck, don't tell the whole hall! You're right. Come on."

We grabbed our slips of card and hurried up to Talendale. He raised an eyebrow.

"You have an answer?"

"Yes, sir. It's knowledge."

"That is correct."

I grinned, and stepped towards the portal, only to find an arm blocking my path. I looked at Talendale uncertainly.

"You worked together," he said. "Before you may pass, you will explain why you chose to do so."

Uh-oh. I shared a look with Sam, who was frozen in place, eyes wide. I straightened and met Talendale's eye.

"A good druid is in harmony with not just the world in which they live, but also those with whom they share it. Cooperation is the key to harmony."

Talendale watched me, unblinking, for a long moment. A really long moment.

"Excellent answer, Ms Eldridge. You may both proceed through the portal."

I stepped through the portal and moved quickly aside so Sam wouldn't crash into me, or tumble back into it.

Portals were tricky. It would ruin everyone's day if he got stuck half-in, half-out.

"How the hell did you know that answer?" he said. I shrugged.

"Made it up. Sounded like something he might like, all that harmony crap."

"Well, looks like we're the only ones who have made it so far."

"Great. What's the next challenge?"

I glanced around, because as far as I could see, we were alone in a deserted corridor, where it intersected with another corridor – giving us a choice of four possible directions. We were somewhere in the bowels of the castle, if I had to guess. Sam pivoted on his heel, sweeping his eyes high and low.

"No idea. This must be part of the test. Which way do you want to go?"

"It could be any of them. We need to choose before we lose our lead."

"Flip a coin?"

He was already reaching into his pocket, but I shook my head. It wasn't like either of us would have one anyway.

"No. You're right, it's part of the test, which means we need to work out the right direction. I bet the others will all send you back to the stadium. The question is, which professor set this challenge?"

"Maybe it's an illusion – a spellcasting test," Sam suggested.

"Could be." It would be just like Atherton to choose a challenge that didn't involve him having to spend any time with the students. On the other hand, as an air element, I was having a hard time picturing him down in the underground warren of the academy.

"Earth element," I said after a second. "It's got to be Ellerby's challenge."

I moved over to one of the walls, and ran my hands over it. Nothing seemed unusual about it.

"Plants, then? Or maybe Swann's challenge?"

I considered it for a moment, then nodded. I couldn't see any trace of plant life down here, and maybe– No, wait. There *was* a plant down here.

"The Tilimeuse Tree!" I gasped. I was so used to seeing its roots and vines entwined throughout the academy's stonework that I'd stopped paying them any attention.

Sam looked dubious.

"Are you sure? I mean, it's everywhere. What are we supposed to do with it?"

"I don't know," I said. "But we'd better decide quickly."

"Okay, the Tilimeuse Tree is attracted to magic, right?"

"It is?"

He looked at me like I'd just said I wasn't sure the sky was blue.

"Hey, I didn't grow up in the magic community!"

"No, but it's your third year here, you might make—"

"More of an effort to integrate. I know. Tell me what else you know about the tree."

He ran his hands over the wooden veins spread through the walls, then took my hand, and pressed it to the wall.

"Do you feel that?"

I started to shake my head, then paused, and cocked it instead.

"What is that?" I could feel the faintest pulsing beneath my palm – maybe it was just my own pulse reflected back at me, but it didn't feel like it. It felt like it was coming from the roots. I slid my hand along the wall, and the pulsing got weaker until I could barely discern it. I pivoted and retraced my steps, and the pulsing got stronger again.

"It's leading us somewhere!"

"Its aura gets stronger the closer to magic it is. I bet the next challenge has a massive amount of magic."

"Sam, you're a genius."

I kept my hand pressed to the wall, and we hurried along the corridor. I had no idea how far behind us the rest of the potentials were, but if they saw what we were doing they'd catch up in a hurry and we'd lose our lead.

The pulsing led us deeper and deeper through the labyrinthine passageways. Sam floated a fireball out in front of us when we hit the darker chambers, so we could still see where we were going. I felt sorry for anyone doing this who didn't have a Fire power. But then maybe my hatred of the dark was because Fire dictated my life. Huh. Something to ponder – later. I pressed on.

"Look!"

I raised my eyes from the wall and saw what Sam was pointing at. Ahead was a glowing portal, and I could make out a figure in front of it. Professor Ellerby.

The portal was giving off so much light that Sam's fireball was completely redundant, and he extinguished it with a curl of his fist. As he did, I heard a shout from behind us in the corridor. Someone was catching us up. More than one someone, if the level of noise was anything to go by.

"Hurry up," I hissed at him, and I dropped my hand from the wall and sprinted towards Ellerby, Sam hot on my heels.

"Congratulations," Ellerby said as we reached her. "You have demonstrated excellent understanding of the nature of the Tilimeuse Tree. You may proceed through the portal… after you have passed my test."

I shared a look with Sam, and saw my own anxiety reflected back at me. I'd fluked a pass on my Botany exam last year, and Sam hadn't done much better. Ellerby gestured to a table beside her, bearing two platters, each piled high with near-identical leaves.

"One set of leaves comes from the highly poisonous Xierhr tree, the other from the harmless Wren tree. You must eat one before you pass. Which will you choose?"

I had no idea. I looked at Sam. He had no idea. Ellerby shot us a sly wink.

"Don't worry," she said in a hushed voice. "Madam Leechington is through the second portal. If you choose wrong, she'll fix you right up."

She gestured to a smaller portal set into the other wall. Somehow, her reassurances did nothing to make me feel better. Just because Leech could regrow fingers, it didn't make losing them any less painful. I suspected the same thing applied to poisons.

"I'll go first," Sam said, squaring his shoulders. "If I get the wrong one, choose the other on your go, and get through the portal."

"No! That's not fair, you're the reason we made it this far."

He stared at something behind me, and I looked back to where I could see the first silhouettes appearing at the far end of the corridor.

"No time to argue," he said, and grabbed one of the leaves from the platter on the right. He shoved it in his mouth, and chewed furiously. My stomach churned as I watched him, scanning his face, trying to see what effect it was having. Suddenly, he gasped and doubled over, clutching his stomach.

"Sam!"

I reached out to him – to do what, I had no idea – but he raised one hand and shoved me away as firmly as he could.

"Go! Before Felicity catches up!"

I looked down the corridor again, and saw he was right – it was Felicity hurrying towards us, and she was almost here. I grabbed a leaf from Ellerby's left platter and shoved it in my mouth. Almost at once, I felt a pleasantly warm tingle inside. I glanced down at my hand, and could make out a faint glow around it, a tell-tale sign of ingesting a Wren tree leaf.

"Very good, through you go," Ellerby said cheerfully, and then to Sam, "We'll just pop you through this portal for Madam Leechington, dear."

I cast one last look at Sam, then dived through the larger of the two portals, with the sound of Felicity's approaching steps ringing in my ears. I hoped she chose the leaves on Ellerby's right platter.

I stumbled out of the portal on the far side, and the glowing on my skin started to fade. I was outside in the grounds, standing beside the academy's large lake. In front of me was Professor Swann. She smiled.

"Lyssa. I can't say I'm entirely surprised you're the first to make it this far."

She'd barely finished speaking when there was a ripple in the portal, and a second figure burst through. Crap. It was Felicity. She gave me a nasty sneer, but then she caught sight of Swann and her expression was all sweetness again.

"Congratulations, girls," Swann said. "Your next challenge is simple."

She gestured to a row ten one-man boats floating in the lake.

"In order to progress, you must each bring a boat to the shore. I wouldn't recommend swimming out to them."

As she spoke, a dark shape breached the surface, and I was pretty sure I could hear the sound of teeth snapping. Yeah, I wasn't going for a dip in that water any time soon. Well, that was easy enough. I was pretty sure I knew a spell that would attract wood towards me. I fixed my eyes on the small boat bobbing about on the surface.

"Tàlaidh fiodh!"

The words echoed back at me, but they sounded hollow, as though they had been stripped of their magic. Across the lake, the boat remained where it was. Felicity shouted a spell of her own, and I flicked a sideways glance in her direction. Her face was a mirror of the frustration and confusion that must have been plastered over mine.

Okay. Her spell wasn't working either. Swann must have done something to us. Light glinted off something at my feet, and I squinted down at it. Metal pieces were scattered around the ground, and I could make out the angular shapes of runes carved into their surface. They were blocking our magic, but there were too many to attempt to collect, and I didn't think that was the point of the test. If I had to guess, I'd say the runes would let only the most primitive of magic through. Elemental powers.

Unlike Felicity, I had a choice of three powers to use. I could use fire to heat the water, speeding and slowing the currents beneath my boat, but that would need a lot of precision at quite a distance. I could use air to push the boat, which seemed like the easiest option and was undoubtedly the one Felicity would choose – but my air power was my newest, and my control wasn't great. Or I could use my water power to move the water beneath the boat itself.

I flung up my hand a split second after Felicity, and my palm immediately started to glow blue. Beside me, Felicity's glowed yellow, and her boat started to cut through the water. Maybe I *should* have attempted to use my air power. Oh well, too late to change my mind now. I commanded the water to move, and the boat rocked violently to one side, taking on a massive wave. Oops. Too much. Too many like that and I'd sink it. I tried again, more gently this time, and the boat lurched forward. Yes!

I saw movement from the corner of my eye, and three more students stepped from the portal. I couldn't afford to let them distract me. Felicity's boat was already in front of mine, and drawing away. I ground my teeth together and my palm glowed more darkly. Carefully, I moved the water, crashing it into the rear of the boat to drive it forwards, whilst keeping enough under the front to make sure I didn't push it under the surface. My eyes flicked to Felicity's boat. Was I imagining it, or was I gaining on her? Felicity clearly didn't think I was imagining it; she let out a noise of frustration and all but stamped her foot like the spoiled princess she was.

I kept gaining on her as our boats floated towards the shore. Behind them, I could see five other boats drifting towards us, and one spinning in a circle. More students had arrived.

My boat was so close I could almost touch it now – and so was Felicity's. With one last push of water, I forced my boat up onto the shore, at the exact same time as its twin.

"Excellent work, girls." Swann beamed at us. "You'll find your next clue inside your boats."

I sprinted forwards and leaned in my boat, plucking the sheet of card from inside. It was completely dry, despite the inch of water it was floating in, so I assumed it was enchanted to repel any water.

It was a map. I could see the lake marked out on it, and the academy in the distance. In the opposite direction, a red 'X' had been drawn. Guessing at the scale by how far apart the lake and the academy were on the map, I estimated the next challenge to be about quarter of a mile away.

I took off at a sprint across the well-kempt grass, determined to regain some of my lead. Felicity quickly fell behind. I'd been training all summer to make sure I was as fit as possible when I got back on Stormclaw, and my training hadn't gone to waste. I set a relentless pace, but by the time I could see Atherton standing at the edge of a copse in the distance, I was barely even breathing hard. Felicity was a long way behind, and the other students, even further. But before long, however many students had made it through the last three challenges would be here. There was no time to waste congratulating myself.

"Ah, Ms Eldridge," Atherton said as I skidded to a halt in front of him. "And here I was thinking we wouldn't be seeing each other this year."

"Sorry to disappoint, sir," I said, with more cheek than was wise considering he was the key to me getting through this next challenge – and he wasn't exactly a fan of mine. He scowled at me, but gestured to a portal beside him.

"This portal will lead you to the final stage of the challenge. You need only enter it."

Well, that seemed anti-climactic. And way, way too easy. I looked at the portal again. It had a strange quality to it, like two images were warring with each other for control. There was a mirror beside it, which seemed completely out of place – not least because it was floating mid-air of its own accord.

"Of course," Atherton added, with a note of smugness in his voice, "it will only take you to the next challenge if you look like Professor Swann. Otherwise... well, you don't want to find out where it will take you if you fail."

No, if the gleam in his eye was anything to go by, I really didn't want to end up wherever it led to if you didn't look like Swann. Dammit. Glamours. I'd always sucked at glamours. Not least because Atherton had spent my entire first year kicking me out of class for entirely made up misdemeanours. Well, mostly made up misdemeanours. Either way, I was screwed – and I could hear the pounding of feet on mud. At least one of the other students was catching up.

I moved to stand in front of the mirror, and brought Swann's face to mind. A glamour wasn't a true transformation, but rather an illusion spell that made you *appear* to look like someone else. A trained druid would be able to see through it, but its true purpose was disguising yourself from mundanes. You know, back in the day when witch burning was an issue. The curriculum didn't get updated often.

I started with my hair, picturing long, blonde locks overlaying my brown ones. In the mirror, however, my hair stayed resolutely mud-coloured, maybe just a shade lighter than it had been. I heard Atherton giving his speech to someone else – though with a whole lot less snark. It wasn't a surprise to see Felicity standing there, his favourite student. She came and joined me at the mirror, but I couldn't see her reflection in it. Unless she'd become a vampire since I last saw her, the mirror must have been enchanted to only show the user's own reflection. That was pretty cool. We could use that enchantment in the girls' bathroom.

In my split second of distraction, my usual hair colour snapped back into existence, like a stretched rubber band being released. I sighed, and set about trying to lighten it again. And that was just the beginning. Eyebrows, nose... I was even too short. More students arrived, until there were about twenty of us clustered around the mirror, all determined to get our glamours perfect. No-one wanted to find out what the price of failure was.

I was trying to change the shape of my lips when Felicity broke away from the mirror, and walked over to the portal. I only knew it was her because of the sneer on her completely-transformed face as she looked and me and flicked her hair back over her shoulder. If I tried to pierce her glamour I'd be able to see her true face, but I didn't have time to waste on that. I watched her only long enough to see her enter the portal, then turned back to the mirror.

Three more students had gone before I was happy that my glamour was good enough to fool the portal. I hoped they weren't too far ahead of me on the final challenge. I bit my lip, sucked in a deep breath, and stepped through the portal.

It dumped me out by the gryff barn, whole and looking like myself again. Alden was standing in front of the barn, next to a row of a dozen metal buckets. A glance to my left told me the paddock was full of gryffs milling around, and that all four of the students who'd beat me here were trying to mount. My heart thudded. I wasn't out of the race yet.

"Lyssa, well done," Alden said, a smile on her ruddy face. "Your final challenge is simple. Mount a gryff of your choice, and get to the stadium. The first rider to pass the finish line will be the winner."

She held out a specialised riding headcollar, with reins attached to it.

"Thanks, Professor," I said, taking it from her with a grin, but as I looked amongst the gryffs in the pen, my grin faded. Stormclaw wasn't there. Alden lowered her voice.

"Didn't think I'd make it that easy, did you?" she said with a knowing look.

"Guess not," I muttered.

"Buck up." Alden shot me a conspiratorial wink. "You're still the best rider here. But, uh, don't tell the others I said so."

My lips twitched, and I grabbed one of the buckets. Then I paused, peering inside it. It was filled with eels. Gryffs *hated* eels. If I tried to feed one from this bucket, it'd probably bite me on principle. I hastily set it back down, and peered in the other buckets, choosing one that was almost overflowing with entire mackerel. Perfect.

I climbed over the stock and rail fence, careful not to spill my bucket on the floor. Behind me, another student stepped out of the portal and started talking to Alden.

I walked into the middle of the herd, running my eyes over the gryffs and watching their reaction to my presence. I couldn't help but notice that one of the other students, a second year Water element called Jimmy, was having a hard time. The gryff he was attempting to approach kept rolling its eyes at him and backing away – probably because even from here I could see he was carrying a bucket load of eels.

I steered well clear of him, and set my sights on a chestnut gryff near the back of the herd. He was plucking strands of grass, then letting them go and watching them fall back to the earth. He was inquisitive. That was a good sign. Usually.

I heard a squeal from the other side of the paddock, and looked up in time to see Felicity land on her backside in the mud, with an agitated gryff rustling its wings above her. I absolutely did not laugh uncharitably under my breath. Well, okay, maybe just a little.

I put her incompetence from my mind and walked slowly towards my chosen gryff, keeping my hands low. From the corner of my eye, I saw the third student – Ben Ackerman – quietly slip his head collar over his gryff's face, and start leading him over to the mounting block.

I clicked my tongue, and the chestnut gryff raised his massive head, several strands of grass hanging comically from the side of his beak. I grinned, and hooked the headcollar over my shoulder, then plucked a handful of grass and let it drop through my fingers. The beast cocked his head, blinking his wide black eyes at me.

"Hey, fella," I said, edging closer. "Sorry to interrupt your game. Want some snacks?"

I lifted the bucket and he stared at it intently. One clawed foot scraped at the floor. I pulled a mackerel from the bucket and showed it to him. He squealed and snaked his head through the air, snapping his sharp beak at the fish. He tossed his head back and gulped it down while I counted my fingers and was mildly surprised to find they were all still there.

"Greedy," I chastised him as I pulled another fish from the bucket. He went to snatch it again.

"Uh-uh," I said, pulling it back. He cocked his head, blinking at me and twitching his ears. He was young, I realised. And probably not fully trained. But the other student was already mounting, and I didn't have time to find another gryff. I'd just have to do the best I could with this guy.

"Back up," I told him, waving my free arm up and down in the air. The gryff clacked his beak, but took a step back and clawed at the grass again.

"Good boy!" I tossed the fish towards him, and he snatched it from the air, again gulping it down. At least he had *some* training. Hopefully enough that he wouldn't throw me off mid-flight.

"Want the rest?"

I set the bucket on the floor between us, and as he lowered his head into it, I slipped the headcollar around his face and buckled it, careful not to catch any of his feathers. I let him finish the fish, stroking and patting his massive shoulder. He kicked the empty bucket over, then butted me in the chest with his huge head.

"Want some more? You've gotta work for them first."

Felicity had managed to corral one of the gryffs to the mounting block without me noticing, and was already climbing on. I didn't have time to waste getting over there, not with my inexperienced gryff when half the herd was in the way. Abandoning the bucket, I took the reins in one hand, and led him over to the fence. I'd done this before, but only ever with Stormclaw, who'd been trained to stand still. I scrambled onto the fence while my gryff pranced beside it, almost yanking the reins right from my hand. Taking a deep breath, I swung one leg over his back, and he leapt away, ripping me from the fence. I launched myself at his neck and clung to it like a hairless monkey, somehow avoiding being tossed on the floor.

A glance around told me what had made him spook – Felicity had just put her gryff into the air, and my boy had his eyes fixed on them, squealing with excitement as he took off at a flat out gallop, following the fence line.

"Up!" I shouted at him as I tried to settle into place with my legs hanging in front of his shoulders. His gallop was nowhere near as comfortable as Stormclaw's, and if he didn't take off soon, he was going to put us right through the fence.

"Up," I called to him again, reaching back to press my hand above his wing. He sunk down on his haunches for a split second, then threw himself into the air and spread his wings, beating them furiously. I crouched forward over his neck, trying not to upset his balance as the ground fell away.

"Wanna go catch them up?" I said, using the reins to gently suggest he turn towards Felicity and her mount. He followed my direction without deciding to throw me off, which I took to be a good sign.

Whether through youthful enthusiasm or natural talent, my mount soon started to gain on Felicity. As we drew closer, I could see Felicity was perched in roughly the right place on her gryff – she'd probably been taught to ride as a kid, long before I'd ever even heard of the majestic beasts – but she wasn't moving with its rhythm, and I could see its motion being upset by her rigid stance.

She glanced back over her shoulder, and her face contorted with fury when she saw me gaining on her. She screamed something to her gryff that was snatched away by the wind, and they started to pull away from us again. Dammit.

"Come on, boy," I urged my beast. Ahead I could see not only Felicity, but the other rider, too. There were only two champions, and I was not going to let Felicity beat me to a place. I wasn't going to let her beat me at all. Her smugness would be more than I could stomach.

I reached down and pressed my hand to his withers. The gryff was tiring under me but he responded anyway, surging forwards again.

"Good boy. Good boy!" I scratched his withers and he twitched an ear towards me.

"You like that, huh? Come on, let's go get some more fish."

His ear twitched again and his wings beat harder, until we drew level with Felicity. My gryff gave a playful squeal, reaching out with his head towards the other gryff. It turned and snapped at him and my beast leapt away, banking hard. I clung to him with arms and legs, fighting desperately to keep from being thrown to the ground below. My legs started to slip until one was hanging down over the abyss. The sound of Felicity's laughter filled my ears; she was well matched with her gryff's spiteful attitude. I gritted my teeth and hauled myself on board. I refused to fall to my death – just to spite that cow.

Her laughter died away as I straightened back in place.

"Come on, you stupid beast!" she shouted to her gryff, slapping him with the end of the reins. He growled, and craned his neck round to glare at her. For a moment I thought he would rip her off his back and toss her to the ground below, but he settled for a snap of his sharp beak, which missed her. Shame.

But their distraction slowed them down, and my gryff pushed in front – no longer interested in playing with the other animal. I could see the stadium in front of us, and the last rider just a length ahead.

I urged my gryff lower, pushing him towards the entrance to the stadium. I could see the crowds in the stands, cheering and screaming as they saw us approaching. My gryff baulked at the sound, then rushed forwards, streaking past Ben and putting us in the lead. Behind, I could hear Felicity screaming something, and the laboured breathing of the other two gryffs, but I couldn't afford to look back. The finish line was just a hundred metres away.

Eighty metres.

The crowd gasped and booed, but I didn't take my eyes from the black and white tape stretched through the air.

Sixty metres.

Someone screamed – a rider, a spectator, I wasn't sure.

Forty metres.

"Come on, boy," I screamed. "Keep going, keep going!"

Twenty metres.

The tape was so close I could almost touch it, the wind was rushing past my face and my numb fingers clung to the reins. The crowd flashed by in a blur, and there was movement on my periphery. I didn't dare look back, I just stared at the tape as it edged closer in slow motion.

My gryff's chest pushed into the tape, and I let loose a scream of triumph and patted him wildly on whatever parts I could reach – his neck, his shoulders, his withers.

"And Lyssa Eldridge takes first place for Fire house."

"Good boy, good boy!" I urged him down towards the ground so he could rest.

"And right behind her, taking the second place is Felicity Hutton for Air house!"

Felicity? I snapped my head round to see her grinning savagely. Behind us, Ben was on the ground halfway across the pitch, limping towards the line with his reins in hand. He must have fallen.

"Dragondale, I give you your champions for the Four Nations Cup – Lyssa Eldridge and Felicity Hutton!"

Oh. Crap.

Chapter Five

Well, that didn't exactly go to plan. So much for dropping out as soon as possible. Damn my competitive streak. Felicity really did bring out the worst in me. I was going to have to work on that before I found some way to get myself killed or expelled. The buzz of winning was starting to wear off by the time I made it back to my common room an hour later, or maybe two — it was hard to keep track of time when people kept cheering every time I walked past.

But not everyone was cheering, and Alden wasn't shy about making her feelings known when I went down to the training paddock the following day to hold Itealta tryouts.

"Have you chosen your replacement for captaincy?" she asked, by way of greeting. I paused, my hand on the barn door.

"Replacement?"

"Well," she said, shoving open the door, "you can hardly captain the team and be a school champion, can you?"

"I can't?"

"Training for the Four Nations Cup will take up all of your spare time — spare time that you already told me you don't have." She sniffed. "You certainly won't have time to captain the Itealta team as well."

She stalked into the barn and started down the aisle.

"Well then I'll drop out of the cup," I said, my voice echoing inside the barn. "I didn't even want to be a champion in the first place."

Alden pivoted on her heel with a speed I wouldn't have imagined her capable of.

"You most certainly will not! You've been declared academy champion, you can't drop out now. The academy wouldn't be allowed to put up a substitute, and I will not have that awful Felicity girl as our only representative. No, you made your decision, and you're old enough to know that actions have consequences."

I looked down at my feet. No Itealta all year, just to be some stupid champion? I was such an idiot, why hadn't I thought about it before putting my name forward?

"I'm sorry, Professor Alden."

She sighed, and her scowl softened into something closer to her usual expression.

"There's nothing to be done about it now." She tutted. "I really had hoped you'd be able to show the talent scouts what you're capable of this year – that's why I made you captain in the first place, you know. It's just such a waste."

"I'll make the time," I tried again. "I can fit them both in."

Alden shook her head, but her expression was sympathetic.

"I'm sorry, but there's a good chance you won't even be here for the matches. Three of the challenges will be at other academies, and if you try to divide your time, you won't do either role justice." She pursed her lips and seemed to consider. "Unless... Well, yes, I think that could work. How would you feel about having a co-captain?"

"A co-captain?"

Alden nodded.

"Or a deputy, if you like. Someone to pick up the slack when you're not around. You'll still be responsible for choosing your team and overseeing training sessions, and if there are any matches when you're not away, you can ride in them. But if your champion duties require you to be elsewhere, your deputy will take charge of things."

"Seriously? I get the best of both worlds?"

"But you have to promise me that you will give priority to your Four Nations Cup training. I mean it, Lyssa. Can't have you letting Dragondale down in front of the entire magical community."

"No pressure, then."

We worked our way down the aisle, tacking up the twelve gryffs Alden had brought in from the field for the tryouts. Aside from Stormclaw, the rest were some of the older and calmer members of the herd. The more highly-strung ones would take hours or even days to accept a new rider and form a bond with them. These gryffs would let any of the students ride them, so that I could assess their skills on the pitch before helping them choose and bond with a mount of their own.

With Alden's help, I led the beasts out into the daylight, and tethered them to the fence, far enough apart that none of them was likely to take a snap at another. I was glad to see the gryff Felicity had ridden yesterday wasn't here. I mentioned it to Alden.

"Darkwing? He's been surly recently – and I imagine his rider yesterday didn't make him any more compliant. There was a lot of discussion about whether she would be disqualified for her conduct."

"What conduct?" I'd been so focussed on getting to the finish line that I hadn't been paying any attention to what was going on behind me, but I remembered the gasps and boos from the crowd.

"Darkwing collided with Ben's gryff mid-air, and took a snap at him – that's why he fell." Alden double-checked the girth strap of one of the tethered gryffs, making sure the saddle wasn't too tight, and continued. "In the end it was decided we couldn't conclusively say she'd done it on purpose, or that she'd known Darkwing would react that way, so we have no choice but to allow her to continue – but it was a near thing."

Knowing Felicity, I suspected that Alden was right, and it had been deliberate. We'd both seen her gryff's reaction when mine got close to him yesterday. There was no way she hadn't known Darkwing would lash out after that. But I kept my thoughts to myself; the first students were arriving for the tryouts.

Amongst them was Devon, who I'd ridden with last year. He was a year younger than me, but he was a good rider, and dedicated. People liked him, and he seemed to have a good eye for the game. Alden caught the direction of my thoughts and nodded her approval.

"You could certainly do worse."

I beckoned him over as I double checked Stormclaw's head collar – wisely, he stayed out of beak range, proving my faith in his gryff-sense wasn't misplaced. I put Alden's proposal to him, and he almost bit my hand off. At least he was enthusiastic.

"You ride left defence, don't you?" I said, and he nodded. "And I ride right wing. So that leaves us with six spaces to fill – but our reserve is going to need to be good on the wing. Sounds like I'm going to miss at least some of the matches."

The rest of the riders had arrived, so we got the first half mounted and sent them off to ride around the paddock, first at a gallop, and then flying fifteen feet up. By the time the second half of the group had ridden as well, we'd already sent four people to the hospital wing for broken bones, and dismissed another six. At this rate, we'd be lucky to have any team at all. And we hadn't even got to the remotely difficult stuff yet.

"Alright," I called to the group. "We're going to try a ramassage. One at a time, you're going to gallop down the field, lean out of your saddle to pick up the ball, then throw it through the hoop at the far end."

It sounded easy when I put it like that, but I knew it was a lot trickier than it sounded. I'd earned my first gryff-related broken bones learning that manoeuvre.

I picked up the Itealta ball – a large round hollow ball roughly the size of a basketball, made of beaten metal with four handles welded onto it, top and bottom, left and right – and tossed it into the middle of the paddock. All of the riders wore gloves, which protected their palms from the impact of catching the ball, but wouldn't do anything to protect misplaced fingers from getting broken. All the more incentive for people to time their pick-ups properly.

The first rider fell out of his saddle, the second got the ball but missed the hoop by a mile. It improved after that, though, and by the time all of the remaining riders had a couple of attempts, I was starting to feel a little more positive about our chances. We had fourteen people left, plus me and Devon. A standard Itealta team was made up for twelve – eight riders, three substitutes and a reserve. That meant we needed to whittle out four more people.

"Training match?" I suggested to Devon, and he nodded and grabbed a helmet. Head injuries took forever for old Leech to heal, and she couldn't bring back the dead, so helmets were a good idea if you were going to be charging around on the back of an animal straight out of mythology.

I strapped on my own helmet and hopped up onto Stormclaw's back.

"Listen up," I called to everyone – somewhat redundantly since they hadn't stopped listening. They were all pretty serious about earning a spot on the team. "We're going to have a little test game. I'll captain one team, Devon the other. We'll switch you through different positions, and don't worry–" I glanced over at the four people who weren't mounted, "–everyone will get a chance to ride."

We'd been riding less than five minutes when it became apparent that one of the people on my team had no spatial awareness whatsoever, when she almost rode her gryff straight into Stormclaw's side. In a high-speed game, everyone needed to be aware of where everyone else was, if they wanted to avoid an accident. I sent her off to switch with one of the others.

We rode for the best part of an hour, until all the gryffs were breathing heavily and all the riders were red-faced and sweating. The tryouts had gone on much longer than planned, and if I wanted to help the new riders select gryffs to bond with, then we needed to wrap things up.

"Alright, everyone, get the gryffs untacked, groomed, and put back in the barn. Me and Devon need to talk, then we'll let everyone know who's in."

There were two riders who I knew I didn't want – Jenny, the girl who'd almost ridden her gryff into Stormclaw, and the hoops, and Ryan – who'd fallen off three times, somehow without managing to injure himself, which was admittedly impressive, but not the sort of skill I was looking for.

Devon agreed with me, and added Miles to the list, who had fumbled a few easy passes.

"Caleb rode left defender last year," I said, "and Kev rode substitute for right attack. I want them both on the team."

Devon nodded. "Tommy rode left wing substitute, but I think Ellie rode it better."

"It's a shame, they're both great riders, but we don't need three wingers. Tommy as first reserve?"

We carried on hammering out the details, until we had a full team. There were three players who'd been on the team last year — five including me and Devon, which meant we had seven new players to bond with gryffs, and integrate into the team. Alden was right. It was going to take a lot of time. I hoped Devon knew what he'd let himself in for.

*

"I still can't believe you get to be captain *and* champion," Sam said the following afternoon, as we headed into Advanced Elemental Manipulation.

"It's not like I wanted both of them," I said, dumping my bag onto a table near the back of the room. "I was going to drop out, remember? You've only got yourself to blame."

"I ate poison for you." He pulled out a seat and dropped into it, pouting.

"Trust me, if I could make you champion in my place, I would. You know Alden's saying I might not even get to ride in any of the games?"

"Well, what did you expect?" Kelsey said, pulling out a textbook.

"Uh, thanks?"

"I just mean that you're lucky Professor Alden is letting you captain the team at all. If she'd turned you down, it would have ruined your hopes of getting signed by a professional Itealta team."

"I know." I slumped my head onto the desk, watching the room through my arms, contemplating exactly how catastrophically I could have screwed things up. Sure, I did know that I wanted to play Itealta professionally, but I knew that didn't want the decision taken out of my hands because of some stupid mistake. What a mess.

"Good afternoon, everyone," Swann said, sweeping her long, blonde hair aside as she turned to face us. "And welcome to your first Advanced Elemental Manipulation class. The clue is in the name – this year I will be expecting you all to stretch your limits, and–"

The door swung open and three more students entered the room. Kayden, Micah, and Harper.

"Sorry, Professor," Kayden said. It seemed like he was the official spokesperson for the group; the rest barely spoke a word, except to each other.

Swann recovered her composure quickly.

"That's quite alright. Dragondale is rather large. It's easy to get lost while you're getting your bearings. Please, take a seat."

The group claimed a table at the back of the room – as they had in every one of our classes – and settled down quickly. Part of me wished one of the trials took place at Braeseth Academy; I'd love to see what sort of academy they'd come from. The other part of me was glad they didn't, given how surly and withdrawn they could be.

"What are the unclassifieds doing here?" Sam asked, from the corner of his mouth.

"Why wouldn't they be?" I asked, and then I realised. "Wait, they can't control elements, can they?"

Kelsey shook her head in answer.

"That's a druid thing."

"Thank you, everyone," Swann called, above the whispers that had started up all over the room. "Now, as I was saying, this year you will be reaching new levels of skill and finesse with your powers. Indeed, most of you have now developed your secondary powers."

She paused and smiled at Kelsey. Kelsey beamed back at her.

"Who here has developed a secondary power over the summer?"

Kelsey's cheeks turned pink, and she raised a hand halfway in the air. Around the room, three more hands went up. Sam's didn't.

"Show offs," he muttered under his breath, and Kelsey pressed her lips together in an apologetic smile.

"And while we're indulging our curiosity…" Swann looked across at the newcomers. "Perhaps you would be so kind as to give us a demonstration of your unique powers?"

The group shared a round of uneasy looks, and Harper leaned her head in and hissed so quietly I could only just make out her words from the table in front of her.

"If she thinks I'm going to perform like a damned circus animal—"

"Harper," Kayden cut her off sternly, with hard look. She looked like she was about to argue, then he muttered something I didn't quite catch. I thought I could make out the word 'integrate'.

She glared at him for a moment longer, then nodded, and got to her feet. She ducked her head, maybe trying to ignore the dozens of people suddenly staring at her. Then she crouched a couple of inches, but before the frown had time to finish forming on my face, she'd launched herself upwards. I blinked, then blinked again. The frown set itself on my face. And still she didn't land. She was perched, upside down, on the ceiling, blonde hair hanging down. There was a long, drawn out moment of absolute silence, then she dropped neatly to the ground, landing and easily absorbing the impact with a bend of her knees. From the freaking ceiling. *Damn.* I bet she'd be badass at Itealta.

She sunk back into her seat, her face set into something that wasn't quite a scowl.

"Well," Swann said, breaking the stunned silence. "That was quite something, Ms…"

She trailed off and raised an eyebrow at her.

"Her name's Harper," Kayden supplied, when it became obvious she wasn't going to answer. "She's, uh, shy."

"Thank you, Harper. Would any of the rest of your group like to share?"

"Sure. I will. I'm Kayden." He didn't get to his feet, but instead leaned back in his chair, and fixed his eyes on the professor. A smirk that bordered on cocky played across his lips. Swann looked intrigued, then confused, then finally she opened her mouth to speak… only no words came out. She tried again, then paused, her lips settling into a smile that didn't reach her eyes. Shit, Kayden could stop people from speaking? That was way cool.

"Imagine doing that to Atherton," Sam said, and I chuckled, because that's exactly what I was imagining. Kelsey didn't look as amused.

"What?" I asked her. "It's funny."

"It's not funny," she hissed, shooting a glance at the unclassified and then back to us. "He could use that power on anyone here, and they wouldn't be able to cast a single spell."

"Shit."

"Yeah, exactly."

Swann coughed and my attention snapped back to her.

"Thank you for that demonstration," she said, but behind her benign smile, there was something else. A tightness around her eyes. She was unnerved. And now that I knew what Kayden's power meant, so was I.

Chapter Six

I was aching from head to toe by the time I made it back to the main hall for dinner on Tuesday evening – I was determined to take my team captain responsibilities seriously – and I found a note waiting for me with Aiden, the kitchen mage. My name was emblazoned on the front of the envelope in gold ink that shimmered in the light. Interesting. But with the smell of hot food in the air, it was not my priority. I asked Aiden for a lasagne, which he conjured from thin air – well, not quite thin air, but close enough. The raw ingredients he used came from the storeroom. He couldn't create food, but he could take meat, fresh vegetables, and herbs, and assemble them into an amazing meal in a matter of seconds, which in my book was much the same thing.

I headed to the Fire quarter, where several long tables were assigned to our elemental house. The elements tended not to mix at mealtimes. It was better that way. It kept food fights to a minimum. I was half-way through the lasagne – which was amazing, by the way – before my mind went back to the letter. I set my fork down, and opened it.

Dear Ms Eldridge,

Please present yourself in my office at seven p.m. sharp for your champion's briefing.

Professor Talendale.

Short and to the point, that was Talendale, alright. And it would have been great, if there was a single clock in the whole academy. Watches, clocks, even phones – none of that stuff worked properly here. So much magic in one place messed with things like that, apparently. And as Talendale was fond of saying, a true druid should be in touch with nature and ought not need to rely on mundane devices such as clocks to tell the hour. Except I did. I mean, I was reasonably accurate, within half an hour or so, but his letter said seven p.m. sharp, and Talendale had a special kind of hatred for tardiness.

Which was when I noticed the page seemed to be vibrating faintly in my hand. That was odd. I flipped it open, and grinned. One the back was a drawing of a clock, and the little inked hands were moving round. Some sort of enchanted clock. I *had* to learn that spell.

My grin turned to a frown. I had fifteen minutes, and it would take me at least ten to make it to Talendale's office. With a groan, I crammed down as much of the lasagne as I could – the food was ridiculously good, especially after a long day working with the gryffs – then dropped my plate back to Aiden and all but sprinted along the corridors, and up the two flights of stone steps.

When I arrived, breathing heavily and with a wicked stitch clawing at my side, Felicity was already there, hand raised to rap on the door.

"Enter," a voice commanded from within. Talendale.

I stepped inside behind Felicity, ignoring the look of derision on her face, because in all honesty it was one of her more benign expressions.

Talendale's office was large – though not as large as the ridiculous door might suggest – and its floor was made of cobblestones, despite being several floors up. If you looked closely, you'd see tiny brown strands scattered through the stones, the walls and the ceiling. I knew, because I'd done exactly that last year. They were roots of the Tilimeuse Tree, and they were more numerous here than anywhere else in the academy, except maybe the library. No surprise, since the tree was attracted to power, and Talendale and the headmasters before him were the most powerful men the academy had ever known. And women. At least, I *thought* there had been a headmistress once, but honestly, I'd never paid all that much attention in history.

Banners of all four elemental houses hung from the walls, and under one of them sat a huge, ornate desk, its legs engraved with intricate patterns that seemed to change each time I came in here.

"Ah, Ms Hutton, Ms Eldridge, how very punctual of you. Thank you for coming."

"Thank you, Professor," Felicity said in a voice so sweet it made my teeth itch. "It's an honour to be here."

"Yeah, that," I said, rolling my eyes. Talendale scowled at me. Oops.

"You could learn a thing or two from Ms Hutton about academy pride."

"Amongst other things," Felicity said. Talendale gave no sign that he had heard.

"You are here, as I am sure you can surmise, to discuss the upcoming Four Nations Cup. We will be joined shortly—" He broke off as another knock came at the door. "Ah, excellent, here they are."

He waved a hand and the door swung inwards. Standing outlined in its frame were Swann and Atherton.

"I have invited your official sponsors to join us," Talendale said, as the two professors stepped inside and the door clanged shut behind them. "They will be responsible for over-seeing your training – though naturally all of us professors will do our utmost to ensure you are prepared and have the best possible chance of coming home covered in glory."

He gave us a wink that looked completely out of place on his usually-stern face, and then it was gone so quickly I couldn't be sure I hadn't imagined it.

"You will train with them at least once a week, more if needed. Officially, your training does not take precedence over your studies, but I'm quite sure if you need to miss a class or two then the professors will be willing to overlook it – so long as you catch up, of course. We can't very well have the Dragondale champions failing their exams now, can we?"

"No, Professor," I mumbled. If academic prowess was a requirement, then maybe they should have chosen a different champion. I wouldn't be standing here at all if it hadn't been for Sam helping me pass Ellerby's challenge.

"Well-rounded knowledge and a developed skillset are essential," Talendale was saying, and I got the sense he'd been talking for a while and would continue to do so. I was right.

I tried not to shuffle my feet too much as he droned on, and probably failed. He drifted out of focus and my eyes rested on the massive wooden desk he stood behind. It was made from the wood of the Tilimeuse Tree, and it was the tree's way of communicating with the headmaster. It was this desk that had first told me I was adopted. If only he would let me use it to find out who my birth mother was, it could have saved me a whole lot of searching last summer, and the one before, and likely the one coming. Discrete searching, of course, because I didn't want my mum – the one who'd raised me – to get her feelings hurt. You'd think with all the magic at my disposal it'd be simple enough to track down a single blood relative, but it seemed like the only person alive who knew was Raphael, and I'd well and truly burned that bridge last year.

"Anyway, enough droning from an old man," Talendale said, startling me from my thoughts. "I shall leave you in the capable hands of your sponsors. Be sure to uphold the good reputation of Dragondale."

"Yes, Professor."

"Thank you, Professor Talendale."

Swann took pity on me – or maybe it was just that I still smelled like a hippogryff. Either way, she agreed that I didn't need to train that night. But she wanted to see me for at least three sessions a week – in addition to my classes, and studying for exams, and taking care of Stormclaw, and captaining the Itealta team. This champion gig was already turning out to be more trouble than it was worth.

*

"Welcome, welcome. Thank you all for coming."

Professor Kaversal was a tall, willowy woman in her fifties, wrapped in a yellow cloak which clashed horrendously with her wiry ginger hair. Her voice was weak and shrill, and she seemed so insubstantial that she might have blown away with the first heavy breeze, or else faded out of existence entirely. I wondered if that was what happened to druids who used too many portals.

That was what we were here for. Every third year Fire and Air element stood clustered in groups in the wide, open grassy space beside the lake. Pockets of exited chatter broke out amongst the groups, and I couldn't help sharing an excited grin with Sam and Kelsey. Finally, we were going to learn how to portal. To be able to travel anywhere in the world, at the blink of an eye – it was the stuff of every kid's fantasy. And as someone who'd never even been able to take a holiday outside of my own country, it was my fantasy, too. There were so many places I wanted to go – Africa, Georgia where my parents had been born, China, Italy… There was a whole world out there, and once I got the hang of portalling, there was nothing to stop me from seeing it all.

Kaversal cleared her throat, though it was so quiet that it took a while for the other students to realise, and then the chatter quickly died down.

"I can see you are all very keen to get started on your first portalling lesson, and I don't blame you. Portalling is an excellent skill, and one that every druid should strive to master, though of course not all will achieve it."

They wouldn't? That was news to me. Anxiety flickered in my gut – what if I was one of the ones who couldn't do it? I pushed the anxiety aside irritably. I was just tired. It had been three weeks since I'd been announced academy champion, and Swann's regime was taking its toll on me. Of course I'd be able to portal. There was no reason to think I wouldn't. I mean, no real reason…

"First, however, we must talk about safety. Portals are very complex, and stepping into a malformed portal can have dangerous consequences."

She wasn't wrong. Last year I'd seen someone get stuck, half in, half out of a portal near the back field. If me and Alden hadn't been heading that way to check on the gryffs, he might not have been found for days. And every apprentice druid knew that if you stepped through a portal without taking care your fingers and toes were inside its boundary, you were likely to lose them. None of which sounded particularly fun to me – nor, apparently, the rest of the group, who became more sombre and attentive.

"We shall start by conjuring a small, simple portal. I will come round and inspect each of them. No-one shall attempt to enter a portal, and for the love of all that is holy, do not poke your fingers into them. Madam Leechington has enough on her schedule today without regrowing dozens of misplaced digits."

I cast another sideways glance at Sam, but he was still grinning from ear to ear, completely undeterred by

Kaversal's warnings. She continued in her wishy-washy tones.

"All of you stand in a line. A long line, facing the lake. Quickly now, quickly now."

Kaversal's voice was devoid of any urgency, so after sharing a confused look, we gradually shuffled into a long line along the bank of the lake, all looking out over the water. I was sure she had her reasons. But if she suggested we started doing the conga, I was out.

"Good, good. Now take three large steps backwards. Yes, that's it, that's it."

Her habit of repeating herself was starting to grate on my nerves, but I kept my irritation to myself. It was probably just the exhaustion. Sam on my left was still grinning like an idiot, and Kelsey on my right was looking pale and a little anxious. Shifter magic and druid magic weren't always compatible, sometimes the mix could be unstable, and it was possible she might not be able to conjure even the most rudimentary portal. Professor Underwood, the other born hybrid at the academy, could portal – but even he couldn't predict if Kelsey would be able to. There were too many variables, and no way of knowing how the two magics had blended inside her.

"Now, when I tell you to – and not before, mind," here she shot a look at Sam, who rolled his eyes in response once she looked away again, "you are going to raise your right hand – your *right* hand – out in front of you, palm forward, like this. Then you are going to picture the very edge of the lake, and you are going to channel your magic through your hand, and through space itself, to connect with your intended destination."

She looked up and down the long line of students and probably saw whole load of very confused faces staring back at her, if everyone else was feeling the way I was. Hold your hand out and think about where you wanted to go? It didn't sound very precise.

"You! Yes, you!"

My head snapped round to the right, and I craned my neck to see down the line of students to see who she was staring at. Noah Howell, from Air house, had his hand extended.

"Put your hand down at once!" It was the closest Kaversal had managed to come to sounding stern, and Noah quickly dropped his hand, flushing red.

"I know you are all very excited," Kaversal continued in her usual sing-song voice, "but please wait until I say you may start – until I say."

Noah mumbled something that I assumed was an apology.

"That's quite alright," Kaversal said. "Now, you will picture only a very small portion of the lake, no bigger than an egg."

Sharna raised her hand in the air above her head, but Kaversal seemed to know what she was going to ask.

"A *chicken's* egg, dear. A chicken's egg."

Sharna lowered her hand again, and Kaversal walked the length of the line, until she reached the end and was no longer standing between any of us and the lake. Probably wise.

"You must stare at a point roughly ten feet in front of you, level with your shoulder – that is where your portal will manifest, if – *if* – you manage to achieve the technique. Are we all ready? Very well, you may raise your right hands, and stare at your spot. Please take care not to project your portal into anyone else's, it... well, let's just say it wouldn't be ideal."

She gave a little chuckle that made me wonder what would happen if someone manifested a portal inside another portal, and then I figured it was probably better that I didn't know. I was nervous enough. I stretched my hand out in front of me and locked my eyes onto a spot a little distance away, directly between me and the lake.

"Picture the very edge of the lake – the size of an egg, remember – and when you are ready, you may imbue it with magic, using the word 'eachlais'."

I stared at my spot and tried to picture a small snippet of the lake there, which was easier said than done. The best I managed was a weak facsimile. Then I reached down to the centre of magic inside myself and urged it up my arm and out of my hand, directly at the spot, whilst saying the trigger word.

Nothing happened.

At least, nothing happened for me. Somewhere further along, a stream of water burst out of the lake and launched itself at a spot ten feet in front of one of the Air students.

"Not to worry, dear, not to worry," Kaversal said to the blushing girl. "That's perfectly normal. I assume your secondary power is quite new? Try to focus on connecting with that point in space, not the water currently occupying it. Try again, everyone."

At least no-one on the Fire side of the line had to worry about that happening, since none of them could control water. Except me. Oh, dammit. One more thing to try not to think about.

"Absolute focus is the key," Kaversal said, shattering my focus. I took a deep breath and extended my hand again. From the corner of my eye, I saw movement.

"Kelsey! Oh my god, Kelsey, you did it!"

And just like that, the tiny glowing blue wavy blob in front of her snapped out of existence.

"Oops." I clamped my hands over my mouth. "Sorry," I mumbled through my fingers. Kelsey turned to grin at me, her eyes sparkling with excitement. I dropped my hands.

"You're such a badass half-breed," I said, from the corner of my mouth.

"Still the most badass half-breed you know?"

I wobbled my hand from side to side, and she elbowed me in the ribs.

"Girls," Kaversal called. "*Focus!*"

Despite our best attempts, an hour later Kelsey was still the only person who'd managed to conjure anything even remotely resembling a portal.

"Not to worry, not to worry," Kaversal said, as we all turned to trudge back to the castle, somewhat disheartened. "It just takes a little practice. We'll meet again next week."

Secretly, I thought it was going to take more than just a little practice. Portalling was *hard*.

Chapter Seven

lright, take him around again, Caleb," I called across the paddock. "Trius manoeuvre."

Caleb rolled his eyes, but touched his heels behind Swiftsky's wings, and took the big animal into the air. He finished one full lap of the paddock before he put the gryff into a steep dive, aiming him at the Itealta ball lying dormant in the short grass. He cut it close, so close that it looked certain they would crash, but at the last second Caleb shouted an instruction, and flung himself sideways. They thudded to the ground with the rider hanging from one side of the saddle, hand outstretched towards the ball. The beast sunk his haunches and leapt back into the air, pumping his wings. The motion threw Caleb back into his seat, ball grasped in one hand.

"Better," I shouted. "Break any fingers this time?"

Caleb circled Swiftsky back round with a shake of his head. Kev leaned over and high-fived him, and Tommy shook his head in disappointment.

"Could one of you at least *try* to have a devastating accident so I can play tomorrow?"

"Well if it's any consolation," I said, "odds are you're going to be riding my position for at least half our games."

"It's not," Kev said, catching the ball that Caleb tossed in his direction.

"Gee, thanks," Tommy said, rolling his eyes.

"Stormclaw's our fastest gryff," Kev said. "We're so screwed without him."

"You're welcome to ride him if you want."

"Nah, you're alright," Kev said, eyeballing my black and gold beast. I snickered. Stormclaw's reputation wasn't entirely undeserved.

"Well, I'm playing in tomorrow's game, and we'll worry about the rest after that."

"Yeah, but tomorrow's just a training match."

"Oi," Devon said, circling Ironclaw round and plucking the ball from Kev's hands. "There's no such thing as 'just'. We're going out there to win tomorrow."

"Aye, aye, Captain," Kev said, snapping off a salute and picking up his reins. Devon glanced over at me and I nodded.

"We've got one last manoeuvre to show you," he said, as I touched my heels to Stormclaw and took him up. The ground fell away beneath us, but we stayed low enough that Devon's voice easily reached me. "It's a Lyssa special, so if it doesn't kill you, it'll probably win us the match."

A groan rose up – Caleb or Quinn, or maybe both. I looked down at Devon, and gave him a curt nod. He tossed the ball high in the air and I pressed my hands to Stormclaw's withers, urging him down, urging him faster.

I fixed my eyes on the ball as it plummeted back toward the earth. There was a flash of movement: Devon was circling Ironclaw round at a lope, coming up behind us on the ground. The ball disappeared beneath Stormclaw's mass. I counted. One. Two. Three.

"Tiolp!"

Stormclaw's wings flared and shoulders dipped as he swung his claws out, and talons scrapped metal with a clunk. I felt rather than saw him snatch the ball from mid-air. I steered left, matching our pace to Devon's, and leaned forwards, perched high over the gryff's neck as I tried to position us directly above my teammate.

"Leig!"

I held my breath for a long second, then a whoop erupted from the rest of the team. A grin spread over my face as I brought Stormclaw round to face them, and Devon rode back to us, the ball clutched firmly in his hands.

"You're crazy, Lyssa," Ellie said, her eyes dancing with excitement.

"Crazy enough to win," Caleb agreed.

"I'm glad you think so," I said, gesturing to Devon to throw me the ball. "Because it's your turn."

We drilled the team on the technique for another hour, until they were all red-faced and sweating, and Quinn had come within a half inch of losing an ear, but eventually all of them managed to perform the manoeuvre. Whether or not they'd be able to pull it off in a match was another matter entirely, but we'd find out about that soon enough. There was no point in working them to exhaustion the day before the game.

"Alright, everyone, great job. Sort your gryffs out, then go get cleaned up."

I led Stormclaw from the training paddock and removed his saddle, leaving just his headcollar on to take him out to the fields. He was already prancing at the end of his lead rope, impatient, no doubt, to get back to Redwing and their foal.

"Alright, alright," I grumbled, as he almost pulled me right over. "Give me a chance to put your saddle away!"

"I'll sort it, Lyssa," Tommy said, nimbly evading a snap of Brightwing's sharp beak. I eyed him dubiously.

"Alright, but if I fall to my death because you tampered with my girth strap, you're cut from the team."

"No sense of humour, some people. What's a little attempted murder between friends?"

I chuckled as I led Stormclaw away, leaving the rest of the team sorting their tack. It was hard to imagine that this time last year, there was a death sentence hanging over him. Harder still to imagine that a little over two years ago, I'd never even known gryffs existed. Or Dragondale. Or magic itself. It was incredible how a couple of years could change the whole world. Or my whole world, anyway. Who knew what the next one would do to it?

"Hi, Lyssa!"

The American accent snapped me out of my musings, and I jerked my head up.

"Oh, hey, Ava! I didn't see you there."

"No, I can see that."

My younger roommate grinned and gestured to the bucket I'd almost walked right into. I glanced inside it, then wished I hadn't. No wonder she'd put it down for a moment. I suspected she wasn't resting her arms so much as her nose.

"Off to feed Dardyr?"

"You know how he is, if I'm late he'll just start snacking on the students."

"Well, if he gets peckish, point him at the Air team."

She chuckled, and hefted the bucket from the ground, causing its contents to slosh precariously.

"Still worried about the match tomorrow?"

"If we get beaten in our first game, we're going to be the laughing stock of the entire academy," I said, falling into step beside her.

"You'll do fine. You've been training nearly every day, and Stormclaw's looking amazing."

She looked the gryff over and he flared his wings, preening under the attention. I rolled my eyes and clutched the rope more tightly in the vain hopes of not being dragged across the entire academy. He pranced on the spot for a moment, tossing his head, then he lunged forward at Ava.

"Stormclaw, no!" I dug my heels in and tried to drag him back, but it was like trying to haul a steam train. There was a clatter as Ava's bucket hit the ground, and I gritted my teeth and yanked harder. Abruptly, he stopped pulling and moved back again, but I was pretty sure it wasn't because of me. I kept my grip on the rope anyway, and tried to see past him to Ava, dreading what I might find.

"It's okay," she called. "I'm okay. Oh, my necklace!"

I twisted round to look up at Stormclaw, and the light glinted off a gold locket hanging from his beak. Great. Bloody magpie of a gryff.

"Put that down, right now," I told him, and he rolled one black eye at me in response, then went right back to clacking his beak softly against the metal. Great. If he ate it, Ava was never going to speak to me again. She wore that thing everywhere. "Stormclaw, give it back. Or no mackerel tonight, I mean it."

He quirked his head at me, then huffed and spat the necklace on the floor.

"Good boy."

I gave his neck a quick scratch, then stooped to retrieve it before he could change his mind. The locket had sprung open, and I found myself staring at a faded photo of a woman's face. The photo was old and grainy, but not a single scratch or mark marred it. I scooped the locket up before it could get damaged, because Ava had obviously been taking very good care of it for a very long time, and I didn't want my oaf of a gryff to ruin it for her.

"I'm sorry," I said, thrusting it into her hands. "I don't think he's damaged it."

"It's fine," she said, snapping it closed and holding it close to her chest for a moment. "Sorry. It's the only thing I have left of my parents."

Of course it was. The one irreplaceable thing she owned, the only thing that had made it through half a dozen foster homes, and Stormclaw had nearly eaten it. I gave him a reproachful glare, stuttering apologies to Ava.

"Honestly, don't worry about it."

She thrust the locket into her pocket, and picked up her bucket, eyeing its spilled contents.

"I'd best head back and get some more food for Dardyr."

"Okay. I really am sorry."

She just smiled and headed back the way she'd come. Never work with kids or animals, they said. I didn't know much about kids, but I was rapidly understanding their hang up about animals. And whichever mundane had come up with that saying hadn't even known about gryffs.

"Come on, you brute," I said, tugging Stormclaw's head up from the bits of dead something now covering my shoes. "Let's get you out to the paddock so I can go take a shower."

By the time I'd emerged from said shower, the common room was awash with excitement. Halloween was always a big deal at Dragondale. I mean, it was to be expected, right – a group of druids, playing with magic and hanging out with creatures straight out of mythology, rubbing shoulders with werewolves, goblins and dragons? Every year, the students threw a massive party, and the professors played deaf and dumb, and spent the night in the staff rooms or their private quarters. For one night a year, there was no-one watching us. And that meant only one thing: party.

I'd missed the party in my first year because I'd been tracking Kelsey down in the Unhallowed Grove. I missed it in my second year because I'd been creeping about, trying to find some way of stopping the Alpha Pack executing Leo. Missing the party was becoming something of a tradition for me. But not tonight. Tonight,

Alex was organising the party, which meant three things. It was going to be loud. It was going to be wild. And everyone was going to get very, very drunk.

On second thoughts, maybe I *should* give it a miss.

"No, you don't," Sharna said, when I mentioned it in our common room after dinner. "Firstly, Alex would *never* let you live it down – you do realise she bunked out of all her classes today to get the dungeon set up? She even managed to get Talendale's permission to portal the Sullen Sirens in.

"Who?"

Sharna rolled her eyes, and looked to Kelsey for help. Kelsey scrawled a note in her book and slammed it shut with finality.

"They're an amazing band. They're not actual sirens. Their lead singer came to Dragondale when she was a student. And I'm going, which means you are, too."

"You're going?"

"Of course I am. Everyone is going. Even Ava... now that I've explained that the drinking age here is eighteen, not twenty-one. You know, for an American foster kid slash outcast, she's very law abiding."

I snorted. Law abiding was the last thing I'd call Ava. She almost got booted last year for breaking every rule there was to go hang out with the dragons. I'm pretty sure the only reason she didn't get punished was because everyone was in shock she hadn't been eaten. Actually, she reminded me a lot of a younger me. Only with a weird accent. And less animal guts on her shoes.

"Alright, I give," I yielded. "I've got a new top I haven't had a chance to wear yet, anyway."

We dedicated the next hour to doing our hair in our dorm, and our makeup, and choosing the perfect outfits that practically no-one would see in the darkened dungeon, and then we re-emerged into the common room. I had gone with my new dark green halter top, and tight black jeans – because a lifetime of being a tom boy wasn't all that compatible with wearing skirts. Kelsey was wearing a short black dress that hugged her in all the right places, and looked stunning against her red hair, which she'd straightened until it fell around her shoulders in a silky curtain. Her heels were more adventurous than mine, because I lacked her natural – or should I say, supernatural – grace, and I didn't fancy turning an ankle in front of half the academy.

The guys' jaws dropped in a manner that was pretty flattering, and we had plenty of offers of escorts to the party. I shot Kelsey a smile, and then we each took hold of one of Sam's arms, and led him out into the hallway past several pairs of envious eyes. Sam grinned.

"This reminds me of a dream I once had, with—"

"Finish that sentence and die," I said sweetly.

Sam knew the way better than either of us, having been at the party both last year and the year before, so we let him guide us, and when the fireballs hanging near the ceiling became more aged and dull, I tossed out a fireball of my own in front of us to light the way.

The party was just getting started when we reached the dungeon, and Alex really had outdone herself. Any nightclub in the country would have killed for half the atmosphere she'd conjured with the subtle lighting and minimalistic props.

Kelsey grabbed my arm and dragged me onto the dance floor as the Sullen Sirens filled the dungeon with their incredible music, despite my protests that I couldn't dance, and the rest of the night passed in a blissful blur.

Chapter Eight

Eugh, I think I'm gonna puke," I groaned, rolling over in my bed the following morning.

"Sh'up," Ava mumbled, pulling her pillow over her head.

"Morning, girls," Kelsey practically chirped. I forced one eye to open and squinted at her where she stood in front of the mirror, already fully dressed and pulling her red hair back into a ponytail.

"Why's she so chipper?" Ava demanded from under her pillow.

"Hybrid healing," I grunted, making a valiant but ultimately doomed attempt to force my other eye open. I gave up and slumped back into my pillow.

"Mongrel," Ava grumbled, then added, "I'm never drinking again."

"Don't blame me because you two over indulged last night," Kelsey said, so brightly that I could actually *hear* her smile.

"Why are you even awake?" If I cracked my eyelids open, I could just about make out the faint orange glow coming in through the window – the sun was still rising.

"I'm, uh, going for a run," Kelsey said. "You should probably get up, too."

"Why?"

"Well, the sun will be up soon, if Ava doesn't feed Dardyr he's probably going to start snacking on the students. And haven't you got an Itealta match to win?"

"Shit!"

I vaulted from my bed and stumbled to the bathroom, one hand clamped over my mouth and the other pressed against the wall to keep me upright. When I emerged a few minutes later, I at least *looked* human, which was probably as good as it was going to get. I tossed on my riding clothes then headed out of our dorm, pounding on the doors of our team's players on my way to the common room. A couple of heads poked out, and a few more people hurled half-hearted abuse in my direction.

"Get up," I yelled back. "Everyone out by the main entrance in fifteen minutes. We're going for a run."

"Great idea," Devon said, from inside the common room. He was already kitted out in his riding gear, and pulling on a pair of running shoes. I peered at him through bleary eyes.

"You look... not hungover," I accused him suspiciously.

"Are you kidding? It's my first game co-captaining the team. I skipped the party last night to make sure I was fresh."

From where I was standing, that seemed like it would have been a good idea. Just the thought of hauling myself round the grounds with the rest of the team brought back my urge to hurl with a vengeance.

"It's a training game," I reminded him.

"Sure is." He started stretching out his legs, grinning ear to ear. "Good thinking, going for a run. Get everyone nice and warmed up."

It turned out he was the only one who felt that way, myself included, and twenty minutes into the run I was pretty sure the team were plotting ways for me to have an unfortunate 'accident' down by the lake. By the time we'd finished, I was sure they were.

"Alright guys, good work," I said, once I'd caught my breath back. "We've got three hours until the game starts. Meet me in the training paddock in two."

The team broke apart and started dragging themselves back towards the castle.

"I'm going for breakfast," Devon said, as we watched the others leave. "Coming?"

I shook my head. This was going to be my first game co-captaining, too. I didn't know whether it was the hangover, or the anxiety, but my stomach was churning way too much to think about food.

"I'm going to start getting the gryffs brought in. I'll see you in a while."

I traipsed down to the barn to grab some head collars, and was surprised to see a figure in the distance heading inside. I hurried down and shoved my head through the door. The earthy scent of hippogryffs crowded my nostrils, and it took my eyes a moment to adjust to the dim lighting inside the barn. Looking out at me over the stall doors were a dozen gryffs I hadn't put there, snorting and shaking out their wings, and halfway down the aisle was the student I'd seen entering. I didn't think it was one of my team, though: they'd all headed back to the castle. Maybe Kelsey popped by to help out? I hadn't seen her on our run, so she must've taken a different route and finished before us. My foot caught on a metal feeding bucket, and the figure jumped and spun around. I recognised her at once.

"Sorry, Paisley, didn't mean to startle you."

"That's okay," the air element said with a shrug, a strained smile on her face. "I just thought I'd bring the gryffs in and save you all some time."

"Thanks," I said, stretching into the stall behind her and scratching Stormclaw behind the ear. "I appreciate it."

She turned red – I guessed she wasn't all that used to people thanking her anymore. Not all that used to people talking to her at all, actually, I'd wager. Things hadn't been easy for her since she'd been turned. That was probably why she'd taken the job working for Alden. The gryffs didn't judge – they hated everyone equally.

"Um, if you don't mind, I'm going to get out of here before everyone else shows up."

"Sure thing, Paisley. Thanks again for bringing them in."

I grabbed Stormclaw's headcollar from the hook outside his stall, and slipped it on his beaked face, then led him out into the early morning air. The light glistened on his feathers, each black outlined in gold, and on the black hair on his hide. He clacked his beak affectionately as I grabbed a brush and set about cleaning the few traces of dirt from him. He stood patiently while I worked, which was a good sign. He might be my favourite gryff in the world, but that didn't mean he didn't have his moods sometimes. Getting thrown in my first match as captain was not in my top ten ways to humiliate myself.

By the time I'd groomed him thoroughly, removing his dead feathers, putting the sheen back in his hide hairs, and working the knots out of his tail, the sun was climbing through the sky and I was recovering from the worst of the hangover's effects. I hauled Stormclaw's tack from the barn and got him fitted out, then climbed up onto his back.

He snorted and sidestepped, and I reached a hand down to pat his broad shoulder.

"Steady there, boy."

He lurched sideways, then grunted and threw himself into a rocky canter. My hips automatically relaxed, preventing me from being thrown all over the place or dislodged from the saddle, just. I frowned, and gently squeezed the reins, asking him to slow. He tossed his head, but came back to a walk. So much for him being in a good mood.

"What's up with you?" I muttered, leaning forward to scratch his neck. He flicked an ear in my direction and flexed his neck. The rest of the team were starting to lead their gryffs out into the paddock, and my stomach lurched as I watched them.

"I'm nervous, enough, okay?" I whispered, my voice hoarse. And that was the problem. I was such a moron. He was just picking up on my nerves and acting out. I sucked in a deep breath, then let it out slowly, straightening in the saddle and stretching out my legs.

"Come on, then, boy. Let's do this."

I circled him round and prepared to lead the team through our last training session before my first match as captain.

It went as well as could be hoped, given that half my team were hung over. The run seemed to have cleared the worst of the cobwebs though, and an hour into the practice they were looking sharp enough that we could at least give the Air team a run for their money. I wasn't expecting miracles in our first game. Anything less than utter humiliation would do just fine for me.

When I led the team out onto the pitch, it was to a small audience that only half-filled the stands. Just the die-hard Itealta fans, and the other students who didn't over-indulge last night.

"Good morning," a voice boomed through the stadium, "and welcome to the first Itealta match of the season. I'm Finn Seddon, and I'll be your commentator today, joined as always by my good friend Adam Wharton."

Adam Wharton was no friend of mine – he'd made it a point to heckle me in every match I'd played in so far, and true to form, he didn't waste time.

"Good to be here, Finn. What an interesting line up we have today. For the first time ever, Fire team will be riding with not one captain, but two. Rumour has it that Eldridge couldn't handle the pressure."

"Now, now, Adam," Finn said, a smile evident in his voice. "Let's not pay too much attention to rumour. Eldridge's record speaks for itself."

"It sure does, Finn. She was lucky not to get a lifetime ban for her conduct last year. Let's hope she doesn't lead the rest of her team into disrepute."

I gritted my teeth and urged Stormclaw up onto his starting platform – a stone plinth that stood a few metres tall. My opposite number was already there waiting for me, a guy by the name of Milo Sutton. I hadn't seen him play before. He was a first year, so he must've been good to get a spot on the team. I gave him a curt nod, then swept my eyes round the pitch – a large, rectangular field with eight plinths lining the edges, and a vertical hoop at either end. The stands ranged all the way round the pitch, and in a normal match they would have been filled to bursting. Even half-filled, the crowd gave a loud cheer as our umpire, Professor Alden, held the Itealta ball aloft, then tossed it in the air and blew her whistle.

I touched my heels to Stormclaw's side, urging him to leap down from the plinth. He raced forward, launching himself towards the ball. We seemed to fall through the air; I glanced behind my leg and saw his wings still tucked against his sides. I opened my mouth to shout at him to fly, but his wings flared a split second later, saving us just before we collided with the ground. The ball was long gone, safely in Devon's hands. I shook my head, and turned Stormclaw around to back him up.

"Come on, boy," I muttered. "Wake up."

Mark Bolton cut Devon off before he could reach the hoop. He looked round to offload the ball but I was still too far behind, and Sutton was sitting in his blindspot. His hesitation cost him – Mark Bolton closed the gap, reached over and grabbed hold of the ball, ripping it from his hands.

"And Bolton has stolen the ball for Air," Adam's amplified voice filled the arena. "Excellent take."

The annoying thing was, it *had* been an excellent take. If we didn't up our game, Air were going to thrash us. I wheeled Stormclaw around and he turned with a grunt, then chased after Mark.

"Bolton has the ball for Air. He passes to Howell. Back to Bolton. He's past the Fire defenders, he's taken them all by surprise down the wing. Where's Eldridge? She's nowhere to be seen. No, there she is, chasing him down, and—"

"Do my eyes deceive me?" Adam crowed. "Or is Bolton *pulling away* from Eldridge? Looks like Stormclaw's reign as the fastest gryff at Dragondale is over."

Oh, that was a low blow. Picking on me? Fine, I was fair game. But my gryff? No chance.

"Let's go, boy," I urged Stormclaw, crouching low over his shoulders. "Faster!"

He responded with a lurch, but there was no way we could close the gap. We were too far behind.

"He's heading to the goal, he's only got the keeper to beat. He shoots, he scores! One-nil to Air!"

The crowd went wild, screaming their delight at the spectacular goal. So much for avoiding utter humiliation.

He'd gone streaking up *my* wing, while I was stuck at the wrong end of the pitch.

"What happened?" Devon asked as he flew Ironclaw alongside us. I shook my head.

"I don't know. It feels like he's holding back."

"Think it could be to do with Redwing and the foal?"

"He's been fine in practice. Maybe he just needed some time to wake up. Come on, let's go even the score."

He cast me a nod and wheeled Ironclaw away. I rubbed Stormclaw's shoulder as he touched down on the plinth again.

"Alright, boy, let's do this."

Whatever his issue was, I hoped he got over it quickly. This might only be a training match, but that didn't mean I wanted to lose.

I crouched over him, fixing my eyes on the ball in Alden's hands. One of my hands held the reins loosely, the other hung down by my side, ready to snatch the ball up. The whistle sounded, loud and shrill, and we launched forward as a team, throwing ourselves through the air. I locked my eyes on the ball as it fell towards the ground and let my body guide Stormclaw towards it. The trius manoeuvre. Stormclaw would touch down, I'd lean right down from the saddle, grab the ball, and be thrown back into place as he launched back into the air. It was dangerous, but we'd trained it hundreds of times.

We were coming in fast, ahead of the rest of the team. From the corner of my eye I saw Devon pull back, leaving me to make the take, ready to flank me when I rose. I dropped the reins and hooked one knee over the large saddle horn.

The ground came flying towards us, but Stormclaw didn't slow his pace.

"Steady, boy!"

He ignored me, his head still low, still diving for the ground. He wasn't flaring his wings. He wasn't getting ready to pull up. We were going to crash. Terror flooded me. I couldn't even use my reins to pull him up, not from this position.

"Stormclaw, up!"

He screeched, the sound filled with panic like he'd realised the same thing I had. His wings flared and he threw his head back, but the ground was too close, it was too late. We hit the ground with the thud of a ton and a half of uncontrolled gryff. His front legs buckled under him and the impact threw me forwards, much too fast. I stretched out an arm and felt it snap as I hit the ground. A scream bubbled in my throat, but the sound never made it out. My head hit the ground, and everything went black.

Chapter Nine

When I came round, it was to the sound of someone fussing over me. I could feel a soft mattress under me, and while my head was foggy, it didn't feel like my brains were leaking out, which meant I had to be alive, and in the hospital wing. Again.

I opened my eyes and blinked Old Leech into focus. The fogginess in my head intensified, and I couldn't stop the groan of pain from slipping through my lips.

"Ah, Ms Eldridge," Leech said, frowning down at me in a way that made me wonder if she was related to Atherton. "I do wish you'd stop using my hospital wing as a hotel. There are several hundred other students here, you know."

"Sorry, Madam Leechington," I croaked, letting my head sink back against the pillow. It really was very soft.

"How's your head?" she asked, scrutinising my face. I don't know why she bothered – the woman was practically a mind reader when it came to pain and sickness. She wouldn't be asking if she didn't already know it felt like I'd been kicked by an elephant.

"Sore," I said.

"That's to be expected. Your skull was cracked in several places. You'd be dead if you weren't wearing a helmet. You also managed to break your left wrist, four fingers, your radius and ulna, collarbone, and shoulder. All fixed now, of course. And there was considerable internal damage from where the gryff fell on top of you."

The gryff fell on... My eyes widened. Stormclaw!

"Is he okay?" I blurted. Leech cut off in the middle of whatever she'd been saying, and the frown came back with a vengeance.

"You riders are all the same," she said, clucking her tongue in obvious disapproval. "You care more for those infernal beasts than you do yourselves."

"Please, Madam Leechington."

She sighed and dusted down her immaculate robes, then rubbed her hand across her forehead. If she didn't answer me soon, I was going to leap up from this bed and throttle her. I just needed to know he was okay.

"He's alive," she said eventually. Only the way she said it, it didn't sound like good news.

"What does that mean? He's okay, right?" I searched her face for the answers her mouth wasn't giving me. She pursed her lips, glanced away and then back again.

"You really ought to speak to Professor Alden. She's far better informed than I. All I can tell you right now is that he has several injuries, and the professor is doing everything she can to tend to them."

"I need to see him." I made to sit up, only to find Leech's hand planted firmly in my chest, which for some reason I couldn't quite fathom was enough to stop me moving.

"Lyssa, you've been in my ward for three days. Your injuries were severe, and you're far too weak to go anywhere."

Three days? That explained why one hand and a pile of blankets were enough to defeat me. But Stormclaw was hurt, and he needed me.

"I have to go. Please."

"You have to rest. If I had my way, you would be under a sleeping spell for at least the next week. But your first trial is in ten days, and I have orders from Professor Talendale that you're not to be put under any enchantment that might jeopardise that."

She folded her arms with a curt shake of her head, and added, "The least I can do is ensure you get as much *natural* rest as possible."

There was absolutely no way I was going to lie in this bed when Stormclaw was hurt and needed me. But appealing to Leech's sympathies wouldn't change her mind. Fortunately, I'd been here often enough to know what would.

"I'll never be able to get back to sleep until I've seen him," I told her, which was true – unless being unconscious counted as sleep, because there was a distinct possibility that was going to happen if my head kept pounding.

Leech exhaled heavily and regarded me through cynical eyes. I tried to keep my face empty of any guile, which was pretty easy since my facial muscles didn't seem to have woken up yet. Eventually, Leech's face grew resigned.

"You will return to this ward the instant you start to feel ill, do you understand?"

"Yes, Madam Leechington."

*

I headed straight for the barn, which took longer than I cared to admit, because every time I moved faster than a snail's pace, the entire castle swam like a mirage and I was struck with the overwhelming urge to puke. Of course, the castle didn't clean itself, and I wasn't feeling up to the job, so I was forced to take a break each time the urge struck, and wait for it to pass.

I wasn't far from the entrance hall when I came across Paisley talking to three girls. I was about to call out a greeting to her when I realised who the three girls were. Felicity, Cecelia, and Imogen. What was she doing talking to them? She might have been friends with Felicity this time last year, but the way the airhead had treated her after she'd been turned was barbaric. Not that it had come as a surprise to me, but then I'd been on the sharp end of Felicity's prejudices from the day I'd first arrived at Dragondale. Paisley hadn't.

I wasn't close enough to hear what they were saying, and I didn't much fancy getting into an argument when walking in a straight line was proving to be a challenge, so I did what any self-respecting woman would do in my shoes. I hung back and snooped from a distance.

Though I couldn't make out the words, there was no mistaking the pleading tone in Paisley's voice, nor Felicity's cruel cackle in reply. Maybe I *should* risk intervening. Sick or not, I wasn't going to stand by and let Felicity pick on Paisley. I pushed myself off the wall and was about to go storming over when Felicity pivoted on her heel in a spray of blonde hair and sashayed away, with the other two following at her heels. Paisley watched them go, her books clutched against her chest, then hung her head and walked off in the opposite direction.

I had no idea what was going on with her, but whatever it was, it'd have to wait. I needed to get to Stormclaw, and I'd wasted enough time hanging around trying not to puke.

Eventually, I made it to the barn and ducked inside. He smelled me before I saw him, and his loud snort and louder squeal drew me to the stall at the end. I heard the clatter of hooves and the scrapping of claws on concrete as he paced and turned, but something about the rhythm wasn't right. As I got closer and looked inside, I saw why.

Stormclaw favoured his front left claw, barely able to put weight on it as he limped round his stall. His left wing hung against his body at a strange angle and his eyes were wide with pain and anger.

A wave of dizziness washed over me, and I grabbed the top of the stall door to keep myself up. My fault. It was all my fault. I knew he wasn't right, and I still made him compete. I should have been paying closer attention. I should have pulled him out. Why had I ridden him in some meaningless game?

"I'm sorry," I whispered. "I'm so sorry."

"Ah, Lyssa, there you are." The gruff voice from behind me made me start, and I turned around to see Alden standing there, a stainless steel bucket in one hand, wearing a bloodstained apron that told me it was feeding time. "I wondered how long it would take you to find your way down here."

She set the bucket on the floor and wiped her hands on her apron.

"What's wrong with him?" I asked.

"He's damaged his shoulder – soft tissue, mostly – it will mend, if he stops pacing long enough. And he's broken his wing. That's going to take longer."

"Can't you just heal him?"

Alden shook her head.

"You know healing magic doesn't work on animals."

"Yeah, I know." I hung my head. Knowing didn't stop me wishing it wasn't true. "Is there anything I can do to help?"

"Professor Talendale doesn't want you doing anything that will put you at risk before the trials."

"That's bullshit!" I burst out... and then I remembered who I was talking to. Shit. I was about to apologise when she said,

"Between you and me, I'm quite inclined to agree. But it is what it is."

"I don't care about the stupid trials," I said. "I never meant to get picked in the first place. Stormclaw is much more important. Please, Professor, tell me how I can help him. If Talendale finds out, I'll tell him I did it behind your back."

"Professor Talendale," she corrected me absently. "If you can get him to take his medication it would be a godsend. No-one else can get anywhere near him."

She picked up the bucket and thrust it towards me. I glanced inside at the half-dozen fish, which all had leaves wrapped around them, or poking out from their guts. I grimaced as I took the bucket: it smelt even worse than usual. No wonder Stormclaw refused to eat it.

"What is it?" I asked, pulling one of the wrapped fish from the bucket, and wrinkling my nose.

"It's humispheria. It has powerful healing properties, and it will help with the pain. Or it would, if we could get it inside him."

I held the vile-smelling fish in my hand as I turned back to Stormclaw. His black and gold feathers that normally shone in the light had lost their sheen, and his chest and legs were caked in mud. They obviously hadn't managed to groom him after his accident. I couldn't blame them for that – grooming any gryff is risky, and Stormclaw had a reputation for being hard to handle even before he was hurt. Still, I couldn't completely bury my reproachful look. Someone should at least have *tried*.

"Here, Stormclaw," I said, holding the fish out over his door. "Come and eat."

He circled awkwardly to face me, then sniffed at the fish in my hand. He snorted loudly, and kicked out with one of his rear hooves, slamming it into the stable wall.

"I know. But it will make you better, I promise."

I offered him the fish again, but he just tossed his head and rolled the whites of his eyes at me.

"Fine. Don't eat," I said, tossing the fish back in the bucket. "Can't say I blame you. I wouldn't want to eat it, either."

I set the bucket back on the floor, and turned to Alden, who had a pitchfork in one hand, and a half-filled wheelbarrow in front of her.

"Can I take him outside? I think it'd do him some good."

"Can't do him any more harm than he's doing to himself being cooped up in here," she said with a shrug. "And you know him better than anyone. I'm afraid I can't lend you a hand, I've got a dozen stalls to get mucked out, and then I have to feed Ares."

I shuddered at the mere mention of the academy's hyper-aggressive gryphon, the half eagle, half lion who was Stormclaw's sire, and who was so aggressive only Alden was allowed anywhere near him.

"Why isn't Paisley doing the stalls?" I asked, frowning as the rest of Alden's words sank in. Alden exhaled heavily and leaned on her pitchfork.

"She quit. Couldn't bear to see Stormclaw in pain. I suppose the poor girl has been through enough trauma for one lifetime."

I couldn't disagree with that. But working with the gryffs had been good for her confidence. And it had kept her away from Felicity. Maybe I'd find time to have that chat with her later – assuming Leech hadn't had me hauled back to the hospital wing by then.

I grabbed Stormclaw's head collar and slipped inside his stall, hoping he didn't decide to crush me against the wall, because there was no way Leech would let me out again this side of Christmas if that happened. Fortunately, despite his bad mood, Stormclaw seemed inclined to be compliant, and lowered his head for me to slip the collar on. Guess he was as sick of being cooped up as I was.

I snagged the bucket and led him out into the sunshine, letting him limp along beside me at his own pace. Every awkward step sent a lance of guilt through me, until I couldn't tell if my nausea was because of my pain or his. I took us inside the deserted training paddock and lifted my hand up to the clip on his lead rope, then paused, giving him a stern look.

"No trying to fly, okay? You're not well enough."

He snorted softly, blowing air over my arm, and I unclipped the rope from his head collar. He butted his head into my chest in his usual affectionate gesture, taking extra care to be gentle, which meant I only staggered back one or two steps. But I was feeling like hell, so I decided to just give up on standing, and park my backside on the grass. On purpose. Definitely on purpose.

Stormclaw fluttered his one good wing against his side and quirked his head at me, then sank to the ground beside me with far more grace than I'd managed. I leaned back against him, scratching his neck.

"They're going to make me take part in the cup soon," I told him, staring up at the sky. "The first trial is at the Irish academy. I'll have to stay there for days, and I can't take you with me. So you have to be a good boy, okay?"

He twisted his head round and took hold of a strand of my hair, playing with it in his beak.

"I mean it. You have to take your medicine so you can get better. And you have to stop trying to bite everyone. And if I get Paisley to come back, you have to be extra nice to her, okay?"

He snorted and scraped at the ground, apparently as much a fan of being told what to do as I was. I rolled my eyes and reached into the bucket, pulling out a fish.

"Come on, Stormclaw. I need you to get better."

The big gryff gave the wrapped fish a look of disgust, then grudgingly took it from my hand, and swallowed it whole.

Chapter Ten

Three days later, a small group of us stood inside Talendale's office, in front of his peculiar Tilimeuse wood desk. To one side was a bookcase that seemed to be perpetually rearranging its contents, and to the other, a tapestry that liked to change colour on occasion. For me, though, the strangest thing was that for once I wasn't in trouble. Well, relatively speaking, anyway.

"Ms Eldridge," Talendale said. "I'm so glad you managed to refrain from injuring yourself again."

His eyes told me he knew I'd been spending time with Stormclaw. Oh well, it wasn't like he could expel me for it, not when I was about to be paraded before the entire magic community.

I could feel rather than see Felicity's smug look, and Atherton at her side was probably wearing its twin. At my side was Professor Swann, and behind me Kelsey and Sam. Each champion was allowed to choose two supporters to join them for the week they would spend at each academy, and frankly if someone had told me that to begin with, I wouldn't have entered in the first place. I could have tagged along with Sam. But it was too late now.

Felicity, of course, had Cecelia and Imogen at her back – no sign of Paisley. Whatever they'd been talking about the other day, it hadn't been Felicity getting over her prejudices.

The eight of us – two champions, four supporters, and two mentors – were to go through the portal together, then Atherton and Swann would formally introduce us to the headmaster of Dryadale, the official druid academy of Ireland. That would be the last we'd see of them until the day before the trial. We were supposed to be joining the students of Dryadale in their classes for the week, learning how they did things – just as I thought I'd found the perfect excuse for a week off studying. Kelsey, of course, was completely buzzing. At least we were excused from homework assignments.

"Very well, then," Talendale said, when he finished droning on in monotone for what seemed like a month. "All that remains is to wish you both the best of luck in your first trials, and to remind you that you carry the honour of Dragondale on your shoulders."

Great. No pressure, then.

"Thank you, Professor," Felicity practically simpered. "We will prove ourselves worthy of Dragondale's noble name."

I shot her a sideways glance, wondering if they taught upper class druids how to brown nose, or if it just came naturally to her.

"Yeah, that," I said, not without a note of sarcasm in my voice. Swann gave me a reproachful look, and I decided diplomacy might be the better part of valour here. Plus, you never knew when you might need to break some rules, so it never hurt to build up some good will with the headmaster. I pasted a more appropriate look on my face, and added, "We'll do our best, Professor."

He nodded solemnly, then waved his hand grandly to his side, and a portal sprung into existence. I eyed it with no small amount of envy – I still hadn't managed to conjure one of the damned things, no matter how many times Kaversal told me it was just a matter of focus.

Our small procession moved through the portal, lead by Atherton and Swann, with the rest of us following behind. Felicity shoved her way in front of me and I saw Sam bristle in response, but I shrugged it off. I was going to see another academy, for crying out loud. I never even dreamed these places existed, and now I get to see not one, but four. People could go their whole lifetimes without being so lucky. I wasn't about to let Felicity piss on my happy. I grabbed hold of my bag and stepped through behind the trio of airheads, and out into....

Oh, shit.

Nah, I'm just kidding you. It was an office, much like Talendale's, minus the uncooperative bookcase, but instead packed with all manner of greenery, with flowers literally growing out of the walls. I stared at them in wonder. There were reds and greens and blues, all flowers I'd never seen before, all stunningly beautiful, peppering the stonework in seemingly random places. I was so caught up in their beauty that it wasn't until Sam coughed and nudged me that I realised someone was speaking. I focussed my attention on the tall man with short dark hair and green eyes, draped in a heavy green cloak. Professor Lynche – the headmaster.

"Good afternoon," he said in a lilting Irish accent, addressing first Swann and then Atherton with a short bow. "It's wonderful to see you both again. I trust you are well?"

They returned his greeting, and then he fixed his eyes on me and Felicity.

"And, of course, you must be Dragondale's champions. Lyssa and Felicity?"

"Yes, sir," Felicity answered, before I could even open my mouth. "I'm Felicity Hutton. It's a pleasure to be here, sir."

Oh, my God. If she kept that up, I was going to puke. I was half-surprised she didn't curtsey.

"Lyssa Eldridge," I said, before tacking on a hasty, "Sir. This is Kelsey, and Sam."

"A pleasure," Lynche said, inclining his head. "I will introduce you to the other students shortly, and have your bags taken to your rooms. I've arranged for you to stay in your elemental dorms. I will escort you personally to the dining hall."

Felicity was already thanking him before I had time to work out whether or not that required a response. Whatever. She could be official spokesperson if she wanted.

"We shall take our leave," Atherton said stiffly. "A pleasure, as always, Professor Lynche."

He inclined his head, and raised a hand.

"Allow me," Lynche said, and a portal swirled into place, without him even lifting a finger. I shared a look with Kelsey – I'd never seen anyone create a portal without needing so much as a hand gesture. Talk about rubbing my nose in it. It wasn't until Atherton and Swann had departed that I got control back of my jaw and snapped it shut.

"Come with me, please," Lynche said with a benign smile, apparently oblivious to the effect of his effortless magic.

We filed behind him as he led us through his maze-like academy. Just what I needed. A whole new place to get lost in. At least this one seemed to be all on the same level. The way Kelsey's nostrils flared told me we were getting closer to the dining hall, though she did her best to quell her body's response. That wasn't like her. I raised a questioning eyebrow before I realised that no-one here, other than maybe Lynche, knew she was a hybrid. Couldn't say I blamed her – she got a clean slate here, if only for a week. Must be nice, after everything she went through last semester.

We stopped in front of a pair of doors, covered in rough bark, where there was a cluster of students. They were standing in small groups – two groups of six, in fact, and a pair. These must be the students from the other academies. I wondered which was which. I wondered what they would be like. Did they do things differently at their academies? And how come they had all arrived before us?

They stepped aside and let Lynche pass, and the headmaster pulled the doors wide. I peered inside to see rows of tables, with hundreds of students seated up and down them. Lynche beckoned us inside, and led us to the front of the hall.

"Good evening, students," he boomed above the excited whispers. All eyes turned on us and I tried not to cringe away. "I know you are all as excited about the Four Nations Cup as I am, so I am thrilled to introduce you to the champions! First, representing the reigning champion, Gryphonvale academy, Aderyn Ellis and Dylan Griffiths."

He beckoned to two of the students from the cluster wearing cloaks emblazoned with a red dragon on a green background, and they stepped forward. Both of them were of a similar build, lean and wiry. The girl, Aderyn, had a very pretty, pale face, framed by a wave of soft brown hair, and I saw more than one guy in the room notice her. The pair gave identical solemn nods to the gathered students, who greeted them with polite applause.

"Next, Alistair Murray and Callum Mitchell from Selkenloch academy."

The two guys who stepped forward were both build like tanks – seriously, what did they feed them up in Scotland? They also inclined their heads solemnly, then one grinned and elbowed the other, whispering something in his ear that I didn't catch, and they both flexed their considerable biceps, earning them a handful of wolf whistles. Sam rolled his eyes.

"Alright, settle down," Lynche said, patting the air with his hands. "You'll have plenty of time to get to know each other later."

The two Scots grinned at that and stepped aside.

"From Dragondale, we have Felicity Hutton and Lyssa Eldridge."

A few whispers swept round the hall as we stepped up, and more than my share of eyes were staring at me with something that went beyond idle curiosity. Great. Just as I thought I'd left all that crap behind. Guess I should have seen it coming, really.

"And finally, show your appreciation, you all know who they are, representing your very own Dryadale academy, Kieran Murphy and Riley O'Dell!"

A massive roar went up, and went on until most of the hall were stamping their feet and pounding their hands on the tables in front of them. I guess home team advantage was really a thing.

Introductions done, Lynche encouraged us to our seats, each with our own element – though I couldn't help but notice more than one pair of eyes was lingering on me.

"Are you going to sit?" Kelsey asked, tugging on my sleeve. "I'm starving."

I snapped my attention back to my own table and took a seat, just as dozens of platters floated through the air, and settled themselves onto the table. Neat trick. I tucked into the food and tried to make polite conversation with our tablemates, but already my stomach was a knot of nerves. Only days from now, our first trial would take place. And if people were staring at me now, it was nothing to how they were going to look at me when they realised how shit at magic I really was.

Chapter Eleven

I'll say one thing for Dryadale: they knew how to throw a party. The food kept coming until long after everyone was stuffed to bursting – though Briana, a bubbly black haired girl with bright green eyes and a tendency to speak every other word as a giggle, was quick to tell us that all the leftover food would be donated to local homeless mundane shelters. Kelsey liked the idea so much that she immediately started planning how she could convince Talendale to do the same.

Once everyone had eaten their fill, the drinking and dancing started, with people breaking into song sporadically. Despite the fact that it was Sunday and we'd all have lessons tomorrow, there were plenty of people who over-indulged, and I'd be lying if I said I wasn't one of them. Well, we were here to make new friends, and learn about their customs, right? And what better way to learn than by partaking?

Of course, the following morning I was starting to regret my community spirit as I pounded on the bathroom door and told Sam to hurry the hell up before I puked on his cloak. It seemed Dryadale wasn't as old fashioned as Dragondale, and the three of us had been put in a mixed dorm. Which was great – except it meant I had to share a bathroom with Sam, and he'd drunk even more than I had last night.

"Hurry up, you two," Kelsey said, carefully placing books in her bag. She was already dressed and looking perfectly healthy. Bloody hybrid. "If you don't get ready soon, we're going to be late for our first class, and what sort of impression is that going to set? The professors here might be really strict, and the students might already be a long way ahead of us, and what if—"

"Take a breath, Kels," I said, swooping in and practically tugging a book from her hands before she turned it to powder. "There isn't a professor alive who doesn't love you, and you're ahead of our whole *year* right now. And we're not going to be late. We'll be ready in a couple of minutes."

Sam emerged from the bathroom, fully dressed and looking just a little green around the edges.

"Just as soon as I puke," I added, and barged past him. Ten minutes later, looking as human as I was going to – which was to say, a damned sight more human than I felt – the three of us emerged from our dorm, caught up to Briana, and followed her out into the corridor. She'd taken up the role of our unofficial guide, and I wasn't about to discourage her. Hell, I still got lost at Dragondale, and I'd had two and a half years to get used to that place. Also, she wasn't as hung over as me, which I took to be a promising sign.

Our first lesson was Advanced Elemental Manipulation, which was taken with the Earth elements. I could get to like this place already – no Felicity and her snide remarks making my life a nightmare. I guess the Waters must have been paired off with the Airs. Rather them than me.

We grabbed a seat with Briana and her friends, Aiden, Sean and Ciara. I vaguely recognised them from last night, though most of it was a blur.

"Nice moves last night," Sean grinned as I dumped my books down. Said moves came back to me in a flash of alcohol and flailing limbs, and I groaned as I slumped into my seat.

"I'm never drinking again."

Sean laughed, a deep, booming sound that was frankly far too cheerful for someone I'd seen drink as much as he did last night. The door opened inwards and one of the Scottish champions – the slightly wirier of the two, Alistair – came in, with two of his friends. They, also, looked too cheerful for people who had been drinking last night. It seemed like the other academies were a lot less inhibited than us.

"How come we got stuck at Dragondale?" I asked, watching Alistair shoot a wink at one of the female students and stop to chat her up. The other academies were definitely more relaxed than ours.

"Because of the patriarchal lines," Kelsey said. "Remember?"

"She was raised by mundanes," Sam said, in response to the confused looks on our new friends faces. Ah, right. They weren't used to me having no clue about all things druid related, and the whole druid world knew about the patriarchal lines. Even me. It just wasn't second nature to think about stuff like that yet.

"Cool," Sean said, with a grin. "Is that like being raised by wolves?"

Aiden landed a slap across the back of his head, and I caught myself about to glance at Kelsey, and instead directed my gaze over to the Scottish contingent as they made their way to an empty table behind us, at the back of the room.

"Wait," Briana said. "The super druid wasn't raised by druids?"

"I'm not a super druid," I said, rolling my eyes. "And no, I didn't know anything about druidry until I got to Dragondale. Honestly, I'm going to be a shit champion. So, you know, don't sabotage me or anything. There's no point."

"She's not wrong," Sam said. "Pure fluke. We only put up with her for the comedy value."

I was spared delivering my witty comeback – which was fortunate – by the door swinging open again, and this time a man in his thirties walked in with a purposeful stride. The yellow cloak draped around his shoulders told me he was an air element, and the way the chatter in the room slowly died away, rather than all at once or not at all, told me he was liked and respected by the students.

"Good morning, sir," a student called to him as he unclasped his cloak and hung it behind the door.

"Ah, good morning, Ronan," the professor returned brightly. "You look like you had a good time last night. If you're going to throw up, kindly do it outside my lecture room."

There were a couple of chuckles, including from Ronan, then the professor swept round to face the class. His eyes caught on a trio from the Scottish academy, and then me, Sam, and Kelsey.

"Ah, our champions. Excellent. I'm Professor Doherty, but you can call me Conor. We're not too formal here. Some of these dolts call me 'sir' as a wind up. Feel free to ignore them."

I felt my lips twitching into a grin. Somehow, I couldn't imagine Atherton telling everyone to use his first name. Things were definitely more relaxed at Dryadale.

He flipped open a book on his desk, then paused and looked over at us again.

"Is one of you... Lyssa Eldridge?"

I felt myself turning red, and I jerked my head in a nod.

"That's me."

He perched on the edge of his desk and regarded me with interest.

"Tell me... and I hope you don't mind me asking... is it true? Do you have control of three elements?"

"Yes, S- I mean, Conor."

Conor exhaled through pursed lips.

"Well, Lyssa, I hate to put you on the spot on your very first day with us, but would you indulge me? I never believed it was possible."

It wasn't like there was any way I could refuse, not with the entire class staring at me. And here I was hoping I could just blend in until the trial. Guess I should have known better.

"Um... sure."

I pulled a bottle of water from my bag and carefully unscrewed the cap, setting both on the table. Start with the crappiest, right? I extended one hand and focused on the anxiety of everyone in the whole damned room staring at me, waiting for me to prove myself a freak, or a liar. No win. My palm glowed yellow, and a gust of wind burst from my palm and blew the bottle cap onto the floor. Then I stretched both arms out in front of me, palms up, and making sure my cloak was well out of the way because setting the damned thing on fire was not going to help my reputation.

But I'd been working on this, and it was pretty cool, even if I did say so myself. I blinked, and my right arm burst into flame. I willed the fire into one long string of flame and wound it around my forearm. Then I stared at the water bottle, exhaled, and focused on drawing the water out in one long stream. I sent that winding around my left forearm. Opposing elements wrapped around me.

There was a gasp from somewhere across the room, and my concentration snapped. The fire went out, and the water fell away from my arm onto my jeans, soaking me right through. Someone snickered, and I gave a bashful grin and a shrug.

"It's a work in progress."

"Very impressive, Lyssa. Thank you."

A couple of the guys who hadn't been paying much attention to me before started sending looks my way, Alistair amongst them. Unfortunately, it was the only interesting thing that happened that day. It seemed that, despite our many differences with Dryadale, our classes were much the same. Kelsey was relieved that she wasn't a mile behind everyone else, and Sam seemed put out that he was having to do just as much work as he would have at Dragondale. For my part, I was just trying to ignore all the unwanted attention I was suddenly getting.

We did a great job of dodging Felicity and the fawning crowd of followers she'd managed to attract – mostly airheads, of course – and it wasn't until Thursday afternoon that we saw her again, in my least favourite class: Spellcraft. I wasn't even taking Spellcraft this year, but both Kelsey and Sam were, and Lynche had put us all in the same classes so we weren't separated. I didn't mind. It would probably be a useful skill to brush up on before the trial, anyway.

"Good afternoon, everyone," the professor said. She was tall and gaunt, but with the same cheerful face most of the professors here seemed to have. Maybe Lynche gave better benefits than Talendale. If I had to guess I'd put her in her mid to late thirties, and she moved with a quiet confidence as she discarded her cloak and took her place at the front of the class.

"For our guests who don't know, my name is Professor Fitchett, and today we will be working on the tàlaidh spell. You will be using it to attract a piece of this wood to you." She gestured to a pile of small branches sitting beside her desk and continued. "It's quite a simple conjuration, so I would like you to experiment with the movement patterns, and see how intricate you can make the spellwork. Would anyone care to demonstrate the basic spell?"

She glanced around the room, and her eyes fell on the two groups of champions.

"Perhaps one of our guests?"

It had been like this in every class we'd been in – everyone wanted to see what we were capable of. I was starting to understand the sullen attitude of the Braeseth students. Harper hadn't been far wrong about them being treated like circus animals, and now I was getting a taste of what it felt like. Like I hadn't had enough of that for one lifetime. I saw Kelsey sink further into her seat beside me. Given her hybrid status, she'd been attention-adverse her whole life, and she was finding the reflected spotlight a struggle.

"I will, Professor. Lyssa Eldridge."

The professor's attention snapped to me, and I saw her interest sharpen. Yeah, yeah, *that* Lyssa Eldridge, I felt like saying. I was getting sick of seeing that look on people's faces. But I'd get over it. They were staring at me because I was supposed to be good, not because I was an outcast. At least, I hoped that was why they were staring at me.

"Thank you, Lyssa. Go ahead."

I rose to my feet, and fixed my eyes on a crooked branch resting at the top of the pile. For good measure, I extended one arm, because I didn't want to cock it up with everyone watching me, then sucked in a deep breath, taking a moment to focus on that place in the pit of my stomach where my magic lived.

"Tàlaidh fiodh!"

The branch wobbled in place, then leapt up from the pile as though it was being pulled by an invisible rope, and raced across the room. It thumped into the palm of my hand with a satisfying thud, and I closed my fingers around it.

"Very good, thank you. Now that we have seen the base spell, I would like each of you to think of three ways to enhance the spellwork, and then attempt to implement them. Off you go."

With relief, I sank back into my chair, because honestly I'd never have lived it down if I messed up a spell that most first years could handle. The rest of the two-hour lesson passed quickly enough, and I left feeling like if we'd had Fitchett as a professor instead of Atherton, I might have actually taken Spellcraft.

"Of course," Felicity said to her entourage as she barged past me on the way out of the lecture room, "anyone could perform the base spell... even Lyssa. It takes someone special to properly elevate the spell. Did you know that Dragondale's Spellcraft professor is my sponsor for the games? He says I'm the best champion Dragondale has selected in decades."

I rolled my eyes at her back as she strutted down the corridor. Never mind that I beat her in the selection trial. No matter. I'd just have to do it all over again.

Chapter Twelve

The day of the trial came round too fast. Atherton and Swann portalled in after breakfast, and each champion was allocated a room in which to do any last-minute preparation. Or any preparation at all, in my case. Of course, it would have been easier to focus if my stomach wasn't being devoured from the inside by a swarm of carnivorous butterflies.

"Try to relax, Lyssa," Swann said, for the eighth time this morning. "You'll be absolutely fine."

"Easy for you to say," I said, breaking off from my pacing for long enough to shoot an irritated look at her, sitting calm and composed in her chair. "You're not the one about to make an idiot of themselves. I barely even know any magic!"

"You earned your place as champion. Out of all of Dragondale, you were the student selected."

"Exactly! That should tell you how flawed the trials are!"

Out of nowhere, a stream of water came flying at my face. I threw my hands up, and the water swerved off to one side, spraying itself against one of the room's large windows. Swann gave me a smug look, and I rolled my eyes.

"I *know* I can use my elemental powers… well, most of the time, anyway. But what if I have to use a spell, and I can't? What if I don't even know what I'm supposed to do? What if—"

Swann clamped her hands on my shoulders and steered me into a seat, parking me firmly there.

"Lyssa, enough," she said, crouching down in front of me. "I believe in you. And Professor Talendale believes in you."

"More fool you," I muttered under my breath, and Swann pretended not to hear.

"It's time you started believing in yourself. When you first came to me, you couldn't even make your palm glow. Look at you now. Every challenge thrown in your path, you've overcome. You've faced the most dangerous criminal in the druidic world – twice – and lived to tell the tale. This is just a competition."

I nodded, and closed my eyes, taking a slow breath. She was right. If I could survive facing down Raphael – and sure, he hadn't wanted to hurt me the first time, but he sure as hell had the second – then I could get through one poxy trial. What was the worst that could happen?

Oh, right. I might look like an idiot in front of everyone.

I heaved a sigh. It didn't matter. I was here now, and there was no backing out of it.

"Are you ready?"

I nodded, and she made a small circle in the air with her palm, and muttered a word. A portal appeared in front of us, and through it I could see a large field — probably an Itealta pitch — and a ring of stands circling it, packed with hundreds of students. My nausea returned with a vengeance. Swann gave me an encouraging smile, and I stepped through, and out into the stadium. A cheer went up from the stands and I grinned up at them, vaguely aware of Swann stepping out of the portal behind me. She squeezed my shoulder, wished me luck, then made her way to the stands.

Around me I could see the other students — Felicity, and the champions from Dryadale, Gryphonvale, and Selkenloch. We were standing in a rough circle, and in the centre of us was a large stone plinth. None of them looked quite as anxious as I felt.

"The final champion has entered the field," a voice boomed around the stadium, no doubt magically enhanced. I did a quick headcount and saw he was right: I was the last one here. That better not be an omen.

Felicity, the closet champion to me, looked at me and sneered.

"Nervous?" she asked. "You should be."

I rolled my eyes, fresh out of witty retorts.

"Good luck, Felicity."

She eyed me suspiciously, but I meant it. I didn't like her, but if one of us could do well, at least Dragondale's reputation wouldn't be too badly tarnished.

"The first trial is a simple race," the commentator said, though the way his voice twisted around the word 'simple' made me think it'd be anything but.

"Each champion will be portalled out, and must race back onto the plinth. The first champion to return will receive eight points, the second seven, right the way through the field. Any champion not returning within one hour – that's one hour – will receive no points."

I glanced at the large, circular stone plinth in front of us, about four foot high. Just get back and jump up. Easy. Right?

Around us, on the outside of our circle, eight portals sprang into existence, one in front of each champion. They looked pitch black, and I wondered if they had been magically tampered with, to disguise what was on the far side. Raphael had done that to a portal last year. Right before he tried to kill me.

"On my mark, champions will have five seconds to enter their portals. The challenge shall begin the moment they cross the threshold. Three. Two. One. Go!"

I sprinted straight at my portal – five seconds wasn't long – but it remained steadfastly black. Crap. One step

away, I took a literal leap of faith, and threw myself
through it.

I skidded to a halt, swivelling my head left and right.
The portal hadn't been disguised. It was pitch black in
here. Shit. I couldn't see a thing. I couldn't even see my
own hand in front of my face. I spun around, but the
portal had disappeared the moment I'd passed through it.
I was trapped here. In the dark. How was I supposed to
escape if I couldn't even see where I–

Oh, wait.

I chuckled at my own idiocy, then conjured a fireball
between my hands. It gave off a faint, comforting orange
glow. That was better. The panic welling in my stomach
faded away. Mostly.

My first priority was to find a way out of wherever I
was. I pushed the ball a few feet in front of me, and saw a
rocky wall just beyond it. I nodded to myself, and steered
the ball to my left, following the wall as it curved round
me. All the way round me. By the time I made it back to
where I'd started, the sinking feeling in my stomach had
made itself at home. The wall ran right the way round me
in a circle, and there was no doorway. I pushed the ball
up above my head, and saw about ten feet above me the
ceiling, also carved of rough rock. Below me, the ground
was dirt. I was in some sort of cave. *Or a tomb.*

I pushed the morbid thought aside and tried to focus on anything other than the terrifying realisation that I was trapped. In the dark. Probably somewhere underground. I wiped my clammy hands on my cloak and tried to swallow the lump in my throat. The fireball in front of me flicked, threatening to go out. I gritted my teeth and focused on it, until the ball stabilised and was blazing again.

Fine. I was trapped. No big deal. There had to be a way out. It wouldn't be much of an entertaining challenge if we all just had to spend an hour sitting in a cave, most of us in the dark.

I push the fireball around the small cave again, examining the walls in more detail. There was definitely no door, or crack or hole in the rock. It was solid. But there was something else, something niggling at the edge of my consciousness, like a familiar smell, or a sensation...

Magic. It was magic. I frowned, and closed my eyes, trying to home in on it. Someone had used magic down here. The more I focused on the sensation, the stronger it became. I turned in a circle, letting the magic call to me. And then I opened my eyes.

I was staring at a spot on the wall, only there was something different about it now. I grinned, and renewed my focus, imbuing my thoughts with my own magic.

Abruptly, the wall faded. It was a glamour. The spell broken, I could see the tunnel it had been hiding, hewn of rough rock. I pushed the fireball out in front of me — because, ew, spiders — and started following it along the trail. A chuckle bubbled up my throat. If I'd known it was going to be this easy, I wouldn't have wasted so much time worrying about it.

You would think, by now, that I'd know better than to think things like that. You'd think I'd have learned my lesson from the hundred or so other times I'd had that exact same thought. But no.

It was the biggest damned snake I'd ever seen.

Its body was easily as wide as my thigh, and its scales glistened black and brown in the flickering light of my fireball. It rose up until its hooded face reached my height, and the rest of its length lay coiled on the packed dirt floor. Its black eyes gleamed as its tongue slipped from its mouth in a loud hiss that echoed back off the walls, so that it sounded like the snake was coming at me from all directions.

My first instinct was to throw the fireball at it. No, wait, that's a lie. My first instinct was to scream like a girl and run back the way I'd come. I didn't do either. Some part of me knew that killing the snake wasn't part of the challenge. The same part of me knew this was the only way out.

The snake swayed hypnotically from side to side, never taking its eyes from me, its thick body pulsating. Screw the trial, if it was me or the snake, I'd choose me. Except I was a druid. Druids protected animals. They didn't harm them if there was another option. Even if that other option involved being eaten.

"Well, this just sucks, doesn't it?"

The snake hissed in apparent agreement.

"Anyway, what gives? I thought St Patrick drove all the snakes out of Ireland. Except you guys were never here to begin with, were you? Not according to natural historians, anyway."

So I used to watch too much TV as a kid. Sue me. I blabbered on.

"Of course, my old Religious Studies teacher used to say it was symbolic. St Patrick didn't drive out any snakes, he drove out pagans. Magic users. Like me."

I frowned as my mind put the new twist on the familiar tale. Well, sure was nice to be wanted. But I had slightly more pressing matters right now, like the gigantic snake blocking the only way out. It had gone completely still, and if I didn't know better, I'd say its reptilian face looked... confused.

"Shit. Of course!"

The snake hissed in agreement with my revelation.

"The snakes were really druids, which means druids were snakes. I am you... and you are me."

I advanced on the creature, and it slithered towards me. Its flared hood had relaxed, and there was a hesitancy about its movements.

"If this doesn't work," I told the creature, who hissed in reply, "I'm going to look like the biggest idiot in the four nations. But that's not going to matter much if you eat me."

I reached the snake, every muscle in my body coiled tight in anticipation of the massive creature striking me, and sucked in a ragged breath.

"Here goes."

I stepped forward, preparing myself to walk right through the snake, cringing in anticipation of the moment my foot would touch it, and it would sink those bright, venomous fangs into me... but it didn't come. My foot landed on solid ground, and I hurried quickly on. I made it a half dozen steps before I pivoted and looked back the way I'd come.

The snake was gone. In its place was... me. Or at least, it looked like me. The pale, dark haired girl in a dishevelled cloak smiled, and spoke, her voice taking on an etheric quality.

"The password is 'Faith.'"

I stared at her – me – slack-jawed for a moment, then I remembered that this trial was a race. I didn't have time to stand around. I spun on my heel and sprinted along the corridor, throwing a fireball in front of me on the run.

The track seemed to slope upwards, and my breath was ragged by the time I saw the solid rock wall blocking the way ahead.

"Faith!" I shouted loudly, not breaking my stride. The wall vanished a second before I hit it, which was great because it would have been seriously embarrassing if I'd knocked myself out. I emerged into daylight to the sound of roars from the crowd: I was back in the arena, which meant…

There! I could see the podium in front of me – five times higher than it had been. My heart skipped a beat. It was empty. No-one had made it to the top yet. But around me, I could see three other figures racing towards it. Shit. I sucked in a deep breath and redoubled my efforts.

Callum made it there first – one of the guys from Selkenloch, Scotland. Dylan – the guy from Gryphonvale – was a dozen paces away, then Felicity, then way back was me. I gritted my teeth and dug deep. No *way* was I letting Felicity beat me.

Callum reached the base of the pillar – now towering over him – and shouted an incantation.

"Fleòdragan!"

His body started to drift upwards, and he grabbed hold of the pillar's rocky surface, using it to control his ascent. *Fleòdragan.* Got it.

Dylan launched himself at the pillar from three strides away, shouting the word mid-air, and landed half-way up it, beside Callum. He grabbed hold of the Scot and ripped him from the pillar's side, then kicked him away. I watched in horror as he drifted up to the sky, out of control.

A loud screech echoed through the arena, and a brown gryff launched up from the ground, a lone rider on its back, in pursuit of the student.

Movement at the plinth jerked my attention back to it as Felicity reached its base and shouted the incantation. Dylan snarled, and fixed his eyes on the airhead. Dammit.

The fireball burst from my hands, striking the plinth right in front of Dylan's face. He swore and stared down at me, anger in his eyes. I threw another fireball, hitting the plinth again between him and Felicity. I had no idea why I was trying to protect the arrogant airhead. All I knew was that what Dylan was doing felt a lot like cheating, and it didn't sit right with me. I didn't care who reached the top first, so long as it wasn't him.

I kept throwing fireballs as I ran the last few steps, landing them on either side of the Welsh champion, above and below him, keeping him trapped in one place. High above me, I saw Felicity haul herself over the plinth's rim.

I reached the base, and shouted the incantation. Nothing happened. I reached inside myself, to the place where my magic lived, and tried to imbue the incantation with my power again. Still nothing. It was like all the magic had been drained out of me, and there was no other way I could get up the plinth.

Suddenly, the floor started falling away beneath me. No, the floor wasn't moving – I was. I looked up and saw Felicity peering over the edge, one hand flaring bright yellow, and her face twisted with concentration. Wind whipped at my clothing as a gale lifted me up, pushing me towards the top of the plinth. My heart raced. One lapse in concentration and she'd drop me.

But she didn't. A moment later, the wind tossed me onto the flat platform, and then died. I laid flat on my back, heart still racing, and stared up at Felicity.

"Thanks," I managed, after a moment, and sat up. "But... why?"

She shrugged.

"Don't go getting ideas. I still think you're a loser. I just don't want Dragondale completely humiliated."

Chapter Thirteen

We returned to Dragondale heroes. First and second place in the first trial – though Swann said I was lucky none of my fireballs hit Dylan or I'd have been eliminated. I thought it was a bit rich that *he* hadn't been eliminated for throwing Callum up into the sky, but whatever. I was too ecstatic to argue. Second place. That was about as far from humiliating yourself as you could get. Felicity, of course, had gone right back to looking down her nose at us lesser mortals, which was fine by me. Nice Felicity creeped me the hell out.

My good mood didn't last long. Stormclaw was still injured, and my being away for a week hadn't helped. His leg was healing up well now that we'd stopped him pacing, but he'd been so agitated that he'd undone all the healing his wing had managed. We needed to find a better way of keeping him calm before he did himself some permanent damage. Unfortunately, we were all coming up empty. He was getting crabbier and crabbier, and he hadn't been the most sociable animal to start with. The next trial was eight weeks away, and while that seemed like forever right now, at the rate he was healing he was still going to be nowhere near recovered by the time I left. He needed someone who could handle him, and I'd only ever seen him show affection to two people other than me. One of them was Leo, but he was back studying at his own academy this year. The other was Paisley.

I caught up with her one afternoon about a week after I got back. We'd just finished Supernatural Zoology, and it was our last lesson of the day. No sooner had Alden announced that the lesson was finished, than Paisley had shoved her books back into her bag and started hurrying back towards the castle. I knew she'd resigned her job with Alden because she couldn't bear to see Stormclaw in pain, but it seemed like she couldn't get away from the barn quickly enough. On the other hand, she was a hybrid, and it was dinner time, so I was probably reading too much into it.

"Paisley, wait up!" I called out, slinging my bag on my back and hurrying after her. She didn't, so I jogged a few steps until I caught up to her.

"Hey, didn't you hear me?"

"Huh? Oh, sorry." She dragged her feet to a stop, not quite looking at me through the waves of dark hair hanging about her face. When she arrived at Dragondale, she'd been a happy, confident girl. Not anymore.

"Look, Paisley, I know things have been difficult for you, since…" I trailed off, not really sure where I was going with that.

"Since your best friend attacked me and ruined my life?"

I took a step back, surprised by the sudden anger in Paisley's voice as she glared at me. I swallowed and scrabbled for something to say, but she cut me off, raising an apologetic hand.

"Sorry. You've been good to me, both of you. And Sam. It's just…"

"Difficult?" I suggested. She nodded. She sighed and we both stood in silence for a moment, neither of us knowing what to say. I'd thought we were friends. Or at least friendly. Ever since Felicity had turned her back on her. But who could blame her if she had some resentment issues and bitterness? She'd lost control of her life, and no matter how much I despised the fact, her future was bleaker than it had been before. There were a lot of doors that would never open for a hybrid. She would always be an outcast.

But that wasn't Kelsey's fault. It was Raphael's. He was the one who'd cast the rage spell on Kelsey. He was the one who was responsible for every single person Kelsey had bitten.

"Look, if there's nothing you need, I really want to get to the canteen," Paisley said, back to avoiding my eye.

"Actually, there is something," I said. "I need you to go back to working for Alden and help out with Stormclaw when I'm not around."

She went even paler under her dark mane, and shook her head, clutching her bag like a shield.

"I'm sorry. I can't. I've got to go."

I grabbed her shoulder as she made to hurry off, and spun her around.

"He needs you, Paisley. Please."

"No. I just… I can't."

"Why not?" I searched her face for the answers she wasn't giving, and saw defeat cloud her eyes. And something else.

"It was my fault," she said, her voice barely audible above the breeze blowing around us. "I'm so, so sorry. Please believe me. I never thought he'd get hurt."

"What was your fault?" I said, but I knew. The look in her eyes was guilt.

"The morning of the game, I gave him something. It was just supposed to make him difficult to handle, so he'd throw you."

"You?" My mouth hung open in horror, and then I was shouting. "You did this to him? He could have been killed, you evil bitch! What were you thinking?"

She shook her head and tried to back off, but my hand was still clamped around her upper arm.

"She just wanted to humiliate you. I didn't know he'd lose control like that, I swear I didn't. She said if I gave him the herbs, she'd let me hang out with them again, but she was just using me. I didn't mean for anyone to get hurt."

"Felicity," I snarled, shaking her. "You nearly killed Stormclaw so you could get back in with Felicity? What the hell sort of druid are you?"

I shoved her away, hard, and stared at her in disgust.

"I actually felt *sorry* for you."

"I didn't ask you to!" she snapped. "And I didn't ask your psycho friend to bite me, either!"

"So you thought you'd take it out on an innocent animal? You make me sick."

My palms pulsed red and Paisley stared at them in horror. A fireball sprung into existence between us.

"Lyssa, stop!"

The voice came from behind me, and I looked back over my shoulder to see Devon sprinting towards us.

"It was her! She poisoned Stormclaw so he'd fall."

I shoved the fireball towards her and she cringed back.

"It wasn't like that, I swear. Lyssa, please!"

"Lyssa, don't do this," Devon said, stepping between us.

"Get out of my way, Devon," I snapped, trying to see past him. "She could have *killed* him!"

"She's not worth it! If you get expelled, who's going to look after Stormclaw?"

His words took the sting out of my fury. He was right. Stormclaw needed me. Paisley would get what was coming to her. The fireball fizzled out and I glared at the hybrid.

"Get out of my sight. Stay away from me, and stay away from Stormclaw."

*

Paisley took my advice to heart, steering well clear of me in the following weeks, although I doubt it was that hard to do, given that when I wasn't in classes or training with Swann, I was stuck in my common room, trying to keep on top of the obscene amount of course work the professors were setting. I'd even taken to bringing work with me when I went to sit with Stormclaw in the evenings. Practically the only time I wasn't glued to a textbook was when I was coaching the Itealta team. It was like the professors were on some sort of mission to make me regret having ever been born, and honestly Felicity and Raphael had already been working on that for the last two years.

"Lyssa, can I speak to you for a moment?" Professor Dougan caught me one afternoon as I was on my way out of his lesson.

"If it's about that assignment, Professor, I know it's late, I just need a couple—"

"Nae, it's not about that."

"Oh."

I watched the rest of the class filter out, my brow furrowed. Kelsey gave me a concerned look as she left, and I just shrugged.

"Careers day is next week," Dougan said, getting straight to the point. I liked that about him. "I noticed dinnae put your name down for the enforcer talk."

"Uh, no, Professor." In truth, I hadn't put my name down for any of the talks. I still had no idea what I wanted to do when I left Dragondale.

"Have y' thought about a career in law enforcement?" Dougan was scrutinising my face, so I shook my head.

"To be honest, Professor, I haven't really had time to think about anything but the trials."

"Aye, I get that, but you cannae afford to neglect your future. In a few months, the trials will be over, and you'll be heading out into the world."

When he put it like that...

"It would be a good idea to know what you're going to do when you get there. I'm sure I'm nae the first person to mention a career in law enforcement to you. You have the right aptitude, and yer marks have been... consistent."

By which he meant I hadn't failed the class yet. But I'd hardly been excelling, either. And I'd meant what I said to Sam and Kelsey at the start of the year: facing down Raphael at the end of last semester was enough danger for me for one lifetime. Not counting the trials, apparently.

"But don't I need Spellcraft to get accepted as an enforcer?"

Dougan grimaced, and inclined his head a fraction.

"You do. But I'm sure if I speak to Professor Atherton, we could arrange something."

I was silent for a moment until the implication sunk in.

"Extra classes?" He had to be kidding. There was just no way! "Professor, my schedule is so full, between the trials, and Stormclaw, and–"

He raised a hand, cutting me off.

"Just come to the careers talk before you make a decision. Besides, I'm sure Professor Alden would be happier if yer had at least one talk booked."

He gave me a knowing look, and I slunk out of the room after scrawling my name on the list.

"Hey, Lyssa, what kept you?" Sam asked, when I caught up to him and Kelsey in the dining hall.

"Dougan," I said, setting my full plate on the table beside his half-empty one. "He wants me to go to the enforcer career talk next week."

I cut off a piece of my lasagne, got it half-way to my mouth, then lowered it again.

"He wants me to have extra lessons with Atherton. Atherton!"

Sam pulled a face, but Kelsey swallowed her bite of burger and got that earnest look on her face that always preceded her trying to convince me to do something that was going to come back to bite me.

"You could at least consider it," she said. "I mean, what harm could it do to go to the talk?"

"Are you in league with Dougan?" I grumbled.

"Well, I'm with Lyssa," Sam said. "Private lessons? With Atherton? No, thank you. I'd drop it if I could. You know, if my family wouldn't disown me."

He shrugged and tossed a french fry in his mouth.

"Look, we're both doing Spellcraft," Kelsey said. "We could help you get caught up."

"It's a waste of time," I said. "I want to work with gryffs, and you said it yourself, I don't need Spellcraft for that."

"So you've signed up for one of Alden's careers talks?" Kelsey asked, looking more relieved than was probably polite.

"Uh, well... That's not the point."

"Lyssa, you have to sign up for something."

"I signed up for everything," Sam said, leaning back in his chair with his arms hooked behind his head.

"You did?"

"Yup. I've got so many that I won't have time for any classes that day. Shame."

I grinned.

"Well, when you put it that way..."

Kelsey scowled at us both, but then her expression softened.

"To be fair, it's not a bad idea. If you're not certain what you want to do, you might as well hear the options. You've got until the end of the semester to decide if you want to swap any subjects – that way you wouldn't have to have extra lessons with Professor Atherton."

And that was how, the following week, I found my schedule packed with nearly a dozen talks – Itealta coaching, Gryff breeding and management, law enforcement, potion making, and healing, amongst others – though I'd only signed up for that last one because Sam was going. I wasn't sure I fancied fixing broken bones and regrowing fingers for a living – although it'd come in handy, spending all my spare time with gryffs.

Dougan seemed to take my appearance as a personal victory. He gave me a curt nod and a half-smile as I made my way into the lecture room he'd commandeered for the purpose, and sunk into a seat at the back. There were about fifteen of us here, so I wasn't going to be as anonymous as I'd hoped. Neither Sam nor Kelsey had signed up for the talk – Sam couldn't, since he hadn't taken Law, and Kelsey had said she already knew what she wanted to do, and Talendale had arranged a talk for her. But she'd refused to tell either of us what it was, because, she'd said, it was a bit ambitious. Her hybrid status probably didn't help with that, and I hadn't wanted to push.

"Welcome, and thank you all for coming," Dougan said. "Now, I could spend the next hour telling you all what being an enforcer entails, but I suspect most of y' already know."

He gestured to the scar on one side of his face, a thick welt that ran from his eyebrow into his hairline.

"I didnae get this cuddlin' bunnies."

There were a few nervous chuckles, and a couple of the guys leaned forwards in their seats. I sank further into mine. A career with gryffs was sounding safer by the second.

"So instead, we're going on a little field trip," Dougan said. "To Daoradh."

There was utter silence for a moment, then all the students started talking at once, in hushed whispers that rose in volume until the whole lecture hall was alive with noise. Daoradh was the underground druidic prison, where the worst of the worst got sent. Few people ever saw it. At least, those who weren't incarcerated there. It was one of the most secure locations in the world, protected by countless wards and spells. It was the stuff of legend.

"Right, everyone up," Dougan said, raising his voice to make himself heard above the noise. "Leave your bags and books at the back of the room. You cannae take any personal possessions with you to Daoradh, and I do mean any."

There was a scraping of chairs as everyone got up and dumped their stuff at the back of the hall.

"We'll just be a minute or two," Dougan said, watching the door.

"Please, Professor," asked Liam, a brawny earth element who as usually in the top half of the class. "What are we waiting for?"

Dougan didn't get a chance to answer, because at that moment, two figures hurried into the room. A ripple of sound ran through the group as they stared at Kayden and Harper. What were they doing here?

"Ah, excellent," Dougan said, beaming. "I'm glad you could make it. Everyone, Kayden and Harper from Braeseth Academy will be joining us today."

Dougan raised his hand and muttered a few words, conjuring a portal in the air beside him. "Listen up, please. I dinnae need to tell you that you are *not* to wander off from the group. Daoradh houses the most dangerous druids in the world. Being allowed to visit is very unusual and I had t' pull a lot of strings to make it happen. Do not let me down."

He gave everyone a stern look that quieted them down, then nodded.

"Right, through you go, single file. Wait for me on the other side."

I was the last to go through, aside from Dougan himself, so when I reached the far side there was already a cluster of students murmuring in hushed voices. In front of them stood a grizzled guy with cropped grey hair, wearing a cloak trimmed in black. He couldn't have been much more than five foot tall, but he was built like a tank. He reached over and shook Dougan's hand.

"Good to see yer again, Dougan." His scarred face creased around the mouth in what might have been a smile, if you were feeling generous. "This sorry group of unfortunates must be the next generation of enforcers."

He snorted, apparently unimpressed, then raised his voice, addressing us all.

"My name is Cochren. I'm a guard here at Daoradh. You've probably heard a lot of stories about t' place. Well, I can tell yer, they're all true. So stay close. Would nae want anything to happen to any of yer."

Janey shivered, and a couple of the guys shared worried looks. Not Kayden, though. He and Harper had that usual cold, shut down look they seemed to wear most of the time when they weren't talking to people. I wondered what they were even doing on this tour. It wasn't like someone who wasn't a druid could become a druid enforcer, right?

"Follow me, then," Cochren said, and turned his back on us.

The group shared a few uncertain glances then Dougan motioned with his hands, ushering us after the guard. I looked amongst the faces, then fell in beside Kayden and Harper, whose heads were bowed close together, talking in hurried whispers. They broke apart quickly as I reached them. Huh. Hope they weren't talking about me.

"Hi, guys," I said, beaming brightly and hoping it didn't feel as fake as it felt. "How's it going?"

Harper gave me a sullen look. Kayden slanted a sideways look at her, then returned my smile, albeit with less enthusiasm.

"Good. We're both interested to see Daoradh. We've heard a lot about it."

"Me, too," I said, as we shuffled through a large door that looked like it was made of solid iron. "Well, not a lot, actually. But, you know, enough to want to take a look."

"We're grateful the professor allowed us to come," Harper said, her voice unconvincing and her face still sullen. I had no idea what her problem was, but it was starting to grate on my nerves. Maybe she was with Kayden – I mean they were pretty much always together – and thought I was trying to move in on her territory. I took a deep breath and reminded myself to try to be charitable. We all suffered from insecurities from time to time. Low self-esteem was a bitch. Of course, occasionally smiling might have helped her cause, but whatever.

I stuck with them – taking care not to let my attention linger on Kayden in any way that might possibly have been construed as interested – as we moved deeper into the prison, and then my attention was diverted. We were heading deep underground, and I could feel the weight of not only the earth hovering above us, but of all the magic that surrounded this place. Dougan said there had never been a breakout – or in – and I could absolutely believe that. The roughly hewn walls practically hummed with power, and I found myself keeping as close to the middle of the gently sloping corridor as I could. Looking ahead, I saw I wasn't the only one – the whole group were moving in single and double file, pressed close together. Conversation had died to a hushed whisper.

After what seemed like an eternity – but clearly wasn't, since we had to be back at Dragondale in time for dinner – Cochren came to a halt in front of a studded door, and turned back to us. The small group clustered round, as much as we could without getting too close to the walls.

"Daoradh is one o' the most secure places in the world. Beyond this doorway, we'll pass through a fear spell. Anyone care to brave it?"

He looked out at us, his expression challenging, and Dougan coughed.

"I don't think–"

"I'll do it," my mouth said, without any permission from me.

Cochren grinned – by which I mean his lips twitched a fraction.

"Ever faced a fear spell, lassie?"

I nodded, recalling the feeling of dread that had taken hold of me last year when I'd visited Leo in Dragondale's second dungeon, the one students weren't supposed to know about. Cochren's eyes narrowed.

"Have ye, now?"

I caught Dougan's look of surprise, too, and cursed myself. No-one other than Talendale and the Alpha of Alphas was supposed to know about my trip to see Leo, or the fact I'd magically drugged one of the alpha pack's guards. Oops. Well, they couldn't punish me twice, right?

Cochren lifted a hand in the direction of the corridor on his left, and a plain-looking door shimmered into existence. I looked from it to the studded door behind him that I assumed we'd been about to enter.

"Uh, what's behind the other door?"

He flashed his teeth in grim amusement.

"Yer don't want to know."

No, I probably didn't. I dipped my chin and stepped towards the plain wooden door set into the rough rock. Just a fear spell, I reminded myself. Deny it three times – and mean it – and it would let me pass. If it was the same as the one at Dragondale. I put my hand on the doorknob, took a breath, and stepped through.

I knew immediately I'd made a massive mistake.

Terror shook the ground beneath me, and a scream started to work its way up my throat. My mouth opened wordlessly, the sounds of my fear trapped inside me. Just a fear spell, I promised myself as tears pricked my eyes.

Just magic. I forced my eyes to focus on the plain door at the far end of the corridor. It was only thirty feet away. Thirty feet. I'd never make it.

I lifted my left foot from the ground and forced it to edge forward, scraping over the round ground. I couldn't lift it higher than that, I'd lose my balance and fall. What was I even doing here? I should go back to the others. I shouldn't be here.

I forced a shuddering breath into my tightly constricted lungs, and scuffed my other foot forward over the rock. *I'm not turning back. I have to keep going.*

I scraped my left foot forward again, not letting it lose contact with the ground as I edged along it. I wanted to stretch my arms out for balance but I didn't dare lift them closer to the walls. The walls. I could feel the magic flowing through them, waiting to bury me. If I kept going, it would collapse in on me, feed on *my* magic, leave me a lifeless husk rotting in this barren place. I scuffed my foot forward. Just keep moving, that's all I had to do. Just had to reach the door. *There's a door behind you. You could just go back to it. No shame in that.* It'd be over that quickly, just turn and run, that was all I had to do. Half a dozen strides and I'd be there.

I caught my head before it could look behind me. Half a dozen strides? I'd only made it half a dozen strides? Dammit. Get a grip, Lyssa. It's a fear spell. It's. Not. Real.

It'd be pretty real if I died here. There's nothing realer than death. I shivered, and pushed myself forwards again. *Keep. Moving. I'm not going back.* The door was only ten feet away now, edging closer with every scuffed step. This was a mistake. What if it was a trap? The hairs on the back of my neck stood on end, or maybe they'd been standing on end the whole time. Maybe Cochren knew what I was, knew who my father was. He was sending me down here to lock me away, in case I turned out like Raphael. Only someone evil could have three powers. It wasn't natural. They wanted to lock me in a cage. If I reached that door, I'd never come out of it again. Never see daylight again. I needed to run while I still could. *Turn back.* I couldn't touch that door. It would end me, swallow me in something worse than death.

I inched a trembling hand through the cold air in front of me, watching my outstretched fingers shake. My breath caught in my throat; if I touched that door, my hand would crumble in front me. I couldn't do it. I needed to turn back. I'd suffocate down here.

No! I'm not turning back.

It was as if some force had been squeezing the air from my lungs and it had suddenly disappeared. I sucked in a grateful breath, and clamped my hand on the door handle, shoving it open. I heard a single pair of hands clapping loudly, and pivoted to see Cochren watching me. He dropped his hands.

"Good job, lassie." To Dougan, he said loudly enough for me to hear, "Looks like some of your kids have got some potential."

I flushed with pride, shoving my hands in my pockets so he couldn't see them shake – it was just the aftereffects of the spell. It'd wear off soon enough.

"Anyone else care to follow yer classmate?"

They all tried, but only one other made it through – Kayden. I didn't know why it surprised me – he'd been through plenty this year. I guess a druidic fear spell wasn't going to hold him back. That didn't stop it holding Harper back, though, I noticed. I grinned at him, and he grinned back before the expression quickly dropped from his face. Cochren performed some ritual that I couldn't make out because my vision and hearing suddenly became hazy, and temporarily blocked the fear spell so the others could pass.

"Yer not a druid, boy," Cochren said when he reached us with the rest of the group. Kayden shook his head.

"No."

Cochren stared at him in silence, the expression on his face unreadable. It didn't look friendly. Then again, nothing about him looked friendly. After a moment, he grunted and turned away.

"This way," he said to the group. "This corridor is enchanted. If you attempt to use magic here, you'll trigger a dozen alarms. So don't."

He stalked along the corridor, and the students followed reluctantly behind him. I feel back in beside Kayden.

"What was that all about?" I asked him.

"They don't want anyone breaking in. Or out."

"No, not that. The look he gave you."

"Oh." He scowled, then shrugged. "In case you hadn't noticed, you druids don't think we're as good as you."

"Not all druids," I said softly.

"No," he conceded, scrutinising my face. "Not all druids."

We caught up with the rest of the group as they left the next corridor, and entered what looked like a large, metal room. Cochren gestured to the walls around him with a grunt.

"The walls are lined with iron and silver – amongst other things. You know why?"

"Shifters," I said, although he hadn't directed his question specifically at me. "It messes with their abilities."

"Aye, lassie," he nodded. "There's enough silver in these walls to prevent them changing. Cuts them off from their strength, too."

"Are there any shifters locked up in here?" someone asked from behind me. Liam, I think. Cochren picked him out from the crowd.

"No, lad. There's nae been a shifter in here for over a century. Cannae be too careful, though."

"Yeah," Kayden muttered sourly under his breath. "Can't forget only druids can be trusted."

"Not all druids, boy," Cochren said sharply, snapping his eyes to the unclassified. Damn, he had good hearing. I made a mental note to watch what I said around him. "Through this door are the most dangerous druids alive."

"Except Raphael."

I didn't hear who said it, but the words sent a shiver through me. *For many years, there has been a cell waiting Raphael at Daoradh, though none have been able to apprehend him.* That was what Talendale had said last year.

"Aye, lad. 'Cept him." He rapped his knuckles on the door behind him. "This door is warded against every known type of magic. It's semi-sentient, and it'll only open for those it knows."

"How do you get through it the first time?" I asked.

"Casing the joint, eh?" He gave a dark chuckle and I shifted my weight from one foot to the other. The more I knew about this place, the less I wanted to be here. Never mind sneaking in. "There's a ritual that involves both blood and magic sacrifice. It leaves its mark on you."

He raised a hand, and I saw a jagged symbol emblazed on his palm in pink scar tissue. I snuck a glance at Dougan's palm, and saw its twin.

"But you won't be doing that today," he said, and I wasn't sure I had entirely imagined the emphasis on *today*. He turned his gaze back on the rest of the group. "This is where the tour ends. Yer professor will escort you back to the surface."

There were a few disappointed whispers, but not from me. I couldn't get out of the place fast enough.

Chapter Fourteen

So, what do you think?" Kelsey asked. "Did any of the talks interest you?"

I leaned back against the wall, stretching my legs out along my bed.

"Well, I know one thing. I'm not going to sign up as an enforcer any time soon. Daoradh scores a solid ten on the creep-scale."

"And you're not just saying that to get out of having extra lessons with Professor Atherton?"

"It's not the *only* reason..."

"It's a good enough reason, if you ask me," Ava said, balling up a sheet of paper and tossing it in the bin.

"How's the assignment coming?" I asked, and she glared at a fresh sheet of paper by way of response, gnawing at her pen.

"You'll get it," Kelsey said, and then to me, "You're going to have to make a decision soon. You've only got until the end of the semester if you want to switch any subjects."

"Kels," I said, "I'm behind enough as it is. If I switched a subject, I'd never get caught up. We're not all as smart as you."

She flushed slightly at the praise, and I could see her formulating some sort of argument to coerce me into making a decision, so I went on the offensive.

"Anyway, enough about my careers talks. Tell me about yours."

Ava stopped gnawing at her pen and glanced over at the redhead. Kelsey made a show of looking out of the window, then grabbed her cloak.

"I'd, um, love to. But I've got to go."

I glanced out of the window and saw the light was fading. Soon, another full moon would rise above the academy, and it would be better for everyone if Kelsey wasn't roaming the halls when it did. But that didn't mean I was letting her off the hook. I hopped off my bed and grabbed my own cloak.

"Where are you going?" Kelsey asked, fumbling with the clasp on her cloak.

"I'll walk you down to the entrance hall." I swung my cloak over my shoulders and pulled the door open.

"Oh. You really don't need to." She avoided my eye as she slipped through the door. "Why don't you, um, stay and help Ava with her assignment?"

Ava looked up hopefully at that, but I shook my head.

"I've got to head down to the fields and bring Stormclaw in, anyway. Alden's letting him run loose with

Redwing and the foal during the day, but she still wants him in at night. Just to be safe."

I stepped out behind her and shut the door.

"Besides, I want to hear all about the talk Talendale lined up for you. That's a first, right?"

She nodded, keeping her eyes on her running shoes as we headed down the hallway and into the deserted common room.

"I– Well, it… It was okay. I'd rather not talk about it."

Great work, Lyssa. Way to put your foot right in it, banging on and on about her 'careers talk'. It wasn't like a hybrid had all that many options, was it? If Kelsey wanted to consider those options in private, then I had absolutely no right to go sticking my nose in. And if she wanted to distract herself by thinking about other peoples' careers, even mine, who was I to judge?

A change of subject was in order, but it took me until we were out of the common room to come up with one.

"How's the training with Underwood coming?"

"Good. I mean, I still can't stop myself changing under the full moon, obviously – that's going to take months or even years of practice – but I can control myself now, mostly, anyway, and Professor Underwood has been giving me extra training to help me learn to shift during the rest of the month."

"That's great." I grinned at her. "Way to show those arrogant full-breeds."

"Well, I haven't quite mastered it yet," she hedged. "Hey, don't you want to go that way, out of the back door?"

"Nah, Stormclaw's been spending a lot of time in the east paddocks recently. I'll try out there first."

"But–" She looked panicked as she groped for words. "Don't you need to go to the barn first? For a head collar?"

I shook my head.

"No, I'll just ride him in. What's up with you tonight?"

"Nothing. What makes you think there's anything up with me tonight? Are you sure you want to come out the front door?"

I arched an eyebrow at her, and she ducked her head and pushed open the door into the entrance hall.

"Ah, hello Kelsey."

"Professor Underwood," Kelsey returned his greeting. I stepped in behind her, and he frowned.

"Hello, Lyssa. What are you doing here?"

"Oh, I'm just going out to see Storm…"

I trailed off as I spotted the other figure – no, figures – in the lobby. Leo was leaning casually against one wall, and the other person was half-hidden behind the professor. But not so hidden that I didn't recognise Paisley's brown mane of hair.

I whirled to face Kelsey.

"Is that why you didn't want me coming this way? Because of her?"

"There will be no need to raise your voice, Lyssa," Underwood said, in a calm tone that belied the sudden stillness of his body. Across the hall, Leo peeled himself from the wall.

"No need to raise my voice? After what she did to Stormclaw?"

"We have all made mistakes, not least you."

"It's her first night in the grove," Kelsey said, her forehead compressed in a worried little frown. "We have to go with her. You see that, don't you?"

"What I see is you siding with the bitch who almost killed my gryff!"

"Language," Underwood snapped. Leo moved quickly, putting himself between me and Kelsey. He glowered down at me.

"She's been beating herself up about this for weeks," he said. "So don't you dare go blaming her. We're doing what has to be done. If Paisley gets out of the grove and makes for the academy, it'll be bad for everyone. Why do you think I'm here?"

"You know what?" I looked from him to Kelsey and back again, my hands balled up by my sides. "I don't care. Do what the hell you want."

I stormed past them and barged through the academy's front doors, out into the grounds. The nerve of them, trying to justify it! Who cared if Paisley couldn't control herself yet? That's what we had a dungeon for, they could have just left her in there. And I had no idea why Kelsey would even want to help Paisley – Paisley obviously hated her. She'd made that clear enough when I confronted her about what she'd done to Stormclaw.

...And Kelsey knew that.

My pace slowed as I neared the east paddocks. Kelsey knew that Paisley held her responsible, and Kelsey was the sort of person who wanted to get on with everyone. Of course she'd want to find some way to make peace with Paisley – even if it hadn't really been her fault in the first place. And I'd treated her like shit for it. God, I was such a bitch. Kelsey was my friend. How could I have spoken to her like that? And the look on her face...

I groaned. I was a horrible person. And now she was going to spend all night risking her neck, thinking I hated her. As if I could ever hate her. If she got hurt tonight because she was beating herself up over what I said, I'd never forgive myself.

I leaned on the post-and-rail fencing surrounding the east paddock – more a visual reminder for the students than an actual attempt to contain the gryffs, since they pretty much just flew wherever they wanted. Except for the ones who were recovering from broken wings and damaged legs caused by psychotic hybrids, of course. I could forgive Kelsey for helping Paisley, but forgive Paisley herself? No chance.

I scanned the paddock in the semi-darkness, looking for the trio of gryffs. Stormclaw hated being separated from his mate and foal, but Alden was adamant he still needed to be stabled overnight if he was going to make a full recovery.

Huh. That was weird. It didn't look like they were here. Maybe they'd headed back towards the main paddocks to fish in the river. I pushed myself off the rail and was about to turn away when a flash of movement caught my eye. Three gryffs were swooping through the skies, one chestnut, one black with a row of brown flight feathers on the underside of its wing – and one black and gold. Dammit.

"Stormclaw!" I called, somewhat redundantly since the trio were already flying towards me. I shook my head as he landed, followed by Redwing, and then Thunderwing, the foal, crashed to the ground in a landing that was all splayed legs and flapping wings. He screeched and shook out his multi-tonal wings, and Redwing butted him gently, then started grooming his feathers with her beak. The foal was six months old now, and the size of a shire horse. And it looked like his daddy couldn't resist helping with his flying lessons.

I shook my head and hopped over the fence, approaching the trio. I gave each of them a quick scratch, counted my fingers – Thunderwing was going through a biting phase – then turned a reproachful eye on Stormclaw.

"Alden would have both our hides if she knew you were flying," I told him, trying to keep my face severe. "How long has your wing been strong enough for that, huh?"

He snorted, and tugged at a strand of hair on my head. Like I'd been expecting an answer. I shook my head and chuckled under my breath.

"Alright, boy, I won't tell if you won't. Come on, let's get you back to the barn. I'll let you back out first thing tomorrow. Promise."

He dropped into a bow and tucked one claw up behind him to make a mounting platform – our signature move – and I scrambled up onto his back, keeping well clear of his wings. He might be healing, but a clumsy kick from me wasn't going to help the process along.

He took off at a steady lope and I settled into place as we moved effortlessly through the academy's well used trails. I wasn't sure exactly when I made the decision, but somewhere along the way I took us off the track that would lead to the barn, and several minutes later, the dark outline of a forest loomed before us. The Unhallowed Grove.

I don't know what I thought I was going to do – I couldn't venture inside to find Kelsey. Stormclaw wouldn't enter the grove, and even if he would, it'd be much too dangerous. Werewolves weren't the only thing that lurked inside the grove's protective perimeter. They were the only thing that could breach it, though.

A howl ripped through the air, rending the evening serenity, and Stormclaw shied sharply to one side, snorting and pawing at the ground.

"Easy, boy," I murmured, patting his feathered neck. I glanced up at the sky, where the full moon hung, shining its pale light. Its spell had already taken hold of Paisley and Kelsey, and I couldn't know for certain which of them had uttered the wretched sound. But it was so mournful, so full of anguish, that I felt sure it had to be Paisley. It was the sound of someone grieving for a wound they knew would never heal. Another howl rent the night air, and in it I could hear her crying for her former life, and for the curse she now lived under.

I turned Stormclaw away. Coming out here had been a mistake. I'd make it up with Kelsey in the morning. Right now, Paisley deserved some privacy.

Chapter Fifteen

Hey Kels," I said, as our redheaded friend caught up to us on our way back to the common room. "Where've you been? You missed dinner."

"Oh, um, I had something to take care of," she said, not meeting my eye.

"More important that dinner?" Sam said, gaping at her. "Are you ill?"

I elbowed him in the ribs, because as usual his sense of tact had deserted him. It wasn't the first time Kelsey had pulled a vanishing act since the last full moon, and she always seemed quiet when she came back. I was starting to get worried, but pushing her wouldn't get anywhere. Especially if it was werewolf stuff. We'd just have to wait for her to decide to open up. That didn't mean I wasn't going to keep a close eye on her in the meantime, though.

"All students, all students."

The sound bounced around me, booming from all sides of the academy's aged corridor. I spun around, looking for the source of it, but Talendale's overly calm tones seemed to be coming from everywhere and nowhere at once. I shot a look at Kelsey and Sam, but before I could voice my confusion, he continued.

"All students, report to the main hall immediately. Please proceed in a calm and orderly manner."

"Do you think something's wrong?" Kelsey asked, a slight tremor in her voice. Sam pressed his lips together grimly.

"Probably just wants to give us all a lecture about remembering to study over Christmas," I said, but I wasn't fooling anyone. That was an emergency announcement and I'd never heard him use one before. Something wasn't right.

Without another word, the three of us turned and headed back to the main hall, picking up several confused and chattering students on the way. We passed Kayden and his usual friends, too, talking in anxious whispers that I couldn't quite make out.

It seemed like most of the academy had beaten us to the hall. Row upon row of chairs occupied the room, and our group grabbed a couple of seats near the back. Standing behind the same lectern he used at the start of the year was Talendale, and behind him stood the four head of elements – Alden, Swann, Atherton and Ellerby – each grim faced and silent. Kelsey glanced at me, her face pale.

"Good evening, students," Talendale said, and immediately the excited whispers filling the hall died down. "I have summoned you here to deliver grave news."

He paused, and from the corner of my eye I saw Harper gnawing at her fingernails. Kayden elbowed her and she let her hands drop back into her lap. I wondered if she was getting a sense of déjà vu.

Talendale took a deep breath before continuing.

"Dryadale academy has been forced to close. Though I am loathe to spread unverified rumour, it would appear the academy has succumbed to a curse. I cannot tell you more at this time."

Stunned silence met his announcement. Another academy had closed. What the hell was going on out there? All at once there was a burst of noise, people talking over each other and shouting questions.

"Who cursed—"

"Is someone attacking—"

"Is Dragondale next?"

I didn't hear who asked that last question, but the whole hall fell silent again at the words. Shit. *Could* we be next? Were we really under attack?

"We have absolutely no reason to assume that, Mr Monroe," Talendale said, his voice completely calm. "For the moment, however, I will ask you all to be vigilant, and report any unusual activity to a professor."

His eyes swept the room, underscoring his words with his silence, before he continued.

"I am sure the matter will be resolved shortly. In the meantime, we will host a number of Dryadale's students here. It does not need to be said that you will treat them with the utmost respect that hospitality demands."

"Where are they going to put them?" I whispered to Kelsey. The spare rooms were already filled with the Braeseth students. She just shrugged and shook her head.

"As there is only one day left of this semester, the majority will join us when they return to study after their break," Talendale said. "Others who were due to remain in their academy over Christmas will join us this evening."

His words prompted another outbreak of whispers. Talk about doing things in a rush. Things must have been bad at Dryadale. I hoped no-one had been hurt. They'd all seemed so friendly when we visited for the trial. Well, most of them, anyway. Talendale coughed in annoyance, and the whispers died down.

"Some will be arriving this evening," Talendale repeated sternly, his glare defying anyone to speak again, "and they will be housed according to their elemental powers. Room assignments will be posted shortly. If you have a spare bed in your dorm you will likely find it occupied. Should that be the case, it will be your responsibility to ensure that your guest finds their way around the academy."

I shared a look with Kelsey. We had a spare bed in our dorm room. It wasn't like we had to worry about keeping her secret anymore — not after last year. But the last thing she needed was someone judging her from inside her own dorm. She put up with enough of that every time she walked down a corridor. Whoever joined us, I'd have to make sure they knew I wouldn't stand for anyone causing my friend problems because of her birthright. Hell, if we were going to get started on birthrights, I was right up the creek without a paddle.

"What about the trials?" It was Dean who asked, earning himself a glare from Talendale, to which he seemed oblivious. A look of irritation flashed over the professor's face, then he sighed in resignation. Several hundred eager pairs of eyes fixed on him, mine amongst them. I mean, it wasn't like I cared, obviously — there were bigger things at stake than some stupid contest, but it *would* be nice to see the other academies. And take Felicity down a peg or two.

"The Four Nations Cup will proceed," Talendale said after a moment. "Though Dryadale will regrettably be forced to withdraw. No more questions. It's getting late and there is much to organise before our guests arrive. Back to your common rooms, please."

The scraping of chairs announced the students dispersing, and I made for the lists posted at the end of the hall beside Alden. Might as well find out what our new roomie was called. Kelsey, Sam and the rest of our little group drifted with me.

"So much for the *Four* Nations Cup," Dean grumbled, scuffing his feet across the scrupulously clean flagstone floor. "There aren't going to be many nations left in it if this keeps up."

"Guess someone didn't like their odds," Sam said.

"Wait." I turned to face him with a frown. "You don't think that's why their academy has been cursed?"

"I was joking. But now that you mention it..." He shrugged. "Why not?"

"Because," Kelsey said, raising both her eyebrows at him in disbelief, "no student has that sort of magic, that's why."

"And professors?"

"Now you're just being ridiculous." She shook her head impatiently, then looked over the heads of the students clustered around the sheet of paper pinned to the wall. "We're sharing with a girl called Chloe."

Hybrid senses. Useful for more than just tracking prey in the woods.

"It's not ridiculous," Sam said. "The professors are hardly saints."

"Do you really think," Kelsey said through gritted teeth and a forced smile, "that this is the best place to talk about it?"

"Oh."

We said our goodbyes to the others and headed for our common room. Dorms were assigned on a single-sex basis – Dragondale was old-fashioned like that – but no-one batted an eyelid about visitors. We'd beaten Ava back here, so it was just the three of us. I spared the remaining empty bed a glance and wondered what Chloe would be like. It was going to be cramped around here for a while.

I shut the door behind us and perched on the edge of my bed, shoving a pile of half-written assignments to one side.

"So?" Sam said, looking at Kelsey.

"Don't look at me," she said. "It's your crazy theory."

"That you obviously agree with," Sam pressed. "Or we wouldn't be here."

He looked around the room with a shudder.

"Much too clean. Where do you girls keep your dirty washing?"

"We wash it," I said, rolling my eyes and making a note not to visit Sam's dorm any time soon. "I don't get it. Why would anyone want to fix the games?"

"Lyssa, Lyssa, Lyssa," Sam sighed theatrically, shaking his head in mock disappointment.

"I swear, if the word 'integrate' is about to come out of your mouth..."

He held up his hands in surrender.

"I'm just saying, the cup is a big deal. It would open a lot of doors for whoever won it. They could walk into pretty much any career, and then there's sponsorships, and apprenticeships, not to mention being famous."

"Okay, I get it. It's a big deal." That probably explained why everyone had been gunning for a place as academy champion – and made me wonder again how on earth I ended up as one. "That doesn't explain why a professor would risk their job over it, though. I mean, I know they care about their students – Atherton excluded – but not enough to throw away their careers."

Kelsey spoke up from her bed, sitting with her back against the wall and her knees tucked up under her chin like a little girl.

"The mentors have a lot to gain, too. It's not uncommon for money to change hands, particularly if the champion's family is wealthy. And mentoring a cup winner opens doors for them, too. Professional coaching, private tuition, there are lots of opportunities for someone with a proven track record. Not all professors want to teach at academies forever. And you're wrong about Atherton. He cares about Felicity."

I absorbed her words in silence, turning them over in my head before speaking again, slowly and carefully.

"You're saying you think Atherton might be involved?"

"No!" She shook her head furiously, blanching at the suggestion, then took a deep breath. "I still don't think a professor is involved. I'm just saying, if you're thinking like that, you can't rule him out."

"The better question, then, is who is struggling enough to need to cheat?"

We all mulled it over. Sam conjured a string of fire and wove it through his fingers absentmindedly as he thought.

"When's the next trial?" he said.

"First week back next semester. Assuming they don't postpone it."

"Then I think we need to take a closer look at the other champions."

Chapter Sixteen

C hristmas passed quickly, Fire won the first Itealta match of the season – though Swann hadn't let me play, slave driver that she was – and we'd barely settled in our new room-mate before we were stepping through a portal in Talendale's office, and into Selkenloch, the druid academy of Scotland.

It was not what I was expecting. I mean, I wasn't completely sure what I *had* been expecting, but this wasn't it. But let's be fair – who expects an academy to be *underwater*, for crying out loud? It was oddly claustrophobic, looking out of the shielded windows and seeing the waters of Loch Ness pressing against them. The whole place was shielded from mundanes, apparently, but everyone we spoke to had a tale about that one time a water dragon slipped out of the academy's shield and scared the crap out of the local mundanes.

The academy itself was carved from underground rock, and through the carved walls of each room, tiny traces of water lobelia grew, which all connected to something called the Dortmannian Plant. Selkenloch's version of the Tilimeuse Tree, I guessed. We weren't going to get time to see much of it. The powers that be had decided the champions would only spend three days here – lessons on the Friday, training on the Saturday, and the trial itself on Sunday, then straight back to our own academies. It seemed like Talendale wasn't the only professor to be feeling twitchy – everyone was taking what had happened to Dryadale seriously. More seriously, I couldn't help but feel, than when it had happened at Braeseth Academy. I shook my head. I'd been spending too much time around Kayden. His bitterness was starting to rub off on me, and I'd had plenty of my own to start with.

"You disagree, Ms Eldridge?"

I blinked my attention back into the lecture room, and found Professor Reid – Selkenloch's history professor – staring at me, along with half the class who'd twisted round in their seats to do the same. Shit. I didn't even have the first idea what he'd been talking about. I'd drifted off some time near the start of the droning lesson.

"I think what Lyssa means, Professor," Kelsey said, shooting me a sideways look that some might have considered reproachful, "is that if Slulk had defeated Krurel, then the battle for Blood River might never have happened in the first place."

"Uh… yeah." I nodded and tried to look like I understood any of what she'd said.

"Interesting point, Ms…"

"Winters."

"Very astute of you both." His slight emphasis on the word 'both' told me he wasn't buying our story in the slightest. Oh, well. Probably wouldn't be the worst thing to happen to me on this trip. "And on that fascinating insight, we finish the class. Please remember, your assignments are due in on Monday. No excuses. You're dismissed."

There was a scraping of chairs as thirty students rose from behind desks, shoving books back into their bags, and chattering about their weekend plans.

"Smooth, lass," a voice said from beside me.

I glanced round to see a tall guy about my age, with dark cropped hair, ridiculously wide biceps, and amused eyes. I recognised him as one of Selkenloch's champions. Alistair. He seemed much more relaxed here in his own academy than last time I'd seen him – then again, we'd been in the middle of a trial, and I hadn't been too relaxed myself.

"That's me," I said. "Smooth and laser focused."

He grinned and gestured to the guy beside him.

"Me and Ollie are heading down to the canteen to grab some lunch. Want to join us?"

I glanced at Sam and Kelsey, but neither of them objected. Probably for the best. I had absolutely no idea where their canteen was, and it wasn't a great idea to be getting lost in an academy where one wrong turn could dump you under a tonne of water.

"Great, sounds good. Assuming you're not scared to be caught fraternising with the competition, that is."

A chuckle rumbled in his throat.

"What makes ye think you're any competition for me?"

"That's fighting talk, Alistair." I returned his grin. His mirth was infectious. "But I seem to recall I'm ahead of you on the leader board."

"Pfft, for now," he said, leading us out of room and into the crowded corridor. "I was just taking it easy on you guys. That cup's got my name written all over it."

"Are you always this modest?"

"Just you wait, Dragondale. You haven't seen anything yet."

"That's true," I said, as he pulled open the door to the canteen. "Because you've been too far behind for me to watch."

I grinned and ducked through the door in front of him, with Sam, Kelsey and Ollie filing in behind. The Selkenloch canteen was like a smaller version of Dragondale's main hall, right down to the tables divided by element in each quarter of the room. They had about half the number of students we did – but whether that was because Scotland was smaller than England, or just because most of them were too smart to want to attend an underwater academy, it was hard to say. It seemed like it maybe wouldn't be polite to bring it up.

We grabbed some food from the kitchen mage and headed to the earth quarter. No-one seemed to care that me, Sam and Kels were at the wrong table, which was refreshing. Or maybe they just didn't think it would be polite to bring it up. Whichever.

"It's a shame about Dryadale having to drop out of the trials," Kelsey said as we made a start on our food. A werewolf focusing on business when there was food in front of her: she was putting me to shame. And she was right. We were supposed to be finding out who might be trying to take out the competition. Since that included me, I should probably take it a bit more seriously. But it was hard to imagine the boyish Scot doing anything like that. I mean, he just wouldn't.

"Yeah, it is," Alistair agreed, setting down his spoon. Probably wise. I wasn't sure it was healthy for humans to eat haggis. "Kieran had a real shot. Still, gives me a better chance of getting my hands on the cup."

Oh.

Sam choked on a mouthful of burger, and Alistair laughed loudly.

"Your face!" His own face grew more sombre. "Seriously though, I'm gutted for them. Kieran is a great guy, he'd been working really hard. Sucks that someone took his shot from him."

I heaved an internal sigh of relief, and took a sip from my glass. See? Good instincts. I had to learn to stop doubting myself. At this rate I was going to end up as cynical as Kayden.

"So...." Alistair said, drawing out the word as he looked between our faces. None of us were going to win a game of poker any time soon. "You think that's what's happening? Someone's trying to take out the competition?"

I opened my mouth to reply, and Sam stomped on my foot. Hard. I glared at him. Jeez, Sam, subtle.

"I don't know, it was just a theory some idiot at Dragondale came up with," I said to Alistair, shooting Sam a sarcastic look and narrowly resisting the urge to poke my tongue out at him. "Seems kinda crazy, if you ask me."

"Yeah," Alistair agreed after a moment, picking up his fork again. "No-one I know could have pulled off a curse like that. It's attacking their primal plant, leeching its energy. If they cannae stop it, the academy will die."

"How do you know about the curse?" I said sharply. More sharply than I'd intended, judging from the look on Alistair's face.

"The same way you do," he said, and he sounded a little defensive – and a little annoyed. "From the Dryadale students."

"Sorry." I slouched in my seat. "Guess I'm just feeling a little jumpy. No offense meant."

"None taken," he said. "If I was sitting second on the leader board, I'd be feeling jumpy, too."

Crap. I hadn't thought of that. Alistair chuckled again.

"Eat up, Dragondale. You're going to need your strength."

He finished the last of his disgusting food, then he and Ollie headed off, leaving the three of us alone.

"What do you think?" Sam said, glancing over his shoulder to make sure no-one was listening in.

"Him?" I said, and shook my head. "No way. He's too nice."

Kelsey gave me a look of stern disapproval, which I took to mean she disagreed with my assessment.

"He's acting nice," she said. "But did you see his face when he was talking about winning the cup?"

"That was just banter!" I protested. "If we're counting that as evidence, then we should just lock me in Daoradh right now – along with half of the other champions."

"That's not something to joke about. Anyway, I'm just saying it's too early to rule anyone out. We need to get to know them better. All of the champions – well, the ones left in, anyway. There's only five of them, it shouldn't be that hard."

"Five?" I frowned as I counted them in my head. Alistair and Callum from Selkenlock, and Dylan and Aderyn from Gryphonvale. "You know I was joking about me being a suspect, right?"

"Felicity," Kelsey said simply.

"Atherton?" We couldn't rule it out, I supposed. And if there was one professor at Dragondale I'd point the finger at, it would be him. Not where he could see me, of course, because I quite liked having fingers. Still, Kelsey was right. Him and Felicity were suspects.

"I volunteer to check out Aderyn," Sam said, leaning back in his chair with a smug smile.

I rolled my eyes but didn't object. Maybe the pretty Welsh girl would fall for his alleged charm. Apparently, some girls were into that.

"Okay," I agreed. "I'll speak to Dylan."

Kelsey shook her head, sending auburn hair tumbling around her shoulders. She paused to tuck a stray lock back behind her ear before she said, "I don't think that will work. The other champions aren't going to relax around you, you're the competition. Besides, someone needs to talk to Felicity."

"Fine," I said through a heavy sigh. She *had* helped me in the last trial, after all. It would give me an in with her. On the other hand, it probably also meant she wasn't guilty. "What about you?"

"I'll speak to Dylan," she said. "And Callum, if I get a chance. The champions will be training all day tomorrow, so we'll have to do it tonight."

"Works for me," Sam said. "I'll take Aderyn for a stroll under the stars."

Kelsey snorted, and Sam gave her a confused look.

"Great idea," I said with a grin, gesturing to the loch floating past the window. "Try not to drown."

Chapter Seventeen

What do you want, Charity?"

"Hi, Felicity," I said, rolling my eyes at the same time as rolling out my shoulders and wondering how badly it would be frowned upon to thump Dragondale's other champion on the morning of the games.

I hadn't been able to get anywhere near her since we got here — she'd spent almost the entire time in the air common room, or training with Atherton. Can you believe he'd even had her meals taken into a lecture room he'd sequestered for her? No, me either. I'd eaten in the canteen with Selkenloch's students like a normal person. Apparently, Felicity didn't do mingling with us lesser mortals.

She looked me up and down like I was something unpleasant she'd stepped in, which was to say in her usual manner. There was absolutely no way she was going to confide anything in me, whether her and Atherton had been involved in cursing Dryadale or not.

"If you think I'm going to help you again," she said through a sneer, "you're mistaken."

"If you think I'm going to need your help, you're the one who's mistaken."

I was wasting my time trying to befriend this airhead. She'd hated me from day one, and that wasn't about to change any time soon.

She laughed, and the sound echoed back at us around the empty lecture room. Her eyes tightened and her lips pressed into a thin line as she glared at me, hands on hips.

"Do you really think you're any sort of threat to me? The professors might think you're some sort of super-druid, but I know the truth. You came from the gutter, and the gutter is where you belong. And by the time this competition is over, everyone is going to know it. That cup is mine and I will destroy anyone who tries to come between it and me."

My heart thudded in my chest and I quickly broke eye contact with her. That was practically a confession. I sucked in a quick breath and forced a practiced nonchalance into my voice.

"Whatever, Felicity. Good luck today."

I turned on my heel and marched out of the room, cramming my hands in my pockets so she wouldn't see them tremble. If Felicity and Atherton really were behind the curses, then I was in trouble. Because there was only one academy they couldn't risk cursing: ours. And that meant I was the only real threat to her getting her hands on the cup. I needed to find Kelsey.

"Ah, Lyssa, there you are. Time to get ready for the trial."

"Professor Swann!"

She frowned, her thin face creased in concern.

"What's wrong? You look pale as a banshee. Pre-trial nerves?"

I opened my mouth to tell her, then thought better of it. It wasn't like I had any proof, and Felicity would just deny having said anything.

"Uh, yeah, I guess."

"After your performance in the last trial? Nonsense. Everyone back at Dragondale knows you'll top the leader board after today."

Oh, great. Now I really was starting to get nervous. I fluked it last time, and I'd never have managed it without Felicity's help. Felicity, who had every reason to want me out of the competition. I was officially screwed, and the butterflies in my stomach knew it.

"Do you have any last-minute questions?"

"Yeah. What the hell am I doing here?"

Swann chuckled, and took me by the elbow – presumably to stop me from bolting. As if I'd give Felicity the satisfaction. I took a deep breath and nodded, exhaling heavily.

"Okay, I'm ready."

"Excellent." Swann beamed at me, then her expression became more serious. "I believe in you, Lyssa. I know you doubt yourself, but you can do this."

She held my eye until I started to feel uncomfortable, then she lifted one arm, muttered something under her breath, and a portal sprang into existence.

"Good luck."

"Thanks, Professor."

I squared my shoulders and stepped through the portal, and out into Selkenloch's stadium. I immediately looked up, expecting a ton of water to crash down on my head, but it was being held back by some sort of force field, so that it formed a dome above our heads. All around me, students cheered from the packed stands. Chuckling my relief at not being drowned and my embarrassment at thinking I might be, I straightened and hoped no-one else had noticed my stupidity. It wasn't like I didn't know they had Itealta games here – it sort of went without saying that they had to have some way to keep the pitch from being flooded. It was probably the same shield that covered the windows – not that I'd ever seen anyone chance opening one.

"...show your appreciation for Dragondale's second champion, Lyssa Eldridge!"

I forced my attention from the dome back onto the crowd, and gave them a small wave. They went wild with excitement, screaming and cheering and stamping their feet. I caught the sneer on Felicity's face from where she stood, just off to one side of me. I guess acknowledging the crowd was beneath Her Royal Haughtiness. Whatever.

I looked round the rest of the ring of competitors – I was the last one here, again – and my eyes snagged on the two empty spaces in the circle. Dryadale's spaces. There was more at stake than just the trial today. If I was right about Felicity, then she would be looking for an opportunity to take me out, especially after her slip. And if she managed it, I would have no way to warn anyone she was the one behind the curses. There would be nothing to stop her and Atherton taking down the other academies. I squared my jaw. I was not going to let that happen.

Inside our circle was a calm stream, completely encircling a small grassy island, just about big enough to support us all. The stream, or perhaps moat would be more accurate – the water didn't seem to be moving – was only a few feet wide. Small enough that it could probably be jumped from a standing start.

"Champions," the announcer said, in his booming voice. "Your task today will be to reach the sanctuary of the island. The first champion to reach it will be declared the winner of this trial."

Why did I get the feeling that wasn't going to be as easy as he made it sound? I eyed the moat, trying to spot any sign of a trap – until my view was blocked by a portal. Of course.

"Champions, prepare to enter your portals and start the challenge. Three, two, one... Go!"

I threw myself through the portal with far less caution than was probably wise for a person jumping through a blank screen into who-knew-where, and who-knew-what. I found myself standing in the middle of a small circle of damp earth, maybe six foot across... and surrounded above and all on sides by water, kept at bay by only a shield that stretched round the edge of the circle, and closed a few feet above me.

Shit. I was at the bottom of the loch.

I took a deep breath, and tried not to think about the tonnes of water pressing in around me. What would happen if I couldn't get out? Would they send someone to find me? What happened if the shield failed? Would anyone know I was drowning? Shit!

Dammit, Lyssa, get a grip. I sucked in another deep breath, calmly and deliberately shutting down the part of my mind that questioned how much air was trapped down here with me. This was no different from the last trial. I'd handled that one just fine.

The portal that had brought me here winked out of existence, plunging me into absolute darkness. I stifled a scream and it came out as a muted yelp. It was fine. I was a freaking druid. A fire element. I focused on my hands and summoned a fireball into existence, careful to keep it from getting too close to the shield – I had no idea if the magic was fireproof, and no inclination to find out.

Okay, time to get out of here. It was the same as the last trial, right? I just had to find the point in the shield that was actually a glamoured pathway, and I'd be out of here in no time.

I'd made it round the circle twice before I was forced to admit there was no glamour. Was it possible Felicity had tampered with my dome to stop me getting out? Did she mean for me to drown down here?

I shook off my paranoia and reminded myself I was supposed to be getting a grip. There was no way anyone could have tampered with any of the domes. Everything to do with the challenges was closely monitored, and she could never have risked it. She had too much to lose. Which meant there wasn't meant to be a glamoured passageway. I was supposed to find another way out.

That made sense. These trials were supposed to be a test of our druidic skills, after all. No point in testing the same skill over and over. Okay, Lyssa, you're trapped under seven cubic kilometres of water, and you need to find your way to an academy which could be anywhere in the Loch. What do you do?

I mulled it over for about a half second. I get out the same way I got here. Portal. Except… well, even with all of Kaversal's lessons, I'd only ever managed two portals, and neither of them stuck around for long enough for me to climb through. If I got stuck, half in, half out, I'd have to be disembarked by a professor, which would mean I was out of the trial. Fine. I'd just have to make sure I didn't get stuck, then.

I raised my right hand, pointing my palm at a spot just in front of the shield, and focused on the middle of the little island in the Itealta field, bringing it into the centre of my mind's eye. I muttered "eachlais" under my breath, willing the portal into existence.

Not so much as a flicker. I stretched out my shoulders, then tried again, forcing all my determination through my hand, and shouting the spellword at the top of my voice.

Nothing. Was there some reason it wasn't working, or was it just my magical incompetence?

It didn't matter. All that mattered was that I wasn't getting out of here through a portal. I needed to find another way, and quickly. The others might have already worked it out my now.

Maybe… maybe I could move the shield? Like, make it come with me as I walked? Well, maybe – if I knew the damned spell for creating a shield strong enough to hold back the entire damned Loch Ness. Which of course I didn't. I mean, who the hell was that powerful? No student I knew.

I stared at the water for a long moment – longer than I could really afford to spare – determined not to admit that I was trapped. By water. Wait. By water! I could control water! Granted, water was a secondary element, and one by rights I shouldn't have been able to control – thanks, Dad – but it was still one of my elements, and I *could* control it. Not an entire loch, sure, but I didn't need to. Just a few square feet at a time, enough room for me to move.

I shivered, and not because it was cold at the bottom of the Loch. If I slipped, if I lost control, I'd drown, probably before anyone could get to me. Go big or go home, right?

I squared my shoulders, and focused on the water pressing at the edge of the shield. My palms glowed blue, and I willed it to move. It sloshed against the shield, then eased back, compressing itself into a roiling mass. Air bubbles were crushed from it, forming an air pocket in the space I'd created. It was working.

Now all I needed was to know where to go – it was pitched black all around except for the light cast from my fireball, and I didn't much fancy wandering the floor of the entire loch until I stumbled across it. I stared out beyond the shield, watching the air and water bubble, and the little traces of marine and plant life drift past. My lips twisted into a smile. The answer was right in front of me, literally. The Dortmannian. It was the Selkenlock's version of the Tilimeuse Tree. Which meant I could feel the pull of the academy's magic along it. If I could just find a piece attached to the main plant.

Acting on a hunch, I crouched down, and pressed my hands to the earth. Its roots had to be underground, and all I needed was a single strand. My fingers dug into the damp silt and I reached out with my magic senses, trying to find anything that pulsed with power. My palms started to tingle, and the earth shifted. What the…

I frowned and started at the moving silt, and then my jaw dropped open. My hands… they were glowing green.

Chapter Eighteen

I had an earth elemental power.

No way. It just wasn't possible. No druid could control four elements, not even Raphael. *And no druid could control three elements before him.*

I shook my head and clamped my jaw shut. I'd deal with whatever the hell this meant later. Right now, I had to find the Dortmannian roots and get out of here. My palms still glowing green, I sought the pulse of power, and immediately I could feel the plant reaching out to me. It was like holding my hands up to a cosy fire – heat prickled pleasantly all over my palms, growing stronger each time I edged further along the root. It would be easy to follow it back to its source – which had to be in the academy. The plants were instinctively attracted to magic and grew strongest where the most magic dwelled.

I got to my feet, wiped the silt from my hands, and stretched my right hand out to the water beyond the shield. It immediately glowed blue, and the water yielded as I took a step towards it. My left palm stayed green, tracking the pulsing roots beneath my feet. Right hand raised in front of me like an extra from a bad vampire movie, I proceeded cautiously forward. All I needed to complete the image was a crucifix.

I moved easily through the shield – it was designed to keep water out, not people in – and the waters of the loch kept retreating from me as I followed the pull of the Dortmannian. I grinned. It was bloody well working.

Water sloshed over my feet and I swore loudly, then redoubled my focus. Distractions were bad. Got it. I kept pressing ahead until I saw a dark shape in the gloom. This time I didn't allow myself to celebrate or feel any emotion except determination to keep the water at bay. One lapse now could kill me. Or at the very least, cost me my place on the leader board.

I made it through the academy's shield without further incident, except for the squelching in my shoes. I took a full half-second to celebrate the fact I hadn't drowned, then I sprinted full pelt round the dry stone track that ran Selkenloch's perimeter, and by the time the Itealta pitch came into sight, I was completely out of breath. A loud cheer greeted my arrival in the stadium, and the other champions looked round at me. I did a quick headcount. They were all here – both the Selkenlochs, both the Gryphonvales, and Felicity. And they didn't all have wet feet.

But none of them had made it to the island yet. And as I got closer, I saw why.

Standing between them, and it, was the most majestic creature I had ever seen. Pure white with a coat that gleamed in the daylight, the beast was tall and lean, with a white mane that flowed halfway down its neck, and a glistening white horn. A unicorn.

I took a step towards it, my feet moving of their own accord. A unicorn. It was incredible, right out of a fairy tale, and it was even more stunning that any depiction I'd ever seen. Hollywood hadn't even come close to capturing their majesty. The way it moved was pure grace, every hoof placed deliberately, as if it was dancing to a music none of us could hear. A chuckle bubbled up from my throat. A unicorn. The national animal of Scotland. I probably should have seen it coming.

And then it snorted, levelled its horn and me, and charged.

I dived aside, hitting the ground hard, and narrowly avoiding being speared on its three foot long horn. I rolled into a crouch as it galloped past me, then leapt back to my feet. A flash of red movement caught my eye, and I saw the long gash in the fabric of my cloak. That had been a nearer miss than I'd thought. And that horn was sharp.

Unicorns are nothing to joke about. That was what Kelsey had said last year, and she wasn't wrong. The creature might be beautiful, but it was deadly. Now I understood why no-one had made it onto the island.

As I watched, the unicorn turned and raced back towards the island, tossing its head and swishing its tail as it eyeballed Aderyn, the pretty girl from Gryphonvale. She backed away and it paid her no more attention. It didn't leap the moat like I'd expected, but ran a circle around its perimeter. We'd be safe once we reached the island. We just had to get past the stabby pony first. Naturally.

"Nice shoes, Dragondale," Alistair said with a grin. I glanced down at my shoes and frowned at him.

"How come you're so dry?"

"I portalled, like any sane druid would."

"If you're so sane, how come you didn't portal your Scottish arse right onto the island?"

"You can't," he said. "Protected by magic. That's the whole point of a moat."

Oh. I should have thought of that. Must've been why they used to surround castles with them.

"Don't worry, Dragondale," he said, clapping me on the shoulder and nodding to Dylan, who was shivering under a layer of drenched clothing. "You're not the only one who didn't work it out."

"I'm not worried," I lied. "Anyway, if you got here so quickly, how come you haven't made it past Lady Amalthea there yet? You're not scared of the pretty pony, are you?"

He looked at me like I'd lost it, which might not have been an entirely unfair conclusion, given the tattered remains of my cloak.

"I mean," I clarified, "Why didn't you just cast a sleep spell on it, or something?"

He looked me up and down, and not in the way a guy does when he's into you.

"You really didnae grow up in our world, did you? The unicorn's horn absorbs magic. But not just that – once it's trapped a spell, it can throw it back at you."

"So, you are scared then?" I taunted, in an effort to cover up the unease sitting in a heavy pool in my stomach.

"Hell yeah, I'm scared of it," he said. "Those things can take down a dragon."

I whistled, keeping one eye on the unicorn as it pawed a rut into the ground with a front hoof, then levelled its horn at Felicity, and charged. She launched herself aside, throwing up a hand as she did – a reflex, I was sure – and blasting air at the beast. Alistair winced. Sure enough, the unicorn tilted its head into the gust and it stopped immediately, then a split second later blasted into Felicity, taking her off her feet.

"Don't use magic," I muttered. "Check."

Which pretty much ruled out all the tools in my box – and apparently everyone else's, too. It was just as well the unicorn was only charging people who looked like they might be about to make a move towards the island, or we'd all be dead by now.

"Hey, Alistair," I said from the corner of my mouth, not daring to take my eyes from the unicorn as it wheeled around. "I've got an idea. If we work together, we can distract it long enough for one of us to make it to the island. Then whoever's on the island can distract it."

"Have ye lost yer mind, Dragondale?"

"You know, I do have a name," I said. He shook his head.

"Not right now you don't. We're competing against each other, and what's to stop you going back on your word when you reach the island? Maybe yer should work with the other Dragondale lass."

"I'd sooner trust you than Felicity." And I wondered what that said about me – or her. "Look, I'll distract it first. Then you distract it when you're safe."

"Then I'll win," he said uncertainly. "You'd be giving up first place."

I shrugged.

"If we stand around, someone else is going to have the same idea, and neither of us will get first place. Besides, I'm already ahead of you, I can afford to spare the points. Just don't double cross me, or I'll turn you into a toad."

He paused for a second, then nodded.

"Alright, Dra– Lyssa."

"Here goes nothing." I moved away from him, waving my arms above my head. "Hey, unicorn!"

It spun around to face me, and I waved my arms again.

"Over here, you dumb beast!" I had no idea why I was trying to get it angry – honestly, it seemed angry enough to start with. Oh well, in for a penny, in for a pound. It snorted as I lowered my arms and held them out in front of me. I pushed my magic into my palms, focusing on all four elements. Swirls of red, blue, yellow, and green light enveloped my hands and forearms, and the whole stadium seemed to fall silent. I took a step towards the unicorn, and it lowered its head, preparing to charge.

"Come on!" I shouted at it, turning up the power pulsing along my arms. I didn't release it – I didn't fancy four elements worth of spells being thrown back in my direction – just kept it swirling around me. The beast took a step towards me, and I tensed, waiting for it to charge.

But it didn't.

The unicorn walked slowly towards me, head held low. Every nerve in my body screamed at me to run, to dive aside before it speared me on its deadly horn, but I was incapable of moving. My legs had completely locked up. I wasn't even sure I could remember how to breathe. Glued to the spot, I could do nothing but watch it cover the ground with effortless grace. But instead of driving that wickedly long horn into me, the unicorn slowed to a stop a few feet from me. Then, it stretched out its nose to my hand, so close that I could feel its warm breath play along my skin, and did something I never could have expected. It sank to its knees.

It seemed like the entire arena was holding its breath with me. I flicked a glance over my shoulder and it was like the world had ground to a halt: no-one was moving, not even the other champions. A freaking unicorn was *kneeling* to me. What the hell?

I drew in a shaky breath and eased closer to the animal. I sank slowly to the ground beside it, until I, too, was on my knees on the damp ground. The unicorn regarded me through eyes that shone with intelligence, and I raised one hand, edging it through the space between us until it was almost touching the animal's glossy white coat. I paused, watching closely, then moved my hand the last fraction of an inch until my fingertips touched against its silken hair. The unicorn exhaled in a loud snort, startling me, and then tossed its head, shaking out its flowing mane, and fixed its eyes on something over my shoulder. I twisted round to see Dylan sprinting towards the island, wet cloak trailing behind him.

Shit! The trial!

I pulled my hand back and leapt to my feet, but Dylan had already reached the moat, and he cleared it in a single bound. Another streak of movement caught my eye from the other direction – Felicity. Dammit!

I started sprinting to the moat, but Felicity had a head start. I gritted my teeth and pushed myself on faster. I was fitter than she was – Itealta practice three times a week saw to that – and within a couple of strides I was gaining ground on her. From the corner of my eye I saw the unicorn lunge to its feet and break into a gallop with an angry snort. I barely had to twist my head round to see its target – Alistair.

I opened my mouth to shout a warning but immediately I saw it wouldn't do any good – there was no time for him to get out of its way. My heart thudded in my chest and I skidded to a halt. If I didn't do something, he was going to get gored.

"Hey, unicorn," I bellowed, my voice ragged with exertion and terror. "Come here!"

The creature wheeled around almost on the spot, and started running at me. Felicity reached the bank, leapt and cleared it easily, taking second place. I ground my teeth together. That was twice she'd beaten me now.

Alistair locked eyes with me, his face pale and his eyes wide, and he recovered enough to give me a curt nod before pushing on towards the bank. The commentator seemed to find his voice as Alistair leapt, and broke the silence of the arena.

"The first three champions are safely across the moat," he said. "Leaving three more to go. No, two now, and I still cannot believe what I am seeing."

Two? I jerked my head up and saw Aderyn on the island. Ah, crap. Just me and the last Scot remaining. And as the unicorn trotted up to me, distracted from its targets again, I could see that he was going to beat me. No. Bloody. Way. I was *not* coming last. Not after I just did the damned impossible.

I eyed the creature, shook my head at my own stupidity, and patted it on the shoulder with more confidence than I felt.

"In for a penny, right?" I muttered, then crouched low, and launched myself up onto the unicorn's back. I landed softly – two and a half years of mounting gryffs having refined my technique – and the unicorn snorted softly and jumped sideways. I rubbed its neck, and twisted to fix my eyes on the island.

"Come on," I said. "Let's go."

The unicorn raced into action, streaking past the remaining champion in three strides – mercifully not goring him on the way – and carried me towards the island.

"I– She–" the commentator spluttered, then tried again. "Lyssa Eldridge is *riding* the unicorn, I did not think it was possible but she's proving us all wrong. And what an incredible leap! She's on the island, she takes fifth place, and breaks every law known to druid-kind."

Chapter Nineteen

reaks every law known to druid-kind. It had seemed pretty cool when he said it like that. It seemed less cool when every single druid in the whole of Selkenloch was staring at me, open-mouthed, everywhere I went, and avoiding my eye, only to talk about me in hurried whispers as soon as I was past. It was like when I developed my opposing elemental powers all over again.

I was pretty relieved to get back to Dragondale late the following morning – or at least I was, right up until I found myself summoned to Talendale's office, 'forthwith'. After checking with Kelsey what the hell that meant, I hurried up to the lofty office, abandoning my half-eaten bowl of pasta with no small amount of regret. What was so urgent that it couldn't wait until after lunch? I mean, it was important to keep my strength up, and honestly, Selkenloch's kitchen mage wasn't a patch on Aiden. It was a relief not to be offered haggis with every meal.

I was still mourning my abandoned food when I raised a hand and knocked twice on the ancient wooden door. It was large enough that several people could enter abreast, and its hinges were broader than my hands. I always felt like a mouse when I stood in front of this door. And on the other side of it, come to that. It opened at a command from Talendale, and I stepped through. As usual, the headmaster was seated behind his ornate desk, its surface engraved with carvings that hadn't been there on my last visit. The desk was made of wood harvested from the Tilimeuse Tree, and there was still a connection between it and the tree. I didn't think the desk itself was sentient, but I wouldn't have ruled it out, either. An open mind was pretty much a prerequisite at Dragondale.

"Ah, Ms Eldridge," Talendale said, rising from his seat. "Thank you for joining us."

Us? I looked around the office, and saw Professor Swann standing by the wall, her yellow cloak and blonde hair making her blend in with the woven Air banner behind her. She inclined her head to me, her face inscrutable.

"We shall begin shortly, as soon as our esteemed guest arrives."

Begin what? When who arrives? I didn't ask my questions aloud, but as usual Talendale seemed to read them from my face. I was never going to have a career as a professional poker player.

"All will be revealed soon. It is best we wait for him before we discuss anything. Please, take a seat."

I gritted my teeth – as if it would have killed him to at least tell me who the hell we were waiting for – and he raised an eyebrow at me. Exhaling slowly, I smoothed out my face, and sunk into the chair in front of the desk – the one that was also made of Tilimeuse wood, and that had freaked me out the first time I'd sat in it. Hell, who was I kidding? It still creeped me out. Druid or no, I hadn't quite got my head around the idea of sentient trees, and possibly-sentient furniture.

I'd only been cringing against the bare wood for a few seconds when a portal sprung into existence in the centre of the room, and out of it stepped a stooped, grey-haired man, whose face was set into deep frown lines. His face graced the back of every textbook here, and his portrait hung in the academy's entrance hall. I'd seen it up close last year, when they were discussing whether my best friend would be locked up for being Raphael's pawn. Cauldwell. Head of the Grand Council, and the single most influential druid alive.

"Good morning, Professor Talendale. Ah, I see you have already summoned Ms Eldridge. Excellent. Shall we get straight down to business?"

I shot Talendale a worried look, which was wasted because his attention was solely on Cauldwell. I shifted my eyes to Swann, who gave me what I took to be an encouraging nod. I probably wasn't about to be expelled or locked in Daoradh, then.

"Indeed," Talendale said, and waved his hand. A chair grew – yeah, grew – right out of the cobblestones, and

Cauldwell inclined his head in gratitude before lowering himself into it with an audible clicking of bones.

"Lyssa," Talendale said, and my head snapped back round to look at him. "As I am sure you have guessed, we have summoned you here to discuss the events of the trial."

"I didn't do anything wrong!" I protested. "I didn't enchant that unicorn or anything, I swear!"

"Quite," Talendale agreed. "To do such a thing would be impossible. The unicorn cannot be enchanted, as I'm sure you have noted from your lessons with Professor Alden."

Oops.

"Nor," Cauldwell said, "does it kneel to a human, nor permit one to ride it."

"I'm human!"

"Yes, you are," Talendale said. "But an unusual one, at that."

"If you've called me here to tell me I'm a freak—" I clamped my jaw shut before I could finish that sentence, and drew in a deep breath through my nose. Losing my temper in front of both Talendale and Cauldwell was not going to help my cause.

"Fiery, isn't she?" Cauldwell observed. "Like her father."

"He's not my father! My father is a lawyer from Georgia, and he's a good man."

Cauldwell regarded me through flat eyes, like he was waiting for a child to finish its temper tantrum. I obliged, and slouched back into my chair. I didn't like being compared to Raphael. I wasn't like him. Not even a little.

"How long have you had four elemental powers?" Talendale said. I twisted round to look at him again.

"I don't – I mean, I didn't – it all happened during the trial. I was just trying to find the Dortmannian Plant."

"You understand the implications?" Cauldwell said, and I pivoted my head back to him. These two were going to make me dizzy.

And the answer to his question was that I'd shoved the revelation in a box and buried it there, giving it as little thought as possible, because it scared me half to death. I picked at the dirt under my nails. No druid had ever manifested four powers. Ever. Yeah, I understood the implications.

"I have more powers than Raphael," I said, not lifting my eyes from my hands. Everyone was right – I *was* a freak. An anomaly amongst anomalies. Yay, me. A realisation struck me hard and fast, out of nowhere, punching the air from my lungs. I gasped sharply and jerked my head up to meet his eye. "You think I'm going to turn bad!"

I leapt to my feet, turning to glare at each of the three silent druids in turn.

"That's why I'm here! You think I can't be trusted, that I'll turn out like *he* did!"

I couldn't quite keep the betrayal from my face as I levelled my eyes on Swann, and I saw hurt and remorse twitch across her face. Her, too. The other two I could understand, but Swann knew me. She trained me nearly every day. How could she think this of me? How could any of them? They thought I was dangerous.

...And I was hardly proving them wrong.

I drew in a shaking breath, and dropped back into the chair, dropping my eyes to the floor again.

"I'm not like him," I told the cobblestones, and then lifted my eyes to meet Talendale's. "Professor, in my first year you told me it's not who we are that matters, but who we choose to surround ourselves with, and that nobility is a learned behaviour. I haven't always made the right choices, but I've always tried to keep from hurting the people around me. I don't intend to change that."

"Well said, young druid," Cauldwell said, surprising me. "It is our job to assume the worst, and from here on, I fear it must be yours to prove us wrong. I most sincerely hope that you shall do so."

I guess 'innocent until proven guilty' was a concept that hadn't reached the Grand Council, but on the other hand, I wasn't rotting in Daoradh so I suppose the notion wasn't entirely wasted on them.

"I will, Head Councilman," I said, silencing my desire to call him on his bullshit.

"The unicorn, at least, believed in your nobility," he said. "We have yet to fully comprehend what that may mean, but rest assured, our best minds are working on it."

I shivered. That didn't reassure me in the slightest. A room full of dusty old men talking about me? Great. Just one more thing to worry about.

"Meanwhile," Cauldwell continued, oblivious to my reaction, "You will be allowed to continue representing your academy in the Four Nations Cup, and you will receive extra tuition from your Elemental Manipulation professor."

Yeah, just what I wanted. Spending more time with *her*. I wisely kept that thought to myself, too. But dammit, I'd trusted her, was it really too much to ask for a little trust in return? Not with her bank details or the keys to her car – if she had either – but just to trust that I wasn't on the brink of turning into a psychopathic killer?

"Yes, Head Councilman," I muttered.

"You are a good druid, Lyssa," Talendale said. "We are more than the sum of our parents, or less, should we choose. You must choose, and I trust you shall do so wisely."

I cocked my head a fraction, regarding him. *He* didn't think I was predestined to turn into Raphael. *He* still thought I had a future, a future of doing good. I was about to thank him when movement caught my eye. Fresh words appeared on the desk between us, engraving themselves into the wood in large letters that were impossible to miss even from where I was sitting. My mouth dropped open as I read them.

GRYPHONVALE HAS FALLEN.

Cauldwell rose swiftly and smoothly to his feet, seemingly discarding fifty years in the blink of an eye.

"I must go to the Grand Council, immediately."

"Lyssa, return to your lessons," Swann said. "At once, please."

"But Professor…"

"Now!" Swann snapped. I couldn't miss the panic on her face. What the hell was going on? A lot more than we knew, that was for sure. I nodded numbly at her, and stumbled from my chair and through the door. As I left, I saw Cauldwell draw a portal in the air, and step through.

If the Grand Council were worried, it could only mean bad news. I needed to speak to Sam and Kelsey. I wasn't breaking Swann's rules, strictly speaking, since my next lesson was a free period, which could only mean one thing: Kelsey would be ensconced in the library, panicking about our exams that were still months away.

When I caught up to her, she had a dozen books scattered around her, and was furiously scribbling notes about Yeriup Fungus, which of course I'd never even heard of. No surprise there. In fact, the only surprise was that Sam was with her. Like me, he tended to give this place a wide berth whenever possible.

I glanced over his shoulder and smiled. Completely ignoring the Gaelic textbook flipped open in front of him, he'd doodled a passable sketch of Professor Thorne being eaten by a dragon – Dardyr, if I wasn't mistaken.

And then I remembered why I'd come here, and the smile fell from my face. I dropped into a seat opposite Kelsey, and shoved some of the books aside.

"Hey, I need–" She broke off when she saw my face. "What's wrong?"

Sam dropped his pen and seemed to notice me for the first time.

"Yeah, you're looking kinda pale."

I glanced round, but Librarian Dawson was behind her desk by the doors, and was paying no attention to us. I lowered my voice to a hiss anyway.

"Gryphonvale has been cursed."

Kelsey blanched, and her pen slipped from behind her fingers, bouncing off her textbook and falling to the floor with a soft thud. She didn't seem to notice it.

"You're sure?"

"I was in Talendale's office when they sent word. Atherton must have got to them after Dylan beat Felicity in the last trial."

Kelsey shook her head.

"No, don't you see? It can't have been them. You can't curse somewhere you've never been."

"You can't?"

Sam tossed a balled-up scrap of paper at me.

"I thought I was the one who flunked Law? You can put a delay on a curse, so it doesn't happen for a couple of weeks after you leave, but you've gotta be there when you cast the curse."

"You have?" Sam was right. I really did need to start paying more attention in lessons. "But I don't get it. If it wasn't them, then who?"

We all fell silent for a moment, because who else would have a reason to attack the academies? Unless…

"Wait. How long does it take to prime a curse? Atherton could have slipped in and out without anyone noticing."

"All of the academies are protected after what happened with Raphael in our first year. No-one can get in without an invite from the academy's headmaster."

She meant when Raphael had posed as a wampus cat called Toby in order to get close to me and raise an army of zombies right under Talendale's nose.

"Fine. Maybe he had an invite. I mean, professors move to different academies sometimes, right? Look at Dougan. Maybe a job interview or something."

Kelsey looked dubious and I couldn't blame her. It was a stretch. I slumped forward onto the table, and idly watched a couple of other students pulling books from shelves. It seemed like Kelsey wasn't the only one taking the end of year exams seriously. I saw Kayden pull down a heavy tome and haul it away to a table, with Micah and Harper in his wake. I wondered what would happen about their end of year exams. They could hardly sit Druidic exams, they didn't have the same powers we did.

"We should talk to Talendale about it," Kelsey said, but even she didn't sound convinced.

"Without proof?" Sam said. "He wouldn't even hear us out."

"Then we need to find some," I said decisively, then winced and ducked my head as Dawson shot a glare in my direction. I lowered my voice and carried on. "There must be a way to track portals that have left the academy. How long can a curse stay primed?"

"Months," Kelsey said. "Longer, maybe, if it was done by a skilled druid."

"There must've been hundreds of portals leaving Dragondale this year. We're never going to be able to prove anything."

"All students, all students," a voice boomed from the walls so loud that I almost fell right out of my seat. "All students, report to the main hall immediately. Please proceed in a calm and orderly manner."

The message repeated itself, but Kelsey was already shoving her notes into her bag, which looked like it was about to burst its seams. A dozen students fell in around us as we hurried out of the library, mostly faces I recognised from our year, as well as a redhead from the Dryadale academy. The three of us headed for the main hall in silence, not wanting to risk continuing our conversation with so many prying ears around us. Some of the other students started speculating, and by the time we made it to the hall and found three seats, I'd pretty much worked out that no-one was going to be surprised when Talendale announced that Gryphonvale had been cursed. Maybe he should have just sent a memo.

"Good morning, students," Talendale boomed when the scraping of chairs had died down. "Thank you for your prompt arrival."

I rolled my eyes. As if anyone would have taken their time getting here, with speculation running rife.

"I'm afraid I am the bearer of further bad news. Both Gryphonvale and Selkenloch academies have been cursed. Dragondale is the only academy to remain unaffected."

Chapter Twenty

Two more academies had fallen. What the hell was going on? I could see my own realisation reflected back at me on Kelsey's face. There was no need to curse Selkenloch. We'd been wrong. Atherton and Felicity weren't behind it.

Talendale raised both hands to silence the sudden uproar, and when that failed, he cleared his throat, but the sound was amplified so loud that it bounced all around the room, and the walls themselves seemed to shake.

"Thank you," he said as the noise died down, fixing a fierce glare on the one or two students still whispering until they, too, fell silent. Behind him, Swann, Alden, Ellerby and Atherton all stood, grim-faced and concerned. And I didn't think Atherton was faking.

"In light of these new attacks, we have decided that for the safety of all of our students, we have no choice but to close Dragondale for the foreseeable future."

Close Dragondale? They couldn't!

"But... what about our exams?" Kelsey whispered, her face so pale and drawn that I thought she might actually faint.

"It'll be okay," I reassured her numbly.

"No, it won't," she snapped, her voice abruptly strong and fierce. "How can it be? If we can't pass our exams, we'll never become qualified druids. Don't you understand what that means?"

I did understand. No qualification, no future. And not just for us. With all of the druid academies out of action, no-one could qualify this year. Or next year. Or any year, until the curses could be lifted, and whoever had cast them had been locked away. And never again, if the primal plants died, taking the academies with them. In short, we were screwed.

"We will begin preparations to evacuate students immediately," Talendale continued. "Rest assured, the professors and protectors of Dragondale will remain on site, and when we find the perpetrator, they will be brought to justice. Please return to your common rooms and await further instructions from your head of element. There will be no need to collect your personal belongings."

We were halfway back to the common room when Kelsey grabbed me and Sam and pulled us into an alcove, letting the rest of the students continue stream past us.

"Did either of you see Kayden, Micah and Harper leave the library?" she asked. I frowned, thinking back. There'd been a small group of us who left there together, but I hadn't seen any of the Braeseth students among them. I glanced at Sam and he shook his head.

"They don't know we're evacuating," I said, a terror thudding in my gut as I realised. "We need to warn them before they get trapped here."

Kelsey nodded, and we forced our way back out into the crowd, this time moving in the opposite direction to them, ignoring the glares we earned as we elbowed our way against the flow. I lost track of Sam and Kelsey but kept forcing my way through until I burst out at the far end of the corridor. Kelsey was already there, and I looked back over my shoulder in time to see Sam burst from the masses, red-faced and panting.

"Let's go," he said, and the three of us took off at a run. I hoped to hell we didn't see any professors, because there was no way they wouldn't send us back to our common room, and the unclassifieds had been having a hard enough time without getting in trouble for skipping a compulsory gathering. Of course, they'd be in a whole lot more trouble if they stayed here and got in the path of the curse.

I could see Kelsey pulling away from us, and ducked my head, forcing myself to sprint faster. I'd been training hard with the Itealta team and for the trials, but even so, there was no way I was keeping up with a druid-werewolf hybrid. She saw it too, and eased off on her pace, but I shook my head.

"Go! We'll catch up!"

She nodded and took off again, moving faster than I'd ever seen her go. Within seconds, she was out of sight. I grabbed Sam's arm and urged him on. He looked like his lungs were about to burst – I knew how he felt – but he kept moving, and eventually, the library doors came into view. There was no sign of Kelsey.

I skidded to a halt outside them and sucked in a lungful of air, then shoved the doors open and stepped inside.

"Lyssa, do—"

Kelsey's voice cut off half-way through her warning, and I spun to see her standing in front of Kayden. The unclassified's face was clouded and his lips twisted into a scowl. Kelsey's lips were still moving, but no sound was coming out. Micah was standing to one side of her, some sort of grey energy swirling around his hand, right next to her face. I started to raise my hand.

"Uh-uh," Micah said. "Don't move, either of you. Nothing would give me greater pleasure."

I lowered my hand to my side.

"What are you doing? We came back here to help you."

"Help us?" Micah sneered. "You druids are all the same, and not one of you has ever wanted to help us."

"You know that's not true," I said, turning my eyes to Kayden. As I did, I saw Kelsey's eyes widen at something other my shoulder. I spun, raising a hand on reflex, and a gust of air blasted from my hand, tossing Harper across the room. She thudded into a wall, and hit the ground, then bounced right back up and rolled onto the balls of her feet, her lips pulled back in a feral snarl.

I readied a fireball in the air between us and she tracked it with her eyes, the rest of her unmoving.

"You obviously don't care much about your friend," Micah said. "Maybe I should just kill her now."

He had one hand clamped on Kelsey's shoulder, and her eyes were wide with panic. I had no idea what he was doing to her, but as I watched her breaths became shorter and faster, like she couldn't get enough air into her lungs. The skin on her face paled and took on a grey tinge.

"Stop!" I shouted, and clenched my fist. The fireball blinked out of existence as if it had never been. "Just stop it."

Micah loosened his grip on Kelsey's shoulder, but kept his hand resting there. She gasped, like a drowning woman bursting through the surface, and the colour started returning to her face.

"No more stupidity," Micah warned. "Or next time I'll keep going. Move away from the doors."

"Okay," I said, shooting a glance at Sam and seeing my own terror reflected on his face. I took a breath and tried to get it under control as I edged slowly away from the door towards them. "Okay. Don't hurt her. Just… tell me what's going on."

I looked past him to Kayden.

"That's far enough," Micah said, and I stopped. I guess he didn't trust us any more than I trusted him. Smart. I kept my eyes on Kayden.

"Talk to me," I said. "Please. Tell me what's going on."

"He's got nothing to say to you," Harper said, straightening and moving to the doors. She slapped one hand on them, and I saw the cracks around the edges go dark, blocking the light from outside. My lips compressed tightly. I didn't know much about unclassified magic, but I was willing to bet she'd just somehow sealed the doors. We weren't getting out of here without help. Except the rest of the academy were busy evacuating. Help wasn't coming.

"It's the only way," Kayden said, his voice barely loud enough to reach me across the room.

"What's the only way?"

"Take her voice, Kayden," Harper snapped.

"He's a big boy," I snapped right back. "He can talk to whoever he wants."

"The only way to be free of druid control," Kayden said, as if he hadn't heard our exchange.

"What's the only way to be free?" Sam asked, his face a frown, but I already knew the answer. Maybe I'd always known it.

"Killing the academies," I said. "It was never Atherton, it was the unclassifieds. They're behind all the attacks. That's why you never wanted to integrate, that's why Harper didn't like you talking to me, isn't it?" I fixed my eyes on Kayden, but he wouldn't meet them. "I thought she was just jealous, but she was scared you'd change your mind, that you'd see we're all human, just like you."

"Ha!" Harper barked. "You're nothing like us. You don't know what it's like to be an outcast. Druids have been looking down on us for generations."

"We don't know what it's like to be outcasts?" I couldn't quite keep the incredulity from my voice. "Have you been paying attention this year? Kelsey's a hybrid, and I'm the first druid to have four elemental powers. Sam's an outcast just for *being near* us. We know exactly what it's like."

"But the others don't," Kayden said, still not looking at me. "We can change it. Redress the balance of power."

"You don't have to explain yourself to her," Harper said. "You've got the curse cube. Activate it and we can get out of here."

For the first time, my eyes caught on the glowing red cube in Kayden's hand. It was small, no bigger than my fist, and now that I was focused on it, I could feel the dark power pulsing from it.

"That's how they've been doing it? The curse is in that box?"

"None of your damned business," Micah snapped, digging his fingers into Kelsey's shoulder.

"I'll take that as a yes then," I said, to no-one in particular. A dozen questions raced through my mind, not least how long we could survive being near the damned thing, and how I was going to get Micah away from Kelsey. The one I asked was,

"Who gave it to you?"

Kayden snapped his head up to look at me, and I pressed on before I lost his attention again.

"I mean, you didn't make it yourself, did you?" I pressed. "I've seen your spellcraft – you're good, but you're not that good. No student is that good. Not even Kelsey."

He glanced at the hybrid when I said her name, and seemed to see what was happening for the first time. His frown deepened, and the curse cube trembled a little in his hands.

"Micah, let her go. No-one's supposed to get hurt."

Micah twisted his lips into a sneer.

"Like I care what happens to some druid apprentice. There's only one druid I give a damn about, and that's—"

"Shut up!" Kayden and Harper shouted at the exact same time, wearing identical masks of panic. It was that, more than Micah's words, that gave me pause. And then I knew what was going on.

"It was him, wasn't it? He was the one who gave you the curse. The one druid you're scared of. My father. Raphael."

"Your... your father?" The curse cube trembled in Kayden's hands.

"Yeah," I snapped. "My father. The druid who set a freaking zombie on Dragondale's students two years ago. The same druid who tried to kill me last time we met."

"I like him better already," Micah said, his fingers still resting on Kelsey's shoulder with an unspoken menace.

"Well, don't get too comfortable. I had a nice little chat with him last year, when he was trying to start a war to wipe out the shifters. That's what he thinks about people who aren't druids. And don't even get me started on what he thinks about people like you."

"You're wrong!" His fingers dug into Kelsey's shoulder and I saw her wince, but no sound made it out of her mouth — Kayden's powers were still muting her. "He respects us! He says we're the future!"

He lifted a hand and flung a ball of swirling grey energy right at me. I dived aside, throwing up my own hands, and a film of green energy spread between them, forming a sort of shield. The grey ball glanced off it and flew across the room, smashing into a bookcase and sending a dozen books crashing to the floor, stray leaves floating through the air around them. I stared at them for a moment, my mouth agape, then dropped my hands and rolled aside. A second grey ball thudded into the ground right where I'd been lying a split second before, and already a third was forming between his hands. Shit. Seriously, some people really had a hard time hearing the truth.

"Unleash the curse!" he bellowed at Kayden, and launched the third ball at me. I threw my hands up again, and the green-tinged shield flexed between them once more. The shield quivered under the force of the attack, stopping the ball mere fractions of an inch from my body. It wasn't going to hold much longer, and I didn't even have a clue how I was doing it. Worse, with the shield keeping both of my hands busy, I couldn't throw an attack of my own, and if I dropped the shield, Micah could get a ball off before I could. It was high noon at the Okay Coral, and I was outgunned. I knew it, and Micah knew it. It was only a matter of time before he landed an attack. But there was one thing he hadn't taken into account.

In his murderous haste, he'd forgotten all about Kelsey. She was still mute, and whatever he'd done to her had left her shaken enough that she couldn't use her elemental powers. I saw her work it out, staring down at her empty hand in dismay, and then she did the only thing left to her – she punched him. Of course, she was a werewolf hybrid.

He crumbled around her fist, hit the ground, and bounced up faster than should have been possible. There was something not right about these kids. He spun around, turning his attention to Kelsey, favouring his right side as he moved. I don't care how tough you are – if you get punched by a freaking werewolf, you're breaking ribs. He was already beaten, he just didn't know it. I gathered a swirling gust of air into my hands, preparing to throw him into the bookshelves. I wasn't sure how much force it would take, and I got the sense it was going to be a fine line between knocking him out and killing him. I didn't want any deaths on my conscience. Not even narcissistic sociopaths like him.

I heard a loud crack from behind me and spun round, spraying air from my hands and throwing furniture across the room. Sam was on the floor. Harper was hanging in the corner of the ceiling like some sort of over-sized spider, and her lips were moving rapidly, casting some sort of spell that was keeping Sam pinned to the ground. He squirmed and shouted as he tried to break free of it, but it was like there was a weight pressing down on him, and he couldn't even lift a hand to defend himself. I glanced back over my shoulder, where Kayden was hurrying down one of the aisles and out of sight, and swore.

I sucked another gust of air into my hands, and blasted it out at the blonde. It hit her squarely and knocked her from her perch. She hit the floor hard, and immediately Sam sprung to his feet, released from the spell.

"Go!" he shouted at me. "I've got her."

A quick glance in Kelsey's direction told me she had the upper hand, too — Micah was down, and it didn't look like he had any fight left in him. I sprinted past them, between the row of books to where I'd seen Kayden. Somehow, I knew where he was going. The restricted section. Curses needed a power source, and what better source than the residual energy of a thousand forbidden spells?

I knew the way from my misadventures two years ago, and it took me less than a minute to reach the small room set aside from the main hall of the library. A figure slipped through the open archway, and I drew a steadying breath, then followed him.

The room was packed with aging, grime-covered books, most of which hadn't been handled in hundreds of years. Knowledge is power, and some powers are forbidden – for good reason. Not all magic is good. The books here could teach you how to enslave a mundane, or raise the dead, or force someone to love you. I suppressed a shudder, and slipped from the shadows, ignoring the ancient tomes beneath the pale fireballs that flickered dully near the ceiling.

Kayden gasped, and spun to face me, the red curse cube pulsating in his shaking hands.

"Easy," I said, showing him my own empty hands. He flinched away, his face pale. Oh, right. Raised hands weren't exactly a sign of peace amongst magic users. I dropped them to my sides.

"You don't want to do this," I said softly.

"It's the right thing to do," he answered, but his voice lacked conviction, and uncertainty played across his face in the flickering light.

"If you believed that, we wouldn't still be standing here. Raphael is using you."

"No, he's not." His jaw hardened and the trembling in his hands steadied. "He says we're equals, and we deserve to be treated like it."

I silenced the laughter that bubbled in my throat before it made it out. The Braeseth students had been laughed at long enough. I knew how that felt.

"You're right. You do deserve to be treated as equals, and I'm sorry that the druid world is too fucked up to see that. Our powers don't make us better than you, or the shifters, or the mundanes."

"So you see why I have to do this, then?"

I shook my head, keeping the rest of me very still. I wasn't sure what would happen if Kayden got spooked while the curse cube was pulsing in his hands, and I didn't want to find out. The thing seemed to be feeding off his emotions.

"This isn't going to solve anything. Trust me, I know. I've lived with these people for nearly three years, and all that curse will do is make them hate you even more."

"No, he said if we bring down the academies, they'll have to treat us better. They won't have all the power anymore. We'll be equals." He sucked in a breath. "I'm sick of hiding in the shadows, Lyssa, cowering under druid rule. Look at what they've done. They can't be in control anymore."

"You're going to start a war," I said. "One you can't possibly win. That's what he wants, can't you see that? Last year he tried to start a war with the shifters. This year he wants us fighting you."

"Why? He's got nothing to gain from that."

This time I couldn't help the bitter bark of laughter.

"The man who wants to be king has nothing to gain? With the druids fighting a war on two fronts, with the entire magic community fighting amongst themselves, he'll be able to seize control. Trust me, you do not want that. I don't care what he's said to you, the man is a monster, and he doesn't want equality. The only thing he's ever wanted is the world bowing at his feet. Use that curse, and you'll give it to him."

"You're lying!"

"Am I? Think about it, it makes sense. More sense than whatever bullshit he spouted about wanting equality. If that was true, why now? Why not years ago? He has been edging the communities closer to war for his entire life, and he's made you a pawn in his plan. There was no other way he could get to the academies, so he lied to you, and he used you, and I'm sorry. But this won't fix anything."

"He... used us." Kayden's voice was hollow as the truth finally sunk in. I nodded gently.

"Just deactivate the curse, Kayden. Let's get out of here."

He nodded and his eyes shut for a brief moment. When they opened again, they were wide with panic.

"I... I can't! It won't shut down."

"Shit. It's feeding off your emotions. He meant for it to go off, even if you changed your mind."

He clenched his jaw, and his expression darkened. I knew the look. I'd worn it myself before now. Betrayal. And fury.

"Don't focus on your hatred," I said. "We'll settle the score with him later, but right now we need to worry about that curse. Can you put it down?"

He crouched down and tried to set the curse cube on the floor, but it stayed resolutely stuck to his hands. I saw the panic flare in his eyes, and the curse cube pulse more brightly in response.

"Take a breath, Kayden," I told him. "I'm going to get you out of this."

He shook his head.

"You need to get out of here. Now. I'll hold it back for as long as I can."

I crouched down beside him.

"Yeah, that's not going to happen. Look at me." I waited patiently for him to meet my eye. "We're going to work through this, together.

His eyes were unnaturally wide and his hands shook around the cube, but he clenched his jaw and nodded.

"Raphael meant for this cube to divide the communities," I said. "But it hasn't. And it won't. Because as long as there are people like you, and people like me, we'll make sure the whole world knows that we are equals, and we won't shut up until they listen. And Raphael? There's nothing he can do to change that. He's already lost."

The red glow flickered, and the cube tumbled from Kayden's hands. I grabbed his arm and hauled him behind me. The curse cube started making a low whining noise, getting louder and louder, and the light leaking out of it grew brighter until the entire room was blazing with it.

"We need to find a professor!" Kayden shouted in my ear above the noise.

"There's no time," I shouted back. "We've got to disarm it ourselves."

"How?"

"I've got no idea."

I held out both my hands, and willed the power of all four elements through them. My arms lit up with a blazing light, swirling red, blue, yellow, and green, and behind me I heard Kayden gasp and stumble back. I ignored him, focusing my attention solely on the curse. I pushed the lights away from me, and they surged towards the curse cube, like iron filings sucked up by a magnet. But instead of making contact, they formed a ball around it, encasing it in their swirling mass. Immediately, the noise died, and the light receded, trapped by the multi-coloured sphere.

What the hell was up with my magic?

Chapter Twenty-One

I f I spent much more time in this room, I was going to be in danger of the Tilimeuse Tree moving my dorm here. Once again, I found myself in Talendale's office, but this time it wasn't just me. Between Talendale, Dougan, Underwood, me, Kelsey, Sam, and the three Braeseth students, it was getting crowded in here. Given that there were only two chairs, and Talendale was in one, most of us had to stand.

That was the least of the unclassifieds' problems. Each of them wore a set of iron and silver shackles around their wrists, engraved with arcane symbols, and connected with a thin silver chain. The shackles and the chains were enchanted. I'd seen Underwood use them last year on Leo, back when everyone thought he was behind the attacks. Apparently they didn't just work on werewolves. Anyone wearing them wouldn't be able to use their magic. As they had last year, the sight of the innocuous silver cuffs sent a shudder through me. It was all too easy to remove someone's magic and leave them vulnerable, as the three captured unclassifieds proved.

Micah and Harper stood glaring at Talendale while Dougan finished sealing the cuffs around their wrists. Micah had a black eye and a split lip, and his nose was swollen and misshapen. He was still favouring his right side as he stood, trying to ease the pressure on what was probably a couple of broken ribs. Kelsey had one hell of a right hook. Harper hadn't escaped unscathed either, and stood with her weight on her left leg, and the beginnings of a bruise starting to show on her jaw. I had no sympathy for either of them. They were lucky we hadn't decided to fight as dirty as they had, or they'd be standing there with burns where their bruises were – if they'd survived the fight at all. They certainly hadn't intended for us to do so.

Kayden was the only one unmarked. He stood with his head bowed, not resisting when Dougan shortened the chain between his cuffs, giving him less movement if he decided to fight back. But it didn't look like he had any fight left in him. His shoulders were hunched, and he kept his eyes on his own feet. He hadn't said a word since the professors had shown up at the library. How they'd known there was trouble was beyond me, but I'd never been so grateful to see a professor as I had when Dougan and Underwood had burst in, taking control of the situation, and hauled all of us up to see Talendale. They'd summoned Atherton to stand guard over the curse cube and whatever weird spell I'd put on it. From the look he'd had on his face when he'd seen it, I was going to have some explaining to do when we were done here. Alone time with Atherton. My favourite.

"The Grand Council has been alerted," Talendale said, rising from behind his desk. My eyes flicked to its surface in time to see several carvings fade and then disappear. "They will no doubt send an enforcer from Daoradh to take the three of them into custody."

"Daoradh?" I looked from Talendale to Kayden and back again in horror. "He made a mistake. He doesn't deserve to be locked up for that!"

"Attempting to destroy the four academies and undermine druid authority is *not* a mistake, Ms Eldridge," Talendale said, peering down his nose at me. "It is the act of a criminal, and Kayden shall be treated as such, as shall his accomplices."

"That's not fair," I protested. "He didn't go through with it, and he only got involved in the first place because Raphael lied to him. It's no different to what happened with Kelsey last year."

I saw Kelsey flinch from the corner of my eye, and shot her an apologetic look. It was still hard for her to think about what she'd done – harder, probably, with Paisley in her face all day, every day.

"It's nae the same," Dougan said, his voice soft. "Kelsey was under a spell. These three acted of their own free will."

"And I'd do it again," Micah snarled, writhing in Underwood's grip. Underwood clenched his hand more firmly around Micah's shoulder, and the unclassified gasped in pain.

"What I'd like to know," Underwood said, "is how Raphael was able to recruit you after you got to Dragondale, when he can't set foot on the grounds."

Micah glared up at him, and his lips twitched in a sneer.

"Aye," Dougan said. "And why he cursed Braeseth. There wasnae anything he needed there."

"Yes, there was." The words burst from my lips as the pieces suddenly came together. "He needed the students. Don't you see? He recruited them *before* they left Braeseth. Before the semester even started. He knew that if Braeseth was shut down, the druid academies would have no choice but to take in their students. The shifters would never have done it, and they wouldn't have had the skills to train them, anyway. No, they had to go to academies that could help them control their magic, and that meant us."

"Is she right, lass?" Dougan said, looking down at Harper.

"Bite me."

"It's true," Kayden said. "He came to us in the summer, and told us we could be free from druid control."

"Coward!"

Kayden didn't react to her, instead lifting his eyes to meet Dougan's over her shoulder.

"What I did was wrong. I'll accept my punishment."

"See?" I blurted. "He's showing remorse. Shouldn't that count for something?"

"Druid laws are nae the same as mundane ones," Dougan said.

"It is for the Grand Council to decide his fate," Talendale said. "He made his choice."

"No, he didn't. Raphael made his choice for him, why can't any of you see that?" I was dangerously close to shouting in my frustration, but I didn't care. This wasn't fair, not any of it. "He was radicalised, and this whole stupid superiority complex druids have is the only reason it was even possible."

Silence fell over the entire office, so absolute that I was sure I could hear the grass growing outside.

"I am most interested to hear you feel that way."

The voice came from behind me, and sent a chill along my spine. I turned round and found myself looking at Head Councilman Cauldwell. When the hell had he portalled in? Ah, screw it. There was probably already a cell waiting for me at Daoradh anyway, for the moment I put a foot wrong.

"She's right," Dougan said. "If something doesnae change, we're going tae be seeing more of this sort of thing. Raphael wants a war, and we've given him hundreds o' willing soldiers."

"This is neither the time nor the place for this discussion, *Professor*," Cauldwell said, glaring at him. I felt some of my ire ease. At least I wasn't the only one who could see problems our injustice was creating.

"I hope there will be one," Underwood said, his hand still on Micah's shoulder. The sneer on the unclassified's face underscored both his and Dougan's point. If something didn't change, there wouldn't be enough cells in Daoradh, but that wouldn't matter, because the druids wouldn't be in control anymore. Sooner or later, Raphael would get the war he wanted.

"We have more pressing matters right now," Cauldwell said, brushing imaginary lint from the front of his cloak. "If such a discussion is to take place, it will be *after* the safety of the academies has been ensured."

His gaze levelled at me, then Sam and Kelsey, and there was no mistaking the look of disdain on his face.

"The Grand Council owes the three of you our thanks for your judicious actions." He sounded as if the words left a bad taste in his mouth, and he didn't meet any of our eyes as he added, "Without you, it is likely that Dragondale, the final remaining academy, would have fallen, and all would have been lost."

"I don't get it," I said, because I didn't think the councilman was prone to hyperbole, but even so, 'all would have been lost' seemed a bit dramatic. "I know the academies falling would have been bad, but…"

I trailed off, not quite sure how to word my question.

"The academies are more than just buildings to which we send our apprentices, Lyssa," Underwood said. "Each academy's primal plant grows directly from an elemental core – the primary power source of that element. Dragondale sits on the core of Fire, Selkenloch of Water, Dryadale of Earth, and Gryphonvale of Air. To corrupt an academy is to weaken that power, and throw the balance out. With the four academies lost, the Grand Council itself would have been weakened, and so would the powers of every druid – all except for one. I believe Raphael's curse would have siphoned some of that power into himself."

Shit. No wonder everyone had been getting bent out of shape about it.

"And his accomplices will pay for their part in it," Cauldwell said, levelling a hard stare at Kayden.

"Professor," I said, turning to Talendale in my desperation. "You know this isn't right. Please. It's not Kayden's fault. He could have set the curse, but he didn't."

"Do not presume to tell your headmaster what he does and does not know," Cauldwell snapped. "And do not think that your sudden increase of power has gone unnoticed, at the exact time your father has been orchestrating the downfall of the academies. The Grand Council will be watching you."

"Oh, like they weren't already." I glared at him, stopping short of rolling my eyes by sheer force of will. "You've been looking for an excuse to blame me for your mistakes all year."

"Lyssa!" Kelsey gasped, and maybe it was the horror etched into her face that snapped me back to my senses. I was standing in the headmaster's office of the only remaining druidic academy in the United Kingdom, having an argument with one of the most powerful druids alive. I was in so much shit. And we *both* needed to get over ourselves.

I held up a hand, cutting off whatever retort Cauldwell was about to make. Outrage flashed across his face, and I spoke up quickly before he could voice it, or have me dragged off to Daoradh for disrespecting him. Or worse, expelled.

"I'm sorry. That was out of line." I exhaled heavily. "I don't know where my powers have come from, but I swear to you, I haven't spoken to Raphael since he tried to kill me last year."

And if I put just a little emphasis on that last part, well, who could blame me? I mean, how many times did I have to say that I wasn't working with that psycho and— Never mind.

Cauldwell cleared his throat.

"Yes, well. Let us give you the benefit of the doubt. For now. We have rather bigger concerns."

Yeah, now that was something we could agree on.

"What happens now?" I asked.

"Now, Ms Eldridge," Cauldwell said, "We go to war."

War. Of course. Why wouldn't the whole druidic world explode the minute I stepped foot into it?

"And the shifters?" Talendale said.

"The shifters?" The words blurted out of my mouth and I darted a look from Cauldwell to Talendale and back. "What about the shifters?"

It was Underwood who answered, his voice sombre.

"The Alpha Pack has been taking an interest since Dryadale fell. If we don't handle our problems, they will."

"They'll fight the Council for control? We can't fight a war on two fronts, can we?"

"No. We can't."

"Three." The word was barely audible, and Kayden didn't look at any of us as he said it. A whole second passed in absolute silence, and then chaos erupted around the office.

"Don't you dare say another word," Micah snarled.

"Shut your mouth, you filthy traitor," Harper screamed, struggling in Dougan's grip and almost managing to wrench free.

Micah slammed his head back into Underwood's face, smearing blood across it. Underwood, taken off guard, staggered back, and Micah wrenched himself free. He wasted no time, throwing himself across the room at Kayden, his face contorted in fury while Harper screamed obscenities and fought against Dougan's grip.

I stared in horror, frozen in shock as Micah grabbed hold of Kayden's head with his manacled hands and slammed it down into his knee. I heard Kayden's nose shatter above the shouting, and saw Micah draw his knee back for a second strike. I raised my hand, but before I could do anything, Kayden tackled him shoulder first, and the pair of them crashed into Talendale's desk and over the other side, missing the headmaster by inches. Talendale leapt to his feet, his face aghast as the grappling pair thudded to the floor amidst flying sheets of paper.

I started to move round the desk, but a shout of pain came from behind me and I spun around. Blood was pumping from Dougan's hand and was smeared around Harper's mouth. Dougan swore and made a grab for her, but she ducked him and made to jump over the desk toward the fray. I raised a hand and with a pulse of yellow energy a gust of air burst from it, hitting her square and tossing her across the room into one of Talendale's bookcases. She hit the ground and made to jump up, but I let loose another burst of air energy, pinning her there.

Movement flashed behind Talendale's desk and I twisted my head round in time to see Micah's cuffs falling away from his wrists. Before I could get my head around what was happening, he tossed the key to Kayden, then raised a hand and shouted,

"Eachlais!"

A portal sprung into existence, and both guys pivoted to look for Harper. I gritted my teeth and forced all of my energy out through my hand, until the wind was buffeting her hair all around her face and tearing at her clothes.

"Go!" she screamed at them, her voice almost lost in the wind.

Cauldwell snapped out of his stupor and raised a hand toward the open portal. He opened his mouth to shout the closing incantation, but Kayden narrowed his eyes at him, and no sound came from the councilman's mouth.

"Go!" Harper roared again.

Kayden and Micah shared the briefest of looks, then dived through the portal, and it snapped shut behind them.

Shit.

Chapter Twenty-Two

Back to your common room, you three," Underwood said. "Wait to be evacuated."

"But Professor—"

He gave me a look that silenced my protests, and I bit down on my tongue.

"We don't have time to discuss this, Lyssa. I am your professor and I am telling you to go back to your common room. Raphael undoubtedly knows we know he's behind the attacks now, thanks to—"

He broke off, but I knew what he'd been about to say. Thanks to me. Because I stood around arguing and defending Kayden, when he'd been planning to betray us. Again. And now he'd escaped, and it was my fault.

"—thanks to this afternoon's events," Underwood finished. "He'll have to make his move soon."

"I agree," Cauldwell said, inclining his head in a curt nod. "I will return to the Grand Council and rally what forces I can."

"I'll take the lass to Daoradh to wait for her trial," Dougan said, his hand wrapped firmly around Harper's upper arm. She sneered at him.

"It doesn't matter. He knows. And the time of the druids is over!"

"Aye, whatever y' say, lass." He glanced over at me as Cauldwell started opening a portal, without loosening his grip on Harper's arm. "Are the three of y' still here?"

"Uh… No, Professor," I said, and nudged Kelsey towards the door. We ducked out of it with Sam behind us, into the stone corridor.

"I'm sorry, Lyssa," Kelsey said, the second the door was shut. "We should have helped when they started fighting. I just froze up, I'm so sorry."

"Kelsey, it's fine," I said, making my way down the stone staircase. "It's not your fault. It's mine. I shouldn't have argued with Cauldwell. If I'd just kept my mouth shut, none of that would have happened."

"It's not your fault, either, Lyssa," Sam said. "There were six other druids in the room, four of them qualified. It wasn't down to you to stop them."

I clenched my jaw as we rounded a corner in the barren castle.

"I was just so sure I was right. Why don't I ever listen to anyone?"

Sam snorted, and Kelsey elbowed him in the ribs, hard enough to make him wince. Hybrid strength, and all that. My stomach was too tied up in knots for me to be amused. Raphael was coming. Tonight, probably.

"We can't beat him," I said, my dull voice cutting across whatever Sam had been saying. He fell silent.

"Raphael is one of the most powerful druids I've ever seen. Maybe stronger than Talendale. Maybe even stronger than Cauldwell."

Sam shrugged.

"Maybe."

"How can you just say that? He's coming here, Sam. To fight Cauldwell and Talendale. To take control of Dragondale and destroy *everything*."

"And that might matter, if they were going to fight alone."

I swallowed and nodded. He was right. Cauldwell was going to bring back anyone he could find to fight. Except the other academies were in disarray and their professors scattered, and Raphael wasn't going to give Cauldwell long enough to raise an army.

"Raphael will bring back up. If Cauldwell can't rally the academies and the enforcers in time, he's going to be outnumbered."

"Not if I have anything to do with it," Sam said, picking up his pace. "Come on, we've got to get to the common room before they evacuate everyone."

I nodded as I realised what he was getting at, but Kelsey shook her head and planted her feet.

"Go on without me," she said. "I've got an idea."

"Where are you going?"

"To find Leo. You said it yourself – we can't fight a war on two fronts. We have to find a way to keep the shifters away tonight. The anti-portal wards must be down right now so Cauldwell can send in his reinforcements. Make sure Professor Talendale doesn't raise them before I'm back."

"But–"

She turned and sprinted in the opposite direction.

"–how the hell am I supposed to do that?" I finished under my breath.

"Come on," Sam said. I cast one last look at the empty space Kelsey had occupied, then took off at a sprint towards the common room.

It took us no time to make it through the deserted corridors, and I was only a little out of breath when I slammed my hand against the Fire common room door and let loose the six pulses that made up our password. Behind me, Sam doubled over, his hands on his knees.

"I gotta get more exercise," he panted.

"Worry about that if we survive tonight."

"Good idea." He gulped air, and stepped through the doorway behind me.

The entire room was packed with dozens of students chattering loudly, shouting over each other to be heard as they talked in panicked and excited voices about the academy's closure.

"Hey, listen up!" I called – and not one person paid the blindest bit of notice. Beside me, Sam sucked in another breath, put his fingers in the corners of his mouth, and let out an ear-splitting whistle. The students nearest to us clapped their hands over their ears, and the room fell silent. I hopped up on a chair so that everyone could see me – and also because it felt kinda cool.

"There's trouble coming. We're going to war, probably tonight, and we're outnumbered."

The chattering started up again and Sam loosed another whistle. Alex glared at him, and he shrugged.

"The professors can't win without our help," I said. "If we don't fight, Dragondale is going to fall."

"War?" one voice shouted from the back of the room, filled with horror.

"We can't fight," another said. "We don't know how!"

"We're not even qualified yet."

The students started talking over each other all at once, and Alex frowned, then jumped up on the chair beside me.

"Oi, listen up, you tossers!" she shouted. "If you're too yellow to fight, then leave! But I thought I was standing in the *Fire* common room."

A few mutters started up, but these ones didn't sound scared. They sounded pissed. And determined. I shot Alex a grateful smile.

"I'm in," a voice called over the muttering. It was Dean, his hand entwined in Sharna's.

"Me, too," she said, putting her other hand over Dean's. I got the feeling she would go anywhere he did.

"And me." Devon was leaning casually against the wall, a languid smile playing across his lips. He shot me a wink.

Not to be outdone by his younger teammate, Caleb stepped forward.

"Yeah, and me."

Suddenly, all around the room people were stepping up and volunteering to stay and fight. A blonde figure pushed past me towards the door. I recognised her.

"Ava," I said, hopping down from the chair. "If you don't want to fight, just stay here until the professors come. It'll be safer. Ava!"

I stared after her as she rushed through the door.

"Well," Alex said, hopping down from the chair and watching the door swing shut. "That sorta undermines our rabble-rousing, but I think we've got a few hooked."

"Don't worry," Sam said. "She'll be fine. The professors will get her out of here."

"Yeah," Alex said. "Keeping the students alive is kinda their job."

"I guess," I said, wondering how anyone was going to track her down in a castle this size.

"Alright, oh fearless leader," Devon said, striding over and clapping a hand down on my shoulder. "What now?"

"Uh…"

The door chose exactly that moment to spring inwards, sparing me from answering the question, and Professor Alden stood outlined in the doorway.

"Alright, everyone, follow me. It's time to get you all portalled back to your homes."

I shared a look with Sam, then sucked in a breath and turned back to Alden.

"We're not going."

"The hell you're not," she said. "Things are going to get very dangerous here tonight."

"Exactly. You need us. All of us. We're staying to fight."

"Fight? Over my dead body." She glared at us, her hands on her hips.

"That's what we're trying to prevent," Sam said. "Professor, we know you're outnumbered, and we can help."

"And how exactly do you think having dozens of unqualified druids running around the castle is going to help?"

"Cannon fodder?" Alex suggested, and I stamped on her foot.

"We can be lookouts," I said. "We can throw potions. And we've got a whole Itealta team ready to form your own flying cavalry."

"Cavalry?" A slow smile spread on Alden's face. I grabbed Devon and thrust him towards her before she could think of any objections.

"I reckon co-captain translates as a sergeant, right? He can help the rest of the team get their gryffs in."

"What about you?" Devon said. I shook my head.

"I've got something else to take care of first, then I'll catch up with you. How about it, Professor? This is our home. Let us fight for it."

She hesitated a moment longer, then nodded.

"Alright. But my first priority is evacuating everyone who doesn't want to be here, and then I need to help the other professors raise the academy's defences."

"I understand." I tried to keep the jubilation from my voice – which was a whole lot easier when I remembered that those defences would keep Kelsey out. I had to get to Talendale and delay him.

"Everyone who wants to leave, follow me," Alden called, and then hurried out of the door, with a handful of students in her wake – mostly first years. Probably for the best. We didn't want anyone accidentally setting fire to our side.

"Itealta team," I shouted, above the noise of everyone moving at once. "And anyone else who can ride, for that matter. Follow Devon down to the barn. Anyone who's good at portals or glamours, go with Alex. You're going to set traps all over the castle. Everyone else, head down to the lab with Sam. We need defensive potions, as many as you can make."

I whirled on my heel, and Sam caught my arm.

"What about you? Where are you going?"

I grinned.

"I'm going to phone a friend."

Chapter Twenty-Three

O r I would have, if phones worked inside the academy. And if I had Alistair's number. But they didn't, and I didn't, so I was going to need to come up with plan B. Quickly. And I needed to stop Talendale raising the academy's defences – that was assuming Kelsey managed to convince the Alpha Pack to give us tonight to fix things, without them trying to lay their problems at her hybrid feet. It wouldn't be the first time.

I could handle one of those things, at least. I took off for Talendale's office at a jog – sprinting was all well and good, but there were a *lot* of stairs leading up to his door, and I didn't want to have to crawl up them. I was in the best shape of my life thanks to Swann's frankly brutal training regime, but I was only human. I would have tried a portal, but if I got stuck half-in, half-out, I was screwed. And my track record with portals was less than stellar.

I was out of breath by the time I made it back to Talendale's office and burst in through the door without any regard for the headmaster's obsession with manners and decorum. Screw propriety, our whole world was about to end.

The headmaster was behind his desk, deep in conversation with Underwood and Atherton.

"I've never seen anything like it, Headmaster. I fear we won't be able to disable it, and there's no telling how long Eldridge's magic will contain—"

Atherton broke off mid-sentence and glared at me, and the other two turned to stare as me as well. The look of fury on Talendale's face froze me to the spot. Maybe I should have knocked after all.

"Ms Eldridge," he said, his voice stiff. "It was made perfectly clear to you that you were to return to your common room."

"Yes, sir. And I did, sir. But..." I took a deep breath and straightened, squaring my shoulders. "Professor, we want to help, and I've got an idea how."

Atherton snorted, and looked down his nose at me. His voice was thick with derision when he spoke.

"Help? How exactly do you propose to do that, given that you've barely even grasped the fundamentals of magic?"

I was getting a sense of déjà vu. I kept my attention on Talendale. Atherton had never liked me, and I didn't think that was about to change now. At least Talendale was fair, even if he was severe sometimes.

"We may not be qualified, but we're well trained. You and the other professors saw to that. Raphael's strong, and he won't come alone. We're going to need every druid we can get if we're going to defend Dragondale."

"We will have fully qualified and better trained druids at our disposal once Councilman Cauldwell returns," Atherton said with a sneer. "What on earth makes you think—"

"Silence."

Talendale's voice wasn't raised, but Atherton immediately deferred to him. If nothing else, I had to admit he was loyal to the academy's headmaster. Talendale wasn't looking at either of us: his eyes were on the desk in front of him, and I could see the etchings reforming themselves into a message, but I couldn't make out the words from where I was standing.

As I watched, Talendale's shoulders stooped, like someone had taken the fight out of him. When he finally lifted his eyes to us, I saw something in them I'd never seen there before. Mortality.

"The Grand Council are not coming," he said softly.

"Headmaster?" Atherton shot a look down at the desk, and then he, too, paled. Unlike Talendale, when he looked up, his eyes were defiant, and his expression resolved. He set his jaw and gave Talendale a stiff nod.

"We will defend Dragondale to the last, no matter the cost."

"Professor?" I looked from Talendale to Atherton and back again. "What's going on? Why aren't they coming?"

"An attack was launched on the Grand Council headquarters," Talendale said, his voice hushed. "They were taken unawares. Dozens were killed, many more injured. They have neither the resources nor the manpower to assist us."

"Raphael?" I asked. Talendale shook his head.

"The shifters. It would seem they tired of waiting for us to resolve the situation."

My heart sank. The shifters. The same ones Kelsey was trying to reason with. She was too late. And she was in danger.

I shook off my fear. She was with Leo, and there was nothing he wouldn't do to keep her safe. Right now, I had to focus on making sure there was a castle here for her to return to. I squared my shoulders, and directed my question to Atherton.

"What do we do, Professor?"

Atherton shook his head again.

"I can't believe I'm about to say this. Tell me your idea, Eldridge."

I filled him in about the Itealta team and the other riders, and the potions, but when I got to the part about bobby-trapping the castle with glamoured portals, his jaw was starting to twitch. At least he wasn't looking pale anymore.

"Is that everything?" he asked, in a tone that suggested he very much hoped it was. But I'd spent two years disappointing him. I wasn't about to change now.

"Two more things. We need to contact the other academies and get them to join us. They have just as much to lose as we do."

"Every spare professor and healer has been summoned to the Grand Council."

"Not the professors," I said. "The students. The champions. Professor Talenale said it himself – the champions were originally meant to protect the academies, back before the cup had even been dreamed up. And we're the best each academy has to offer, right?"

"Little full of ourselves?" He arched an eyebrow and I shrugged, forcing a cocky grin onto my face.

"Well, a unicorn did bow to me."

He sighed, but I thought I saw his lips twitch in amusement.

"And the second thing?"

I grimaced, but there was no getting out of it. I had to make sure Kelsey was safe, and she'd only asked me to do one thing.

"Kelsey went to the shifters. We have to keep the wards down long enough for her to get back."

"Absolutely not. We'd be leaving an open invitation for Raphael to walk straight in here."

"Oh, please. We all know he's going to get in one or way another. And we can't just leave Kelsey out there."

Talendale sank into his seat behind his desk, startling me – I'd all but forgotten he was there.

"She will likely be safer out there than in here tonight. The wards will be raised."

"But Professor!"

He cut me off with a raised hand, and I bit my tongue. Nothing good ever came from talking over him.

"I have made my decision. However," he looked across at Atherton, some of the strength returning to his voice. "We will first summon every ally we might raise – including the champions of each academy, should they be willing."

He placed one hand on the desk of Tilimeuse wood, and lines started racing frantically across its surface. Atherton inclined his head, his lips pressed together.

"As you wish, Headmaster."

"Lyssa," Talendale said, without looking up from the etchings flying across his desk. "Go and join your classmates. Tonight, I fear the hopes of Dragondale and the entire druidic world will rest on your young shoulders."

Great, no pressure then.

"Um, Professor Atherton? Any chance of a portal out to the barn? You know, because it's kinda hard to run with the weight of the whole academy on my shoulders."

"You'd best hope this year's exams are postponed, Ms Eldridge."

Nonetheless, he raised an arm, muttered a word under his breath, and a portal sprang into place in front of the door. It looked so easy when he did it. Atherton was right. If the exams went ahead on schedule, I was screwed. And if I saved the academy, only to get held back a year, I was not going to be impressed. Oh well. Best take care of the saving the academy part first.

I stepped into the portal and emerged outside the old red and gold barn by the paddock. The night air hit my lungs in a shock of cold, and I wrapped my cloak tighter around me and clapped my hands together, wishing I'd thought to bring gloves.

There were nearly twenty students in the paddock, all in various stages of tacking up some of the academy's gryffs. I scanned the beasts' faces – I recognised each of them, having worked with most of them during my first two years here. Good animals, all of them. Fast, and brave – and sure, cantankerous, but that wasn't a bad quality in an animal you were about to ride to war on. *Ride to war.* That was a helluva thing.

"Lyssa!"

Devon made his way over to me from amidst the mass, with Ironclaw prancing behind him on the end of his lead rope. I looked him over with a critical eye.

"He looks a little fired up."

"They all are. The students, too. Here, I brought you these."

He held out a pair of thick brown riding gloves, lined with the hair of some animal I'd never heard of. I took them with a grateful smile, and thrust my hands inside before any of my fingers had a chance to freeze right off.

"Thanks." I glanced around the cluster of gryffs again and raised a hopeful eyebrow. "Stormclaw?"

"Sorry. He took a snap at Jensen's face, then took off towards the grove. You want to go look for him?"

I pursed my lips and thought about it for a moment, then exhaled in heavy white cloud, and shook my head ruefully.

"No. We don't have time. It's probably for the best anyway. He's not exactly fit right now. He's barely recovered from his injury. So who am I riding?"

"This guy," Devon said, pointing me at a chestnut gryff, who stood plucking blades of grass, and watching them fall to the floor. "Firefly."

The young gryff I'd ridden in the Four Nations Cup try outs. It seemed like a lifetime ago, back when my biggest concern had been not making an idiot of myself in front of the entire academy.

"Hey, fella," I said, stepping softly across the ground between us. "Remember me?"

He snorted softly, and thrust a blade of grass out towards me.

"Uh... thanks."

Someone had already tacked him up, so I led him over to the fence and climbed up and onto his back. He snorted again and pranced two steps sideways, then shook out his massive chestnut wings with a rustle of feathers and settled down.

"Good boy," I said, rubbing his neck. He wouldn't have been my first choice – nothing quite came close to the bond me and Stormclaw shared – but the inexperienced young animal was the best I had. "We'll get through this together, right?"

He stamped a rear hoof, jostling me in the saddle.

"Right. Great."

I wheeled him around, and looked out at the cluster of students and their Itealta gryffs. They were no army, that was for damned sure. But beggars can't be choosers.

"Alright, everyone," I called above the sound of creaking leather and rustling feathers. "Mount up. We've got a war to win."

Chapter Twenty-Four

We separated the students into four smaller groups to patrol the grounds. I didn't know when Raphael would come, but we'd be ready for him when he did. I made sure each group had at least one person who could portal, because if any of us came across Raphael or his foot soldiers, we were going to need a way to warn Talendale, and quickly. Too bad magic and electricity were so incompatible, because a couple of radios would have made our lives a whole lot easier right about now.

I circled Firefly around, and called over Devon, Caleb, and Ellie – our most experienced riders, and the captains of the other three scouting parties.

"I'm going to lead my group north," I said. "We'll cover from the lake to the gryff barn. Ellie, head west, from the gryff barn to the Unhallowed Grove. Devon, go south, from the Grove to the dragon pit, and Caleb, take east, from the dragon pit back to the lake. We can't be everywhere at once, but if we each stick to our quadrants, we'll catch any large groups. Every thirty minutes send a rider to the centre of the grounds – the Tilimeuse Tree – to check in. If you run into trouble and you need back up, send four fireballs up above your location. Understand?"

Everyone shared a round of terse nods, then the other three riders wheeled their gryffs around and headed back to their groups. I turned back to my own trio of students as Devon took his group into the air.

"Alright," I called to them. "Let's go!"

I touched my foot just under his wing, and clicked my tongue a couple of times.

"Come on, Firefly, let's fly."

He tossed his head up and leapt five feet forwards, then broke out into a bumpy canter. I rolled my eyes and wrapped one hand around my saddle horn as he splayed out his wings, sunk his haunches, and leapt up towards the sky. After a few awkward beats of his wings, the motion smoothed out, and somehow I was still on board – just about. I released my grip on the saddle horn and took up the reins in both hands, gently guiding him out towards the lake. I risked a glance over my left shoulder for long enough to see Kev and Quinn on my left wing, and Tommy on my right. Firefly banked hard to the left and I twisted back round, inwardly cursing my luck to be on the inexperienced young gryff when Stormclaw was out there somewhere.

But that wasn't Firefly's fault. I lowered a hand to scratch his neck, and he flicked an ear back to me. The thrumming in his throat was snatched away in the cold night air, and lost beneath the beating of wings.

It didn't take us long to reach the lake – the academy's grounds were vast, but gryffs were fast on the ground and even faster in the air, even inexperienced ones like Firefly.

"Spread out," I shouted back to the others. "But stay within eyesight."

They nodded and fanned out, so that I could just make out Tommy on my right and Quinn on my left, and Kev was just a faint shadow in the distance. I led them through a sweep of our quadrant, flicking my eyes between the ground and the sky. By now, Atherton was sure to have the academy's wards back up. We'd be able to portal around within the grounds, but no-one would be able to portal from outside. In theory. Raphael had had two years to find a way to smash through the wards, and I had a feeling that if he wanted in, nothing was going to keep him out.

A shrill whistle sounded from my left wing. I glanced across at Quinn and she pointed down at the ground. I could see it then: a small dark shape barely visible against the treeline. A lone figure.

I dipped my head in a tight nod, trying to ignore the frantic pounding in my chest. I took a moment to loosen my stranglehold on the reins and ease the tension in my hips. Getting thrown off would only make it easier for whoever was down there to kill me. Shit. There was someone down there who might try to kill me.

"Down, Firefly," I croaked, and pointed the gryff towards the dark figure. He took us down and broke into his choppy canter, bouncing across the ground at breakneck speed towards the figure. I tugged softly on his reins, steering him wide – I didn't want to get within striking range, not until I knew what I was dealing with. How was I going to defend myself? I barely knew any defensive spells. What if Firefly wasn't fast enough to dodge? Maybe I should have told Quinn to portal to warn Talendale. What if we were all injured and there was no-one to—

"Lyssa!"

The figure on the ground waved his arms above his head, and I tugged Firefly back towards him, earning myself a grunt of disapproval from the gryff, and squeezed him back into a trot. My brow furrowed as I pulled the gryff to a halt in front of the figure.

"Alistair?"

"Heard ye were having a battle, and I didnae want t' miss all the fun. Got a spare gryff?"

I shook my head and my lips curved into a small grin.

"Uh…"

"Y' look a little pale there. Should I have come waving a white flag?"

"Funny. You'd best hop up here before someone takes a pot shot at you."

He eyed Firefly critically.

"You sure that's a good idea? He doesnae look all that trained."

It was hard to argue with that, while Firefly pranced around underneath me, tearing up clumps of damp grass with his talons. He really did have a bit of an obsession.

"Well, you're welcome to walk…"

I stretched down and offered him my arm. He ran his eye over Firefly's restless outline again, then shrugged and jumped up to grab my hand, and scrambled onto the gryff's back behind me. Firefly snorted, startled, and leapt forward.

"You might wanna hold on back there."

I clicked my tongue and urged Firefly up into the air.

"Did you come alone?" I shouted back over my shoulder.

"Nae, I bought Callum an' a few other idiots from Selkendale. They're up at yer castle." He glanced around him. "It's a wee bit weird, with nae Loch above ye."

I chuckled dryly.

"We make do. Any word from the other champions?"

"Not yet, lass. Yer headmaster was tryin' t' get a hold o' them when I portalled in."

We were reaching the edge of our quadrant. With our little pitstop, it must be about time to send someone in to report back to the other scouting parties. I considered sending one of the other three riders, but it probably made more sense to go myself, that way I could pass on what Alistair had told me. And with a bit of luck, we might spot a stray gryff on the way. I signalled the rest of the group to do another lap, and then circled away and took us the centre of the grounds.

The Tree of Tilimeuse stood taller than the academy itself, dominating a large grassy clearing, and its trunk was broad enough to have hidden a small building. I had no idea what type of tree it was, but I'd never seen another like it. The dark brown bark was mottled silver in places, and the star-shaped leaves that adorned it all year round were an odd mix of greens, oranges, reds and browns, as though it was every season at once. The smallest of them was at least the size of my head.

Alistair gave a low whistle as I brought Firefly to a halt at the foot of the behemoth.

"Some tree."

He wasn't wrong. I'd seen it from the air, of course, but I'd never seen it up close before. Very few students were ever allowed to approach the tree, and I'd never been one of them. But the rules didn't apply right now.

"Looks like we've beaten the others back here," I said, snapping myself out of my awestruck stupor. "We'd best make sure it's secure."

I clicked my tongue a couple of times and trotted Firefly in a wide circle around the trunk, looking up into the branches and out into the bushes on the edge of the clearing for any sign on movement. Only when I was certain we were completely alone did I bring the gryff back to a halt. I tossed the reins back to Alistair, and vaulted from the saddle.

I could feel the steady thrumming of raw power in the ground beneath my feet – the Tilimeuse's roots ran through every inch of Dragondale, drawn to the academy's power, or I supposed, the power on which the academy had been built. The tree itself was sentient: it communicated with Talendale through his desk made from its wood and maintained some sort of connection to the outside world. It knew the genealogy of every druid in all of England and advised the headmaster when it was time for new students to study at the academy. If it wasn't for this tree, I might never had known I was a druid. But it wasn't infallible: when I first arrived, it hadn't been able to sense whether I was a Fire or a Water – though granted I'd possessed both elemental powers at the time – and it hadn't been able to tell Talendale who my father was.

Though…

I cocked my head and looked up at the ancient tree.

Though it might know who my mother was. And if we defeated Raphael tonight, it might be the only one left who did. Hell, even if we didn't beat him, even if he destroyed us, I wanted to know. If I died tonight, it would be knowing who I truly was. I'd given so much to Dragondale over the last three years. Didn't I at least deserve that much in return?

I'd edged closer to the tree without realising, and now I was less than an arm's length from its trunk. I didn't know how to communicate with it. I'd never seen it done, and it wasn't the sort of thing they taught in class. But instinctively I raised a hand, and tentatively reached out to it.

The tree's power reached out to me in return. It was the strangest sensation, like a magnet drawing my hand closer and closer, until I could feel the gentle heat leaking from the bark, and then my trembling hand made contact with the rough bark.

Nothing happened.

I exhaled a shaky laugh. What had I been expecting – bright lights and a talking tree? Yeah, right.

But there had to be a way to communicate with it, and not just through Talendale's desk. I knew he came down here every week, and I was pretty sure he didn't do it just to admire the view.

I took a breath and reached deep inside me to the place my magic lived. The magic flowed up my arm and into the tree, and immediately I felt the tree's magic flowing back into me, bringing with it the sense of peace, and the feel of warm, damp earth around my feet and between my toes. I inhaled again and felt the refreshing trickle of water quenching my thirst, and the gentle summer breeze rustling my leaves... Wait, my *leaves*?

A slow smile spread over my face. I was feeling what the tree felt. I focused on the warm air tugging softly at my hair, and the feeling of a full, content belly, and returned the sensations to the tree. We were communicating. It was a start.

I closed my eyes, let go of the sensations, and pictured the tree in my mind, then let that image fade, too. Immediately, it was replaced by an image of me, standing in front of the tree with my eyes closed, one hand resting lightly on its bark. The image drifted out of focus and I paused, trying to work out the best way to convey what I wanted. After a moment, I pictured the tree shrinking back to a seed, and tried to imagine the tree that had created that seed. In return, the tree sent back an image of me as a baby. The image disappeared almost at once, replaced by an image of Raphael.

I almost broke my connection to the Tilimeuse in my shock. The tree didn't know about Raphael. Or it hadn't.

Had it learned? Exactly how sentient was it? His image faded, and my attention sharpened. In his place, a slight, mousey-haired woman came into focus. I felt a pang of disappointment that I couldn't quite explain. I guess I'd been hoping, I don't know, that I'd recognise her or something. Stupid, right? I mean, she did seem a *little* familiar, I supposed, like maybe I'd seen her before... or maybe not. I was just seeing what I wanted to see.

And then I saw something I definitely did *not* want to see. The image of the woman faded to a pallid grey, and she sank into the soft earth beneath her feet until she was covered. Buried.

I gasped and yanked my hand from the tree.

"Lyssa! Are y' okay?"

I heard a soft thud as Alistair jumped off the gryff, but I couldn't quite bring him into focus.

"She's dead."

"I dinnae understand, lass. Who's dead?"

"My mum." I blinked, and this time the haze lifted from his worried face. "She's dead. All this time, I've been looking for her, and..."

I took a deep breath, and shook my head, trying to dislodge the memory of the grey and withered woman from my mind. I didn't quite manage it.

"I'm sorry."

"Yeah." I coughed awkwardly, clearing my throat, and scuffed my feet in the dirt.

"We've got company."

He pointed at something in the sky, and I followed the direction of his hand as the silhouette of a gryff emerged from the darkness, and a second later, another from the opposite direction. I made a lunge for Firefly's reins before he decided to take off and joined them, scanning the skies for the third rider. Maybe Ellie was just running late.

The other two landed and came to a halt beside me, not bothering to dismount.

"All clear out by the pit," Tyler said.

"No movement in our quadrant, either," Luke said, patting his black gryff's neck.

I nodded to them both. Firefly snorted and leapt towards the night-coloured beast, dragging me behind him. I dug my heels in and gritted my teeth, and let out something that wasn't entirely unsnort-like myself. This animal was going to be the death of me. He came to a stop and looked at me in what I could have sworn was surprise, as if he'd forgotten I was there and holding onto his reins.

"Don't pull that face at me," I scolded him under my breath, then turned my attention back to the two riders.

"Alistair portalled out to our quadrant. He brought a few friends, they're up at the castle getting ready to defend it. No sign of Raphael or his men yet. I–"

A dark, swirling patch opened up in the sky, and whatever I'd been about to say went right out of my mind. A gryff burst out of the portal, a rider hunched over its withers and urging it on. My hand was already tingling with energy by the time I recognised Nicole on the back of one of Alden's gryffs. She swung the beast round and it dived towards the ground.

"Intruders!" she shouted as the beast thudded into the dirt. "Intruders have breached the wards by the grove!"

Her gryff spun in a tight circle, tossing its head in agitation.

"Raphael's men?" I asked.

"Unless we're at war with someone else I don't know about!"

Fair point. I tapped Firefly's shoulder, and he crouched down enough for me to grab hold of the saddle and swing myself up onto his back. I reached a hand down and hauled Alistair up behind me.

"Portal up to the castle," I told Nicole. "Tell Talendale everything. Get him to send people to help. You two, get back to your groups, and get them to the grove, as quick as you can. Alistair, can you open me a portal back to the lake?"

Alistair nodded. I urged Firefly forward and lined him up with the portal that sprung into existence in front of us.

I'd have to deal with the revelation about my mum later. Right now, I had to stop my dad from killing everyone.

Chapter Twenty-Five

It took only minutes to gather up the other riders, but if there were already intruders here at Dragondale, then that could be minutes too long. We exploded from a portal at the edge of the Grove, with the twelve other riders that made up our scouting parties on my tail. It wasn't much of an army, but Devon needed whatever help he could get. We had to hold them off until Talendale sent help from the castle.

"Down there!" Alistair shouted over my shoulder. I followed the direction of his arm and saw a gryff circling restlessly down on the ground below. I urged Firefly down towards him, and as we got closer, I could make out the outline of a figure on the floor. I vaulted from Firefly's back as soon as his hooves touched the ground, without bothering to wait for him to stop, and ran towards the figure. The gryff squealed and lashed out at me with a talon, and I recognised him at once. Swiftstorm. I ducked under his beak and raced to the downed rider, skidding to a halt in the dirt beside him. He was out cold, and blood was soaking through his robes, pumping from four long gashes along his torso. There was only one thing that could have done this. A werewolf.

I jammed two fingers against his neck and felt a faint pulse. He was alive. Just.

"It's Jay," I shouted to Alistair. "He's hurt pretty bad."

Swiftstorm screeched at me again and flared his wings, trying to drive me back from his rider. I rolled away, narrowly avoiding taking a hooked beak to the shoulder. The pair had been bonded since the start of last semester, thank God. Anything could have happened while he was lying here, unconscious, if his gryff hadn't been standing guard over him.

"It's okay," I soothed the beast, raising a placating hand towards his neck. "It's okay. I'm here to help. We're going to help him."

The gryff rolled his eyes at me and snorted loudly, but allowed me to take hold of his reins and lead him out of the way. I hooked his reins over a low-hanging tree branch and gave them a quick tug to make sure they wouldn't come loose.

"Portal Jay to the hospital wing," I told Alistair, accepting his hand and hauling myself back onto Firefly. He handed me the reins with a curt nod and hopped down, keeping a close eye on Swiftstorm as he moved to Jay's side.

I twisted round in my saddle to the uneasy looking riders behind me, and set my jaw. I was going to have to be confident enough for all of us. Which would have been fine if I hadn't been shitting myself. This was real. People could get hurt. Could… die.

I swallowed, and pushed the thought from my mind. Whatever was going to happen, getting scared wasn't going to help.

"Come on," I called to them, picking up my reins. "Let's go."

I touched my hand to Firefly's shoulders and he leapt into motion, galloping for two choppy strides before he stretched out his wings and propelled us into the sky. I hunched over his shoulders and we raced through the night, the other riders on our tail.

"Up ahead!" Quinn shouted, pulling up on my wing. Firefly snorted and banked away from the noise, and I hauled him back on track with a grimace.

"I see them," I shouted back. On the ground were eight werewolves – no, nine – harrying the three remaining gryff riders. One of them had landed and was being backed up by three of the wolves, but whoever it was didn't take off. As I swooped down low, I saw why. It was Devon, and his gryff was injured, trailing one wing. He couldn't fly. And if he couldn't take off, it was only a matter of time until one of the massive wolves pulled Devon to the ground, and it would be over.

"Faster," I screamed at Firefly, and with a wild screech he raced towards the ground, talons outstretched.

We passed just above one of the wolves, Firefly's claws missing it by inches as it ducked, then snapped its jaws at us. Cursing, I took Firefly up again then swung him around for another pass. All around me, the riders flew low to attack the shifters, driving them back from our three injured friends.

The wolves fell back and started to regroup, and a shiver ran through me as we drew close again. We outnumbered them, but that might not count for much. The wolves were bigger, stronger, and faster than us, and they healed in nearly no time. And none of us were carrying silver weapons.

But we had one advantage. We could fly. They couldn't.

"You okay?" I shouted to Devon, circling Firefly back round, and touching down to the ground beside him.

"Ironclaw is injured," he said. "He can't fly."

Right. We didn't all have that advantage. Gryffs might be fast, but an injured one wasn't about to outrun a werewolf, not on the ground. Ironclaw was lathered in sweat from trying to outmanoeuvre the shifters, and Devon didn't look in much better shape.

"Nicole's gone to the castle," I told him. "We just have to hold them off until Talendale sends help."

The other riders had landed in a cluster around us, so I raised my voice loud enough for them all to hear.

"Listen up! Ironclaw is hurt, and they're not going to stop coming for him. But we outnumber them. Caleb, Tommy, and Luke, stay in a circle around Devon. Don't let any of those shifters get close to him."

"Forget about me," Devon said, shaking his head. "I'm not important."

"No chance. We've still got one Itealta game left this season, I need my co-captain pulling his damned weight. Everyone else, on my tail. We'll drive them back from the air."

I looked round the fifteen students and got the distinct feeling I was about to be riding into battle on my own.

"We don't have to beat them," I called out. "We just have to hold them back until help arrives. If you've survived Atherton all year, you can sure as hell survive a couple of puppy dogs!"

A couple of nervous laughs broke out and a few people shared uneasy looks. The gryffs, picking up on their uncertainty, pranced on the spot and tossed their heads. I felt Firefly's shoulders twitching, and gave him a heavy pat on the neck. He exhaled in a snort, and settled down. If I could fool him, I could fool them, right?

"Look at them!" I jerked my chin at the werewolves, who were snarling and air snapping in our direction, bearing their vicious teeth that could curse a druid with a single bite, and claws that could shred even a gryff's skin, and... "Okay, forget that. Look at me. I'm not the most skilled fighter here, and I'm not the best rider. But I'm going out there. If I can do this, you can too!"

There was no rousing cheer, no battle cry like in the movies. There was just the sound of rustling feathers, and the wind blowing through the trees. I circled my mount one last time to face the army of invaders.

"Firefly, up!"

He launched into the air with a flap of his mighty wings, and I could only hope the other riders were following in our wake, because if I was doing this by myself, it would really *suck.*

Of the nine shifters, each covered in slabs of muscle and heavy fur, I set my eyes on the largest, more fearsome looking of the pack. Go big or go home, right?

I drew in a shaking breath and exhaled a white cloud into the dusk. I could do this. I *had* to do this. If I faltered now, our whole makeshift cavalry would be routed, and I would not cower while these savages tore apart the one place I could be who I truly was. No damned way.

"Down, Firefly!"

I stared at the heavy grey wolf, his claws dripping blood, and his muzzle pulled back in a feral sneer that set my teeth on edge. To hell with just driving them back, I wanted to hit him so hard that he'd run right out of our academy with his tail between his legs.

Firefly tucked his wings to his flanks, sending us into a nosedive. For once, the young gryff was on the same page as me. We plummeted towards the ground, towards the deadly pack, towards the waiting teeth of what could only be the alpha werewolf, until I could see the feral glare in his eyes, and still we dove. And dove.

"Now, Firefly! *Tiolp!*"

Huge russet wings flared on either side of me, jolting me in the saddle as our downward spiral abruptly came to a halt. His shoulders flexed, and though I couldn't see it, I knew he was extending his talons towards the alpha. I felt a thud travel through his body as his claws struck flesh.

"Go!"

He beat his wings and I pivoted to look behind us. The alpha wolf snarled and leapt up towards us, blood streaming from two talon gashes on his face. Good. That was for Devon. I dropped my reins, and conjured a ball of fire between my hands. A flick of my wrist sent it flying through the air towards the beast. With a growl, he dodged aside, snapping his teeth at us as Firefly carried us further from his reach. I whooped with joy, adrenaline pulsing through my body as the beast fell away and we carried on, untouched.

I turned Firefly mid-air as three more of the riders rose from their attacks. Blood glistened on one set of talons, and the howls of enraged wolves followed us through the dim sky.

Emboldened by our success, the rest of the riders urged their beasts from the floor, and raced at the wolves.

The shifters had barely recovered from our first pass, and now eight more pairs of talons were striking at them. They ducked and snarled, leapt and snapped, but every one of our riders made it safely past them, and more than one of them landed a strike on the intruders. Three of the riders turned and threw fireballs as if they have been the metal Itealta balls I'd drilled them with for hours every week, and they threw with deadly accuracy. One of the wolves threw itself aside, narrowly dodging the flames, but the other two balls found their targets, and loud yelps mingled with the snarling, and snapping of teeth, and the beating of wings.

I was so proud of them that when they reached us, I didn't even call them out for staying behind on the first attack. To be fair, the whole idea probably sounded pretty suicidal until you saw someone pull it off. And after, come to that. Bloody hell, we just charged a bunch of pissed off werewolves – and lived to tell the tale.

Now we had to do it again.

And this time, they'd be ready for us. But I didn't plan on hitting them in two waves again. We'd go all at once, with every rider targeting a different wolf. I was about to call the other riders to me when I saw a dark shape emerging from the gloom. I frowned, watching its progress as it headed straight for us. A gryff and rider – Nicole. It had to be. I scanned the sky behind her, and my heart sunk into my stomach. She was alone. Talendale hadn't sent anyone.

As I took up the reins, my shoulders felt so heavy it seemed a miracle that Firefly didn't plummet to the earth below. Nicole rode high above the battlefield, right towards me. I looked to the worried faces left and right of me as she reached us.

"Sorry, Lyssa," she said, and her defeated voice barely carried across the air between us. "He can't spare anyone."

The last grain of hope died in my chest. No-one was coming.

I dipped my chin in acknowledgement of her words, unable to find my own to answer her. We were on our own. A handful of unqualified students against nine deadly werewolves.

"What now?"

Quinn's voice came from behind me, and she didn't sound scared. She wasn't pleading for some impossible way out. She was ready to follow my lead. And I'd be damned if I was going to let her down. We weren't just students, we were druid apprentices riding flying beasts straight out of mythology. And we were more than a match for the nine mangy curs down below us. We'd already proved it once. I squared my jaw and turned to her.

"We fight. We protect Dragondale, and everything it stands for. Ready? Again!"

I urged Firefly on. With a ragged cheer conjured from adrenaline and determination, the others followed behind us, and as one we raced towards the cluster of shifters.

We were met face on by the pack of snarling, horse-sized wolves, their hackles raised and teeth bared. I picked out the grizzled grey alpha again, and sent Firefly after him. If we could make that one wolf run, the whole pack would follow him.

"Tiolp!" I screamed, and heard my cry echoed all around me. Wings flared, claws grabbed, and wolves dodged, leapt, and snapped. I couldn't see the grey wolf beneath me, but I didn't feel the jolt of a solid hit. We must've missed him. Dammit! Shrill yelps filled the air, which meant at least some of the riders had had more luck than me.

"Go, Firefly," I shouted, urging him up with my hands and voice. He gathered his wings, preparing to launch us back into the sky, and then something thudded into us and he faltered, the impact nearly tossing me from the saddle. He squealed in pain and kicked out with his hind legs, his jerking movements throwing me onto the saddle horn hard enough to knock the wind from me.

I looked down, gasping, frantically trying to see what was going on, but I couldn't see a thing past his flailing limbs. But I didn't need to. There was only one thing that could be making him react with such terror – he'd been bitten. Badly.

My stomach lurched as he bucked under me again. Worse, in his panic he was flying low, and I could see a black wolf fixing its yellow eyes on us.

"Come on, Firefly," I screamed above the snarling and snapping of jaws. "Go! Up, up!"

Finally, he seemed to regain some control of himself and spread his wings. Too late. It was too late. The black wolf leapt at the gryff's scaly front legs, disappearing from my sight the moment its feet left the ground.

I felt the wolf slam into us and latch on, trying to drag us to the ground. Firefly screamed in pain, lashing out with all four of his legs as he tried desperately to dislodge the wolf's grip. He reared right back, and the force flung my legs from around him. A scream burst from my lips and I snatched at the saddle horn, managing to wrap the fingers of one hand around it.

The grizzled grey wolf leapt at me and I threw up my other hand, slamming a gust of air into his chest and tossing him back like he weighed nothing. Terror pumped through my veins, amplifying my powers   , and I flung a fireball at the black wolf, landing a solid blow to his shoulder. He yelped and fell to the ground with a heavy thud.

Panting, I hauled myself back into the saddle as Firefly straightened out, but the pack could sense weakness, and another of them threw itself at my injured gryff. He squealed in terror and beat his wings, hurtling us through the darkening sky.

"Easy boy, easy," I called to him, but his ears didn't so much as flick back to me in recognition of my words. He carried us beyond the reach of the wolves, banking and swerving and threatening to dislodge me from the saddle with each turn. I tugged at the reins, fighting to steady him, but he tossed his head, evading my touch, and raced on, straight past Devon and the others, almost bouncing me from his back as he spooked at some imagined danger. I dropped the reins – they weren't helping – and clung to the saddle horn with both hands, trying to wedge myself deep down into the saddle.

"Down!" I shouted to Firefly, but he showed no sign of hearing me as he raced on through the sky, bucking and kicking his legs as he tried to escape from the pain of the bites.

And then he suddenly *did* start going down – much too fast, much too close to the trees.

"No, Firefly! Steady!"

I prised one hand from the horn and snatched up the reins, trying to turn his face away from the treeline, but he threw his head down with a screech and pulled them right out of my hands, almost pulling me from the saddle with them.

"Shit!" I latched onto the horn again with both hands and swallowed a gulp of air. "Leave your head alone. Got it."

I wrapped my legs tight against his heaving ribcage as the ground rushed up towards us, hunkering down over his shoulders and screwing my eyes shut as we crashed through the treetops. Branches whipped at my arms and shoulders as we plummeted to the earth, completely out of control in the foliage where there wasn't enough room for Firefly to use his wings.

We hit the ground hard, and Firefly's front legs buckled under him. The force flung me from the saddle, and I flew through the air. A scream rattled inside my chest but my breath was caught in my throat, and I didn't have control of a single one of my muscles as I hurtled past a broad-trunked oak, missing it by inches.

I slammed into the dirt beyond it, and the breath rushed from me in a strangled cry that turned into a groan of pain as my brain caught up with my body. Shit. Ow. That hurt. I groaned again, ran a quick mental inventory. Everything hurt, but I didn't think anything was broken. Tentatively, I lifted my head from the mud.

Firefly was gone. I could see a trail of broken branches and plucked feathers leading deeper into the forest. I wasn't going to be seeing him again any time soon. Great.

Rustling sounded from off to my left, and I snapped my head round, my eyes darting over the tree, searching for its source. A pair of yellow orbs stared at me from the foliage, unblinking. A split second later, they were joined by another pair, and as they emerged from the gloom, I could make out the faces of the black wolf, and the grizzled grey alpha. Their lips curled back in identical snarls as they advanced on me.

I scrambled backwards in the dirt until my back thudded into a tree. Shit. They must have followed us out here, their instincts urging them to chase down their injured prey. And now Firefly was gone, and I was on my own.

And I was fucked.

Chapter Twenty-Six

I swallowed, and scrabbled against the tree, using it to pull me to my feet, not daring to take my eyes from the advancing werewolves. My hands trembled, but I pushed them out in front of me, and conjured a fireball.

The grey shifter rumbled deep in his throat — unmistakably a laugh – and the black wolf's tongue lolled from one side of his mouth as they continued towards me, undeterred. And why would they be? I'd landed a direct hit on the black wolf not five minutes ago, yet here he was, completely healed, walking on the leg that should have been a smouldering wreck. I understood for the first time, truly understood, why shifters were so feared and shunned by the rest of the magical communities. They were relentless killing machines. Unstoppable. And one druid apprentice was nothing more than a lamb to them. My heart sank. Devon and the riders stood no chance against the rest of the pack – I'd sent them all to their deaths. It would only be a matter of time until they were overwhelmed by the wolves – but I wouldn't be around long enough to see it.

I set my jaw. If all I could achieve with my death was buying them some time to escape, so be it.

"Come on, then," I snarled. "I'm not afraid of you."

It was a blatant lie, and we all knew it. But the difference between courage and cowardice was in deciding what to do with that fear, and I was going to shove it right down their lycanthropic throats. I hoped my bones caught in their damned teeth.

I put all of my fear and fury into the fireball, and flung it straight at the grey shifter. It smashed into his shoulder in an explosion of red flames, but he didn't so much as break his stride. I sucked in a desperate breath of air past the lump that had formed in my throat, and started to form another fireball.

As if by some unspoken agreement, the two wolves broke into a run, devouring the short distance between us in a few rapid strides. The black leapt first, and for a split second I watched, frozen in horror, as his body arced through the air at me, teeth bared and claws outstretched. At the last moment, I flung myself aside, sending a lance of pain through my shoulder as I hit the dirt for the second time. The wolf smashed into the tree I'd been leaning against, and the whole damned thing shook from the force. My eyes widened, but I didn't have time to process it before a grey flash streaked through the air. I rolled aside, and the shifter's lunge missed me by inches, his yellowed fangs snapping closed right in front of my face.

I yelped in terror, then sent a gust of air from my hand, spraying dust and mud into his eyes. He flinched back, snapping blindly, and I leapt to my feet. I'd barely got my legs under me and ready to run when there was another snarl, and the black wolf landed in front of me. I backed away, flicking my eyes frantically between the two shifters. The grey shook his head one last time then started to advance in tandem with the black, the pair of them flanking me and driving me out of the trees, where my last hope of running and hiding would be gone. If they pushed me out there, this would end quick and bloody.

I bared my teeth in a snarl of my own as I reached the edge of the treeline. If I was going down, it was on my own terms. I passed one hand over the other in a circular motion as I conjured another fireball, bigger and more powerful than the last. One shot. That was all I'd get before they took me out, but I was going to make it a good one.

They took their time advancing on me, drawing out the moment of their victory. I waited, barely drawing breath, and fixed my eyes on the grey alpha. I wasn't going to give him time to dodge this one. A square hit, right between the eyes, with the most powerful fireball I'd ever made. One final 'fuck you' to the bastard who was going to kill me and destroy my home. It was all I had, and I was going to take it.

Three steps. Two steps. One.

The shadow passed directly above me, blotting out the setting sun for a long second, and at first I thought one of the wolves had leapt early, but they were both still in front of me, frozen in place. A screech split the air, so loud it drove every thought from my mind other than the sudden and unrelenting pain in my eardrums. My hands clamped themselves over my ears, abandoning my fireball to nothingness as they tried to blot out the hideous sound. A heavy thud behind me shook the ground and I pulled my hands from the side of my head, twisting round slowly, but I already knew what I would see. There was only one creature that could make a noise like that.

"Good boy, Dardyr," Ava said, patting the dragon's neck with one gloved hand.

"Ava," I gasped. "I thought you left!"

"And miss out on all the fun?" she said, her lips pulled back in a smile that was nine tenths terrifying.

A twig snapped in front of me and I twisted my head back round barely in time to see the grey leap at me. I threw myself backwards, diving between Dardyr's massive scaled legs and hoping to hell I wasn't swapping one messy death for another.

The wolf landed short and started to circle around the monstrous dragon, assessing it with cold, calculating eyes. The black shifter circled us in the opposite direction, leaping nimbly aside as Dardyr lashed out with his long tail. At a word from Ava, Dardyr snorted a stream of fire at the grey alpha in front of him, setting light to the stubby blades of grass as the wolf dodged aside and out of his eyeline. I realised the problem at once – with me under his legs, Ava couldn't turn the dragon for risk of squashing me, and he couldn't fight what he couldn't see.

My eyes flicked between the two snarling wolves, both fully focused on the new, more deadly threat, and I seized my moment, sprinting from the cover of the beast to the treeline beyond. Dardyr spun immediately, stretching his neck down low to take a snap at the grey wolf. I saw the black wolf take in the rider's vulnerability with a glance.

"Ava, look out!" I screamed, but I was too late. The shifter leapt through the air, aiming for the spot where Ava crouched on the dragon's back, holding on with both hands. He crashed into her, ripping her from the beast's back, and the pair of them crashed to the ground in a tangle of hair, fur, limbs, and fangs.

I raced towards them, peppering the shifter with half a dozen fireballs as I ran, but they glanced off him without leaving so much as a mark. Beneath him, Ava grappled frantically, fending him off with her hands and feet, but she was no match for the werewolf, and his teeth edged closer and closer to her face.

Dardyr loosed a scream of fury and twisted round to the pair. His head snaked out and his gaping jaws clamped shut around the wolf. He plucked it from Ava as though it was made of feather, and flung it into a tree. The trunk snapped under the impact with an almighty crack, and the wolf tumbled to the ground, unmoving.

The grey alpha looked from us to his downed companion, and without another sound, turned and took off through the trees. I watched him go, then rushed over to Ava, keeping one wary eye on Dardyr in case he decided I was a threat, too.

"Are you okay?" I reached a hand down to Ava and helped her onto her feet, eyeing the claw marks across her chest and neck.

"Uh, yeah, I think so," she said, nodding unsteadily, and then threw an affectionate look towards the dragon. "It didn't bite me. Thanks to this guy."

"Yeah, he's quite something," I agreed. "I don't think these are deep, but you should get them checked out."

She snorted.

"We're in the middle of a war, Lyssa. I think they'll keep."

"Oh, right." I looked over at the downed wolf, still unmoving. Ava followed my gaze.

"Do you think he's..."

"I don't see how anything could have survived that," I said. Something caught my eye; a flash of gold around his paw, and I edged closer.

"Let's not find out, yeah?" Ava said, but I ignored her. As I got closer, I recognised the gold strand tangled in his paws, with an intricately decorated gold oval hanging from it. Ava's necklace. It must've snagged on his claws when he was attacking her. She loved that thing, and it was the least I could do, seeing as she'd just saved my life and all.

I crouched down next to the wolf, trying not to look too closely at his curved claws, each longer than my fingers and three times as wide, as I tugged the chain loose. The locket had popped open, either in the struggle or when Dardyr had thrown him, and I frowned at the photo inside it. A photo of a very familiar face. A face I'd seen earlier this evening, at the Tilimeuse Tree. This was where I'd seen it before!

"Where... where did you get this photo?" I asked, my voice trembling.

Ava clutched at her neck and seemed to realise for the first time that it was missing. She came closer, and looked at the image over my shoulder.

"That's my mom," she said. "I mean, my birth mom. I never knew her. And that's a photo of my sister. I never knew her, either."

I noticed the second photo set into the opposite side of the locket for the first time – two little girls sitting together, one a baby, and the other maybe a year or eighteen months. I stared at the photos, my mouth open. When eventually I regained control of my jaw, my voice didn't sound like my own.

"Ava, that's… that's *my* birth mother." Who'd been in America at some point, who'd given me up for adoption and insisted I was raised in this country, and…

"I don't understand," Ava said, and I shook my head.

"Neither do I. I think… I think we might be *sisters*."

We stared at each other in silence, our faces identical masks of shock, until Dardyr slashed his tail into the ground impatiently.

"Oh my God," Ava said, snapping out of it faster than me, her eyes wide with panic. "We don't have time. Talendale sent me to find you. Raphael's people are trying to force the front gate. We've got to go!"

She grabbed my hand and towed me towards the dragon, and we'd made it out of the trees again before I came to my senses and pulled back.

"Ava, I can't. Devon and the others need me. There are other wolves, they portalled in, and–"

Ava shook her head impatiently, cutting me off.

"The gates are our priority. A few shifters might have managed to portal in, but if they break the wards over the front gates, they're going to march a whole army in here. Talendale thinks your magic can help hold them."

I cast one last look towards where I'd last seen the rest of the gryff riders, then dipped my chin in a nod.

"Okay. Let's go. Wait, my gryff ran off."

"You don't need him," Ava said, with something of her old grin. "Dardyr awaits."

"You've got to be kidding."

She wasn't. She scrambled nimbly onto the dragon's back and perched between the spikes along his shoulders without any saddle or tack — because dragon riders were bloody insane — and stretched a hand down towards me.

I could only assume insanity must be a family trait as I accepted her hand, and let her pull me up behind her.

"Fly, Dardyr," she said, and the beast spread his massive leathery wings, and took to the skies. I wrapped my hands around two of his spine spikes until my fingers turned white, and pressed myself nearly flat to his scaly body, clinging on like some sort circus monkey as he swept through the skies. Each beat of his wings lifted us a dozen feet in the air and then down again, so that it was like riding a boat through a choppy sea — only there was no water beneath us, and if I fell, I wouldn't be swimming, I'd be plummeting straight to the ground below.

"Hold on," Ava yelled, her words almost drowned out by the rushing of the air around us. Hold on? What the hell did she think I was doing back here, bloody backflips? But I didn't say it aloud, because I was pretty sure opening my mouth right now wasn't going to end well.

And then Dardyr banked left, hard. My legs slipped along his scaled back and I bit back a surprised yelp, scrabbling desperately until my feet hooked onto one of his spikes, and latching onto it until we levelled out again.

"I thought you were used to flying!" Ava called back with a laugh, looking not even the least bit worried by our near brush with certain death.

"On a *hippogryff*," I growled back, hauling myself back into a more stable position, as much as it was possible to be stable on the back of a freaking flying lizard.

"Look, up ahead!"

I prised myself up enough to glance over her shoulder to where she was pointing – yeah, pointing. She was on a damned dragon that was tossing us about so much I was getting seasick, and she let go with one hand to point. Bloody dragon riders. Nuts, the lot of them.

And then I saw what she was pointing at, and all other thoughts vanished from my mind. The academy's main gates were up ahead, and dozens of students and professors were there, spread out in defensive positions. Circling above them was another dragon – Paethio, by the looks of it. Ethan might have been a womanising prat, but if nothing else, he took his duties as a dragon rider seriously, and on any other day the pair would have been a reassuring sight.

But there was nothing that could reassure me because hammering spell after spell at the warded iron gates was a sight from my worst nightmares. Raphael's army. There had to be a hundred of them – more, maybe – and they weren't here to talk. Even from up here I could feel the hatred pouring off of them. And they weren't just students from Braeseth Academy. It looked like Raphael had done one hell of a job stirring up hatred in the magical community. Except... The thought niggled at me, the same one that had been harrying me for weeks now. Except you can't create that much raw hatred overnight, or even in a year, or a decade. This was the sort of hatred that built up quietly over generations, until someone ignited it. The druids' own arrogance had given Raphael his army. The way they – we – lorded it up over the other communities, laying down our laws and expecting others to bend to them. But when you bend a branch too far, it does one of two things. It breaks – or it comes back to smack you in the face.

Flying above the masses was the biggest bird I'd ever seen, shaped like an eagle but matching Dardyr for size. It screeched its fury as it flew back and forth above the army, controlled by a bridle wrapped around its beaked face. Perched on its back was a cloaked figure, and though I couldn't make it out from this far away, I knew it could only be one person.

"Where the hell did Raphael get a rokh?" I shouted to Ava, but she just shook her head.

"I don't know, but it looks hungry."

I shuddered. Rokhs fed exclusively on human flesh, and I for one did not want to become an appetiser.

"On, Dardyr," Ava called to the dragon, and he beat his wings harder and faster, racing towards the gates and the waiting armies.

We were almost there where it happened.

With a flash of bright blue light, the wards shattered, and the force flung the gates from their hinges. A cry went up, and the army surged through the opening, swarming the people beyond.

342

Chapter Twenty-Seven

My heart sank into my stomach as invaders poured into Dragondale, charging straight for our ragged cluster of defenders.

"We're too late!"

Ava shook her head, her lips pressed together in a grimace.

"No, we're just in time. Get ready."

Before I had time to work out exactly what she meant by that, Dardyr tucked his wings back and went into a dive, swooping down low towards the battlefield.

An energy ball zipped past on our left, missing Dardyr's wing by inches. He banked right, then homed in on the woman throwing them. She flung another energy ball at us and hit Dardyr square on the nose. He bellowed in fury, and we were close enough to see the woman's eyes widen as the dragon kept on coming. He snatched her up without landing, and I squeezed my eyes tight as he tossed her aside, the same way as he had the wolf. Then I forced myself to open them again. These people were here to take Dragondale any way they could, and they were more than happy to go through us. If we held back, they'd kill us all. This wasn't the time to get squeamish.

I prised one hand from Dardyr's spine spikes and conjured a fireball. Another flurry of energy balls blasted our way before I could loose it, one of them missing me by inches, and the others smacking into the dragon's thick, scaled skin.

"Dammit!" Ava cursed, as Dardyr bellowed again. Another dragon swooped close to us, and Ethan shook his head and gestured frantically up.

"Ava, take him up! He's too vulnerable this low!"

Ava swore again but guided her dragon higher up.

"We're useless up here," she seethed, watching the fight play out across the battlefield.

"Can't he breathe fire on them?"

"Sure, if you don't mind killing half of our people too."

"Shit."

"Yeah."

We flew in silence for a moment, too high up to do anything useful. I tried conjuring a couple of fireballs, but they were useless over such a long distance, burning down to barely an ember by the time they reached anyone and causing nothing worse than a couple of singed hairs. Meanwhile, our friends and our professors were down there, risking their lives, fighting a battle that they couldn't win.

"There's got to be something we can do."

"There is," Ava said. "But Talendale's not going to like it."

"I don't get the sense you're going to let that stop you."

"Family trait, right?" she said, grinning back at me over her shoulder.

"We are going to talk about that when this is over. So don't die, got it?"

"Got it," she said, and I could hear the smile in her voice. She was an orphan, she'd grown up in foster care – this must have been an even bigger deal for her than it was for me. I mean, sure, Raphael wasn't winning father of the year any time soon, but I'd known I had a blood relative, even one who wanted me dead. And I had a mum, and a dad, and a baby sister back in Halewich, because family was more than just blood. Ava had grown up with no-one, just a succession of group homes and foster carers, and from the sounds of it, none of them had been all that good to her. Discovering after all these years that she had family? I couldn't even begin to imagine what she was feeling right now.

But now wasn't the time to think about that.

"Good," I said. "What's the plan?"

"I'm going to make some swoop attacks with Dardyr. We've done them a few times in training, I think we can get in and out fast enough that he's not in any danger."

"You know what? I think this is my stop. Because frankly falling off a dragon is not in my top ten ways to die."

"You're probably more use down there than you are up here," she agreed, steering the dragon towards a small clearing. "And Dardyr can manoeuvre more easily if we're not worrying about dropping you."

"Uh… thanks."

"Just…" she broke off for a moment. "Just be careful, okay?"

"Promise," I said, and then gritted my teeth as the ground rushed up to meet us, and we thudded down onto it hard enough that a couple of nearby saplings shook. I was never going to complain about a bumpy landing on a gryff again.

I clambered down from Dardyr's back, almost landing flat on my face because it was a *lot* further down from a dragon than it was from a gryff.

"I'm okay," I called up to Ava, then scrambled out of the way of the dragon's legs. "Go. And good luck."

I wrenched my eyes from her and darted towards the battle. Air and dust buffeted me as Dardyr shook out his leathery wings and took to the sky again, taking one of my only blood relatives off to fight against the other. Ava was my sister. What the hell was I supposed to do with that?

An energy ball smacked into the ground by my feet, reminding me that I had other things to worry about right now. Like surviving long enough to have that chat with her. I flung a couple of fireballs to discourage anyone else from thinking I was a soft target, then zig-zagged my way into the fray. It was chaos everywhere, people running and ducking and throwing fire and air and energy at each other, shouting curses and counter-curses, screaming in fury and in pain.

I recognised the Dragondale uniform: a small group of students were clustered around a professor, and I made for them. Dougan was an impressive sight, slinging curses and fireballs at one invader after another. His years working as an enforcer hadn't been wasted. Around him, Sam, Paisley, and Felicity were throwing potions at anyone who ventured close, covering Dougan while he single-handedly carved a hole in the attacking army. I didn't stop to question where the two girls had come from, or what they were doing here when I'd have expected them to be cowering as far away from Dragondale as possible. I didn't even stop to warn them I was coming, which in hindsight may have been a mistake. Paisley spun and drew back her arm, aiming a potion at me as I sprinted towards them.

"It's me," I shouted, at the same time as Sam spotted me and grabbed her arm, sending the potion smashing into the ground.

"Lyssa," she gasped, her wide eyes finally taking me in. "I'm sorry, I—"

"It's fine," I said, hoping no-one else could hear the tremble in my voice as I looked at the now-dead grass and boiling mud. "No harm done. Just... look before you throw, okay?"

She nodded, and Dougan twisted round to look at me over his shoulder.

"Lyssa," he said, nodding his head in greeting. "What happened to your cavalry?"

He spun forwards again in time to throw his hands up and deflect an energy ball, sending it flying right back at the hooded figure who'd thrown it.

"They're still out there," I said. "We found some werewolves."

"Shifters?" Dougan's eyes widened. "In the academy?"

"Yeah. We were holding our own, but... And then Ava found me, she said you needed help up here."

"She wasnae wrong." He broke off to throw a fireball at a man running straight for us. The flames caught on his boot and he fell to the floor, patting at them frantically. "We're pretty badly outnumbered."

"Where did they all come from?" A fireball thudded into the ground in front of us, missing my feet by inches. I stared at it in horror for a moment before I snapped out of my shellshock and stamped it out. Unclassifieds couldn't throw fire. No-one could, except for— "Are there druids out there?"

"Aye," Dougan said, and his lips pressed together in a grim line as he deflected another attack.

"*Why* are there druids out there?" I heard the hysterical edge to my voice and sucked in a breath, trying to control my terror. "I mean, where did they come from?"

"Well, I don't know about all of them," Dougan said, throwing another fireball with a grunt, and nodding with grim satisfaction as his target went down. "But that one was locked up in Daoradh."

"Daoradh? There was a break-out? But no-one has ever broken out of there!"

"Until now." He threw two more fireballs in quick succession, then added, "We think it was an inside job."

My reply died on my tongue. Harper. She let herself be taken. Dammit, we'd known she was working with Raphael, how had this happened?

"It's my fault," Dougan said. "I should nae have let them come on the tour."

"And if you hadn't, you'd just have proved that everything Raphael had told them was right."

"Aye, and then what?" he asked wryly. "They'd have stormed the front gates?"

Well, he had me there. Fortunately, I was spared from answering by an energy ball that almost took my head off my shoulders. I dived aside and rolled up into a crouch as it passed through the space my head had been occupying a split second before, and tossed a stream of air in the direction it had come from, knocking the man to the floor. Dougan hammered three fireballs into him while he was down, and there was no way he was getting up again after that. I tore my eyes from the burning body and looked at Dougan in horror, my mouth open.

He'd killed him. Without hesitation.

"Now's nae the time to be pulling yer punches, lass," he said softly, and I snapped my mouth shut and squared my jaw. He was right, of course. I knew it. But knowing and seeing were two different things entirely, and I'd seen more death tonight than I'd seen – or wanted to see – in my entire life. But if I kept holding back, it would be my friends who were on the funeral pyre when this was done. Innocent people, not those who'd chosen to attack an academy full of *students* because they didn't like the hand they'd been dealt. Sure, what the druids had done to them was wrong, but so was this. Killing innocent people to further their goals was cowardly, the act of a terrorist, and I *would* defend my home, as all those around me were doing. Even Talendale was holding the front line. And I watched in awe for a moment as the old man threw curses and evaded attacks with the athleticism of someone half his age, seemingly emanating a glow of power, like an aura around him.

Then a flash of movement caught my eye. A cloaked figure, approaching him from behind. I didn't shout a warning – it would have been drowned out in the chaos of the battle. Instead, I raised one hand, and conjured a fireball. I wasn't pulling my punches anymore.

"Lyssa, no!"

Dougan grabbed my arm and my fireball went wide, smashing into an aged tree and scorching the bark. The figure reached Talendale and bent its head to speak in his ear. Talendale nodded in response, and my stomach churned. He wasn't an attacker. He was on our side, and I nearly killed him.

"From the council," Dougan said, and as he did, I recognised the black trim to the man's cloak, marking him as an enforcer of the circle. Good. Not good that I almost killed him, obviously. Good that they were here. This is what they were trained for, and if they were half as good as Dougan, then this battle might not be a suicide mission after all. Maybe they could take down Raphael. I scanned the skies, looking for the horrific outline of the rokh, but it was nowhere to be seen. Then I heard a scream from off to my left, and caught sight of the bird tearing someone in half – our side or theirs, I couldn't tell. I tried to look away, but my eyes were intent on capturing every detail of the grisly, barbaric death, and the blood splatters across the hellion's maw and neck, and–

I gasped.

"Raphael's gone!"

"What?" Sam turned to me, and Dougan stared scanning the battlefield.

"There's no rider on the rokh. He's gone."

"I suppose it's too much to hope it ate him?" Sam suggested.

"Aye," Dougan said. "A rokh won't turn on its master. He's here somewhere."

"What, you think he just got off his gigantic murderous eagle so he could fight on foot? Does that sound anything like the Raphael you know?"

"Actually, I've never met him, lass."

"Me, either."

"Well, I have! And I'm telling you, if he's not on that bird, he's up to something!" I spun to face Paisley. "Can you track his scent?"

She paled, and avoided my eye.

"Lyssa, I…"

"Can you?" I demanded. "Because this is bigger than you not liking part of who you are, and–" I swallowed, and forced myself to continue. "And it's bigger than what happened between us at Halloween."

It took everything I had not to say, 'what you did to Stormclaw', but I made the effort, because there was too much at stake to be rubbing salt into old wounds.

"Old grudges aren't going to count for a damned thing if we all die here today," I said. "I forgive you, okay? I understand why you did it, I always did. I know what it's like to want to fit in. But we need to work together right now, okay?"

Paisley closed her eyes and exhaled slowly, and then nodded.

"I'll need to change," she said. "I can't– I need to be in my wolf form to track. I haven't exactly embraced my beast side."

"You can control your shift?" I asked, and she nodded.

"The hard part is *not* shifting. It always has been."

"Alright then, let's go. Those trees over there?"

I pointed to a copse of trees just away from the main of the battle, and she nodded again.

"I'm coming too," Felicity said, and for once, her voice wasn't mocking. If anything, she sounded... almost scared. I turned to meet her eye, about to turn her down flat when I saw the look of determination on her face. "I wasn't made a champion by chance. I want to help, Ch– Lyssa."

I chewed over her words for a moment, but we didn't have time to stand around arguing. I'd find out whether or not she could be trusted to watch my back soon enough.

"Okay. Let's go."

Sam started to move with us, and I planted a hand firmly on his chest.

"No. You need to stay here, Sam. Someone has to help Dou– I mean, *Professor* Doug–"

"Would yer just get out o' here?" Dougan cut me off, rolling his eyes in exasperation at my sudden onset of propriety. I nodded.

"Good idea. Come on."

The three of us raced towards the copse, zig-zagging and keeping our heads low until we were far enough away that no-one was paying any attention to us. Paisley darted into the cover of the trees, and I heard the whisper of fabric and the soft thuds of her clothing hitting the floor. I turned my back on the trees, and saw Felicity working hard to keep the revulsion from her face.

"Are you sure you can do this?" I asked her, keeping my voice low. "No-one would think any less of you if you wanted out."

"I don't have to like half-breeds to understand how she can help," Felicity said sharply. "The same can be said of how I feel about you."

"Right."

Well, it was reassuring at least to know that Felicity was still the same judgemental bitch she'd always been. War or no, some things would never change.

Chapter Twenty-Eight

It was nearly a full minute before Paisley's cries of pain became snarls of rage, and then she burst from the trees, teeth bared and hackles raised. Felicity gasped and took a step back, and I narrowed my eyes. For all her hatred, I bet she'd never even seen a werewolf. Paisley was smaller than the wolves we'd fought in the clearing, smaller even, I thought, than Kelsey – maybe because she'd been bitten, or maybe because she was still fighting the wolf in here, I didn't know. I just hoped her nose worked as well.

A squeal sounded from the trees, and right behind the wolf, a black and gold hippogryff burst through the foliage, wings and head raised high in fury.

"Stormclaw!"

He skidded to a halt, kicking up mud and stones, then lowered his head and nuzzled Paisley. Slowly, her hackles went down, and her lips closed over her yellowed fangs. I guess I wasn't the only one Stormclaw had a bond with anymore.

"So that's what you've been getting up in your spare time, huh?" I said, patting his neck. He thrummed in his throat and butted his head against my chest.

"Cute reunion," Felicity said, her voice loaded with enough sarcasm to down an elephant. "Can it wait until after the war?"

"Alright, don't get your knickers in a twist. How about it, Stormclaw, mount up?"

He sank down into the mounting position, and tucked one claw up behind him, forming a mounting platform. I wasted no time scrambling up onto his back, and held a hand down to Felicity. She raised an eyebrow and took a step back.

"Oh, no. I'm not riding bareback again. And I'm not getting on that animal. He's savage."

"You want to run along behind and hope you have time to catch up? Come on, you can hold onto me, you'll be fine."

Felicity hesitated for another moment, then reached up and grabbed my hand. I hauled her onto Stormclaw's back behind me, and fixed my eyes on Paisley.

"Let's go!"

Paisley ran with her nose a few inches above the floor, covering the ground faster than any human could have run. Stormclaw followed behind her without needing any instruction from me, as though he knew exactly what we were doing, and what was at stake. Sitting astride him as we raced through the academy felt like coming home. My legs hung on either side of his neck, resting against his powerful shoulder muscles as I perched on his withers. Not even the gravity of the situation could fully steal away my joy of riding him. Felicity, on the other hand, seemed to be doing her very best, her hands clinging to my shoulders in a death grip, and her knees digging into the small of my back.

"Try to relax," I called back to her.

"Easy for you to say," she grumbled, but I felt her grip ease up just a fraction. She'd been riding gryffs since before she could walk, like any well-bred brat of a druid family, and she knew that relaxing her body was her best chance of staying on board. And mine, too.

Paisley led us away from the battle through the falling night, across open meadows and through wooded areas that slowed our progress, occasionally letting out a huff or a rumble as the trail changed direction. We'd been running in silence for a long time – long enough that I was starting to worry that Paisley was following the wrong scent – when I recognised the track we were following. The small, sparse wood we were running through was as familiar to me as the back of my hand, and any moment now we would hit a trail that I had walked every day I'd been at Dragondale. Realisation hit me with blinding clarity, and then with horror. The track we were heading for lead to the gryff barn in one direction, and in the other, to the academy's back entrance – the academy's unguarded back entrance. Raphael was going inside the castle itself.

"He's going to the library!" I shouted, and Paisley lifted her head from the scent to look back at me, stumbling over the uneven ground as she did.

"Why would he be going there?" Felicity shouted back, apparently forgetting that her mouth was right by my ear. I winced, and then said,

"The curse cube. It has to be. He's going to finish what Kayden started!"

Felicity cursed, and Paisley ducked her head back to the trail and doubled her speed, so that it took all my balance and skill to stay on Stormclaw's back as he galloped after her. I was so focused on moving with him as we charged along the track that I didn't hear anything until the bushes on my right rustled and then parted, and the grizzled grey wolf exploded onto the track in front of us, snarling and snapping his teeth. Stormclaw spooked and reared up, clawing the air with his front talons in panic. I threw myself forward, wrapping my arms around his neck to keep from tumbling off his back. A scream burst from Felicity's lips and she dug her fingers into my shoulders as she tried desperately to hold on.

"Down, Stormclaw!" I shouted, leaning all my weight forwards, and he slammed his talons into the ground, missing the wily old wolf by inches. Three more wolves burst from the trees in his wake, two of them snapping at Stormclaw's heels while a third locked its eyes onto Paisley.

"Run!" I screamed, and urged Stormclaw forward. Paisley didn't need to be told twice and took off at a break-neck sprint. The grey alpha leapt aside before we trampled him and Stormclaw tore over the track behind Paisley. The wolves pounded along the track behind us, and Felicity's hand left my shoulder for long enough to throw bolts of air at them. I twisted round in time to see a wolf take a blast of air to the chest and tumbled backwards, head over heels, only to shake itself off and bound back into the chase.

Four more wolves leapt from between the trees on either side of the track, flanking us and snapping whenever they got close enough. This had to be the whole pack. Where were Devon and the other riders – what had happened to them? I really hoped the wolves had just given them the slip. I *knew* I should have gone back to them!

"Lyssa, look out!" Felicity screamed, as a wolf threw itself at Stormclaw's face. He shied sideways, almost unseating us both, then snapped at the wolf, gouging a red line from its back with his hooked beak. The wolf hit the dirt but was back in the chase in seconds. We couldn't stop them on our own.

If we could just get out of the woods, I could take Stormclaw into the air and tell him to pick Paisley up in his talons. I was pretty sure he could do it without hurting her, at least, not more than she could heal in a minute or two. But with these branches overhead, and trees on either side of the track, there was no room for him to unfurl his wings.

A wolf leapt at my leg and I hiked it up higher so his teeth snapped shut around empty air, then fired a blast of air into his chest, tossing him aside. He bounced off a tree with a yelp, but just like Felicity's wolf, he sprung straight back into action and started chasing us down again.

"It's no good," Felicity shouted. "They just keep coming back!"

"Just hang on," I screamed, urging Stormclaw on until we were riding right on Paisley's tail, protecting her back from the other wolves. She'd refused to embrace her wolf-form for months, there was no way she could hold her own in a fight against stronger, more experienced shifters who outnumbered us two to one. I could see open space just beyond the trees ahead, we just had to make it a bit further, and then we could grab Paisley and get out of there. Except... Stormclaw had never grabbed a living person in his talons. What if he grabbed her too hard and killed her? What if he couldn't fly with the weight of the three of us? He wasn't fully recovered from his injury yet, there was a chance he might not make it.

I set my jaw and fixed my eyes on the opening ahead. If we didn't try, we were all dead. There was no way we could survive even a minute in a straight fight against eight shifters. There was no other choice. We had to try.

The wolves seemed to know what we were planning, and redoubled their efforts. A scarred, chocolate-coloured wolf lunged at Paisley, and I hammered a fireball into his chest. The force of the blow tossed him aside, but I knew it would be only moments until he was back on our tails again. We just had to hold them off, just a bit longer, we were only a handful of strides from the opening now, just a few more seconds. We were going to make it!

"Go on, Stormclaw," I urged. "You can—"

My words cut off as a wolf threw itself at one of his scaled front legs, finding its mark and latching on. Stormclaw stumbled, and I felt myself thrown through the air for the second time. I hurtled towards the ground, vaguely aware of Felicity crashing into the earth somewhere ahead of me. I hit the floor hard and rolled, trying to absorb some of the impact, and finished up on my back. A grizzled grey face filled my entire range of vision, its mouth open wide as it lunged for me. I threw up both hands in blind panic. A jet of fire shot from one, and a gust of air from the other, burning the wolf and throwing him back at the same time. I stared at my hands in shock. I didn't know what I'd been planning to do, but it sure as hell hadn't been that – whatever *that* was.

A scream came from somewhere to my left and I jumped up, throwing three fireballs at the wolf closing in on Felicity. Snarls erupted from my right, and I could see a flash of Paisley's brown fur against with white as she fought with one of the pack. From the corner of my eye, I could see Stormclaw scraping the ground with one claw, ears pinned flat to his skull in rage, surrounded by three more of the beasts.

"Stormclaw, fly!" I shouted, as I tossed three more fireballs at three different wolves. At least he could survive this, even if the rest of us couldn't. Movement flashed behind him as he took to the air: an oval of darkness that didn't quite match the surrounding darkness. A portal. More of the pack had come. I dropped my hand. We were finished.

A redheaded figure stepped through the portal – human. A massive black wolf followed, landing just in front of her, teeth bared and hackles raised.

"Kelsey! Leo!"

I didn't know whether to hug her or curse her for coming here – to her own certain death. Leo took in the scene with a single glance, and threw himself into the fray, tackling the grey alpha to the ground.

More wolves leapt from the portal, six or seven of them, and raced into the battle. Kelsey hurried over to me and Felicity.

"What's going on?" I gasped. "Who are all these wolves?"

"The alpha pack sent them. They don't want Raphael in control any more than we do. They're trying to rally as many wolves as they can."

"But the pack…" I gestured to the battle; a snarling mass of fur and teeth.

"A rogue pack. They defied the Alpha of Alphas' command. We'd have come sooner but portals aren't working properly. Too much magic flying around. We're lucky we didn't end up the other side of the castle."

"The castle!" I threw a frantic glance over my shoulder at the dark outline. "Raphael's heading there, he's after the curse cube!"

"Go!" Kelsey glanced back at the fight. "We've got this."

Without another word, she raced towards the fighting wolves and leapt gracefully through the air. Her clothes burst from her as she erupted in fur and her entire body changed shape in a split second. She hit the ground fully in her wolf form, her clothes landing in tatters around her. I gaped at her in shock – I'd had no idea she was *that* good – and she glanced back over her shoulder, giving a meaningful nod at the castle. Right.

"Come on," I said, tugging at Felicity's arm. She snapped her horror-struck gaze from the feral battle and dipped her chin. We took off at a sprint, running on nothing but adrenaline and desperation, until the sounds of the fight faded behind us, and we rounded the last corner to the academy's back door.

I saw a cluster of figures around it and skidded to a halt. The six of them turned to face us, then one stepped forward with a grin.

"Late to the party again, Dragondale?" Alistair said. "Come on. We've got a dark druid to destroy."

Chapter Twenty-Nine

How did you know he was coming here?" I asked, pulling off the remains of my shredded cloak and tossing it aside. It turned out being thrown from two gryffs and attacked by a pack of werewolves wasn't good for your wardrobe. Who knew?

Alistair shook his head.

"We didn't. We followed him here. What we don't know is what he wants in there, when the battle's going down near the main gates."

"There's a curse cube in the library, the same as the ones he used to bring down the other academies. If he can hook it directly to our primal plant, he won't just curse the academy, he'll kill it outright, and take control of the final elemental core."

"Shit."

"Yeah." I looked round the circle of champions. Each of us had our own skills and weaknesses, but we'd all being chosen to represent our academies for a reason: we were the best they had to offer. Still, Dragondale was our home, mine and Felicity's. They didn't owe us anything.

"None of you have to be here," I said. "No-one's going to think any less of you for walking away or waiting for help to come."

"Are you scared we're going to take all your glory?" Aderyn said in her lilting welsh accent, a smile tugging at the corners of her mouth.

"If the welsh aren't going to welsh," said Kieran, "then neither are we."

"Yer already know we're in," Alistair grinned. "Besides, he's with the scum who cursed Selkenloch. We've got a score tae settle."

"How many others does he have with him?" Felicity asked, trying to sound unconcerned as she brushed some of the dirt from her cloak, and not quite pulling it off.

"About twenty, from what I saw," Callum said, glancing round at the others. They nodded their agreement.

"Too bad," I said. "If he'd brought a few more friends, it might have been a fair fight. Come on."

I pressed my hand to the door and sent a long pulse of energy through it. It swung inwards, and the eight of us moved through the corridor in silence. I swept my eyes left and right, my hands hanging loose by my sides and ready to conjure a fireball at the first sign of movement.

"How far?" Riley hissed.

"Not far. Second corridor on the right, then third on the left."

"Figures she'd know the way to the library," Alistair said with a smirk, shooting me a mischievous look. I snorted.

"I don't know why. Every time I go there someone tries to kill me."

"Well, it'd be a shame t' ruin yer record…"

He checked the first corridor, hand drawn back, then beckoned us on past it. It was eerily quiet in here, with no-one in the building except the eight of us… plus Raphael and his small army.

"Stop!" I hissed, as Riley prepared to duck into the next corridor. She froze, hand pulled back, and snapped her head round to me. I stalked closer, eyeing the corridor that had never been there on the dozens of times I'd passed along this hallway before.

"Glamour," Dylan said, his eyes slightly out of focus as he looked at the turning. I nodded.

"Alex and her group must have laid glamoured portals down this way."

Riley let out a low whistle, eyeing the portal she almost walked through.

"She's good."

"Where exactly do these portals lead?" Alistair asked as we pressed on towards the next turning.

"Have you ever met a gryphon?"

"You Dragondale lot don't mess around, do you?"

"Remember that next time you're thinking about saving the world without me. This way."

I led them down the right corridor, and hurried the rest of the way, only hanging back long enough to check for movement at each opening we passed. We rounded the last corner, and the library's doors loomed ahead.

My stride faltered as they came into sight. The air was humming with magic, some of it mine, some of it not. Raphael was here, I could all but taste his power. My father. The first druid ever to manifest three elemental powers. But I was the first druid to manifest all four.

I set my jaw, squared my shoulders, and walked towards them.

And stopped again. The man beyond this door tried to kill me last year. He failed not because he hadn't been strong enough, and sure as hell not because he'd had a sudden attack of compassion. Just because he'd underestimated me. It was too much to hope he'd make the same mistake twice.

But I wasn't facing him alone this time. And it wasn't just my life on the line if we failed. If Raphael was allowed to activate the curse cube, the fate of every druid in the country, even the world, would be affected. My friends. My *sister*. Everyone. We could not fail.

I sucked in a deep breath, steadied my shaking hand, and blasted a jet of air at the doors, slamming them open.

The library was exactly how we'd left it – books and tables strewn all across the room, torn sheets decorated the floor, and more than one bloody red patch staining the ground. Except now, it was host to a small army.

"I should have known you'd come. You can't help sticking your nose where it's not needed."

I picked the blonde with the lank hair out from the large semi-circle of unclassifieds taking up defensive stances. She was standing front and centre, with Kayden and Micah on either side of her.

"Harper," I said. "I should have known you'd come back. Vermin always do."

"I see you've found some friends." She cocked her head to one side, and a smile played across her lips. "Too bad you're outnumbered."

"Too bad you're outclassed. I beat you once, I can do it again."

"Ladies," a deep, rumbling voice cut across us, and my heart skipped a beat. Raphael stepped from the shadows at the back of the room. The curse cube was glowing in his hands, no longer surrounded by the strange web my magic had woven around it. He saw me notice.

"It was very impressive magic," he said. "Intricate. Almost… elegant. I will give you one more chance, Lyssa. Take your rightful place by my side."

"Never." I spat the word at him, the anger coiled in my stomach surprising even me. He pressed his lips together and shook his head.

"I'm disappointed, but I cannot say I am surprised. So be it. Step aside."

"I'm not going to let you do this, Raphael. We're not going to let you do this."

I felt the others forming their own defensive line beside me, cutting Raphael off from his only way out of the library. He tsked, and turned to his small army.

I saw him mouth the words, 'kill them', but no sound came out. He frowned, then uttered the command again, and again, no sound escaped past his lips. Realisation darkened his eyes at the same time as it widened mine. He turned to Kayden, a fireball appearing in his hand in the blink of an eye, but the unclassified was already moving. He ignored my hand beckoning him towards us, and raced straight for Raphael.

"No!" I screamed, as Kayden dived for the curse cube. Raphael threw his fireball, and Kayden tried to dodge, but he wasn't fast enough. It scored just a glancing blow to his leg, but even so, the force of it threw him clear across the room. He crashed into the wall and hit the floor, unmoving. There was absolute silence for a long, drawn-out moment, and then chaos erupted.

The small army ran forwards, some conjuring energy balls, some using types of magic I'd never seen before, and some drawing knives from their belts. The champions held their ground. I saw Felicity's palm glow yellow, and as the first energy ball flew towards our ranks, she directed a blast of air at it and sent it spiralling back towards our attackers, scattering several of them. I stared at her, open-mouthed. Where the hell had she picked up that trick?

"Lyssa!" Alistair shouted from behind me, and I ducked reflexively, throwing up my arms to protect my face. Something burned across my forearm, and a trickle of blood leaked from it. One of Raphael's foot soldiers was closing in on me, pulling another knife from his belt. I threw a fireball at the weapon and he dropped it, clutching his hand with a cry of pain. I conjured a second ball, but before I could throw it, I saw Harper duck away from the battle and make for where Kayden lay unconscious, a flash of silver in her hands.

I forgot all about my attacker and ran straight for her, barging through the scattered unclassifieds, ducking an energy ball someone threw at my head, and leaping over another. There was a scream as one of them hit someone behind me, and I could only hope it was one of the attackers who'd been hit.

Harper reached Kayden and dropped into a crouch over his body. I broke into a sprint over the last few feet separating us and threw myself at her. We smashed into the floor and rolled, the force of my tackle sending us tumbling away from the downed student. Her hands gripped my wrists as we came to a stop with her on top, and I struggled desperately to free my hands. She grinned down at me as I bucked and kicked, trying to fight my way out from under her before she could work out how to attack me while her hands were tied up holding onto me.

It was no good. She was stronger than me, and we both knew it. But unlike her, I hadn't grown up relying on magic my whole life. I lifted my head up, opened my mouth, and sank my teeth into the back of her hand. She howled in pain and jerked her hand away from me, losing her grip on my wrist.

"You bitch! I'm going to—"

I didn't wait around to find out what she was going to do. The second my hand was free, I aimed a full-strength blast of air at her, sending her flying across the room. She crashed into a bookcase and hit the floor hard.

I leapt to my feet, racing over to Kayden and skidded down beside him. I heard movement behind me and spun round, fireball in hand.

"Whoa, easy lass!"

My eyes flickered across Alistair's face, and then back down to Kayden. The hilt of a knife was sticking up from the middle of his chest, and blood had soaked through his clothing and pooled all around him. His face was pale, and his eyes vacant and lifeless as they stared up at the ceiling.

"I'm sorry," Alistair said.

"He came back here for us. To stop this. He tried to warn us about the Daoradh breakout, and when that didn't work, he went back to Raphael to try to stop this. All of this."

I gestured all around at the fighting group, the bodies on the floor, the screams of pain and panic and anger and desperation. After everything he'd been through, he'd still wanted the factions to unite, not fight amongst themselves. To stop Raphael from upending our world. I squared my jaw and rose to my feet. I wasn't going to let his death be for nothing.

"Where is he?"

"Where's who?"

An energy ball zipped at my head. I raised a hand, effortlessly sending it aside with a blast of air. Alistair's eyes widened.

"Where's Raphael?" I ground out. He shook his head.

"He got past us. He's in his wampus form and he's got the cube."

"He didn't portal?"

"Too much magic. They're nae stable."

Which meant I couldn't go by portal, either – even if I had been capable of creating one. Dammit.

"Go," Alistair said. "We'll cover yer long enough to get out o' here."

"You're already outnumbered." I glanced down at Kayden and got that sick feeling in the pit of my stomach again. This wasn't just some trial for the dumb cup. People were dying.

"He's right," Felicity called, and I jerked my head up to see her tossing one of the unclassifieds across the room. "We'll hold them off. I hate to admit it, but you're our best chance of stopping him. But this doesn't mean I like you."

I looked between them for a long moment, and nodded my head. They knew what was at stake here, and they'd made their choice. I didn't have any right to stop them.

"On three," Alistair said, locking eyes with Felicity. "One... Two... Three!"

The pair of them spun and started throwing fire and air at everyone between me and the door. I tucked my head down and sprinted, locking my eyes onto the narrow opening. An energy ball flew over my head, missing me by inches, exploding against the doorframe, and then another. There was a loud crash from behind me, and the energy balls stop coming.

I threw one last look over my shoulder at the chaos of the battle, and then dived out into the corridor, and pounded along the ancient stone hallways. How much of a head start had Raphael had? And how long would it take him to activate the curse cube once he reached the Tilimeuse Tree?

I swore, and pushed myself harder. There was no way I could make it there in time. I was fit, but I couldn't outrun a damned wampus. I threw myself into the academy's back door, and out into the grounds, and almost ran straight into the answer.

Chapter Thirty

Stormclaw! Am I ever glad to see you, boy."

With that strange intuitive streak of his, he seemed to understand my urgency, and dropped down into a crouch, lifting his uninjured claw for me to scramble up on, and then onto his back. I hooked my legs over his shoulders.

"Wait, your leg! You're hurt, can you run?"

The hippogryff snorted in what I was sure was derision, and then spread his wings on either side of him.

"Right. You don't need to run. Got it."

With two massive beats of his feathered wings, we rose up into the skies. I turned him towards the Tilimeuse Tree in the centre of the grounds, and we raced through the night air. I shivered violently, wishing I still had my cloak, shredded or not, and tried to press myself as close to him as possible for warmth. I was going to have a hard time saving the academy if I froze stiff and plummeted to my death first. Good job we were flying low enough that I was probably just going to break all my bones if I fell. That sounded like fun.

In the distance, I saw the silvered branches of the Tilimeuse Tree stretching up into the night, stark against the dark skyline.

"Come on," I called to Stormclaw, urging him on with my hands and legs. Below us, nearing the tree, I could make out a tawny cat that could almost have been mistaken for a lion – if it wasn't for its six legs and two tails, and the glowing cube in its mouth.

Raphael.

He was a skin walker, not a shifter – his transformation was the result of a spell he'd learned – which meant his senses were only a muted version of a true wampus cat. I didn't think he'd caught our scent yet. But there was no time to sneak up on him, not if we wanted to stop him before he fully-activated the cube.

Stormclaw swooped down towards the tree, and below us, the cat's form distorted and changed before my eyes, until Raphael was standing there, holding the glowing curse cube in his hands. The gryff touched down lightly, with a grunt of pain as his talon took his weight, and I vaulted from his back. Raphael spun around, the light from the cube casting shadows over his face.

"You don't know when to quit, do you?" he demanded.

"I guess it's a family trait."

"I am beyond expecting you to understand. You have already proved yourself incapable of higher reasoning. But this must be done to ensure the supremacy of the druid race."

"We're not better than any of the other magical races. Or the mundane ones, for that matter."

"You dare to compare me to a mundane?" His voice rose in anger. There never had been any question where my temper came from. "I am nothing like those lowly animals!"

"That's why my mother hid us amongst them," I said, fighting to keep my voice casual while every muscle in my body twitched and screamed at me to run. "She knew you'd be too blinded by your hatred to ever look for us there."

"Us?" His voice was low and dangerous, and his entire body had gone still. I could feel the menace leaking from him.

"Oh, you didn't know? After she left you, after she *got away* from you, she found someone else. She fell in love with him."

"She loved me!"

I laughed, it felt like coughing up razor blades, but I forced the sound from my throat anyway.

"How could she? You don't even know what love is. You're not capable of understanding it. She never loved you. She *hated* you. Why do you think she went to such length to make sure you never found us – found me?"

"Where is she now?"

"Dead." My voice had a strange, empty ring to it, and the word hung in the air between us. I watched the closest thing I'd ever seen to grief pass over Raphael's face.

"How?"

It was time to change the subject before he realised I didn't have a clue, just the grey image the Tilimeuse Tree planted in my mind. I gestured around me.

"Is this your idea of a family reunion? Because, you know, there better ways to catch up."

"Ah. You don't know, either."

"No, I don't," I snapped, my voice hot with anger. "You took that from me, and I'll be damned if I'm going to let you take my home, too."

"Let me? My, my, what high opinions you have of yourself."

"Another family trait, I guess."

The fireball flew at my head so quickly I barely had time to see it coming. I flung up a hand and deflected it with a gust of air that sent it flying into the distance.

"You learn fast," Raphael said. "You could have been powerful. Your death will be a waste."

"We'll see about that," I said, and flung a fireball of my own. Raphael swatted it aside with embarrassing ease. Crap. He threw two more of his own in quick succession. I dived aside and hit the dirt, reigniting the dull ache of a hundred bruises all over my body. So much for keeping him talking until help arrived. If help was even coming. I really sucked at making plans.

I rolled and came up in a crouch, barely avoiding another fireball, and glanced back at the smouldering spot I'd been lying in a split second before. Raphael wasn't holding back. He'd meant that to kill me. I hurled another fireball and sprinted towards the tree, throwing two more on the run. He raised a hand and sent all three into the dirt, his expression bored. He was bored. I was barely staying alive here, and he was *bored*. I was so far beyond screwed it would have been laughable if the future of the whole druidic world hadn't been hanging in the balance.

He spun another fireball in my direction, and this time I didn't get my hand up in time. The ball thudded into my hip, the force of it throwing me through the air. I hit the ground hard, pain screaming through my entire body and bursting out of my lips in an agonised howl.

Raphael turned away from me and started muttering an incantation over the curse box. I swallowed my pain. This was it. This was my moment. I lifted one hand, ignoring the whimpers that were still spilling from my lips, and focused on conjuring a fireball. Nothing happened. No fireball. Not so much as a flicker. I gritted my teeth as another wave of agony washed over me, and tried then again, but my hand stayed resolutely empty, my palm mocking me with its ordinary-coloured flesh. No matter how I tried, I couldn't gather my scattered energy. Every time I got close, the pain broke through and shattered my focus, leaving me gasping in the dirt, the smell of charred skin heavy in my nostrils. My charred skin. My stomach heaved, and I didn't dare look down at my hip. It didn't matter. Once I got out of here, Madam Leechington would heal it. I just had to stop Raphael. Somehow.

I tried to sit up and focus my eyes on him, but the movement sent a lance of agony through me and I sank back, panting. Too painful. That wasn't going to happen. My head pounded ferociously and my vision swam. I raised a hand to it and something hot and sticky leaked over my fingers. I must've hit my head when he threw me. I bit down hard on my lip, and rolled over onto my uninjured side. The movement pulled at the fabric stuck to my burned skin, and I screwed my eyes shut, willing the agony to fade. Blacking out seemed like a good idea right about now. I could just wake up in a nice, warm, soft hospital bed, with Leech lecturing me about reckless behaviour and diverting her attention from patients who really needed it.

Except if I didn't find a way to stop Raphael, there would be no hospital wing, no Dragondale academy, and very probably, no me. He wasn't exactly vying for father of the year anymore. The only reason he hadn't finished me off was because he thought I was already done. He was making a habit of underestimating me. I was going to have to punish him for that. Maybe just a little nap first.

I sank back into the dirt. I'd spent a lot of time in the dirt today. I was going to have to wash my clothes when I got in. Except my cloak. I was just going to buy a new one of those, and then I was going to stop getting thrown off hippogryffs. I didn't like riding very much anymore. It wasn't much fun when you kept getting beat up. My head hurt. I rested it on the ground and stared up at the sky. The stars had come out. That was nice. It was cold. Except my hip. I whimpered again. My hip was so hot, it hurt so bad.

The wind changed direction, disturbing my almost-nap with the irritating, repetitive sound it carried my way. A voice, chanting. Raphael's voice. I groaned. He was going to activate the damned cube and plug it into the tree somehow, and the nap I wanted would become a permanent state. I groaned again and hauled my head out of the mud. No rest for the wicked. Who knew getting hit by a fireball hurt this damned much? Geez.

I paused to get my breath, disappointed to discover I was only halfway to sitting up and leaned back on my elbows for a moment. I rolled my head back in frustration – I was sure I hadn't always been this much of a wimp. A flash of movement caught my eye in the treeline. I squinted, trying to make out the dark shadow shifting between them, but the more I tried to focus, the more blurred it became, until I couldn't make it out entirely. I blinked. The head injury. Maybe I was seeing things. But I'd been sure…

Raphael's chanting rose in pitch, building towards a crescendo. Whatever he was doing to the cube, it was almost done. Time was running out. *Come on, Lyssa, dammit! Show a little spine!* Clamping my teeth down on my lip so hard I almost bit right through it, I forced myself to sit the rest of the way up. The sudden surge of pain made my head spin, but I wasn't going to let it stop me. I tried for another fireball, but still nothing. No matter. I wasn't going to let that stop me, either. I was going to stop Raphael from activating the curse cube even if I had to walk over there and knock him out.

Only… ow. Yeah, walking wasn't such a great plan right now. I managed to get into a crouch, but when it came to pushing myself up into a stand, it felt like someone was setting my hip on fire all over again. I collapsed back into a crumbled heap. No way was I getting up without some help.

Raphael turned to glance at me over his shoulder. Shit. He must have heard me fall. He frowned – I guess he'd already written me off. See? Underestimating me, all the time. What sort of parental example is that? He didn't throw another fireball, which was just as well, because I was in no state to dodge one right now. He could have finished me off with a flick of his hand, but he hadn't. Not that I wasn't grateful, but he didn't seem the sort to leave unfinished business. And then I got it. The curse cube was floating in the air between him and the tree, and both of his hands were tied up in the spell.

If there was one thing I'd learned in Atherton's classes – and let's be fair, there probably was only one thing I'd learned – it was that you never, ever interrupted a spell once you'd started. For the low-level stuff, it'd just leave you feeling a little queasy and lightheaded, but the more complex and powerful the spell, the more dangerous it got. And Raphael's take-over-the-world spell was as powerful as they came. If he stopped now, it could be deadly. If only I wasn't busy lying in a heap on the floor.

"Looks like I'm not the only one stuck here," I said. "Too bad your little army is too busy having its ass kicked to come help you."

He eyed me with derision, and I couldn't be certain I wasn't slurring my words a little. It was hard to decide which hurt most, my hip, my head, or my ego, but I couldn't afford to focus on that. I had to make Raphael stop the spell. I made another attempt to push myself up from the floor, but it was doomed to failed.

"What sort of self-respecting super villain runs out of minions, anyway? Guess your recruitment power isn't quite what it was before I thwarted your plans. Twice. Well, three times after tonight."

He raised an eyebrow in what I took for amusement, and to be fair, three times was going to be a stretch, what with the plethora of injuries and the fact he was the most powerful man in druidic history. What can I say? I've always been an optimist.

"You tried to stir up trouble with the shifters, too, didn't you? You knew we couldn't fight a war on two fronts. And I guess it would have been win-win for you – if the shifters had reduced our numbers, the better your chances of beating us. And if we'd defeated them, well, it's no secret that you want them wiped out. And either way, we'd have kept each other tied up while you waltzed in and took control. Do you want to know where you went wrong?"

It had been too much to hope for that he'd actually let his temper get the better of him while he was working, but like I said, I was an optimist. He was just too disciplined. He didn't even falter in the incantation. He didn't even turn to *look* at me. That was probably a mistake.

The big gryff moved in near-silence across the damp ground, favouring his front leg as he crept towards me, with his usual instinctive understanding of the situation. I kept talking as Stormclaw moved closer, figuring if I suddenly shut up it might make him suspicious enough to turn around.

"Unlike you, we have friends in the pack. People who actually care about us, people who have a vested interest in not going to war."

Stormclaw dropped into a mounting bow beside me and raised one claw. I looked at him helplessly. There was absolutely no way I could scramble up onto his claw. It was too high from down here, and I couldn't get to my feet. Stormclaw quirked his head at me and blinked his bird-like eyes. Then, he did something I've never seen a gryff do. He sank right to the ground beside me, stretching himself out flat. I shuffled forwards through the dirt, biting back a hiss of pain.

"See, that's the trouble with having underlings instead of friends," I said. "Your underlings only do their jobs, and only for as long as they think you're going to win."

I slivered on top of Stormclaw, and grabbed two big handfuls of his neck feathers. He wasn't going to thank me for that, but I figured he'd forgive me so long as none of them actually came out.

"Friends, on the other hand, have your back. Stormclaw, up!"

Raphael spun on his heel to face me as Stormclaw lurched to his feet. I clung to him as he moved, just managing to get my legs into position on either side of his neck. Pain shot along my hip, and I couldn't hold back a strangled cry, but I managed to stay on board. For a moment I thought Raphael was going to break his focus and speak, or blast us with another fireball, but he did neither. Instead, he sped up his incantation, and the cube started to drift through the air towards the Tilimeuse Tree. If it got there, we were finished.

"Stormclaw, go!" I aimed him straight at Raphael. If I interrupted the spell, the backlash could kill us all. If I didn't, it would destroy Dragondale. There was no choice to make.

The black and gold beast surged forwards, and Raphael's eyes went wide. The cube edged closer to the tree, but it felt like we were moving in slow motion. We were never going to make it. The injured gryff's gait tossed me around on his back, each movement sending fire lancing through my wounds.

I lifted one hand from Stormclaw's neck, and with a scream of pain and terror and frustration and pure fury, I conjured a fireball. It was streaked with blue and green and yellow, so that the swirling mass of flames seemed to pulse with the power of all four elements. We were only six feet away when the ball flew from my hand, and struck Raphael squarely in the chest. The force threw him backwards and the curse cube froze mid-air. The glow surrounding it dimmed for a heartbeat, and then bright light flashed out of it in a shockwave, the force of the energy smashing into me and Stormclaw. I felt his legs buckle underneath him, and then I was catapulted through the air like a ragdoll, and smashed into the ground besides the unmoving body of Raphael. A split second later, the cube's light blinked out, and it fell to the floor, spent.

The night started to close in on me, and as I lost my tenuous grip on consciousness, one last thought drifted through my mind:

I really *need to stop riding gryffs.*

Chapter Thirty-One

I think she's waking up!"

"Ow, no need to shout," I mumbled. Or at least I tried to. I wasn't entirely sure that the sounds that made it out of my mouth could have passed for words. I opened one eye a crack, but everything was too blurry to make out much beyond vague shapes, and my ears were still ringing from the oddly-familiar voice announcing my return to the world of the living. My sense of smell was about the only thing that seemed to be working right now, and it told me I knew this place. It smelled like home. More specifically, it smelled like Dragondale's medical wing.

Well, I wasn't dead, and we'd all survived long enough for me to wind up here. Again. That was something, I supposed.

"Stormclaw?" I croaked.

"Exactly how many times do you intend to wind up in my wing asking about that animal?"

Madam Leechington leaned over me, coming into focus for a second before blurring out again.

"Give me some room to work, please," she said brusquely over her shoulder.

"Sorry, Madam Leechington," a voice replied, and this time I recognised it. "Is she okay?"

"Ava?"

"I'm right here, Lyssa," she said.

"And you shouldn't be," hmphed Leechington. "As for how she is, I would be able to answer you faster if you stopped interrupting my work."

Her matronly frame came back into focus, and this time she didn't blur out again. Her hands fussed around, projecting tiny pulses of energy at me here and there, which bounced back to her hands. She frowned slightly as she interpreted their feedback, which might have been concerning if I didn't know that the frown was as much a part of her uniform as the white robes. When it came to me, at least.

"You had a nasty accident," Madam Leechington said, peering at my face. "How much of it do you remember?"

It was my turn to frown, wrinkling up my forehead as I tried to remember what had happened right before I got here.

"Raphael. The curse."

"Quite. You're lucky not to be dead, interrupting a spell like that. The backlash could have killed you. You were very foolish." Her expression softened. "And very brave."

"Stormclaw?" I asked again. Leechington straightened and huffed out a sigh.

"Yes, as I understand it that wretched animal is alive and getting better by the day. Do you know how many fingers I've had to reattach in the last two weeks?"

My lips spread themselves into a smile. Stormclaw must be on the mend if he was taking snaps at people. Then Leech's words sunk in.

"Wait. Two weeks? How long have I been out for?"

"A little under two months."

"Two months? Are you joking?"

"I do not joke, Ms Eldridge," Leechington said sternly, crossing her arms over her chest. "As I said, you are lucky to be alive. Now, if you think you can resist the urge to put yourself in mortal danger for five minutes, I must inform Professor Talendale you're awake."

"I don't think she likes me much," I mumbled, as the healer turned on her heel and bustled away.

"Could have fooled me," Ava said. "She's been fussing around you non-stop since you got here."

"Professional pride," I grunted, trying and failing to lever myself into a sitting position.

"You should probably take it easy," Ava said, concern creasing her forehead.

"I've been doing that for two months. I want to sit up."

Ava chewed her lip for a moment, then nodded and slid an arm behind my shoulders. With her help, we managed to get me sitting and leaning back against the headboard. She handed me a glass of water, and I drank deeply before handing it back to her and speaking again.

"Not to sound ungrateful, but where are Sam and Kelsey?" A sudden thought hit me like a punch to the gut, and my head started spinning. "Are they... They're not..."

I couldn't quite get the words out as I searched Ava's face. She opened her mouth in an 'o' of surprise as she caught my meaning, then quickly rushed to reassure me.

"No. No, they're fine. They're just in class at the moment. Professor Talendale excused me from lessons so I could stay with you as much as I wanted... since we're related."

I leaned my head back against the headboard and closed my eyes in relief, waiting for the dizziness to pass. They were okay. They'd both survived the events of last— Of two months ago. That was going to take some getting used to. And it wasn't the only thing.

"I'm sorry. Is it okay that I'm... do you want me to leave?"

I snapped my eyes open to see Ava looking anxious, chewing at her lip again. Guilt flushed through me. She'd misunderstood my reaction. I could see the rejection all over her face. I'd barely had time to process the fact that she was my sister, but she had. For two whole months.

I'd had family before, but she never had, not really. And now she thought I was rejecting her.

"Don't be silly," I said, lifting my hand and putting it on hers. It felt like trying to weightlift a hippogryff. "Of course I want you here. You're family. And thank you, for staying."

Her face relaxed, and she dropped back into a chair that had been set up next to my bed. She really had been spending a lot of time here.

"I hope you're not falling behind on your studies, though, not for me."

She hefted a book from the floor and gave me a small smile.

"Courtesy of Professor Atherton. He threatened to drag me off to the dungeon if I didn't keep up with his work."

"Ah, of course." Far be it for Atherton to remember that people were human and needed to be cut a bit slack occasionally.

I gnawed on my lip for a moment, and then said;

"Did you know her? Our mum."

Her lips pressed together, and her hand moved to her locket, her fingers playing unconsciously across its intricate design. She shook her head.

"I'm sorry. Her and my dad died when I was a baby. Her name was Violet."

"Violet." I rolled the word around my mouth. My mum's name was Violet.

"She had no other family, at least, that's what the adoption agency said. That's how we ended up in the system. I was supposed to be adopted by a couple here in England, but it fell through and I ended up in care, in Georgia."

Georgia. That's where my parents, my adoptive parents, had been from, before they moved to England. When I found out I was adopted, they'd said they moved here for me, that it was a request in my birth mother's will. I guess she'd wanted us both to be raised here, in her home country. Near to Dragondale. A mix up at the airport meant the few things I'd had of my birth mother's had been lost.

"It's a lot to take in, I know," Ava said, entwining her hands and looking off to one side. Abruptly, she stooped to pick something up from the floor. "This is for you. I had a copy made."

She placed a small scrap of paper in my hand. My mother's face smiled up at me from a copy of the photo Ava kept in her locket.

"Thank you," I said, my voice a raspy whisper. Ava placed her hand over mine, giving it a small squeeze.

I heard the click of a door closing, and Ava twisted her head round to look at something out of my eyeline, then quickly got to her feet. I tried to follow the direction of her gaze, but my head refused to co-operate. I'd forgotten how much fun it was waking up after you'd been out for a couple of weeks. Or months.

"Professor Talendale," Ava said, inclining her head in greeting. I frowned. That was way too respectful for any sister of mine. We were going to have to work on bringing out her rebellious streak.

"Good afternoon, Ava," Professor Talendale said in reply, stepping into my line of sight. "I believe they are serving lunch in the main hall. Perhaps you would care to go and join your friends. I understand you've been missing quite a few meals recently, and we can't have that."

His tone was benign, but I couldn't miss the instruction to leave us alone. Ava didn't miss it either.

"Yes, Professor. See you later, Lyssa."

"Bye," I mumbled, as she hurried off.

"Ah, Lyssa," Professor Talendale said once we were alone, shaking his head mournfully. "I seem to recall you made me a promise that we wouldn't keep having these end of year chats. Though I must confess I am rather glad you seem incapable of keeping that promise."

There was a twinkle in his eye. I wouldn't have gone so far as to call it pride, but I figured I wasn't being expelled, and I'd take that win any day of the week. He sank into the seat Ava had recently vacated, and folded his hands neatly in his lap.

"It was quite the thing you did," he said quietly. "Very brave."

I wasn't quite sure how to respond to that, so I stared down at my immaculately clean hands – no gryff grime coating them, no leather cleaner from looking after the tack. No dirt to pick from under my nails.

"Professor," I said after a long moment of examining nothing. "How are the others? Did they..." I swallowed. "Did they survive?"

It was a stupid question, I knew that. We had taken fatalities even before I'd gone up against Raphael.

"We lost sixteen lives," Talendale said. "Seven druids, and nine shifters."

"Who?" I croaked. For a moment I didn't think he would answer me, then he seemed to come to a decision.

"The riders Quinn and Caleb," he said, watching me closely. "Ian and Christopher. And the champions Aderyn, Kieran, and Callum."

I blinked hard, and tried to swallow the lump in my throat that was threatening to suffocate me. They'd been my friends. Classmates. I'd sent over half of them to their deaths. And the champions...

"They died protecting me. Kayden, too."

"They died doing what had to be done to stop Raphael," Talendale said sternly, meeting my eye and holding it. "Lyssa, were it not for your actions, there would have been many more deaths that night."

I couldn't see it that way. Maybe in time, maybe when their faces weren't fresh behind my eyelids, maybe when I couldn't hear my instructions to them ringing in my ears. But not right now. I swallowed the damned lump again, and asked the question that had been nagging me since I awoke.

"What about Raphael?"

"Captured," Talendale said. "Along with many of his followers – those who survived the assault."

"He's alive?"

"Indeed, though it does not seem possible. It would seem he is more powerful than even we had anticipated. Ah, it would appear you have another visitor."

He rose from his seat and gave a curt bow to the newcomer. Frustratingly, I had to wait until he came into my eyeline before I could see who the visitor was, and when he did, I gave a little gasp.

"Caul– I mean, Head Councilman Cauldwell."

Maybe I wasn't the right person to teach Ava about rebelliousness after all. Cauldwell's face took on the usual disgruntled expression it got whenever he looked at me – that is, as though he was wondering why I wasn't locked in Daoradh, and if there was anything he could do to change that. And then he did something that took me by surprise. He extended his hand to me.

Tentatively, half-expecting it to turn into a snake and bite me, because honestly that seemed more likely than this, I lifted my hand from the bed and accepted his. His grip was firm, and the handshake was brief. I was relieved. The snake might have been less dangerous.

"We owe you a great debt, Ms Eldridge. The four primal plants have survived, and their academies restored to their former state. It is not often I speak these words, so heed them. I misjudged you, and you have my personal gratitude."

I was dreaming. I died when Stormclaw threw me. That was the only logical explanation. I was dead. This was the afterlife. Except Cauldwell was no angel.

"Thank you?" I ventured, making it into a question.

"I did not become the head of the Grand Council by blindly ignoring that which is right in front of me. You were a great asset to Dragondale on the night of the battle. A great asset."

I really wasn't used to having praise heaped on me – the opposite, usually – and I squirmed uncomfortably.

"I am aware you are still recovering from your injuries, so I will keep this brief. I am here to offer you a job, once you complete the formality of your exams, of course. I would like you to accept a position within the enforcers – a career to which I believe you are uniquely suited."

A *job*? I frowned. With the enforcers? I said the first thing that came into my head.

"I didn't take Spellcrafting."

"Well, no matter. There will, of course, be a good deal more studying before you qualify as an enforcer, and I have no doubt that our instructors could bring you up to speed in that time. You need not make a decision right now. Think it over, and come back to me by the end of the year. Professor Talendale knows how to reach me."

"Um, okay." It wasn't exactly a fitting thing to say to an offer like that, but hey, I'd just survived the lethal backlash of a curse. I was a little off my game. Cauldwell nodded once, wrapped his cloak from him, and swept from the room. Talendale looked down at me with a smile. I frowned.

"Wait, did he just say exams?"

That hardly seemed fair. We'd just saved the entire academy, surely we could cancel exams this year?

"In five weeks. Plenty of time for you to catch up to your classmates."

Sure, if I was Kelsey, maybe. I mean, I'd been behind in half the subjects to start with, before I took a two-month siesta. My head was hurting just thinking about it.

"I think I need to sleep," I said.

"Quite," Talendale agreed. "And so you shall. Certainly Madam Leechington won't thank me for keeping you from your rest. But I must impose on her hospitality a moment longer."

I blinked. I had no idea what he was going on about, and I was really starting to feel tired. Talendale took a slow breath.

"In light of these... recent events, the Grand Council deemed it appropriate to cancel the remaining trials in the Four Nations Cup. However, your fellow surviving champions pleaded for one last trial, in honour of your fallen comrades. Their argument was most compelling. Dragondale will play host to the final challenge. Do you wish to compete?"

"Do I– Yes!" I straightened a little in my bed. "Yes, Professor. Very much."

Three of them were dead, their funerals no doubt long since carried out. This was the only way I could pay my respects, and I would take to the field one last time, even if I had to crawl.

Talendale nodded.

"Excellent. We shall schedule it for the weekend after the exams, because I fear you do not need any further distractions from your studies."

Yeah, he was probably right about that. On the other hand, I was already wondering if I could convince Professor Swann to give me some extra training while I was stuck here.

"And, of course," Talendale added, with a glimmer in his eye, "We want to be sure Dragondale's champion is fully recovered."

Chapter Thirty-Two

It was a long five weeks before the exams. Kelsey, Ava, and Sam all visited me in the hospital wing regularly to help with my revision in the first fortnight – though, truth be told, Sam was more of a hinderance than a help – until Leechington agreed I could return to my dorm and my usual schedule, so long as I reported back to her the moment I felt ill. It was like déjà vu, right down to visiting Stormclaw, though at least this time round he was faring a lot better. Paisley had taken over his care during the last week of my stay, and consequently Madam Leechington was no longer complaining about dealing with extra injuries caused by cantankerous beasts. I slipped down to the paddocks to see Firefly, too. He'd turned up the day after the battle, showered Alden with blades of grass while she bandaged his leg, and had made a full recovery.

Going back to class was weird – there were empty seats in most of our lessons, and I felt a little bit sick every time I accidentally set eyes on one of them. The professors seemed determined to drag us all up to examination standard kicking and screaming, so I didn't have too much time to dwell, and before I knew it, exam day was upon us. I was glad all over again that we'd dropped a couple of lessons at the start of the year, so that I only had five exams. Any more than that and I think my head would have exploded, and I wasn't sure even Old Leech could fix that.

Druidic Law was a written exam, and it had lasted so long I was pretty sure I'd given myself carpal tunnel by the time we finished, but at least I hadn't spent half the time chewing the top of my pen like Liam. That had to be a good sign.

Fortunately, the other four exams were all practical. Unfortunately, they were insanely hard. For potions, Professor Brennan dumped a mass of grey goop in front of me, and told me to fix it. I was allowed to ask him three questions about the potion – though sadly that didn't include 'What went wrong?' and 'How can I fix it?' I knew, because I tried. Well, if you don't ask, you don't get, right? But in this case, if you asked, you still didn't get. In the end, I settled for asking what the potion was intended to do, which ingredients had been added, and how long ago the potion had been started. And then I proceeded to dump half the contents of the room into the potion, in the hopes of making it look more like the product of science and magic, and less like yesterday's leftover porridge. Whether I succeeded was a matter of opinion.

Botany was better. Ellerby put five plants in front of me, told me to identify the one that could be used to cure creeping rot, and grow it an inch. The small bushy plants were all similar, but I knew that the one with the jagged leaves would induce vomiting, and the one with the darker green leaves was an anticoagulant – it would make the rot spread faster. But the one with the slight scent of pine smoke when you rubbed its leaves was an anti-inflammatory – and if it was crushed with pepper seeds and ingested, it would reduce the swelling and let the rot leak out. I transferred it into a limestone soil, warmed a small can of water and then trickled it into the pot, and directed a steady pulse of heat at the plant for the next hour. We weren't allowed to measure our plants, but I was feeling pretty confident by the time I left.

Next was Supernatural Zoology, and it was a cakewalk. I mean, when a unicorn had bowed to you, handling a shug monkey was nothing. Alden had even looked impressed by the time I finished.

Our last exam was Advanced Elemental Manipulation, and Swann had already warned me what to expect. Now that I was showing four elemental powers, the Grand Council had decided that I should be tested on each, but that my tertiary and quaternary powers only needed to be tested to a second-year standard. Which was great, because I had precious little control of my Earth power, what with having only discovered it a few days before I spent two months unconscious. But if nothing else, battling an all-powerful super-druid and his army gives you ample opportunity to hone your skills. The exam didn't give me too many problems. I wasn't getting a perfect pass any time soon, but I was pretty sure Swann wouldn't fail me, either.

And then, abruptly, exams were done, and that part of my life at Dragondale was over. No more classes, no more studying. Soon, I'd be leaving here, saying goodbye to my classmates, most of whom I'd probably never see again. There was an air of quiet melancholy that mingled with the excitement and anticipation of the third years. Our future was awaiting us, but to meet it, we'd have to say goodbye to a big part of our past.

Talendale didn't allow me to ride in the final Itealta game of the season – apparently the Four Nations Cup took priority, and for once I didn't disagree. Devon and the rest of the Fires did a great job without me, lifting the Itealta cup for the third year running. They wore black armbands, and dedicated both the game and the cup to Quinn and Caleb, a solemn reminder of the sacrifices some had made so we could be here. True to her word, Alden arranged for a talent scout from the Essex Hornets – the country's top team – to be there, and I couldn't help but feel that when Devon graduated, there would be a position in one of the professional teams awaiting him. Knowing the sacrifice he was asking of me, Talendale had personally vouched for my skill as a rider to the talent scout, and Alden explained I'd trained the team, and would have been riding had I not been called by more pressing duties on the international stage.

No pressure, then.

But when the morning of the final trial came around, on the last Saturday of term, the atmosphere was different to how it had been before. At the other trials, each of the champions had been gunning for first place, and the home crowd had cheered on their own champions with almost religious zeal.

When we gathered in the centre of the stadium to start the final challenge, there was no animosity. The five of us stood shoulder to shoulder, and the stadium fell silent as we paid our respects to those who weren't here today. Then Alistair raised his head and shot me a wink.

"Don't think this means I'm going tae go easy on you, lass."

With dramatic flair, Talendale unveiled the cup, standing on a plinth in the middle of the stadium, so close I could almost touch it. The crowd went wild, screaming and stamping their feet. That cup belonged in our trophy room.

"The first champion to lift the cup will be deemed the winner," the commentator announced, "and his or her name will go down in history as the Supreme Champion of the Four Nations Cup!"

More cheering burst from the crowd, echoing around the packed arena, and I fixed my eyes on the magnificent cup. It stood three feet tall and was made of polished gold that reflected the sunlight in a thousand glittering orbs around the arena. I could feel the faint pulse of magic woven into the metal, and the names of former supreme champions seemed to swirl in its surface. My name could be the next to join them.

"Champions, please move to the north end of the field."

We did so, and immediately a ring of fire sprung up around the cup, shooting thirty feet into the air. The flames were orange and gold, streaked with hints of black. They were no ordinary flames. That was dragon fire.

"Guess I won't be using my fire power to put those flames out," I muttered.

"Or my water power," Riley agreed, sounding just a little regretful.

"Champions," the commentator called. "You will find what you need to get through the fire in a sealed chamber. The chamber you have been assigned, and the difficulty of what lies within, has been determined according to your current ranking in the Four Nations Cup. Should you decide to withdraw, send three long energy pulses into the air, and your mentor will extract you."

I nodded to myself. Get to the chamber, grab whatever would get me through the dragon fire, get back here before everyone else. Easy, right? Except I was pretty sure I didn't rank near the top, not after getting distracted by the unicorn.

"Entering chamber one, with an impressive fifteen points, Felicity Hutton of Dragondale academy. Entering chambers two and three, tied on a respectable twelve points, Alistair Murray of Selkenloch, and Dylan Griffiths of Gryphonvale. Chamber four goes to Lyssa Eldridge of Dragondale with eleven points. And lastly, entering the final, most dangerous chamber, Riley O'Dell of Dryadale, who competed in only one trial, and earned five points."

Second hardest chamber. Great. A blank portal appeared in front of me before I had time to dwell on that too much. Probably for the best.

"Three. Two. One. Go!"

I raced forward and dived through my portal with considerably less caution than I should have done. Second hardest chamber? I should have known something nasty was going to be lurking on the far side. But even so, I'd never have expected what was waiting for me.

The roar was like a shockwave through the air, shaking the ground beneath me – literally. I sucked in a deep breath as the trembling stopped, and stared across the open plain at the massive beast that had the head and wings of an eagle, and the body of a lion. A really, really pissed off lion.

Ares.

Alden's psychotic pet gryphon. I let out a low breath, then immediately froze as he snorted loudly, his breath kicking up a cloud of dust, and turned his black eyes on me. Oh, shit. I so did *not* want to end up as his next meal.

…But I wasn't about to send up a panic pulse just yet.

The beast turned his massive bulk, moving with a feline grace, lashing his leonine tail through the dirt. I needed to keep him busy long enough to look around this place, preferably before he started getting ideas about lunch. The enclosure was about an acre – a lot of ground to cover on two legs, but not so much when you had four legs and wings. And a deadly set of talons. It was important not to forget those.

Most of it was dust and dirt, and the remains of what looked like some sort of animal. I couldn't see anything that looked like it would protect me from dragon fire, but I guessed it wasn't exactly going to be lying in plain sight.

Ares huffed up another cloud of dust, lowered his head, and started stalking towards me. Uh-oh, time to go.

I held out my hand and directed a blast of air at his feet, throwing up a huge cloud of dust in his eyes. He snarled, snapping his sharp beak at the dust cloud, and I took advantage of his distraction to dart across the enclosure, putting some space between us – and hopefully keeping it there. Alden had once told me that Ares was the most dangerous animal at Dragondale, and nothing I'd seen since then had convinced me she was exaggerating.

I managed to make it the whole way round the perimeter without being mauled, pausing every hundred yards or so to blast more dust at the deadly beast and discourage him from getting too interested in me, but by the time I made the last sprint, he'd given up attacking the dust, and started paying more attention to the person causing it. Worse, I hadn't found a thing on the perimeter run. It looked like the entire enclosure was barren – except for the carcass. There was nothing for it, I was going to have to find a way to get close to the remains of his last meal without becoming his next one. And I didn't figure Ares for the sharing, caring type.

I took a step towards the carcass, and immediately Ares froze, other than his long tail that lashed the air as he tracked me with his eyes. He bellowed a furious roar and I clamped my hands over my ears. No animal needed to be that damned loud. But loud was the least of my problems. I prised my hands loose, and as I did, the gryphon stretched out his powerful wings and beat them a half dozen times. Dust billowed round the entire enclosure, and by the time it cleared enough for me to see him again, he was streaking through the air, graceful in flight. He landed beside the carcass with a thud that shook the earth under my feet, and loosed another mighty roar.

There was nothing for it. I was going to have to lure him away. There was no way this was going to end well.

"Hey, Ares!" I shouted waving my arms at him. "You want seconds?"

He spun round with a guttural grunt than sent shivers through me, but I forced myself to wave my arms above my head again and ignore the tremble in my voice.

"Come and get me, you dumb beast!"

He charged, his muscular legs devouring the ground beneath him, and I suddenly realised it wasn't the luring part that was going to be difficult. I threw up another cloud of dust, but this time he charged right through it, his dark eyes unblinking and fixed on me.

Looked like it would be plan B. Too bad I hadn't planned that far in advance. I threw up a wall of fire in front of me, and Ares skidded to a halt, then loped in a circle and took to the air. Crap. Time to go.

I clenched my fist and opened a hole in the wall of fire, darting straight through it. Ares bellowed in rage and swooped down at me. I threw one hand over my head and projected a dome of fire above me. Ares bellowed again and rose back up into the air, tracking me from way too close for comfort. A split second of distraction, and he'd be on me. So it was a really bad time to stumble.

I crashed right over the carcass and hit the ground in a gory heap. Great. Now I smelled like lunch, too. This just kept getting better. The fire above me flickered and went out. Ares screeched in renewed fury and victory, and dived towards me. I scanned the carcass frantically, trying to find whatever I'd just risked my life for, and for a heart-stopping moment, I thought I'd misjudged and the gryphon would crush the life from me for getting between him and his kill before anyone could stop him. I could smell his rancid breath, and his entire bulk blotted out the sun as he closed in on me, talons extended towards my head.

Wait, there! I saw it hanging from the exposed rib cage – a black leather drawstring pouch. I reached out through the cloud of dust kicked up by the gryphon's wings and snagged it, just as one of his talons touched my back and–

The scream that burst from my lips was fear rather than pain, and it took me a second to process that not only was I not being shredded by a pissed off Ares, I was no longer in the gryphon enclosure, either. Result.

I rolled over onto my back, gasping, my hand still wound tightly around the pouch.

"No time for a nap, Dragondale," a voice called cheerfully, and my eyes snapped open to see Alistair loping past me, his own pouch dangling from his hand. Shit. He was right. I'd have to savour being alive later. Right now, I had a trial to win.

I hauled myself to my feet, looking around me for the first time. Of course. A weary smile spread over my face. I knew exactly where we were. I'd been here hundreds of times before. The gryff barn.

The training paddock was filled with over a dozen gryffs, just as it had been that day of the tryouts. It seemed like another lifetime.

Alden had pulled the best and the bravest of our herd from the field. No surprise. After all, we were going to be asking them to fly through fire.

I took a second to scan the faces – both gryff and human. I counted three other people, and frowned.

"Where's Felicity?" I called to Alistair, as I pulled myself over the fence.

"Pulsed out," he called back, grabbing a set of reins. I snagged one too. The gryffs were all wearing adapted head collars already, they just needed reins to be attached. There were no saddles to be seen. Looked like we were going to be finishing the challenge bareback.

I had no idea what had happened to Felicity to make her forfeit the challenge when she'd had the easiest animal, but I didn't have time to worry about that now. Not if I was going to get to the cup first. Alistair and Dylan were already approaching their chosen gryffs, and Riley was trying to haul herself over the fence, one leg dripping blood.

I searched amongst the gryffs for the outline I'd spotted moments before, and there he was, off in one corner, his feathers shining black and laced with gold.

"Stormclaw!" I called.

He quirked his head to one side, then squealed and came trotting over to me, barging one of the other gryffs aside. I gave him a quick pat on the neck, then hooked the reins on his bridle and opened my leather pouch, already knowing what I would find inside. I reached in and removed the two shimmering green discs that were just small enough to fit in the palm of my hand. Dragon scales. I crammed one in my back pocket and slipped the other into a small sleeve on Stormclaw's headcollar. Now we could fly straight through the dragon fire without being burned.

I grabbed the reins and led him to the nearest fence. As I did, I heard the loud flapping of wings and saw Alistair take to the skies on Riverquil. Cursing, I climbed up the fence and scrambled onto Stormclaw's back. So much for never riding a gryff again.

"Up, Stormclaw!" I shouted, still scrabbling to get my legs in place. He spread his wings and took us into the air, chasing after Riverquil with a squeal of delight. Below me, I heard the other two riders urging their gryffs to follow us. It was going to be close.

The stadium wasn't far from the gryff barn – if I wanted to overtake Alistair then I didn't have long to do it. And I *really* wanted to overtake Alistair.

"Come on, boy," I urged Stormclaw on, and I felt him gather himself under me and push forward. Already the stadium was in sight, and Riverquil was just a single length in front of us. Stormclaw beat his wings harder, and steadily we gained on the leading pair, until we were neck and neck. I twisted my head round and shot a grin at him.

"No time for a leisurely ride, Selkenloch," I shouted, my words carrying above the beating of gryff wings and the rushing of the wind around us. He laughed, and crouched low over Riverquil's shoulders, urging him on as we flew over the top of the stands and into the stadium.

The roar of the dragon fire was surpassed by the roar of the crowd as they sighted us, and we were neck and neck as we swooped towards the ring of fire. In tandem, we rode straight at it. I screwed my eyes closed, hoping I hadn't misjudged the positioning of the scales as we rode at the deadly flames. Sweat broke out all over my body as we burst through them, and it was a full second until I realised we hadn't caught fire. We'd done it. We were through. I touched Stormclaw to the ground at the same time as Alistair landed Riverquil, breathing a loud sigh of relief. I pulled him to a halt, and looked over at the Scot. As we met eyes, a silent understanding passed between us.

I vaulted from Stormclaw's back, but made no effort to grab the gleaming gold cup. Beside me, Alistair did the same, and we both stood calmly with our gryffs as a handful of seconds later, Dylan plunged through the fire, Riley behind him. They saw us standing there and a look of confusion passed over their faces before they, too, nodded in understanding, and dismounted on the far side of the cup.

"For Callum, Kieran and Aderyn," I said. We bowed our heads for a moment, and then stepped to the cup, Alistair and me both reaching a hand towards one handle, and Riley and Dylan the other. As one, we seized the handles, and between the four of us, hefted the cup into the air to the roars and cheers of the crowd. I looked at the other three champions, and my face split into a grin.

The four druid academies of England, Scotland, Ireland, and Wales were united, as we always should have been.

Chapter Thirty-Three

Come on, get up!"

I groaned and rolled over in my bed, pulling my pillow over my head in an effort to blot out Kelsey's voice.

"Don't wanna," I mumbled into my bedding.

"We can't be late, it's results day!"

"She's not going to let you go back to sleep," Ava said. "You might as well just give in and get up."

She was right, of course. Results day to Kelsey was like Christmas to a five-year-old. I dragged the pillow off my head and stared up at the ceiling. Results day. That meant it was our last day here at Dragondale. Ever. In a few hours, I'd be stepping through a portal, and I'd never be coming back. It was like high school all over again, except here, for a little while at least, I'd truly fit in. Dragondale was my home. I was going to miss it.

"Hurry up, Lyssa!"

"Alright, alright," I groaned, staggering out of my bed and stumbling into the bathroom. It was possible that I might have over indulged last night, just slightly. But hey, I'd just become joint winner of the Four Nations Cup, and if that wasn't an excuse for a party, I didn't know what was. The rest of the academy seemed to agree with me, and honestly, I couldn't remember anything much past about nine. And now I was paying the price.

By the time I made it out of the bathroom, Kelsey was pacing up and down by the door, and Ava was doodling dragons on her notepad. It wouldn't be her last year here. She still had third year ahead of her, and after that she'd stick around, and eventually get a job here, so she could be close to Dardyr. The life of a dragon rider – it wasn't all glamour and battles. But some part of me wished my future was laid out for me like that: no uncertainty, no decisions to make. It turned out the talent scout had come back, and he'd seen me ride yesterday. And he'd offered me a place on the team, as a professional Itealta player for the Essex Hornets. Three more job offers came in last night at dinner – doors opened by my new status as joint cup winner and druid celebrity.

Rolling her eyes, Kelsey grabbed my arm and hauled me bodily through the door. When we reached the common room, Sam was already there waiting for us, looking every bit as bad I as felt. He looked me up and down with bleary eyes, his expression telling me that my attempts to look at least halfway human were failing miserably. He shook his head sadly and tutted.

"Yeah, yeah," I mumbled. "You don't look so pretty yourself."

"Ouch. I'm wounded."

"Both of your wounds are entirely self-inflicted," Kelsey said, and then added with a little more sympathy, "Come on, let's get you some breakfast."

"Please don't mention food."

Despite my objections, by the time we'd made it to our seats in the main hall with plates of food and unhealthy amounts of coffee in front of us, I was starting to feel more like myself – which was to say, a jumbled mess of nerves and anxiety. But at least the jumbled mess wasn't in danger of puking any time soon.

Talendale's lectern was set at the head of the hall, currently deserted, and Kelsey kept darting looks at it after every other mouthful of food.

"Would you stop doing that?" Sam said. "You're making me dizzy. Besides, what have you even got to worry about? You get a perfect 4.0 every year."

"Yes, and if I don't maintain my grade, I won't get–"

She cut off abruptly, clamping her lips together.

"You won't get what?" I asked, curiosity getting the better of me. "Come on, spill it. Where've you been sneaking off to all year?"

"Oh. You, um, you noticed that?"

I rolled my eyes.

"Kelsey, I love you dearly, but you're about as subtle as an elephant doing tap dance."

"Well, I didn't want to jinx it," she said, using her fork to push food around her plate instead of eating it — which was basically unheard of. Werewolf appetite and all that. Whatever was on her mind, it was big. I waited patiently.

"I've been visiting with the council. With Head Councilman Cauldwell."

"You... what?" That was not what I'd been expecting her to say. The guy tried to have her killed last year, with barely any evidence, without even hearing her out — because she was a hybrid.

"If I graduate Dragondale with a 4.0, I'll become the youngest druid to join the Grand Council. And the first ever hybrid."

My jaw popped open.

"Kels, that's massive. That's..."

"Insane? Unrealistic? Impossible?" she suggested, stabbing at her bacon.

"Everything I always knew you were capable of," I finished. She dropped her fork and grabbed me in a hug, almost crushing the life from me with her werewolf strength, until I coughed and spluttered. She hastily unwrapped her arms from around me.

"Oops, sorry."

"Never apologise for who you are. You, Kelsey Winters, are going to change the course of history."

"Hey, does that mean," Sam asked, from between mouthfuls of toast, "that you can change my grades if I fail?"

Kelsey poked at her food again.

"I'm not going to be changing grades or history if I flunked Elemental Manipulation. You know I struggle with my second elemental power."

"You've never flunked an exam in your life. It'll be fine. Just... breathe."

She took my advice and sucked in a deep breath. Her lips fluttered into what was almost a smile, and probably as much as she was going to manage before she got her results. Now that I knew what was hanging in the balance, I didn't blame her.

"Anyway, enough about me," she said. "Have you decided what you're going to do?"

"Yeah," Sam said, gulping down a mouthful of coffee. "Must be nice having more options than you know what to do with."

"That's the problem, though. I don't know what to do with them all." I took a swig of my coffee. "Or at least, I didn't."

"So, you've decided, have you? Can I have one of the jobs you don't want?"

"I told you mine," Kelsey said, with a teasing smile. I huffed out a sigh and slumped forward onto one elbow.

If I said it out loud, it was going to be real. Well, I supposed I was going to have to sooner or later.

"I've decided to join the circle. As an enforcer."

Sam groaned, and Kelsey held her hand out to him, palm up.

"Pay up," she said.

"Wait, you guys took a bet on me?"

"How could you turn down the chance to ride with the Hornets?" Sam grumbled.

"I don't know. I thought it was everything I wanted." I picked up my mug, realised it was empty, and set it down again. "But the battle against Raphael... it made me realise. I want to do more than just ride gryffs. I want to protect people. I want to make the world a better place. A safer place. And there's only one way I know how to do that."

"Well, I think it's a great idea," Kelsey said. "The circle will be lucky to have you."

I was about to express my doubts to that sentiment when Talendale stood, approached the lectern, and cleared his throat. Silence immediately fell over the entire hall.

"Good morning, students," he began. "And congratulations on reaching the conclusion of another academic year."

I felt Kelsey tense beside me, and reached out to take her hand. This was it. The head of each elemental house collected a stack of envelopes from Talendale and came to stand in their quarter. Kelsey didn't seem capable of tearing her eyes from the pile of envelopes Alden carried towards us.

"You will receive your exam results momentarily. But first, a few words. This has been a trying year for us all, and there are those who did not survive it. We shall forever remember them in the heart of Dragondale, and carry them with us in our spirits. For as long as we live on, so too shall they."

He bowed his head, and I felt a pang of guilt and sadness as I looked around at the empty seats, and thought about the students who would never graduate, and the families who would not be reunited tonight. Our graduation had not come without a price.

"In honour of them," he said, raising his head to sweep the room with his imperious gaze, "it falls to you to achieve greatness in your time here at Dragondale. But for some of you, that time has come to an end. Soon, you will leave our hallowed halls, and find your own way in the magical community. It remains only to tell you how proud I am of each and every one of you. Though you may leave Dragondale, Dragondale will forever be a part of you."

He looked between each of the four head of houses, and nodded once.

"Very well, then. Without further ado, we shall distribute your results."

He raised both hands high in the air and muttered a word that I didn't quite catch, and the envelopes flew from the professors' hands, racing along the tables and skidding to a halt in front of their owners. I reached out to pick up the one marked 'Lyssa Eldridge' with trembling hands, and then paused.

"You, first," I said to Sam.

"Oh, no," he said. "Not this time. You're going first."

I looked to Kelsey for help, but she just nodded. Traitor.

"Fine," I sighed. I didn't know why I cared so much. Cauldwell had promised me a position with the enforcers regardless of my results. Of course, he hadn't specified what that position would be, and I didn't fancy spending my entire career scrubbing floors. I ripped the top off the envelope, pulled the single sheet from within and unfolded it. My eyes scanned it, top to bottom, left to right, then I stared at it, unblinking.

Sam reached over and yanked it from my hands.

"I don't believe it," he said, not lifting his eyes to Kelsey who was practically twitching with impatience.

"She slept through two months of lessons, and still passed every subject."

"And here I was thinking sleeping through all the excitement was your speciality," I said, plucking the sheet from his hands.

"Trust me, there was nothing exciting about two months of Gaelic."

Yeah, that I could believe.

"Alright, your turn," Kelsey said. He opened his mouth to object, then snapped it closed again, and nodded with all the stoicism of a hero marching to the gallows. He ripped the flap, and yanked the sheet from inside.

"I… I don't…"

"You don't what?" I asked, rising a little in my seat and craning my neck to try to read his results.

"I… Well, I passed! I mean, they're not great passes, but I passed everything." A grin spread on his face. "I'm graduating."

"That's brilliant! Well done." I turned to Kelsey, who'd gone uncharacteristically quiet, staring at the white envelope in her trembling hands. "Kels?"

"I don't think I can."

"Of course you can. You're the same Kelsey who took on a pack of rogue werewolves."

She nodded, biting her lip, and peeled up the flap and extracted the single sheet within. She exhaled slowly, and then unfolded it.

"Well?"

Her face lit up in a grin.

"I did it! Another 4.0. I'm joining the Grand Council. I can't believe it!"

"I can." I reached over and gave her a hug. "I knew you could do it."

"Well done, Kels," Sam said.

"So that's it, then. We're all graduating."

I looked at my two best friends, and felt another pang of sadness. We'd never sit here again, studying for classes or getting exam results. Everything was going to change. I said as much, but Kelsey shook her head.

"The important things won't change at all. We'll always have our magic, and we'll always have each other. We'll see each other all the time. Even more than we did last summer, now that we can all portal."

"I guess you're right," I said. "It just feels weird, knowing that were not going to be here anymore. My life has changed so much in the last three years."

I couldn't quite keep my eyes from darting to Ava as she celebrated with her friends. Life had changed so much for us both. Kelsey caught the direction of my gaze.

"Will the two of you stay in touch?"

I had two living blood relatives, and one of those wanted me dead. There was no way I was losing touch with the other. And Ava, well, she didn't have any other family at all. She felt the same way.

"She's going to stay with me this summer – in between looking after Dardyr, obviously. I've already arranged it with my parents. And she'll visit at Christmas. She's got a home with us for as long as she wants one."

"I guess this is it, then," Sam said. "Back to our dorms one last time to pack our bags, and then out into that big wide world waiting for us – where I hope the pair of you will remember your less academically-inclined friend when you're rich and famous."

We gathered our plates and prepared to leave the hall for the last time. I couldn't help but feel a sense of loss for what I was leaving behind, but there was a spark of excitement deep inside me as I thought about what the future held.

I knew one thing with absolute certainty: though my time at Dragondale had come to an end, my adventures were   just   beginning.

A note from the author

Thanks for joining me for Lyssa's final year at the Dragondale Academy of Druidic Magic. I hope you enjoyed it as much as I did. This series is now finished, but watch this space to find out about her adventures at the enforcer training academy later this year.

Meanwhile, if you enjoyed this book, I'd be really grateful if you would take a moment to leave me a review.

Sign up to my newsletter by visiting www.cschurton.com to be kept up to date with my new releases and received exclusive content.

There's one thing I love almost as much as writing, and that's hearing from people who have read and enjoyed my books. If you've got a question or a comment about the series, you can connect with me and other like-minded people over in my readers' group at

www.facebook.com/groups/CSChurtonReaders

Printed in Great Britain
by Amazon

52746171R00251